SAGE EMPRESS II

BOOKS IN THE PHOENIX FEATHER SERIES

The Phoenix Feather Arc:

Fledglings

Redbark

Firebolt

Dragon and Phoenix

The Sagacious Arc:

Tribute

Sage Empress I

SAGE EMPRESS II

SHERWOOD SMITH

BOOK VIEW CAFE

BOOK VIEW CAFE

SAGE EMPRESS II
Copyright © 2024 by Sherwood Smith

Published by Book View Café
304 S. Jones Blvd., Suite 2906
Las Vegas, NV 89107
www.bookviewcafe.com

ISBN: 978-1-63632-256-8

This is a work of fiction. Any references to historical events, real people, or real locales are used fictitiously. Other names, characters, places, and incidents are productions of the authors' imagination, and any resemblance to actual events or locales or persons, living or dead, is entirely coincidental.

Cover Design by Victoria Davies
Interior Design by Marissa Doyle

Discover other books by Sherwood Smith at
www.Sherwoodsmith.net

For Bruce and Brad, just out of reach

With gratitude to my readers at Patreon for their enthusiasm and comments. And special thanks to Rachel Neumeier, heroic beta reader, Jennifer Stevenson, BVC's heroic formatter extraordinaire, and Marissa Doyle, who with equal heroism and grace formats my print books.

ONE

Spring departed, cherries fell,
and butterflies flit and flew in pairs
when she sailed in good faith
toward vaulting mountain
crowned in sunrise pink…

I MUST ADMIT THAT some of the private amusement I find in writing this history of my own life is digging into the most pompous of the many, many poems that have appeared about me. Some are merely guilty of the official obsequiousness that seems impossible to avoid, but the most noisome are those written full of empty flattery, no doubt with an eye to largesse. I trust that in years to come they will be forgotten.

My favorites are the satiric ones. Especially the ephemera written by On Lu—when I can catch them.

Private amusement aside, I must dip my brush and continue my tale. I believe I left myself rising into the air to escape my dear brother's well-meant intent to keep me safely stuffed in a small cabin aboard the grand prince's fleet leader—that same brother I'd sought ever since leaving my home.

This leave-taking ripped my heart in two. I knelt on Sagacious Blade and soared over the sea, weeping with all the passion of sixteen years. After three of those years spent wondering, and worrying, and during this past year listening to travelers as I carried dishes at the Three Kingfishers Inn, I'd finally found my brother — just to leave him without so much as a farewell.

And I left Koi, who had been with me since leaving the imperial island.

When I stood on that flagship, I was so very certain I was right to escape being closed up in a cabin as supernumerary baggage, but as soon as I soared into the sky — avoiding looking down at the vast blackness of the sea — I was severely tempted to turn back.

"Did I do right to leave them?" I asked Granny Zim, who had remained silent all this time. "Ought I to go back?" As I said it, my heart knotted, for I knew that I'd be shut up on that ship, then shut up again whenever it reached Imperial Grand Uncle Yiulo's current stronghold. "Was Koi right to stay?" Koi had relegated himself to the invisible chains of servanthood, after three years of freedom. I knew that he had made that decision out of loyalty, friendship, and conviction of its rightness.

"My Bu, if you merely seek comfort, turn not to me. Whatever you do, you still possess your wit, your heart, and your hands," spoke the voice behind my inner ear, through Sagacious Blade, the sword in which her soul dwelt.

I had to accept the rightness of that answer. Perhaps someone more clever than I would make a success of being immured in a silken veil of feminine respectability in a fortress, but I was convinced I could only act to free my parents if I myself were free.

How? That had to be my next task.

I was so overwhelmed by my own doubts and regrets that I had paid little heed to the steadily rising wind as I sought the *Pangolin*, the gallant wanderer ship that a number of us had wrested from slavers and made our own. I was only aware of expending a fury of Essence to keep myself from wobbling right off that sword into the sea.

Through blurred, stinging eyes I swept the vast, dark sea until I saw our converted trader. As promised, lamps had been set out along the deck. One snuffed out by the rising wind from the oncoming storm that had begun blotting the stars from the sky. One of the crew struggled to relight the lamp as I fought the gusts in descending. I nearly crashed into a racketing sail, took my gaze briefly from the lamp on the deck — and promptly tumbled down, the sword clattering beside me. If I had not trained for a third of my sixteen years in how to fall, I might have done worse than jarring myself painfully, as a couple of crew recoiled in alarm.

"It's Pangolin Ren," the gunner's eldest grandson shouted. "She's back!" He added in a tone of question, "Alone?"

Dinek, our captain, nineteen but with years of experience aboard a tea trader behind her, dashed out of the galley. "Ren?"

I got painfully to my feet—and the wind nearly flattened me again.

"Inside," she shouted.

We bent into the gale, me clutching Sagacious Blade until we reached the galley. The other Pangolins not on duty had gathered there, staring back.

"Where's the sailboat?" Fan, our marine captain, asked.

"Where's Brother Koi?" Jai demanded. Even taller than Fan, who was otherwise our largest Pangolin, Jai was nearly my age, and as volatile as a landslide. "Did you abandon him? And where did you come from—?"

Dinek held up a hand. She barely reached the middle of Jai's chest, her round face dominated by prominent rabbit teeth, and her voice was quite high, but there was a tautness to her posture that halted everyone, as the sound of the wind rose to a wail. The ship had begun to rise and plunge through increasing waves.

Fan said urgently, "This storm is coming on fast."

"The crew has it in hand. I'll go out to con the ship when I need to, but first I want to understand what happened." Dinek turned a furrowed brow to me. "We all left the Tiger Islands to stop at Dawn's Placid Sea Harbor so that you could warn Governor Huyun about some imperial prince being there, disguised as a general. We expected you to return to us as soon as you passed on the message. Instead, you vanished, and On came to get us. He said we had to sail before the duke's entire fleet chased us, and you were off to Tiger Island again, *flying on your sword*."

I turned to On, who lounged against a wall, his arms crossed, his long hair lying damp and tousled over his arms. Had he been outside, watching for Koi's and my return? In my exhaustion, I could not fight against that strange sense of the world of spirits and Essence and other things humans usually lived without awareness of, as his un-foxlike face was overlaid with the insouciant grin of the fox-spirit that lay in his ancestry.

"You didn't tell me not to," he said lightly.

"Why should she keep that from us?" Dinek asked.

Outside a wave crashed over the rail, sending foaming water

streaming down the deck. A few worried looks turned Dinek's way. "The crew has the ship," she said shortly. And to me, "Pangolin Ren, I need to understand. We all agreed to rescue Aku Orchid from being forced into marriage. Then, within a day, suddenly we might be chased by the duke of the very island we regard as our home port, because you think he's plotting against a couple of the warring imperial princes, and you have to save them? This was not our decision."

Dinek and Fan stood shoulder to shoulder, one tall and broad, one short, their expressions similar: not just wariness, but hurt.

I was far too tired to think. I tucked my cold fingers in my armpits as I said, "This wretched fool begs forgiveness." I began to bow, and staggered.

Fan reached forward and caught my elbow. "None of that courtly nonsense, Ren—ay! You're shivering! It's not that cold out. Are you sick?"

"Not sick. Tired." I spilled words as rapidly as breath and tongue permitted: "Koi stayed to protect my brother, who was on the grand prince's ship. I—we—were afraid that he was to be sent to that false peace conference, instead of the grand prince's grandson. And we were *right*. I'm sure it was no peace conference."

"But what has that to do with us?" Jai muttered. "The imperials can kill each other and I'd stand by and cheer."

"That's right!"

"Yes!"

"Except it's not just them. It's all the innocent people of Tiger Eye Bay." I scrubbed my hands over my face, and turned back to Dinek, who seemed determined to hold this tribunal before going out to command the ship. "I believe that Governor Huyun Shandek used the pretense of a peace conference to plot against both the grand prince's representative—who I was more sure by the hour would be my brother, in the place of the grand prince's precious grandson—and the imperial crown prince. Which, if successful, would provoke the emperor into retaliating against Ji Jiang and his innocent island."

Dinek nodded slowly, bracing herself against a barrel. "I can see saving an innocent town. And I understand filial loyalty. But why did you never tell us about this missing brother?"

"Your brother being…?" On prompted, with a wicked smile.

He knew very well that I was hiding my identity. As I was certain he was doing. But *he* had not put the Pangolins into this new, precarious position. However inadvertently, I had dragged them very near the whirlpool of imperial conflict, and I owed them the truth.

"Lan Banti." I sighed, then said, "I may as well confess that I am Lan Renti."

"But...Lan is the name of the imperial dynasty," one of the Hat brothers said.

"That makes you..." Fan said slowly.

"A princess?" Dinek asked.

"Fifth rank. The lowest."

"Then Pangolin is not your family? But the sword? Ay! It's a charmed sword, is that it? Inherited?"

"Yes. And yes, though the imperial family does not know about it. Charmed swords are forbidden to anyone but the emperor. It came down through my mother's family —"

The wind rose to a shriek as the ship shuddered.

Dinek tipped her head back, her bare feet planted wide, toes tense as if they were going to root into the wooden deck. Then she said, "All hands."

That meant every one of us. We'd practiced the "all hands" command as diligently as Fan ran the martial arts sparring on the foredeck every day.

Dinek threw open the galley door and vanished outside, followed by the rest of us, temporarily leaving the subject of my actions — and my identity — in the galley.

We ran to our stations. Mine was to be part of a human chain at one of the sail ropes. I knew very little about ship navigation beyond the fact that great currents in the ocean carried the ship, countered by the wind on the sails. Left alone, a wooden ship bobbles along like a twig in a stream, as wood floats. But in a storm such as this, the danger was not only the screaming winds but the enormous waves. Too much sail made the ship awkward, and might lead to broken masts, in which case the waves would spin us about before overwhelming us; too little sail would be ineffectual, with the same end.

Dinek had taught us a system by which arm signals conveyed orders having to do with raising and lowering sails, and with maintaining the helm — at which all the gunner's crew stood now, with various ropes attached to the hull to take some of the strain.

We stood in the horizontal rain, which veered between warm to icy. We pulled when told, loosed when told, our feet braced against the madly slanting deck. Water broke over the rail at intervals, rushing down and away, but we were bound securely—all except On, who somehow clung to the upper reaches, tending the whipping ropes.

I was so exhausted that after each rush of water my knees wanted to buckle. I longed for rest. I think I even slept in the two, three breath-long intervals between waves, my mind slipping inadvertently into the place between our world of the senses and that of the unseen. Streamers of light shot through the tearing winds, and dragons of air, of water, of lightning, tumbled and spilt the clouds, taming them slowly as rain diminished to a steady fall. The waves lowered from cliff-high monsters to foam-crested billows, until the ship settled to a less frantic rhythm, and we were dismissed.

I had trouble peeling my numb fingers from the rope. Then came the daunting climb to the second level, where my cabin was.

I reached it at last, shedding harness, sword, carryall, and sodden clothes at each step, until I fell into the bunk, and down into a well of darkness and dreams.

I woke to bright sunlight filtering in the tightly closed window, whose thick, oiled paper shed a disagreeably inescapable light on the mess I'd left on the deck. Wearily I rose and stepped over it. It took all my strength put on the clean clothes I'd left in my trunk. At least the lengthy scouring we'd all received in that rain left my skin clean.

It had been merely a couple of days since I'd last opened that trunk, but so much had happened that it felt like years had passed. A weight on my heart reminded me of last night's confession.

I began to finger-comb my still-wet hair as I tried to think about those years' worth of decisions and consequences. I'd found my brother. He was alive, and he had a sense of purpose that was at heart the same as mine, but his path was not mine. And I'd been unable to convince him otherwise.

If I couldn't convince him, how did I expect to succeed with anyone else?

This question pressed on me as I skewered my hair with my wooden hairpin, then I dropped my hands and left to face the others.

The ship rolled gently in light airs. I had no sense of how far we had been blown by the storm, but Dinek knew. She was forward near the bow, watching as three crew clambered above, doing something with one of the sails. But when she saw me, she called, "Bind it tight!" and crossed the deck. As she neared, I could see how tired she was, eyes marked and red-rimmed, jaw set in the way that meant each step was a conscious effort. She said, "You look as destroyed as I feel."

That surprised a laugh out of me. "I hope it's the storm and not my actions that destroyed you."

"Both," she said, with no courtly face-saving. "We're going to have to replace that spar, as soon as we can. Another blow like last night's might bring down that sail altogether."

"Are we completely lost?" I asked.

"No. We've been blown clear out to the Great Sea. That's good because it's unlikely anyone will find us. It's not good because we'll have to make up our westing before we run out of stores." She sniffed the air, as if that told her where we were. Maybe it did, though I saw nothing but ocean.

She then indicated the dining cabin off the galley, where congee sat warming, and tea as well. We both dished our share up, and sat cross-legged on the women's side.

Dinek picked up her spoon. "I understand rescuing a brother. If I knew where mine is, I'd want to go rescue him at once. I also understand hiding your identity. A lot of gallant wanderers have to hide their identities, though I don't know how many are hidden imperials."

I caught myself bowing in apology, and quickly changed that to the gallant wanderer hand clasp.

"Ay," she said, narrowed gaze on my hands. "Fan's stomach is full of teeth because we might find ourselves trapped in imperial troubles that we did not want. But when your brother is a prince, it seems ... how can I say it? When I think *prince*, I'm imagining a grand parade full of banners and gongs and many loud instruments, and everyone lined up at the sides of the road on their knees. But when I think *brother*, I think of my own brother who looks like me, who knows every harbor along three trade routes without a glance at a chart. I don't think of those two things together, brother and prince. You do."

"My brother never had a parade," I said—then remembered that First Brother had actually had one, when he won first rank at the Imperial Examination.

And my wicked Cousin Xianti, now Imperial Crown Prince Xianti, had forced the Imperial Guard to parade my family through the length of the imperial palace to the prison, in order to humiliate them.

Dinek sighed. "Perhaps I said it wrong. Princes are apt to

bring imperial troubles in their train, whether they get parades or not."

I could not deny that.

"But there is no imperial trouble following us," I said. "The plot against the princes was spoiled. In fact, that storm sweeping on us would have spoiled it even if I hadn't warned them."

"Then you are certain no princes will be chasing us?"

"I can't promise that," I said, my mind going straight to Xianti, the vindictive one. Yiuti was on his way back to his grandfather—with my brother—I was very certain. Xianti... No, why would he chase after me, especially if they were blown all over the ocean by the storm? Far more likely he'd return to the imperial island. And—if he'd believed me—start conspiring against Governor Huyun Shandek.

Dinek said, "Here's my biggest worry. If Governor Huyun was secretly plotting, and you spoiled it, is he going to be chasing us?"

"I don't think so," I said. "Because there's no way for him to know it was I who spoiled his plot. All I said to him was that I'd recognized Xianti. And when he told me about the supposed peace conference, I didn't say anything at all. I warned Ji Jiang, but never said my name. Finally, no one saw Koi and me warn the grand prince's fleet. We caught them well outside the bay. Then the storm came."

Dinek's shoulders relaxed. "Then you didn't tell the governor your true identity."

"I did not," I said. "He knew me as Pangolin Ren."

Dinek knuckled her eyes. "Ah, I am so glad. I don't want to have to give up the Celestial Chart if there are warrants for our arrest, because I told Hat Dove to meet us there when she finishes investigating. But she'd know to return to one of the other Hat trade houses," she muttered—mostly to herself, I think.

Then, to me, with an awkward diffidence, "Thank you for turning out in the storm."

"You said all hands," I said, puzzled.

"But..." Dinek looked away, then back, diffidently. Awkwardly. "Fan said, if you don't want to drill with us, you needn't."

And there it was, the ghost of rank rising between us. I was not going to escape it, though I forced myself to fetch Sagacious Blade and join the others doing our martial forms, just to show everyone that I was merely one of the crew. In a sense I'd brought this awkwardness on myself, not so much by my revealing my identity, but through the decisions I'd made that necessitated my revealing that identity.

Because Dinek was right. Those warring princes were not distant figures to me. I knew all three of them—one being Second Brother Banti.

My reluctant muscles had warmed when Fan said, "Good enough. We'll have some sparring."

I stepped into the shade of a mast with a weary sigh. Even when I wasn't tired, I loathed sparring. But Fan looked around, then skewered me with a glare. "Someone," she said, "didn't tell us about light skills expert enough to fly a sword."

And every face turned to me.

I reddened brighter than a dragon fruit in mid-summer. "Yesterday was my first time," I protested. "Ah. The day before."

"Oh." Fan's scowl of moral outrage eased at that, her thick brows climbing toward her hairline. "How do you do it? Can you teach us? Or is it an Essence skill?"

The others stood about with the ship's swords, some laying them down on the deck, others eyeing the blades with skepticism, wonder, suspicion.

"It's very much an Essence thing," I said. "And I'm still terrible at it. You saw how I fell off last night. Heights make me dizzy."

The crew looked at me with varying expressions, mostly disappointment. "You mean you can't teach us? Is it akin to On's light skills, then? He says his light skills are not Essence skills. He doesn't know any. He jumps up to the top of the sail, and says, 'Just do it.'" She pointed overhead.

"His Essence skill is innate," I said. "It can't be taught. Mine isn't innate. That is, I have a talent for it, in a way, but I've also been studying very hard to use it."

One of Fan's brows quirked. "So it's real, then, that royal blood is blessed?"

"Not that I know," I said. "At least, there's no Essence talent in the rest of my father's family that I know of. It might be somewhere farther back on my mother's side."

The Pangolins accepted that with a nod here, a muttered, "Ay," there.

Fan sighed. "I thought you'd be able to give us a defense better than our cannon. Because what if our gunpowder gets wet? Or we run out?"

"Gunpowder's still more trustworthy, if you ask me," said wizened, scarred Ayep Vu, our gunner—survivor of what looked to me like countless mishaps with this lethal form of brimstone. "Using Essence for anything is like asking for lightning to strike right where you want it. At least with gunpowder, you know what you have."

Behind him, his three grandsons nodded in firm agreement. "Though I wouldn't mind learning to fly a sword," mumbled Three, the youngest of them.

One of his elder brothers—twins, named Day and Night—cuffed him gently for speaking out of turn, and Three sighed. Being the youngest meant being the lowest no matter what level or circle one was born in, it seemed.

Fan ignored the gunners and chewed a weapon-scarred knuckle. "All right. Yet. Seems to me, even one person on a flying sword could be a good defense, if needed. So you better get to practicing. Ah, Princess. If you want to listen to this humble … Dinek!" Fan called over her shoulder. "What was the rest of it?"

"This humble wretch of no talent," Dinek called from the helm.

Fan's lip curled. "Do I really have to call myself a wretch?" she asked me. "Is that what you expect?"

I said, "When have I ever expected anyone to call themselves a wretch, or anything else? I told you, I was the lowest ranking princess in the imperial palace." I gritted my teeth, then added, "For that matter, I'm very certain even that rank was annulled when the new imperial crown prince…" Here I made a spitting sound to the side. "…had my family arrested and demoted. Rescuing them is the goal for my brother and for me."

Sparring was momentarily forgotten.

"Is that what you expect of us?" Jai asked.

"I don't expect anything of you," I said. "It's *my* goal. I don't know how to do it. Yet. When I do, I'll tell everyone here before I leave to do it."

Looks semaphored between the others, and then Fan cleared her throat. "That's fair. That's gallant wanderer justice. But before that, we still need defense. So, my suggestion is, you practice on your sword instead of sparring, until you get it right."

I agreed. She was right. It was foolish not to practice a skill that had already proven to be vitally important in the single day since I'd first used it.

Though Fan divided the others into sparring pairs, I felt them watching me out of the sides of their eyes as I placed Sagacious Blade on the deck, knelt on it, crouched over, and fixed my gaze determinedly on a spot a few paces away.

Tired as I was, we had a clear, warm day, and it was so easy to bring handfuls of Essence to me, unlike the strain of the previous night. I only rose a palm's breadth from the deck, and slowly glided to the spot. Then I picked up the sword, turned it around, and repeated another straight line. Once, twice, and I felt the others' interest turning back to their bouts.

After a short time, On landed lightly next to me, his thin, expressive brows lifted in question. "Are you angry that I told the others?"

"Why?" I said. "It seems to me that you saved my life. If you hadn't figured out where I'd gone, and got the rest to sail after me, I would either have had to expire in that storm while trying to find a place to land, or else I'd have had to return to the firedragon ships."

"At least you'd have your brother. And Koi."

"Except that I'd be locked up because what else do you do with a girl on a warship?" I retorted. "I don't blame my brother. I don't even blame Yiuti, little as I trust him. Custom and propriety require it. Pushing against that is leveling a mountain with a spoon." Which can be done, I thought to myself. But more effectively done by many willing hands with many spoons.

I turned the sword about, then knelt on it to go the other way. "My regret is that everything I did was like trying to draw water with a basket. Utterly useless."

"You didn't know that the storm was coming," On said. He'd been working with fighting fans instead of his knives. He spread one now, holding it with two fingers as he watched the wind batter it.

"I hope Ji Jiang didn't say anything, once the storm was over," I admitted, picked up the sword, turned it around, knelt on it, and fixed my gaze firmly on a spot on the deck at a distance of twenty paces.

Consequences, Father had always instructed us. *You must consider the consequences of all your actions.* I'd forgotten that one completely as soon as On had suggested that the bannerless ships filling Tiger Eye Bay were actually seaworthy, and perhaps poised for attack.

Ayah! Forget it! Not a life had been lost. Not even an arrow shot. Xianti's ships were either safe and snug in harbor or blown southward, and my brother and the firedragons ships had been chased by those winds clear out into the Great Sea, where the whales sing.

I was able to sleep far better that night.

And over the following stretch of days, as Dinek guided our wounded ship carefully back to Mountain Peony Island, and then along its southern shore to Cloud Terrace Harbor, I kept working diligently each day at mastering the art of riding my sword.

I was beginning to learn how to turn it by leaning, instead of landing, picking it up, and physically placing the point in the other direction, when we spotted the beautiful temple on the eastern promontory of the harbor. But once we came in sight of other ships, specifically the diligent Huyun guard ships with their green and gold banners, I put Sagacious Blade away. As I told Fan, "My being useful at defense will only happen if others aren't expecting to see someone on a flying sword, and watching the skies with arrows nocked."

Fan exclaimed, "You are very right." And, to the others, "No one outside of us is to know about our flying princess."

Everyone agreed with the kind of fervency that came with the realization that blabbing about certain things was more likely to bring trouble falling on one's head instead of golden coins, even Jai. He said, "At least that blabbermouth Ke stayed back in Dawn's Placid Sea Harbor."

No one disagreed. I rather liked Ke, the ambitious dancer who had first alerted us to the plight of her boss's niece, Aku Orchid. But Dinek had been right to say about her that she was like grass on the walls — grows everywhere it wants to. It did not surprise me that she'd refused to rejoin the ship after the failure of our rescue. To her it would seem only practical to remain on the eastern side of the island to take her chances in a new environment, instead of returning empty-handed to her boss.

She was leaving that to us.

I stood at the rail with Fan as Dinek conned the ship into the harbor. It was always so important to Dinek to bring the *Pangolin* to a flawless anchorage. Fan stood beside me, a sizable figure shadowing me from the brilliant early summer sun. She sighed. "When I think it's we who have to go tell Madam Aku that she went to all that trouble and expense for nothing, instead of Ke, whose idea it was, I want to haul Ke back here and slap her face off."

I said, with no enthusiasm, "I supposed I ought to do it."

"No, but I thank you for the thought on Dinek's behalf. She perceives it as her duty. She hopes that hearing that Orchid is in child, and has a garden all of her own now, will help somewhat."

"And she can always go visit her, once the child is born," I said.

"That's right."

As we spoke, both of us ranged our gazes over the bay. No green-clad guards came out in force toward us. Some did watch us come in, but that was as usual. A few of those waved a hello, and once, Fan waved back. "I think we're really all right," she said at last, with satisfaction.

Ay! She had been worried a little as well.

The sails came down and the anchor let go, which meant the ship could be left except for one on board. We let down the longboat, and rowed for the wharf.

Dinek said with a sigh, "I'll report our arrival to the magistrate, and stop by Madam Aku's emporium on my way back down to the Celestial Chart. I take it you're off to Three Kingfishers, Ren?"

"Yes," I said.

Dinek turned to the others, who all had their various favorite places to stay—except for On, who apparently bounced between several lively shoreside inns, or friends, according to Dinek.

I glanced at him as he lay back in the longboat, head on the gunwale, face sunward, his long hair drifting over the edge of the boat to trail its ends in the water. The nine-tailed fox I sometimes saw was completely hidden, leaving only his entirely normal, some would even say pleasing, features.

He seemed to sense my gaze, but I turned my attention to the wharf as he stirred, and a heartbeat or two later we bumped up against the pilings.

Dinek paid off the wharf tender for our spot, and we all hefted our carryalls, and climbed to the weathered planking. I headed across the street toward the Three Kingfishers. It had merely been a little over Phoenix Moon month since we left, but it felt in some ways like a year.

The Pangolins parted in several directions. I took off alone, weaving through the crowds of busy people. Prosperous people. Not a refugee or beggar in sight, the street clean-swept, the houses in their tiers, cut into the mountainside, clean and bright as if newly washed in a spring rain.

There seemed to be more greens about, in their black hats with the kingfisher feathers, than usual, but then Three Kingfishers had always been a favorite haunt of the guards. "Keep them happy, and they watch out for us," Ma Shao had said many a time over the past year and a half. "Besides, we know how lucky we are to have a good governor in these wicked times."

The inn was scarcely fifty paces from the wharf. I hefted my harness over my shoulder, bracing against the weight. Once again I'd have to get used to my sword and carryall over my shoulder. Question: when? I was now free. The missions were over.

How was I to go about rescuing my parents?

I walked into the inn, its interior dim after the brightness outside. It smelled delicious — Ma Shao was cooking her pepper fish again. The place was full of custom, mostly greens, some of whom turned. A couple waved greetings to me, men I'd served countless times.

"You're back, Ren," called Commander Nan, sitting at a table with five other guards.

"I am," I said.

"Good sailing?" another called.

"Except for a dragon storm ten days ago."

"We had it here as well," someone else commented. "Blew wooden signs clean down the street and out to sea. Glad you made it safe."

"Me," another commented, "you'll never see me set foot on a ship unless it's orders. We don't have fins, we humans."

That raised a genial laugh. I laughed with them, and passed into the back room, my thumb unslinging my carryall.

Ma Shao was there, with her daughter Fia, who squinted at me. "Ren?"

"I'm back. Is there still room up at the attic?"

Ma Shao gave me an odd smile. "You'll want to step into Autumn," she said.

"Autumn?" I repeated. Though I knew what it was — the inn's finest room, with the view out over the sea. Its name was properly a bit of poetry about autumn chrysanthemums, but as in many things, people are apt to shorten impractical phrases to a simple word.

I was going to set my things down, but her manner was tense enough to prompt me not to assume the liberty, and so I turned about, ran up the stairs, and to the doorway carved with chrysanthemums over a harvest moon.

I slid it back, and stepped inside, and stared.

Seated at the table, with the inn's finest porcelain tea service before him, was Governor Huyun Shandek, dressed in layers of mauve silk embroidered with dragonflies and bamboo shoots. "Welcome back," he said, with an inviting gesture to the empty seat opposite him.

Behind me, the door slid shut, and two guards stood there, hands to their sword hilts.

Two

*Though prideful brocade streamed with dragons' gold
And heavily mounted generals rode in rows,
She commanded the skies.
Whose banners fly now?*

HUYUN SHANDEK WAS DRESSED for a court entertainment, his hair worn in the scholar's mode, half pulled up into a pearl-edged clasp, the rest loose, a night-black shadow against rich mauve silk. Jade on one finger, as well as at his belt, carved in the ancient mode's longevity character, a long tassel in deep green depending from it.

These signs of civilized elegance conflicted with the military aspect of the two guards standing at attention at my back.

My heart galloped as fast as my thoughts. Remembering my error the first time we met, I did not bow at all, but sat down, taking care to slide Sagacious Blade to one side of the chair.

Huyun Shandek was *here*. Waiting for *me*.

The fact that he knew of our arrival would not be a surprise, if there had been orders to the coastal patrol to watch for the *Pangolin*'s banner. The fact that those orders would be issued, necessitating a pigeon solely to carry news of our sighting, and then the presumably busy governor coming down from his palace on top of the mountain to this inn, was the surprise.

Whom did he assume he faced?

"Welcome back, Pangolin Ren," he said, one hand sliding along his sleeve in perfect court form as he poured out fresh tea. With a smile he pushed the cup toward me as I allowed myself an inward trickle of relief at hearing myself addressed as Pangolin Ren. He went on in a friendly manner, "A toast to your surviving the dragon storm."

I refrained from the correct courtly reaction, which would be a bow as I took the cup with two hands, mindful of my own silken sleeves. But I no longer wore silk, and my sleeves were modest, narrow, and practical. I fingered the cup with one hand, slinging the other over the arm of my chair. "Thank you, Governor Huyun," I said with the gallant wanderer version of politeness, then slurped my tea.

I told him nothing, I told him nothing, I reassured myself: on that first meeting I only warned him of Imperial Crown Prince Xianti's presence in Tiger Eye Bay. The important part—Granny Zim telling me he was lying to my face when he told me about the peace conference he had little to do with—was not heard by him.

"Innkeeper Shao is to be commended for the excellence of her Long Mountain Leaf," he commented, and I suppressed the instinct to bow politely on her behalf. He then went on, "We would have been sorry to lose promising independents such as you and your … the Pangolins are not really a sect, are they? Pangolin. So very rare a family, only yourself as representative. No others by that name within all the Inner Islands."

"Small family," I said, remembering that I'd told him that I'd lived in the south, on the imperial island. Which had given me a good excuse—so I thought—to recognize Xianti. "We've moved quite a bit. Especially in recent years. Because of the troubles," I said—which was all true enough. In a sense. And, hoping to get away from the subject of my nonexistent Pangolin relatives. "We Pangolins aboard the ship all got separated from our families. We do not think of ourselves as a sect. Only as shipmates."

"Ayah, of course. When first you graced this island, you had only just wrested that ship from criminals who had attempted to enslave you, as I recollect?"

I fought against a courtly bow of acquiescence. Hearing the court cadences in his speech and seeing his courtly manner kept prompting long-trained muscles to respond correctly. "That's right," I said, fingering my empty cup in a very uncourtly way.

"We barely escaped ahead of them when your patrol ships came up."

"And a couple weeks back, there you were on the east coast, before Kraken Boat Day. What brought you there again?"

"We took a commission. Two commissions, actually, but one was a personal favor since we were delivering silkworms to a customer on a nearby island."

Governor Huyun gave a slow nod as he poured out more tea and saluted me with his cup. "The other was bringing presents to the new wife of the small islands' governor, I believe?"

My heart thumped. What had Ji Jiang said about my self-appointed mission? Which had turned out to be useless…

"Sent by her aunt," I said.

"Is that when you chanced to witness the august presence of the imperial crown prince?"

"Yes."

The governor then said, mildly, "He appears to have changed his mind about the peace conference, judging by the fact that he set sail before the dragon storm moved in to sweep the bay."

"That must have been after we set sail," I said. "We never saw the imperial banner flying on any ships before the storm overtook us."

We both drank tea; Huyun Shandek then said, "I am relieved to report that he and his fleet survived, as you and your companions did. I wonder if you've chanced to witness any of the other august imperial family? Have you any observations about them to offer, by chance?"

Granny Zim said in that mysterious place behind my ear, "Ah, Bu, he is very angry with you, but equally unsure."

I found it profoundly more disturbing that I could see no sign of any of it.

Though I squashed the impulse to respond with courtly manner, I was thoroughly in court mode insofar as using the control Mother and Father had worked so hard to inculcate in us, to firmly suppress any outward reaction. I kept my voice blank as I said, "I don't like to repeat hearsay."

Huyun Shandek laughed. It wasn't loud. But humor crinkled his eyes as well as his smile as he said, "Nor I. But I've heard it."

His tone invited comment, but I drank my tea and waited.

He said, "Back to you. Before our unaccountable interruption when we first met—and I apologize for the lengthy delay, which seems to have necessitated your precipitate departure—I believe I invited your honored and ever more interesting self to grace my poor domicile with your presence."

"That was very kind," I began. "But I had to report back to my ship." Eventually...

He interjected smoothly into the pause, not quite an interruption, "I'd hoped to get a closer glimpse of your family artifact." He smiled in invitation. "Is there perhaps a chance now?"

"It's not a question," Granny Zim whispered to me.

"I know," I thought back to her. It was in all ways except the thinnest veneer of politeness, an order.

My heart was still racing. But I'd been in this situation before. I drew Sagacious Blade, and offered it on my palm, hilt toward him.

He took it with grave thanks and held it up, turning it this way and that in the light slanting through the open window. The blade shone with rich bronze highlights, the scales clear, but the white stone—usually so brilliant—gleamed with the nacreous dullness of a fish's eye.

He hefted the blade with the ease of sword training, and ran a hand slowly over the etched scales. He then looked past me to one of the silent men standing at the door. "Master Tuleg?"

The elder of the two guards came forward, bowed, and held out his hands. His face was long, with the absorbed expression of the scholar, though he was dressed in the Huyun guard green. The governor handed him Sagacious Blade. He held it, head bowed, then whispered Essence charms. My skin prickled subtly as Essence motes whirled around, but the blade repelled them. Or rather, it did not absorb them.

He handed the sword back to the duke with another bow. "My lord governor, this blade is inert. There is no charm left on it. Not even a trick illusion of fire of the sort they use in plays."

"Ah," said the duke. "No illusion can blast ancient rock from a formidable reef. It does seem that the mysterious Snow Crane monk was mostly responsible for that remarkable display, then. It is my misfortune that he'd moved on to wherever traveling monks go by the time I'd had occasion to attempt an interview."

Huyun Shandek offered the sword back to me then glanced at the door as he said, "I will leave first. I expect we'll meet again."

The two guards instantly effaced themselves with crisp bows, and slid open the doors. Out walked the duke with silent step, his train brushing over the clean, shining floor behind him.

I sank back into my chair, relief rolling off me in waves. "His affinities are air and fire, and he's so affable, and I know he's well-liked by all. Are you sure he was lying to me before, Granny Zim?" I asked inwardly.

"That young man's voice is filled with a sea of ambition," Granny Zim replied.

'Young' man—he had at least ten years on me.

Ten years of experience.

I shrugged that away as irrelevant right now. "You once told me I had a lake of ambition, though I still don't truly feel it. Maybe one doesn't? Is it bad or good to have lakes of ambition? Or seas?"

"Bad or good? Ayah, my Bu, such words at times are nearly meaningless. Nearly, but not all. I will say this. Your lake is water, which is coming into balance with your fire and metal nature. Think of a watered sword: the metal is forged in fire, but needs water to remain sharp and flexible. Whereas that young man's sea is liquid stone. Fire and stone can become..."

"Fire mountains," I said. "I think I understand. Fire mountains explode. I could see Xianti as a fire mountain of ambition. But Huyun Shandek is so popular with everybody. Not just the rich and noble, and the guards. The folk along the street all like him, too. Ma Shao likes him, and she's Falcon raised! They all say that he's a good governor, and everything I've seen of this island testifies to order and prosperity."

It occurred to me that Mother would highly approve of Governor Huyun Shandek. He was the sort of man she would have tried to arrange a marriage for me with. The idea was ... odd. Even though there was utterly no possibility of that happening, I could not help but wonder what that might have been like.

"I know nothing of his governance," Granny Zim said. "I can only repeat that one specific: he lied to you about having nothing to do with the peace conference. He enjoyed lying to you."

And *that* was why I felt odd. Unsettled. I tried to shrug the matter away. At least the dragon storm had swept away his putative plot.

It was time to go downstairs, and get back to the normal life of the Three Kingfishers. I gathered the dishes together, as I knew I'd likely be sent back up to do it anyway, and carried them down to the kitchen.

Ma Shao said briskly, "Ah, here you are, Ren. Good, good, put those dishes over there. How surprised I was, to have the duke walk in himself! And to ask for you! What an honor for this humble house! I trust it will bring more custom. Are you to leave us, then?"

"No," I said a little too emphatically. "It seems he wanted to see my sword for himself," I added—rather inanely, but Ma Shao was not the woman to question the vagaries of high rank.

"Ayah, of course he would! The famous Pangolin sword that gave us a passage through that dreadful reef. A meritorious deed, one that deserves meritorious acknowledgment. And your luck is our luck! So much custom his visit brought in today!" She looked around at the others on staff.

"I told you, Ma," Fia said softly, "we ought to save Ren's bed place, and her shelf."

"And did I not agree? Ren, your place awaits you!"

Ma Shao continued to gloat happily over all the attention and coinage brought in that day, intermittently insisting I go to take my things up to the attic. Not until the dinner rush began did she actually let me leave, which afforded me scant moments to fling my belongings in their old place, then race down to tend to the tables.

By the next day, things had fallen into the old pattern. That included Ma Shao sending me on errands that Fia had difficulty with, which was anything that required reading or the seeing of detail at close hand.

That day, as I walked out in the summer brightness, I felt as if I was watched. I tried to scold myself out of that sense. I never carried my sword, which I knew was of far more interest to our neighbors than I was. I was only doing errands for the inn. Yet the back of my neck still crawled, enough so that twice, I sat down. First on a bench under a parasol tree here, and second beneath a sweet-smelling fringe tree full of delicate flowers that gave me the rare itch to embroider them on silk.

I glanced around the street ever so idly, and saw no one out of place. Everyone going about their own lives, with no apparent interest in mine. I got up, wishing that such instincts weren't like omens, only useful in hindsight. Perhaps I was being foolish, but I resolved not to retreat to my secret place to train until I was absolutely certain that sense of hidden eyes was imaginary.

On my way back, I discovered Dinek coming up from the wharf, probably on her way back from rowing out to the ship. "Ren!" she called, and on my greeting her, I asked how the visit to Madam Aku had gone. "I would have helped you," I said, "but I got detained."

Dinek exclaimed, "No, no, no," as she wiped an arm over her damp forehead. "As it happens, she wasn't even there. She's sold the Rose Parasol to the owner of one of the theater groups, and it's now made over solely for plays and concerts. I was told Madam Aku got a letter from her niece not long after we left, and now she's gone to Tiger Eye Bay to set up shop there, where she can visit her niece and the child." She wiped her forehead again. "Have you by any chance seen On?"

I did not hide my surprise. "Are we leaving soon?"

"Ay! No, the ship isn't going anywhere until I get that spar replaced, and Fan returns."

"Fan? Returns?"

"I thought you saw them yesterday? They were right behind you, going inside." She pointed over her shoulder at the Three Kingfishers.

"I was summoned upstairs. The governor was there..." I gave her a brief summary of that interview.

She listened with a frown of distraction between her brows. "It sounds as if nothing came of his plot. Good, good, good. As I passed on my way to the Celestial Chart, I remember thinking that there were a lot of guards lounging around for an ordinary workday! What a relief there was no trouble after all. Anyway, Fan went with Jai up to the Falcon scrape in hopes that that Master Sima Koi talked about is still there. It's just that On told one of the Ayep boys to register him at the Bamboo, where a lot of sailors and wharf laborers stay, but he's not there. As usual. He's worse than a bird, flitting here and there between all the places where scholars go to spout poetry or play their games, if he's not on some yacht doing those things." She sighed. "If the greens were to suddenly take it into their heads to investigate us, and come after me, holding me responsible for not knowing where my crew is, what would I say?"

"The truth, that he vanishes to visit his scholar friends," I said.

Dinek gave a short sigh. "True, true, true." I had already noticed that she liked things squared properly. Which is a good quality in a ship captain. "One comfort, he always turns up. Who knows how he hears we're about to sail. Now I'm off to the lumber yard. It's the watchful sparrow that gets the cricket."

She sped off, leaving me wondering what orders the duke might have issued after he left. Two years ago, there had been followers watching me after our arrival and the story had spread about my sword blasting a way through the reef ahead of criminals. I knew a little about the arduous work of investigation. Father had talked often about it, as a necessary part of his work as Imperial Chief Censor. First Brother, as well. The reminder of my guiltless brother blinded by that villainous Xianti brought the usual surge of grief and anger, to be consciously dismissed. Anger begets only more anger, I reminded myself.

Nothing assuages grief except time.

I went about my tasks in an orderly manner, without contravening the smallest law. As before, surely I'd soon bore them into dropping any shadows assigned to follow me.

When I got back to the Three Kingfishers, it was in time for household practice out in the yard. I joined with a will—I needed to work hard enough to settle all those memories and emotions I'd stirred up like mud at the bottom of a pool. I also needed to get back to my own secluded place to work on my Essence skills, and to practice on the sword. But not until I was certain that I wasn't being watched.

Over the next few days, I tended tables at the inn, only going out with basket or abacus when Ma Shao sent me. I resisted the impulse to turn suddenly and search behind me—a thing I'd read countless times in the gallant wanderer tales was sure to raise suspicion. Only guilty people looked behind them.

Last time, my shadows had been obvious, once the Watcher, the Falcon observer who was in charge of the Falcons in any domicile, had pointed them out. One had sat on the other side of the street, fishing. I was reluctant to bring any more attention to myself than I already got by asking the current Watcher, a rather somber man who also did some of the heavy labor around the inn. But on the third day, I approached him after our yard practice. "Is the inn being spied on?"

He blinked at me. "By?"

"The greens." I blushed at the astonishment on his face.

Then, as I'd dreaded, he gave me a suspicious look. "No. Have you done something that warrants the magistrates' attention?"

"No," I said. "I just wondered."

He grunted a negative, and went to clean his practice sword and rack it.

Late the next morning a couple of entertainment girls my age entered the Three Kingfishers, taking one of the tables near the window. They reminded me of peacocks or parrots — birds of brilliant feather — out of place in so plain an inn as this one, with their bright layers of floating gauze, dangles on tiny chains glinting in their complicated hair twists, and their cheeks and lips rouged. Entertainers tended to stay closer to their own places of work, where they could get customers to spend money. Maybe they were off-duty, here just to sample plain fare, rather than the fancy foods that were rumored to be on offer at those places.

"What can I get you? The day's dish is spicy clam and seaweed."

"I'll have that," one said. The other nodded, and when I came back with tea and bowls, they were carrying on a teasing flirtation with some young guards at a table nearby.

I set the dishes down, and the one with the blacker hair exclaimed, "Ay! Looks so tasty! Sister Oriole was right about this place."

Mindful of Ma Shao, I said, "You ought to bring her back some time," and made to turn away.

The girl put her hand out. "You look like someone who might enjoy a good play." Her wide-set eyes were what they call apricot-shaped, her best feature.

"I do?"

"You ought to come see Sister Oriole in *The Five Handsome Scholars*, at the Rose Parasol," said the other. She, too, had apricot eyes. Sisters? "It's full of toothsome dancers. If you like watching men dance — oops, oh I am so clumsy." She used a fold of her gauze to scrub at a little spilled tea.

"I can get you more."

"No, no, don't trouble yourself," the girl said, tapping a finger insistently in a few drops that she had not mopped up.

As I looked down, puzzled, she used her forefinger to sketch the character for *On*. Surprised — intrigued — I said, "I don't usually go to plays."

"Why not begin now? While you're still young?"

"Yes, before you know it, you'll be doddering around wishing you'd had more fun when you could!"

"My next afternoon off is in two days," I said—and both nodded brightly, a little too vigorously, and picked up their spoons to attack their soup.

I left them, and tended the rest of the customers as the pair ate, flirted, paid, and then left in a swirl of gauzes. What was that all about, I wondered. Did On send them on a bet?

Two days later, I paid to enter the Rose Parasol, feeling awkward as one does when everyone else in a crowd knows the etiquette of a place. I was also aware of a lingering trace of grief, even guilt. I had little experience of plays, though I'd heard many poetry recitations and musical entertainments in court. My place had always been as far from the performance square as possible as I was invariably lowest and least in rank. Mother had regarded plays as vulgar and frivolous. My expectation was therefore of vulgarity and frivolousness, perhaps with a lot of romantic sentiment of the most boring kind—floods of tears and wailing for lovers with whom only the briefest glance had been exchanged before fate threw duty and dire circumstance in the way of happiness. The title of this play being *The Five Handsome Scholars*, I expected five versions of the same thing.

Instead, five separate stories expertly wove together. While the most noble of the five scholars did indeed suffer tragedy while uttering the most lofty poetry, the other four stories differed greatly, two of them vying for laughter. All this set to the most ravishing music, with catchy songs, and oh, the dancing!

When male dancers came out, I assumed that On might somehow be among them. Of course he would be the one who leaped the highest. But that dancer was too tall, the second one too broad, and so on. None of these expert, enthralling dancing men was On—so I found myself drawn into the stories, laughing and listening with the rest of the avid audience.

Until suddenly it was over.

I looked around, bewildered. I sat on a bench up in the crowded balcony with others who'd paid a modest charge. He was not among us, or even down below at the tables. Slowly people got up, talking and laughing. One or two humming songs. I hadn't seen the apricot-eyed sisters, though I thought that during one of the dances I recognized one.

I began to shuffle out, until I found myself walking next to another girl, who wore her night-black hair in typical fox ears, her servant robe dull blue. She stepped closer to me, and as we approached the door, closer still. As we passed through, she whispered, "Ren, you've got two spies shadowing you. Leave your window open tonight. First Turtle hour."

Then we were through, and with a flicker of modest blue sleeves, she vanished into the dispersing crowd. It was then that my astonished mind caught up, and I recognized On's voice in that whisper. Why the disguise?

And so, my instinct was right.

Intensely curious—and even more intensely self-conscious—I scarcely dared to look right or left as I proceeded back down the street to the Three Kingfishers.

THREE

In those days when Ghost Moon shone full on the vast ocean —
When pearls wept tears, and in the summer sun, jade gave off
smoke —
That was when feeling wakened, though she petitioned the moons,
could it not wait?

STRICTLY SPEAKING THE REST of the evening was my own, but I offered to help, as I felt less exposed among the others. When at last we closed up and the tables were clean and set for morning, I retreated to the attic.

At that particular time, there were no Falcons staying with us. Fia, no longer considered a child, had a room in her family's wing at the back of the house overlooking the yard. The two sharing the women's side of the attic with me were the poultry girl taking over from Ma Shao's mother, whose knees were getting too stiff for chasing chickens, and the laundry woman, young and strong. She was invariably asleep withing a single breath of lying down.

I whispered to the poultry girl, who—two years younger than I, regarded me as an elder—"I'm leaving the window wide so it doesn't get stuffy."

She accepted that with a tucked chin, and curled up in her corner.

I had to keep myself awake through the slow Dragon hours until Turtle, but I did this by sinking into memory of Essence lessons.

I was roused by a slight scrape on the tiles outside the open window. I pushed the window wider and peered out. A silhouette crouched nearby, profile familiar before a weakly moonlit face turned my way. That was On.

I eased out, feeling my way toward On. How I hated heights! I had to ignore that dropping sensation in the pit of my stomach and the back of my knees until I reached him. "You're still in your disguise."

"I'm living this way right now."

We spoke in whispers. "Disguised as a girl?"

> *"Parasols and paulownias grow together,*
> *And mated ring-neck ducks glide side by side.*

How do you think I escaped my snake of a guardian?"

"Ay!"

"The Xuan cousins helped me. You met them a couple days ago. They think you're my latest flirt, and they were on a romantic mission."

I did not know how to respond to 'latest flirt' so I ignored it, and said, "I thought they might be related."

"Their mothers were twins, and they were born within a month of each other, so even though they had different fathers, they like to think of each other as twins. Especially as they only have each other."

I had often thought about what it might be like to have a sister, but I did not say so. My regrets over my family—how reminders always hurt—were a heart-wound that refused to heal. I said, "Why are you in disguise?"

"Because the other day, when we rowed in from *Pangolin*, there were two rings of guards surrounding your inn."

"What? I thought…"

"You thought that many greens had a day off?" On chuckled under his breath. "What a picnic you must think their lives are."

I said stiffly, "I wouldn't recognize two rings of guards as such."

"Maybe you should learn," he retorted, dead serious now. "I overheard gossip that the duke himself was upstairs. Interviewing you?"

"Yes."

"I got back into my old disguise, just in case, but the greens are not after me. Ren, you've got two very good spies watching your every move. What exactly happened with the duke?"

I told him everything, including what Granny Zim said. I ended with, "He called me Pangolin Ren, and his Essence expert got no response from Sagacious Blade. I don't think he's sure that I'm the one who warned Xianti. I was watched for a time after our initial arrival on this island."

He stared up at the moon, profile a frown.

My nerves flared painfully. "Can you teach me how to spot the spies?"

"It's easy, but exasperating. Go down one of the shopping streets. When you pass a vendor selling glass or metal or even very shiny enameled things that reflect, get a look behind you. Don't be obvious about it. The good ones won't be obvious to you. So you do it again. And again. If you see a familiar face, good chance that's your spy. If it happens on another day, you've definitely got a shadow. Yours are very good."

"Not those sent by Commander Nan." I describe the fisher from two years before. "From the duke?"

"Yes."

"Then, could he know who I am? He doesn't trust me, for certain."

"Since he got a message that the imperial crown prince survived the storm, that means your true name could have been mentioned in that message. You did say the imperial prince recognized you."

"He did."

"If he did, and he mentioned you in his communication with Huyun Shandek, then our Handsome Huyun surely is very angry at the mysterious princess who turned up in Tiger Eye Bay and warned the crown prince. But he can't know that was you—unless the prince recognized the sword? Or described it?"

"He would never have recognized it. The imperial family did not know I had it. And it was dark in that room. Our fight was barely a single exchange. He can't have seen the sword in detail, especially since I froze his meridians."

On gave a slow nod. "That makes sense. We can hope the duke can't be sure that you and the princess are the same, but I wouldn't count on it."

"That's no comfort."

"It ought to keep you wary. There's more. Just found out yesterday that the duke is in the habit of taking a yacht to Crescent Island once or twice a year."

"Crescent...?" Then I had it. "That island on the other side of the reef. The one we were to be sold as slaves from?"

"Yes. And yes."

"Does he have an estate or retreat or summer house there?"

"That's just it. There's nothing there. Except the fishing villages along the north side, and that one old trade bay on the south side, supposedly unused except by a few traders, since the previous dynasty."

I said doubtfully, "Are you saying he participates in the slave auction? I can't believe it. What I mean is, everything he does is talked about, and surely if he bought slaves who were seized from groups of refugees, that sort of gossip would be all over. That's a different matter from contract slaves—which I hate, but it's legal."

"True."

"Also. He left Cygnet and those other people alone at the Snow Crane temple. I've never heard of any of those women or children being enslaved again."

On lifted a shoulder. "Who would know? It's not as if they have advocates before the imperial throne."

That hit me like an invisible blow. I said uneasily, "But there would be *some* sort of talk, I'd think. There were so many of them."

"True," On conceded. "It's possible that their sheer number protected them, because yes, there was still talk when we arrived almost two years after you first landed here, about the girl with the blade of fire who slashed her way through the reef, saving a hundred or more captives. There's a good chance that the Snow Crane temple got them all safely situated as the duke smiled benevolently and took all the merit to himself."

I remembered the eel monk, and this time I agreed wholly. If anyone could protect those people without hurting anyone in the process, I felt sure he would be the one.

On added, "From what the Pangolins said about Cygnet during our tea run, she alone would have brought in a huge trunk of gold. That kind of gossip also travels. And you're right, I heard nothing of the sort."

"Cygnet is still here. She teaches at a school at one of the temples. That much I know. I think MiMi, at the magisterial kitchen, would have passed the word if anything had happened to her. If Cygnet was friends with anyone, it was with MiMi."

"So Dinek told us. Back to the governor's travels. According to the Rose Parasol dancers, he always takes a fast yacht in preference to military scouts when he wants to go to the eastern end of the island, or anywhere else, so to the dancers, there's no difference between his trips for governmental affairs and jaunts for fun. There is a lot of competition among the entertainment houses for the privilege of providing entertainers for his yacht, because he is generous with rewards."

"I remember he went to investigate that bay on the south side of Crescent Island, or at least Commander Nan said he did. Maybe he started checking on that bay since then, to see that those slavers and their buyers don't slither back."

"According to the girls, he's been sailing there once or twice a year for eight or ten years."

"It still could be an inspection," I said. "He might have gone at the wrong times to catch the slavers. Didn't we learn that the slavers were only there once or twice a year for a brief time? We'd have to find out if his visits were at the same time or different times. But again, I can't believe he'd be buying slaves twice a year. Ay, I wish Koi was back with us! He'd tell us exactly what he overheard that night. We would not have known the duke's name then, but Koi might remember having heard it, now that he knows who he is."

On shrugged, his earrings glinting in the weak moonlight. "There's more."

"More?"

"In light of that interview you had with the duke, there's gossip about the duke being granted an imperial princess for a marriage alliance."

"Granted," I repeated—but I knew that that could mean many things. If the emperor told a mere duke that said duke would be delighted to be honored with the hand of one of the imperial princesses, what could that duke say but yes?

And in any case… "When?" I asked.

"No word, except the talk all assumed it was imminent. You'd know better than I about that. Wouldn't that entail weeks of preparation, and the summoning of a grand fleet as honor guard?"

"Yes." I was trying to remember things I'd paid scant attention to as a child, and apply them to now. "Whichever princess it is, she'd know me at a glance. The only one I could trust would be Taisa. I need to be somewhere else by the time that happens," I muttered. "As for the honor guard…"

My mind skipped back and forth from the events earlier in the month to now. I said, "There was no *result* of the duke's plot. If there was a plot. The storm saw its end. But there might be *consequences*. Ay! I ought to have thought of that. Xianti would have been furious. He'd believe the plot on scant evidence, I feel sure, because it's exactly the sort of treachery he'd do himself. Oh, what if I was wrong? Granny Zim in the sword told me the duke was lying, but I'm the one who put together circumstantial evidence into the plot..."

"Remember, I was there. The circumstantial evidence was mighty convincing," On said.

"And you didn't hear the sword. What convinced you that he was lying?"

"It was the way he was laughing inside," On said flatly. "Gloating. Especially at the end. When he told you to stay put while he went to get servants, or guards, or whoever it was who was supposed to lock you up. He didn't act surprised. He didn't ask the questions that anyone else might have asked. But he wanted to get you boxed, which suggested that he did not want your helpful warning carried to anyone else. And that suggests plot if anything does."

I considered that, then said, "I got that same sense that he was laughing behind a fan the other day."

"Whatever he knows or doesn't know about your origin, Ren, you had better confront the fact that you've become a piece in the imperial game. Huyun Shandek likes the game. I don't trust him as far as a pig flies."

"Imperial game," I repeated.

"It's a game to them all," On retorted, his voice low and heated with passion. "But they'll surely call it an art, the way my snake of a guardian did.

> *In ancient days, they fought from ship to land,*
> *the dragon banner raised on high —*
> *They've all become the wind-blown dust...*

Can you imagine calling a street of burned houses and unburied corpses everywhere an art? Two days before my guardian launched his war in my name, I tried to tell him that art meant poetry and painting. Music. Ay! I'm telling this backwards."

I'd never seen him so disturbed as he briefly but vividly described being a small child when he woke up to shouts, clashes, flames, and before he was grabbed and carried away, he had to see his own family lying sprawled in the wreckage of his home, weltering in their blood.

As he spoke, he plunged his hand into his clothing, and pulled forth an object, which he held out on his palm. In the dim light I made out the subtle glisten of a jade ornament. Even in that weak light I could see that it was very fine, carved exquisitely—the sort of ornament princes carried. My brothers had them. "My brother pressed that into my hand before he went out to help defend the house. He thought they were brigands, there to steal," he said in a soft voice. "I was so small that my brother seemed next thing to an adult, and of course he'd go fight alongside our father. He was *twelve*."

He put the jade away, and his voice lowered. "The only other artifact I have. No, had. Was a three-fold screen, depicting the two moons touching at New Year's, and the twelve earthly branches beyond. The single thing saved out of my house, by my mother's nanny. Who he saved, I suspect merely because she would do the labor of caring for me. He wanted to dispose of it because of scorch marks, but my nanny begged him not to because my mother had made it. When Nanny died, he ordered the servants to carry it away but I said it was art. In spite of the scorch marks. You know what he said? He said that art was for women. Men's art was war."

"That sounds exactly like something Xianti would say," I responded with hearty disgust.

"Ay, it's one of the earliest precepts in Liad Il's *The Way of the Blade*. Only when he wrote it, he was actually talking about methods for limiting destruction in order to gain the most effect."

"I know nothing about Liad Il except his name. My brothers had to read him. Oh, and my horrible imperial Cousin Xianti quoted him constantly." I turned to On, and added, "Apparently Liad Il was part of your education, too?"

On sat back on his elbows, nose pointed up toward the sky. "I thought you would have guessed by now. I'm pretty sure Koi did. But he was kind enough to pretend he didn't." He sighed. "However, this situation isn't kind. To either of us."

If my brother had read Liad Il, then Koi would have, too. Also, they would have heard all the names of the people the emperor regarded with suspicion in the never-ending struggle around the throne.

Game. Art.

It seemed that in this case, the emperor had reason for suspicion—

And I had it. "On. Sheion?"

On laughed.

"Do not ask for my full name —
The tide strews sand, their bones are cold...

Not much of a disguise, eh?"

"*You're* the Upstart Prince!"

"Only I tried not to start... No. Not the least funny. Lan Renti, permit me to introduce one unhumble, thoroughly useless, Kwai Sheion, the last of a long and venerable ancestry. And ghost of many names since."

"How... What..." I couldn't lay my tongue to one of the questions streaming through my mind.

"The only way I thought I could stop a war led in my name was to run. I ran. But that didn't stop my uncle's war in my name. I guess he assumed he could always catch me once he won. Or that I would come crawling back, lured by golden dragon banners."

His quiet voice was so bitter that my nerves chilled.

"I joined the refugees fleeing in advance of attack. Happened to defend the Xuan cousins from a pack of two-legged wolves preying on the wretched poor. The cousins in return taught me the art of being a girl. That's how I disappeared without a trace — twice, my uncle's searchers passed right by us." On uttered a short, sour laugh. "He had his battle anyway. And died in it."

Now I had the context: his guardian was the uncle who was defeated by Ji Jiang at the eastern end of this island. Who years before that, motivated by revenge — and ambition — had saved only a very small boy and a nanny out of his entire family and dependents during an imperially-ordered slaughter.

I could tell by the rue beneath On's insouciant tone that these memories still galled him, and I began to comprehend why On, a skilled martial artist, regarded war with visceral hatred. He said, "Enough about me. You've got to consider what to do if the duke figures out who you are."

"I never thought to check if there is a wanted poster for me," I said, sickened. I'd never gone to look at the notice board because I'd been afraid to see Second Brother staring out of one.

"No. I checked. After all, you're young — younger than I am — and you've done nothing that the emperor can point to as criminal. Being part of a criminal family of course can be enough, except your branch of the Lans is so very highly regarded, from what I could discover. It won't bring any merit whatever to the emperor to publish your name all over, or for

Huyun Shandek to have you dragged down the main street in chains."

"Instead, he'd have spies watching me, while he gloated, thinking that I believe I'm hiding."

"Keep your allies close, and your enemies closer. That's another of the Liad Il precepts," On said.

"Even I've heard that one. Read it, in gallant wanderer tales."

"So the earnest Pangolin Ren, who had never attended a play, likes gallant wanderer tales?" On pretended surprise,

"I liked my first play very much," I said stiffly. I was not in the mood for teasing, unsettled as I was. But then On had lived with far worse experience, and threat, all his life. Rather than express my affront, I changed the subject. "I think I need to understand more. They all consider war a game. Not just the governor. It's Xianti. The emperor. The grand prince, and ayah! Especially his grandson Yiuti. My second brother—I don't think he sees war as a game so much as that it's inevitable. There *has* to be a way around that way of thinking. War, a *game*."

My mind flashed back to Circle. Which I had never thought of as a war game. To me, it was far more interesting when seen in the light of the natural circle of trade, the north producing things the south needed, and the south making things the north needed. Ship travel the lifeblood of this great circle. "I need to learn more…"

"And I have to finish my new play. *How* that arrogant tiger up in his pretty palace will hate it. He's going to hate it so much. Yes. It needs to circulate right before that princess comes…"

The starlight had gone, clouds smothering the dim light as a drizzle began to fall, chilling me to shudders. It didn't seem to bother On, though his clothing was much lighter than mine.

"You're shivering," he said abruptly. "And I'm braying like the donkey in my play. I'll go."

"Wait!"

He'd risen. He paused, a mere silhouette, barely discernable against the darkness. I asked, "Do I have watchers at night?"

He laughed. "I wouldn't be here right now if you did." Then he made a warding motion. "That sounded arrogant. It's always easier to spot the spies who watch elsewhere, and I know how to look for them."

"I'm going to try to learn to spot them, but will you tell me when, or if, the spies go away? Will I see you if I go to the Rose Parasol?"

"Maybe, though I'm not always awake in afternoons. This life means strange hours. But if you want to exchange news, begin attending plays. Or leave that window open. I sometimes escape to the open air on nights I don't earn my keep."

He ran lightly over the tiles, soaring between the roofs in a way that made my insides clench. I returned to the attic, my mind resounding with everything I had learned during that swift, soft-spoken conversation, at times barely audible above the gentle pat of rain.

Yes, he had lived with a worse burden than mine all his life. There surely were wanted posters issued under his true name.

I shed my wet clothes before wrapping myself in my bedding, where I lay wide awake.

And restless. So restless.

Now I wanted to get up and go outside again. To…?

It had never occurred to me to exercise at night. The proper and orderly progression of a day still guided me, an unquestioned order that I'd learned from my parents.

But what was to stop me from getting back to earnest work at night instead of day? Though I loathed heights, I'd managed to fly in spite of that. I'd fixed my gaze on my target, and not on the ground falling away below. I could do that from the roof, surely.

I'd have to. Because I had become a piece in their game.

FOUR

To the lofty peaks of great Mt. Lir the capital bowed down —
Three princes carved the empire into wintry ruin
Until the qilin empress dispersed the clouds,
To clear the ruin where the Immortal's Path ascends.
She soared to the summit to study
Unseen by warships in motion below.

FIRST, I HAD TO master and implement the lesson for the illusion charm that would blur me so that no one who was not looking directly for me would notice me. It took concentration to perform, and to sustain, but I was determined to make that into habit: if I was tempted to skip it, being tired at night, I had only to remember, *Huyun Shandek likely knows who you are.*

I began resuming my light skills practice tentatively, because I did not like being on the roof. I was never going to like being on the roof.

The world is so different when seen from the air. There's a sense of mirror reflection, light reflecting light, and life reflecting life—the unimaginable life of the stars above, and below the window-lights of those awake, lamps at the front of carriages, and in the swinging lamps of patrols in their ceaseless march. The rest of the worlds above and below slumber, indistinct shades of black and deep blue.

The first time I dared to look about me while balancing slowly a finger's width above the roof tiles, I was surprised by the sense that this view was familiar, I think from dreams. I cannot explain that, so I don't try. I can state with confidence that I seemed to think more clearly when I could see all the way to the horizon.

I learned that though the Essence charm on the sword enabled it to lift me, it did not actually guide my flight. I did. The sword's point gave me a focus to guide by. Which was why those first long flights were successful—I kept my eyes on the horizon, then when I neared my goal, and my gaze found it, unconsciously my body followed. By forcing myself to circle the roof gargoyles, round and round, then back again the other way, I learned to guide with my body.

Kneeling actually made guiding more difficult. I discovered that it was easier to stand and guide from shoulder or hip, as we correct without thought when walking. The sword's charm made me feel light as a leaf, but I still had to raise the sword with inner Essence, and propel it along. I discovered that riding air currents aided me.

When next I noticed On's light skills, I became aware that his brief periods airborne were different from mine in that they described the same arc as a thrown object. He could not go in a straight line. The Essence he'd inherited from that long-ago ancestor gave him only bursts, but he did it on his own, whereas I needed the sword. But my Essence sustained the flight.

At first I saw little of On, though I began attending the plays as a regular thing, my spy shadows diligently following me. One was a girl maybe two years older than I, or no more than twenty, I think, though I never saw her full on, only briefly in reflection. The other was an older man of the sort you saw everywhere selling steam buns or sugar sculptures. Not that he had wares, but he often wore an apron and carried a basket. It took me the longest to be certain of him.

I went back to see the *Five Handsome Scholars* three more times. I noticed a lot of other girls and young women were also return customers, judging by the way they sometimes sang the songs right along with those on stage. On my third visit, I spotted On, as Sister Oriole, among the dancers in the background. He was not the best, but neither was he the worst. Far from it. He danced with an exuberance that I found more entrancing than the formidable skills and perfectly articulated poses of the premier dancers. I don't know if it was my imagination, but I sensed that he had to keep himself from soaring upward.

He spotted me as well, for that night, he bounded along the rooftops toward me as I went about my regular practice — proving incidentally that the "invisibility" charm did not make one invisible to anyone looking for one.

"You came to the play! Did you have news?" he asked when he neared.

"No. I thought I would go see the plays as a regular thing, so that my visits would not seem suspicious."

"Good idea. What did you think of my dancing?" He struck a coy pose.

"You were in the group at the back. I wasn't sure it was you, at first."

"I'm lucky not to have inherited an obvious throat-knuckle, but I'm not good enough to be a primary dancer even if my throat were as flat as a woman's," On replied. "Male dancing is easier, a matter of strength, and some martial forms adapted to music. The girls have it far harder."

"Oh, I had enough lessons to understand that," I said, and memory brought a vivid image of beautiful Cousin Arati, graceful and controlled to the arch of her little finger. And what did all her beauty and training net her? Married summarily to a rough general and taken off to the west, away from her family. Poor soul, I sometimes thought of her, hoping she'd found a semblance of happiness.

On said, "The Xuan cousins taught me some of the traditional dances, so I can fill in the background when needed." He shrugged a gauze-draped shoulder. "Don't worry about me. Or is that sober expression for something, or someone, altogether different?"

I could not explain why his talk of dance had arrowed my thoughts straight to marriage. It was at once too irrelevant and yet too intimate, so I said, "I wish I knew how much I'm being watched. That is, to what larger purpose."

"Meaning?" He perched on the tiles of the slanted roof as easily as sitting on a floor cushion.

"I need to learn more," I said. "I was very well taught for a child of twelve. But I'm no longer twelve. Every subject I try to contemplate presents me with a wall of my own ignorance. Yet if I go to a bookstore to repair that, are the spies going to demand an accounting of what I buy from the bookseller?"

"Of course they will," On said. "Buy a variety of things. Hide what you want among them. That should puzzle your watchers."

"I don't want to puzzle them. I want to bore them. And my earnings do not extend to profligate buying."

"What do you want to study? Maybe I can help."

"You can't."

"Why not?"

"Because you were educated to think in terms of war," I said. "I know you hate war, but I don't think a military path is the only one. I need to learn, oh, the things I ought to have been learning, had Mother been able to keep teaching me. I feel sure she would have begun teaching me which islands are known for what they trade, for their customs, and their history. How the empire fts together properly — in peace."

On gave a slow nod.

> "Battlefields and beacons — the imperial summons —
> Sea-lanes and cloudy mountains clogged with booted dust.
> There's few enough scholars left to their brushes,
> Earning tassels as merit, rather than kills.

Leaving aside my education, and you're not wrong, what are you going to do with what you learn?"

"Find a way to rescue my family other than more fighting," I said, and then added defensively, "which I know sounds just as arrogant as the duke laughing at me behind his invisible fan as I pretended to be Pangolin Ren. I know I'm just sixteen. I have no power. No worth to any of these others who play their 'game.' I'm merely another piece on the board. But I intend to try."

On turned to me, half his face in shadow. The other half visible only in weak light from the paper lamps still burning a couple of stores down. "I learned not to discount age, or how one person, however powerless, can change everything."

"How?" I asked, because he seemed to want to talk.

He settled his gauzy robe around him, fists resting on his knees. It was not at all a feminine pose, though I'd seen him mincing and sidling with the dancers as demurely as any of them, earlier.

"The day I learned that," he said, "was a rarity in that my usual watchers were not there. My bodyguard never came into the library with me and my tutor, and as for the tutor, that venerable grouch was irritated with me because I'd left my inkstone behind once too often. So he sent me back to fetch it."

On explained rapidly, with quick gestures, how that journey meant crossing the back garden, which was quite secluded, almost a separate estate from the front where his guardian lived. It was an excuse to leap the walls, which he enjoyed far more than lessons. He'd already learned to hide the extent of his talent, which meant taking a circuitous route so that no one would see him leap.

"I landed near the back entrance only used by servants, climbed through the open window, and passed by the cool room containing jars of rice and oil and dried beans and the like. Where I saw movement. Here I found myself face to face with a boy a year or so younger than I. I saw my own startlement mirrored in his face. Not just that. Fear, too. We both stood still as I took in the fact that his servant gray robe fit quite ill, and was that a bare foot under the dragging hem? Servants all wore house slippers, which kept their steps noiseless."

I gave a nod—it had been the same in the imperial palace.

"I'd backed a few steps, but he froze, one hand having dropped something into the jar. A pungent smell on the air reminded me of emetic herbs, which I'd taken once when I'd eaten too many candied haws. *Are you poisoning us?* I asked, indignant—it did not occur to me then that being wary of poison was not a part of regular life for everyone. He gave me a quick shake of the head. *It's medicine.* I pointed at my backside. *It smells like downward-draining herbs.*"

On paused, then shook his head, and went on with his tale. "He admitted that he'd been told it was medicine, but I think that doubt had already set in because we stared at once another, long enough for me to see his gnawed knuckles, and the hollows in his cheeks that meant not enough food. Of course there was fear. I also knew, even at my very young age, that any outsider caught within the palace or grounds would be put to death. The truth of those rules was written in the air around the marching guards, in the high walls, in the gargoyles scowling from the roof into the demon world to hold demons at bay. Fear, I expected. It was his doubt that appealed to me. Though at that time I could not have put my own doubt into words, I sensed that this intruder was beginning to question whatever orders had caused this encounter."

"Had he already dosed the jar?" I asked.

"He had. He admitted it, though by then he was ghost-pale with terror. So I told him to run. He took a step or two, then I think hunger forced him back, and he said, *But I was promised two silvers if I did the job properly!*"

"Oh," I said, flinching. I knew that story.

On uttered a breath of a laugh. "I can see you've read the same tales. I said to him, *Two silvers, to do a job they should have done? Don't you listen to the stories about Jong Siang?* And when he protested that he did, I said, *Then you should know that in the stories, they promise a lot of silver or gold to make sure you return so they can...* And I drew my finger across my throat."

Even though this had happened years ago, I found myself breathing easier in the knowledge that On had not condemned this unknown boy to certain death.

"I told him to help himself to the buns cooling nearby, and go. He stuffed buns into his filthy clothes and scrambled through the window. Then I had the problem of what to do about the jar, because I also knew that if I told the cook that there was probably poison, and my guardian found out I hadn't done anything about the perpetrator, I'd get a fearful beating. So I put my back to the jar, and tipped it until it crashed, spilling the pickled cabbage that everyone prized so much. The sound of the crash brought servants running from the cooking area. By then I had splashed myself liberally, my eyes watering as I howled that I'd slipped and fell."

"You saved the household," I said.

"Yes, but. I knew now that I, powerless, was still a target. I was constantly being told how important I was, how imperial my blood. Later I wondered if the target that day might have been my guardian. In any case, someone was willing to poison an entire household to get to us. And they used a child younger than me. I never overlook how important one person can be. I'm asking you again, what do you want to do with the knowledge?"

"I am so ignorant that I don't yet know," I admitted. "Only that I need to learn. And find a way to rescue my family without adding to the strife. But at least as pressing is the possibility of one of the imperial princesses appearing. Is there any talk of when?"

"Not yet, though much speculation. Some insist that no one travels during Hungry Ghost Month, which would mean late summer."

Mother and Father had both insisted that "Hungry Ghost Month" — between Phoenix Moon's sixth and seventh months — was an invention of ignorant commoners, because that was the time when the two moons are farthest apart in their circle, leaving the sky mostly filled with stars.

"The imperials would pay no attention to Hungry Ghost

Month," I said firmly.

He shrugged. "Another thing. I know you don't want to think in terms of war. Neither do I. But sometimes you have to in order to know what you need to counter."

I hated hearing this, and whined, "I don't want to study military writers to figure this out."

"You don't have to. You've got me," he said, flashing that fox-grin. It was gone in a heartbeat. "Let's discuss what the emperor likely wants by this sudden move."

I said, "I did think about that. If Xianti believed me, it would infuriate the emperor. It surprised me that the governor, also a duke, wasn't summoned to the court."

"The emperor might be spread too thin to risk being turned down with some specious excuse—usually illness in the family," On said. "If the emperor fears he's losing prestige he's most likely to reinforce his prestige by launching an invasion. Sending a princess would cost less. And Huyun Shandek can't spurn her without losing face in court circles. As well as inviting an excuse for retribution that will look righteous in the court's eyes."

"Spread too thin… This might not be solely an imperial slap in the face for daring to plot against Xianti. The emperor might need something that he hasn't been able to get, only now he has a … a moral hold, so to speak."

"Exactly."

"Which would be what?"

"The most obvious choice is conscription. In order to make war, you need men. We know that the imperial prince rode all over the imperial island snatching men away from their villages. That's not something you can do more than once in ten years, if you take everyone over ten."

"Conscription," I repeated, thinking back. "How Huyun Shandek would hate that. Especially if…"

"What?"

"If those ships he's building in the lake below the Falcon scrape are meant to be sea hawks rather than traders."

On said, "You still think he was intending to invade the imperial island if his plot was successful?"

"Why kill the crown prince, and another prince with a claim to the throne, unless he meant to take it himself?" I asked. "It doesn't take any strategy books to see that."

"Actually, it mostly does," On said with another quick grin. "But let that pass. The imperial crown prince would certainly have seen that, after you revealed the plot. So he—or the emperor—might intend to ally with this island by demanding proof of loyalty in a bride-present of the island's resources. Whereas the choice his grace the governor has is to give in, or be invaded. Unless he can negotiate his way out of it."

All that seemed obvious once On laid it out. I could also see that there was little I could do to prevent yet more tragedy, and said so.

"Ayah, remember influence," On said. "Not that I was successful when I tried to block my uncle by removing myself. But that was because I'd overestimated my importance."

"You were raised to think you were irreplaceable," I said.

He lifted his chin. "Thank you for that. And it's true. But I failed to stop that battle. Doesn't mean you'll fail. But warding off bloodshed means finding the right influence." He jumped to his feet, yawning. "I'll scout some books and leave them outside this window. Be sure to look."

FIVE

*She read that under the mantle of Heaven
Spring turns all things to art,
And art turns all things to love.*

HE WAS AS GOOD as his promise.

Two days later, I found a grubby, much-used history of the island lying outside the window. I smuggled it in and read it. When I was done, I wondered what to do with it, lest it raise questions. I tried putting it outside the window again—and in the morning it was gone. I found out next time we met that he sneaked into one of the schools for merchants' boys who wanted to test into public service, took the books, then put them back after I read them.

That was our pattern for a while, as work parties went about refurbishing an already orderly street, and incidentally stiffening shoreline defenses. The gossip was that the emperor's imperial niece was to make a visit to the duke's mother, Dowager Duchess Huyun.

The press of urgency to be elsewhere intensified each day, even seeping into my dreams. Meanwhile my shadows remained diligent. After one especially sleepless night, I sought Dinek, and mindful of the spies, asked her to go with me to the theater, where it would be difficult to be overheard.

She was clearly surprised, but accepted with alacrity, and it was clear that she really enjoyed any kind of entertainment. As we filed out, I murmured to her, "Is there a chance of a tea run soon?"

She shot me a sympathetic glance, then said with an air of puzzlement, "Last week, it seemed there might be three tea runs coming up, but suddenly I'm getting ambiguous words. Everyone at the Chart is still nice, but they don't quite look at me when they tell me that this run or that run is a problem, or already promised to someone's aunt's brother's boss—an old debt—and the like."

"Is there a sense that they want to keep the *Pangolin* here?" I asked.

She studied me. "It's possible, but there've been no orders."

I sighed, then whispered, "Can you just slip the anchor-cable, and sail?"

"No." She raised a hand. "We'd never get past the promontory." She frowned. "I need Fan to tell me for certain, but it seems that the patrols are more vigilant than ever out to sea, as if they expect pirates or the like. Fan is much better at defensive thinking."

But Fan was at the Falcon scrape—which, I remembered from Koi's words, had been donated by the duke's mother. Dinek and I parted, with me thinking about the fact that all the martial arts sects were registered. We'd heard that the very first day we arrived. At the time it meant nothing, but now I wondered how much the duke kept track of their movements.

There was the duke's mother again. Koi had told me that she was a duchess who never used that title, just like the duke preferred 'Governor' over 'Duke.' All Koi knew about her was that she'd once been saved by Falcons, back when it was only women, and so she'd made that distant palace retreat over to the Falcons. That argued for a grateful personality. But how grateful?

Or rather, was she like her son, liked by all, but with unspoken ambitions? If I met her without Sagacious Blade at hand, would I even know if she was laughing behind an invisible fan at me?

I said to Dinek before we parted, "If I just vanish, you'll know I had to."

She gave me a tiny, unhappy nod—and not two days later, she turned up at the Three Kingfishers, loudly calling for a meal, but her eyes kept ranging over the room, and to the windows.

I served her, my mind racing. It was clear she had news, and we had to be able to talk. The only time I had free would be during the dead hours mid-afternoon. I said, "I need to get something from my trunk on the *Pangolin*."

Looking immensely relieved, she said, "I'll row you out."

The fact that she made herself available on the spot testified to urgency, and I had to strictly control my impatience until at last we were bumping over the waters. When we both felt that we were safe from listeners, she said, "Dove came back last night. She says that there are more questions, but because of our experiences on Crescent Island, she chased one line of inquiry. Ren, I don't even know what to say or believe, but Dove is adamant that the slavers on Crescent Island are still operating. And do you know who gets half the profits?"

Sick at heart—but not surprised—I said, "Governor Huyun Shandek."

Dinek's face was crimson from rowing in the heat of summer. "How did you know?"

Now that we were on the water, I told her everything, leaving out only On's personal history and his name, which were his to tell. I finished, "If the governor's planning to join the fight for the dragon throne, then he'd need a fortune, and selling people is one of the most lucrative commodities, with no investment at all if you steal them."

Dinek actually shivered. "Dove says that trunks of gold are brought out, guised as provisions, while all the singing and dancing is going on, and stored in the hold. That's only one source. Dove says there might be more… She thinks it might have been going on for a long time, maybe generations. This is the way the island gets rid of its miscreants and refugees, but it has expanded a great deal ever since the troubles broke out. Oh, here we are at the *Pangolin*. Should we go aboard?"

"I'm being watched, so we must."

And I clambered aboard behind Dinek. I fetched my heavy winter tunic, which I did not want, but I felt that I had to have something in hand. Dinek looked decidedly unhappy when we descended to the boat. "I don't know what to do. An invasion?"

"I'm sorry to say I have no solutions. I'm also sorry to have gotten us into this whirlpool. I thought we'd escaped."

Dinek sighed. "But if the governor truly is bent on rebelling against the emperor, then invasion was going to happen anyway."

We rowed largely in silence back, Dinek grim. Before we neared the wharf, I said, "I will only seek you out if I find a way around our difficulties."

"What way?" She gave me a look. "Ren, what can even a princess do? You're sixteen! How can you avert a war?"

"I don't know, but I mean to try."

How indeed?

That night, when I was about to go out to practice flying Sagacious Blade and think, I heard the mutter of thunder in the distance, and closer by, heavy splats of rain. The arrival of sixth month meant summer storms, everyone said.

I pulled my head back in and sat on my bedding, mulling Essence lessons and ships. I was deft with the charm that blurred my surroundings. Could that extend to an entire ship? Oh, I knew it was possible, that it had happened for years — and that Essence masters had ways to counter that charm, regularly performed in ship engagements. I'd thought such talismans far beyond my abilities. But now?

It was time to sink back into memories, and listen to the Essence guidance again. I discovered that the charm existed, and I knew that I could sustain it, if I did nothing else. But there was also raising a fog. As long as there was water, it could be mixed with a little fire, and spun into vapor. Fire was the simplest of all Essence charms for me, especially during the day. This charm to raise fog was easy — as long as I had enough water. I had to resist the impulse to enfog the building, which would definitely bring notice.

It occurred to me a day or so later that I had not seen On for several days. I decided to attend the theater again, as I had time free.

When I got there, I discovered a great stir. Far more finely dressed nobles than I'd ever seen on the island disembarked from decorated carriages, guards in clan colors clearing gawkers out of the way as they went inside.

I found someone my age in the crowd. She was dressed like me, so I approached her, and after a polite greeting, asked was there something special happening?

She turned to me, eyes wide with excitement. "Yes, they say her grace Madam Duchess has come down from her mountain. She's here to see the play!"

"She is?" I asked, peering around.

"Ayoh, not *here*. Yet. You can be sure the greens will clear us all out of the way." The girl laughed. "But she is in Cloud Terrace, it's said to make ready for the imperial princess, who is coming to court Handsome Huyun Shandek."

My stomach dropped. "Which imperial princess? Has

anyone said?"

Her eyes rounded. "An imperial princess," she repeated, as if they were all more or less alike.

I thanked her, suspected that more questions might draw notice, and wormed further into the crowd to confuse my spies.

I very much wanted to get a glimpse of Madam Duchess—but so did everyone else, it seemed, and all the places had been sold out since morning. I turned away, and began to thread through the crowd back toward the street when a drift of silk brushed my hand, and a pair of girls strolled by, one carrying an umbrella. The other passed so close to me her robe fluttered against me—and her fingers pressed a wadded-up bit of paper into my hand.

I looked up, but the two had their backs to me, and vanished into the crowd. My heart jolted. I kept moving, until I was inadvertently stopped behind the broad back of an egg-seller bearing two baskets, and taking advantage of the crowd to bawl, "Eggs! Fresh-laid! Two tin, eight for five!"

Using his back as a cover, I fingered open the note, and read: *Around back.*

I tore the paper to tiny bits and dropped it underfoot as I slowly edged around the egg-seller. How would I shake my spy?

Then I remembered that I had a huge crowd to hide in. This was a perfect opportunity to see how well my charm for going unnoticed worked during daytime. I knew that the charm was less effective if someone searched carefully, but perhaps that was more difficult to do in a crowd?

Time to find out.

I was faster with the charm by now. Between one step and another I performed it, and then darted this way and that through the thinning crowd. By the way no one reacted, I became convinced I was no more noticeable than a gust of breeze.

To make certain, once I'd made my way down the narrow alley between the Rose Parasol and the shoe store next to it, I waited behind a climbing wisteria for the spies to appear. I was pretty certain I glimpsed the back of Apron Man, who was moving slowly through the crowd, pausing as a swarm of children raced and rambled by.

Satisfied that I'd escaped his notice, however briefly, I ran to the discreet door at the back, and relaxed the charm. On opened it himself. He was dressed in vivid wedding colors of red and green, with fine blue trim, his face and eyes rouged and painted.

"You look very…" I began, then shut my teeth with a click as my mind caught up with the fact that I was making a personal remark uninvited. Men did such things to women, of course, all the time, but from my earliest days I'd been exhorted to believe that only wicked women trespassed so against men. Women were judged by their beauty as well as their birth and accomplishments; men had a wider range of possible capacities to be evaluated by.

"Fetching? Handsome? Not ridiculous," he finished. "You'd insult Xuan Wuyang's artistry, then. Come in. I have to get you stashed before the call to the stage."

"You will be performing?"

"We all are," he said, beckoning. "Did you come to see me?"

"I came to talk to you, but I want to see you perform. I also very much want to see Madam Duchess. Perhaps meet her."

"Oh? No, it'll have to wait," he said to himself as he led me along narrow passages, through a riot of color—performers darting in all directions, scenes being carried, fabric and flags, lanterns.

"Why the chaos?" I asked.

"Change of play." Here he paused for dramatic effect, his wide eyes reflecting the lamps that we passed. "Someone asked Madam if she likes tragedies. She said that there were too many tragedies in life at present. And next thing we all knew, the play that had been rehearsed for weeks vanished into the air, and Owner in desperation is bringing out one of my efforts." He grinned. "The *Scholarly Duel*—*The Scholars' Duel*, still not quite sure about what to call it—is my second play. That no one would look at because no one has heard of me. Me as On Lu," he corrected as we ducked under a rolled rug being carried by two muscular men. "Mysterious On Lu, the hermit scholar. Lu for—"

"I know. Lu for the great poet-warrior who wandered about dispensing justice and posting poems exposing corrupt governors and others in powerful positions."

"You might have stopped your education at eleven or twelve, but at least you were reading the right things," On said cheerfully. "Right now, I'm merely Oriole. Too poor and insignificant for a family name."

We stepped over some spilled silver-painted bamboo swords as I asked, "Do you always remember which of the many yous you are?"

"Yes," he said. "Except if I drink too much. I try to keep my drinker selves simple, a poor but well-born fourth and fifth son studying for the Imperial Examination."

"Madness," I commented.

"What do you expect of someone who spins lives and histories out of air?" He flashed me a mocking glance before shoving me into a narrow space between a set frame and a stack of boxes of masks. He swung a curtain of gauze down in front of me. "You won't see anything yet; however once they light the lanterns, the gauze will be nearly invisible. And you'll get a very good view of the duke's mother." He ran off.

It was just as he said. A line of dancers brought out glowing paper lanterns, and more were hung above. The gauze was not quite invisible, but conveyed a shimmering effect.

This play was possible to put on at the last moment because so much of it was a duel through quotations of the ancients. Not Kanda so much as Ar Laq and especially the gadfly Mek Mak, poetry all these actors had grown up reciting until it was effortless. These duels were enchantingly woven with lots of music and dance, most of the latter done by Xuan Suanek and Wuyang, the cousins On had befriended. As orphans, former refugees, they'd never had a hope of notice among so many, but now their several years with On paid off: he had worked out so much of the dance of his plays with them that they knew every note and step.

The most interesting aspect was how much of On I recognized in it. Though the play was what I considered, at the time, dauntingly erudite (and now I recognize that it was dreadfully slow, infested with far too many shopworn clever quotations, especially from Mek Mak), but the dancing nearly made up for it. The stage was always in motion, with scenes coming and going, dancers leaping and whirling, songs sung from the heavens and from the demons in the underworld as the usual scholars, retiring maidens, jolly innkeepers, scowling fathers, and wicked thieves cavorted.

I could see the duke's mother right in front, at a table set with fine things. She looked very young in the flattering golden light, a handsome woman with a strong resemblance to the duke. She laughed when the audience laughed, and clapped with fervor at the dancing, yet everything about her demeanor revealed court training.

I needed Granny Zim to get past that polite curtain to her real thoughts. Though I reminded myself that Granny Zim did not actually read minds. She heard real motivations and intentions in words, tone, breathing. That, after many, many years of hearing so many voices, not only of those who wielded Sagacious Blade, but those in reach of the wielder's ears.

Watching from where I sat nearly on the stage, I was at once a part of the play and yet detached from it. The actors sometimes spoke or sang within arm's length from me. Once, as the Evil Demon whirled and leaped, my gauze fluttered.

I had no part in it, and yet when the audience laughed as poem clashed with poem, and dancers reacted with each verbal hit as if struck, tumbling gracefully about the stage while the speaker preened, my heart sped with exhilaration. I could feel the actors and dancers' elation intensifying, which sharpened movements and lilted voices—causing yet more delight from the watchers.

It was so like an infusion of Essence that I shut my eyes. Yes, there it was. I sensed the proximity of that strange lake of glowing Essence. It had not been evoked by a single skilled expert, but by every person on stage, whose joy in performing deepened the effect. This was art, being made by all. Though it was ephemeral in the physical sense, the intensity of this shared experience echoed in mounting elation between players and audience.

The effect was, I gradually came to see, so much like On himself, dynamic with hidden mockeries, but generous enough to bring misty smiles before the happy close.

Everyone rose to their feet, smiling and clapping, the air charged with shared enchantment. Then the spell broke like a bubble. The actors were all in movement, and shielded by them, I emerged from my cramped spot, as On appeared out of nowhere. "What did you think?" He spoke close to my ear, as everyone was talking.

"I need to speak to her," I said. "Without my spies. Can you get me to her?"

On's gaze diffused, and I understood that in the triumph of his moment, he had forgotten all about the larger problem. Art had prevailed, then I'd brought back the real world. But I had been ungenerous. "The play was *wonderful*," I said. "I didn't just see it, I felt it. And I could feel everyone feeling it."

His smile widened. He gave me a quick nod. "Might be tonight. Prepared to fly? It's the only way you will get away from that inn without notice."

"Yes," I said, though as always my innards clenched at the

idea. Then, remembering my spies, I said reluctantly, "I'd better go."

"I'll show you the way, but first I need to give both my hermit and Xuan Suanek a spark for the wildfire of gossip. It's on our way."

So saying, he slipped a fan from his sleeve, and spread it, casting me a grin. I saw a poem written on it in fine calligraphy.

On plunged into the crowd, turning and ducking expertly as I stumbled behind him, until he arrived at the place the crowd was thickest. With an apology here and a twitch there, he was through, and in the wispy voice of Sister Oriole, abashedly approached the more vivacious of the two Xuan cousins. "I was told to offer you this."

"Ayah," Suanek replied, taking the fan, and twirling it expertly before pausing. "What does it say? Whom is it from?"

"I can't read," Oriole said in her breathy whisper that somehow carried to all avid ears. "I didn't see him, only heard his voice above my ear, and when I turned he was gone."

"What does it say?"

"Read it out?"

The crowd exhorted Suanek, a circle of excitement. Suanek turned about gracefully, smiling down at the fan, then began softly,

> *"Her hair a fragrant cloud, sleek as cicada's wing*
> *Caught fast by a golden hairpin…"*

She stopped, blushed, touched her hairpin, and the voices rose louder, every eye on her. On backed out skillfully, unnoticed, and I followed until he pointed in one direction, then was gone, swallowed by the crowd.

I blundered my way out, after many false starts, and joined the huge crowd streaming from the Rose Parasol. I caught sight of the new owner, a tall man with gray in his mustache and beard, beaming proudly as the audience dispersed. Then I got that back-of-the neck sensation—my spy had spotted me.

I returned at a sedate pace to the inn, filled with images: the smooth, lovely face of the duke's mother; the avid crowd leaning over the balconies as they called exhortations to their favorite among the "scholars"; Suanek expertly shifting the audience's attention from the play to her as she teased them with the poem on the fan.

The united power of a crowd.

Six

Compassion's essence draws good fortune —
With this thought she dared the citadel.
A branch in the wind cannot be still —
For how could she hold back a tide of blood?

IN SPITE OF HIS night of triumph, On did not forget what I'd asked.

He was back just before we closed, bringing the Xuan cousins and a couple of other young women. The two cousins, flushed and bright-eyed with glee, were the principal talkers. On sat quietly, and as I served them I observed him being Oriole among others, two of whom I don't believe knew he wasn't a girl.

They drank a great deal, and Ma Shao kept the doors open as the coinage flowed with the wine. When his companions' faces were thoroughly red, On got up and made the gesture indicating the privy. I began industriously scrubbing a table between him and the door.

As he passed, he whispered, "Hour. Roof."

Tonight? We couldn't possibly be visiting the dowager. He must have something to tell me. Questions churned inside me. An hour later, we'd barely closed up down below when I trudged upstairs.

My reward for volunteering to serve till closing time was to find my two attic-mates already sound asleep, for laundry and chickens both demanded early rising.

I went to the window, and found On outside — to my surprise, he was not clad in his Oriole clothes, but he'd put up his hair in the man's hair clasp, and wore ink-stained, ragged scholar's robes. "Madam Duchess wants to meet the playwright," he whispered with a glance inside. "Who is rumored to be a hermit."

"Rumored?"

"I started that rumor myself," he replied with that fox grin. "Counting on the respected magistrates having better things to do than chase all over the mountain just to register a single scholarly hermit. But this very same hermit will make an exception for so exalted and respected a lady — if the interview can be private. She agreed, appointing any time during the last Dragon hour." He had carried a wadded-up ball of cloth with him. "Put this on. It's almost first Turtle. We'll have to hurry."

Surprised, I shook out a long tunic robe, slitted up the side for riding — a guard's robe, except it was even more ragged than the one On wore. It had patches at elbows and various other places.

"The only way I could think to get you in was to say that I'd bring my one servant, with me since childhood."

I pulled the robe around me. It was clean, its smell reminding me of the Rose Parasol — sweet candle-wax and cedarwood. A costume? I brought out Sagacious Blade. Clasping the sheath with one hand, I stepped on the blade, charmed myself to be unnoticed, then said, "Do you want to be charmed against notice?"

He glanced back at me. "Can you take the charm off again?"

"Yes."

"Good, then we'll be faster as we won't have to avoid the outer perimeter guards."

I passed my palm an arm's length from him, uttering the charm. He frowned. "I don't see anything different. Except are the lights blurry? Or is that how wildly tired I am? I should not have drunk even that one glass of wine."

"No, the blur is part of the charm. I don't know why it is."

He said, "I have an idea how to approach her. If it works, what questions do you want to ask her?"

I froze, questions blooming. So many questions. Any answer she might give would no doubt bring more questions.

He shifted on the tiles, a small sound that brought me back to myself. "I think, to start, if she knows why the emperor is sending an imperial princess now, nearly Ghost Moon Month, when traditionally travel is considered inauspicious."

He said nothing more, just ran along the roof's overhang so that no one below would hear his steps. I followed on the sword as he leaped over to the next building. I breathed away the familiar wringing of nerve and muscle, and glided after him. He sprang in arcs from roof to tree to roof up the street toward the magisterial building, and then to the next level up, where the great gates of the wealthy estates faced south, each gate guarded by the much-coveted stone lions only granted to the fifth rank and above. Each right-hand lion posed a paw on a symbol of the family's chief merit: a scroll for a scholar, a drum for a general, and so on.

Midway along these was a grand palace with the highest walls—guarded by the winged qilin only granted to princes. That surprised me—but then I remembered that the Ti family had governed this island before the Huyuns, back when the highest-ranking governor was related to an emperor. Interesting that no one had quietly replaced those qilin with lions—but then who would dare say anything?

We sailed over the heads of vigilant guards to the western, or women's side, and then alighted inside a court. Whoever came to the door of this court would assume we had been passed through by the guards. Who thinks to look up unless warned?

Still I was extremely uneasy, aware that on the other side of the central garden, Huyun Shandek dwelt, and he'd recognize me in a heartbeat.

I sheathed Sagacious Blade, removed the charm from On, then myself, and he knocked at the door. It was opened by a gray-haired woman in the soft gray of servants; I was to realize before long that Madam preferred her Falcon guards about her, who also functioned as servants.

"Name?"

"Please tell her grace that the hermit is here," On said, his gaze on the ground. In the golden lamplight pouring out, I noticed that he'd inked his fingers.

"She is expecting you."

We were brought into a chamber hung with silken screens depicting pairs of black-neck cranes in flight over snowy mountains. All the windows had been pushed outward to the length of the carved sticks, to coax a breeze from the sultry air.

Two more women stood in the background, alert and

armed. Their eyes tracked us as we entered and bowed. These women had martial aspects, but they wore fine servant gray trimmed with green, and no blue Falcon headbands.

Dowager Duchess Huyun—Ti Lanek without her married title—sat behind a low table carved with lotus patterns. She gestured toward a cushion, onto which On plopped cross-legged, as a third woman, gray-robed as the others, brought in chilled juice of mango and tartberry. On helped himself as one of the women poured out tea.

Then Madam said, "I am honored by your visit, O poet of talent and mystery. But before you honor me with your wit, may this mother presume to inquire of one young enough to be her son, why this ragged garb—are you in need?"

On bowed. "Many thanks for your benevolent concern. This foolish wastrel is not in need, in that earnings invariably go by preference to inkstones and paper, rather than clothing. And to wine, too much wine," he added. "A donkey cannot live in a palace, and a fool cannot bide among a town's manifold temptations."

Madam had reached for a pouch that clinked richly, but she withdrew her hand. "Then a reward might not be welcome?"

"The thought is reward enough for me," he said with an elegant bow.

> *"On the heights, no one knows the deeds of men —*
> *The hermit delights in clouds and mountains.*

But I must admit to a weakness for words as well as wine."

Madam laid her hand in her lap, chuckling softly. She was quite handsome, her smile kind. The resemblance to her son was very strong. His smile was kind, too. But how much kindness lay behind it? "Then it is true, what they say, that the mysterious hermit who gave us so much wit from the ancients the other night truly lives on moonlight, poetry, and the scent of apricot blossoms?"

On bowed again. "All three of these are alike in offering their beauties to any who delight in the senses—without obligation. If your grace would indulge my favorite game, a question for a question? So much more entertaining than cold metal of whatever color."

"Ayah," Madam said, chuckling. Then, "My honored guest permitted me to begin with two questions," she said, bowing slightly. "Is it not your turn? Though I am wondering what so talented a poet could possibly wish to ask a poor old woman who seldom steps in the city if she can avoid it."

On said, "I will comply, but first petition for your generous forbearance at what I fear is a trespass."

"Forgiven, for rarely am I so intrigued. It is a sensation I find myself enjoying." She gave a nodding bow and sipped from behind her sleeve, a courtly habit. He bowed back, sipped from behind his fan, then said, "Might the wise and benevolent Madam be inclined to enlighten this ignorant scribbler about why the emperor so abruptly proposed this marriage alliance?"

My heart thumped. Madam blinked, as if she had expected anything but that. Her lips parted, and she took a quick peek toward the door, then back, hesitating. One of the women gave her head a tiny shake.

Madam relaxed a trifle, then said, "This poor, talentless seeker of wisdom is desolated to disappoint you, young qilin: I must confess I do not myself know. My son might be better informed, but as I, merely a woman, know nothing of imperial matters, I would have to send to him for enlightenment."

On held up a hand, then glanced at me.

I was inclined to believe her, but I did not trust myself. I asked Granny Zim internally, who whispered behind my ear, "This woman believes what she says."

On glanced toward the nearest window. I wondered if he, like me, had mentally measured the distance in case we had need of a quick escape, then he said, "This poor scribbler dares to remind her grace that it is her turn for a question."

Madam's eyes had narrowed. "This old recluse perhaps erroneously suspects a hidden context. Do *you* know the reason for this unseasonable imperial honor, young hermit?"

On glanced up at me, and this time her gaze followed, brows lifting in question as On said, "Only a foolish guess. But my companion here can explain, if your grace permits."

I'd studied each face. If the women standing vigilantly at exits and entrances were Falcons, there was a chance they would not go running off to find the governor, as long as they detected no threat to their madam. Though I already knew that the Falcons were inclined in the governor's favor—certainly those born and raised on this island were, like the Watcher on duty this year at Three Kingfishers. But the sect as a whole cherished its independence.

I said, "I believe that the emperor was angered by a report. About his grace, Governor Huyun Shandek..."

His mother looked her inquiry.

"She is anxious, this mother," Granny Zim said. "Ayoh, that brings back memories. One of my boys was little better than a wastrel, but still my heart burned if he was hurt, and my instinct was to defend him even when I was angriest with him."

I pulled my attention back, and reordered my words at this reminder that the duke who I considered very nearly an enemy was to her a precious son. I explained — in courtly terms — about the imperial crown prince, the grand prince, the putative peace meeting — the ships waiting in the bay, and then the storm that swept the plot away. But not the knowledge of it.

Then I waited, balanced on my toes, hand on the hilt of Sagacious Blade. Madam's face had gone as blank as any courtier's, then she let out a slow, quiet breath. "Have you proof?"

"None," I said. "Except that when I first approached the governor to warn him — as I thought — that the imperial crown prince was walking about in the guise of a general, he tried to invite me to stay."

On then said, "He was in the process of summoning servants to ensure a stay..."

"When I left," I finished.

Madam raised one hand to cover her eyes. Then she looked up. "Who are you?"

Even in retrospect, it's impossible to say what might have happened had I chosen to prevaricate. The obvious answer — the one On had kindly furnished me — was to claim I was an unnamed orphan, raised to take care of the hermit writer. Or I could have claimed to be Pangolin Ren, though I was so afraid of Huyun Shandek finding me in his house that my neck still tightened. But I had brought these questions to her. I had told her a truth about her son, however unpalatable it might be. It seemed right to tell her truth about me.

"This insignificant one was born Lan Renti, raised in the imperial palace, who had to run when my family was..." My throat tightened, and I could not get the words out.

On murmured into the silence:

> "My heart perceives, that secret and seen are sundered —
> But how's enduring different, then and now?"

Madam glanced his way, and said, softly, "*Mending then the bonds that this world breaks...*" And to me, "I knew your respected mother, I believe. Is not her much-esteemed name Gu Fua?"

"Yes," I said, barely above a whisper, for now it was my turn to be taken utterly by surprise.

Madam gave me a tremulous smile. "She saved my life. It was during the competition for crown princess — this was under Emperor Lan Yanshar, you understand." She bowed politely to the south.

"Might this ignorant daughter inquire what happened?" I asked.

She half-rose, and beckoned me forward. "Child, your rank is above mine, though I am your elder. Please sit."

Everything had changed. It had been so long since I'd been in a courtly social situation that I'd become used to gallant wanderers' habit of all sitting on the same level, or at most, with an acknowledged leader a little raised, so that all could see. In court, of course, only servants stand, but with lowered gazes, and at the edges of the room, which effectively relegates them to furniture. This distinction is so profound that it never occurs to courtiers to think of the heads of breathing furniture being above those of rank. Otherwise, courtiers sit ranked in space as they are in birth or merit.

Right now, we were quietly engaged in a short but still complicated dance of manners. I could ignore her request and stay with gallant wanderer usage, and yet I'd assumed the speech with which I'd been raised. Though I was not dressed for court, my instinct urged me strongly to bow to tradition. Certainly to refuse outright would be to deny her face, as I stood over her.

I made a full court bow, lowest-ranking princess to a duchess and an elder, then dropped down beside On, Sagacious Blade laid by my side.

Her countenance relaxed a trifle, and I understood then that with this adjustment to courtly manners, she could navigate properly. She said, "Word whispered among us that I was the leading candidate, until I was given anonymously a gift of poisoned candied rose petals, in a beautiful box, with verses about my beauty, as if a prince had written them. As it happens, I don't like candied rose petals, but my maid, barely fifteen, adored them. I gave them to her and she was dead within an hour. The imperial physicians insisted she had brought the illness with her, but the word 'poison' whispered among us. Though we could of course make no direct accusation, for who in the imperial palace would believe us? If we made a noise, might not we be silenced in some other way? It was your mother who dared to act, sending one of her own maids to me, my dearest, loyal Minsa."

Here, a glance over her shoulder toward one of the women. "I had never heard of the Falcons before then. She was the only one who discovered that the box had been sent by she who was to become empress. There were two more attempts against me, which Minsa foiled. By then I was so frightened that I pretended to be ill, and I was dropped from the competition—something I never regretted afterward. I came to regard the empress's venality as a favor, for I later heard that she lived very much in the shadow of the dowager empress. As for me, I was soon married to Governor Huyun. I tried to show my gratitude to Minsa and the Falcons in bestowing one of our oldest Ti family palaces on them for a scrape."

I exclaimed, "It is your renowned and illustrious family whose name provided our generation name!"

Color bloomed in her face as she said, "Perhaps. The Ti family certainly has crossed the imperial dynastic lines in the past, and I do believe the Ti family deserved its venerable reputation, but then we are all a little prejudiced toward our own, are we not?" Then she seemed to reconsider the implications—specifically what had happened to my own family, through our relations—and raised her hands. "Ay! Do not answer that, dear child. I have blundered. This is the cost of leading the life of a recluse. One forgets that a quick tongue is sometimes one's only defense. And I was never very quick. But I wish to say that I admired your mother, who was merciful to us all, and I will be forever grateful to her for introducing to me the Falcons."

At this, the women in the room then gave me the gallant wanderer salute. I returned it from where I sat.

Then Madam said, leaning forward a little, "Child, honor me with your insight, which I am certain is great, considering your respected mother. You will know these princesses. Is the one they are sending likely to be an aid to my son?"

How to answer *that?*

To gain a little time to think, I said, "Ah, might I trouble your grace by asking which princess is to be sent?"

"To be sent? She is nearly here, is what I am told. Thus I am in Cloud Terrace to begin arranging a suitable welcome, and such entertainments as our humble island might offer," Madam said. "To answer your very sensible question, who could it be but the only princess left who is granddaughter of the former emperor through the crown prince and princess, and not by a consort, as the present emperor has no daughters?"

"Siarti? Or Liarti, her younger sister?"

"It is my understanding that the latter is already married. It is only the elder who is still unwed."

I said carefully, "It's been several years since I was in company with Imperial Cousin Siarti, but at that time, I would confidently say that if she thinks that your son, through any children they might have, would bring her back to proximity to the dragon throne, she would favor the match."

"Then she would be a loyal wife?"

I considered Siarti, then said slowly, picking each word, "It has been four years since we saw one another. Everyone might change. But the cousin I knew then would come here to spy for her brother, I think. Yet...if she came to believe that the governor had a better chance at taking the dragon throne, she would favor him, for that would make her an empress, something she cannot be if her brother might someday inherit." And, with conviction, "The imperial princess I knew then would do anything to anybody in order to sit on the phoenix throne."

"As did her grandmother. I continue to pray that my innocent maid, who had been with me as a child and ought to be here now, went on to a better life." Madam gave a slow nod. "So you believe that my son is making a bid for the dragon throne?"

"I do," I said.

She looked away, her hands tightly gripped. Then she said, "It does not surprise me that he's said nothing to me. Ever since he returned from his visit to the imperial island ten years ago, he has been less forthcoming, though he's always been my devoted son," she added quickly. "A natural reticence to be expected when a boy begins to wear a man's hair clasp! If he has imperial plans, it does not surprise me, as many were the reports of bad governing on the imperial island and elsewhere. Increasing ills. My husband was respected for the benevolence and expertise of his governance, which he in his turn taught to his son." She narrowed her eyes, studying me. "He would make a good emperor, though I would not wage a war to put him there. However, war, it seems, is already upon us. Have you proof to offer to support your allegations against my son?"

"One thing only," I said. "And it's indirect. This was discovered by ... an investigator I know."

"Ay, your venerable father was Chief Censor. You would know about such things," she murmured. "Go on."

"It's just that raising an army and the ships to carry them is very expensive, and it seems he has been raising funds by his share of profits from the selling of refugees seized by slavers."

A vein beat in her smooth forehead, otherwise she showed no visual reaction.

Finally, Madam spoke. "My much-mourned husband — in so many ways the most admirable of governors — believed that selling criminals and beggars was the most humane solution to crowds of refugees, who quickly turn to crime. On this one thing we did disagree. I know from our archives that when my Ti forebears ruled this island, there was no such law."

I had definitely ventured onto a bridge of knives!

"This ignorant one is aware of her lack of years and experience," I said, and I meant to choose my words but they streamed out of me, pushed by still-simmering memory. "Within that experience has been a close acquaintance with refugees, some from the imperial island. From commoner to merchant to ninth-level nobles, before their villages were raided of their men. All with different education. And intent. Most were women and children. Snatched as slaves, and hauled away to be sold, while the imperial prince's own men looked on. I was one of these," I added — trying to keep my voice smooth.

"Ay!" she exclaimed. "But they set you free, of course?"

"They did not. We occasioned our own escape."

"Ayah," she breathed, and once again the fingers pressed to her eyes. "I confess I do not know what is right. My esteemed husband, so selfless and hard-working as governor, so well loved, was very convincing about such people needing a firm hand...but that is, perhaps, a debate for another time and place." She shook her head slowly. "Right now, the most pressing question before me is about this imperial princess. She is like her grandmother the empress, then?"

"Very like," I said. "Or, she was when last I saw her. And I have heard worse since, but that was in reference to the treatment of my own family."

Madam nodded. "Such a one is exactly what I would do anything to avoid for my son. But my opinion will not be sought," she finished briskly. "By imperial edict, this imperial princess is coming, my son fears that she comes with an army behind her, the wedding being an excuse for an invasion. Now I understand the reason why Shandek has been preparing for that, as quietly as possible, while furbishing the city in honor of the prospective bride."

Not so quietly, I thought, if Dinek had noticed the

reinforcing of defenses.

Madam said, "Either choice seems bitter aloe, and I, recluse and ignorant of great affairs, do not see a way to avoid such profound tragedy. Ay, I almost wish you had not come, for terrible news is only worth hearing if one can avoid the terror. And I can do nothing, now, except die. Then my worries are at least over."

Her servants made little motions of dismay, regret, and warding; I heard the distress in her voice, yet the words "except die" brought an image from my childhood reading. There had been a story very similar to this situation in one of those old tales about the wily Jong Siang and his 110 heroes, among whom was my favorite, Xue Two-Swords.

"I beg forgiveness." I rose to my knees to bow in full court mode. "There might be a solution…"

Madam gave me a startled glance, eyes so wide I could see the reflection of the lamp in each. "My child?"

My heart began thumping. Ordinarily I would not dare to propose a deal with an elder, especially from my precarious position. But I had seen how disturbed she was to hear about the Crescent Island slave auction.

I said, "If this presumptuous and ignorant one could be permitted to put forward a possible trade…"

"Speak, child, please," Madam said with great dignity.

"I would propose a ruse. I think that I would have to find help for you…" I turned to On—and caught a smile that curled at the edges. He had, after all, read those same tales. He said, "The spider-demon plague story?"

"Spider-*demon*?" Madam repeated.

"Yes, but there would be no demons involved," I said. "Only some trickery with meridians, and charms, and perhaps some dyes. We'd give it a different name. And a terrifying appearance. It's not a permanent solution, alas. But it would grant time. In my turn, I presume to beg your interference on behalf of the refugees being sold on Crescent Island. And other places."

"Ay, I already intend to do something about that," Madam stated with quiet dignity.

"I like this woman," Granny Zim said. "Her conviction rings like a bell."

"Though I am a recluse, and only a woman, I am also a daughter of the Ti family, and I may safely attest that my influence through my family's holdings in this island are considerable. But that, as you say, is for another time. I can promise I will do what must be done to put an end to this lamentable practice…here."

That left the rest of the imperial world. But it was a start.

"What is this ruse?" she asked. "Though I dearly love a play—indeed, seeing plays is about the only thing that happily draws me out of seclusion—I cannot act."

"You will not have to, except to be dead," I said. "I shall count upon the hermit to arrange for some fellow victims to this mysterious plague."

On said with gory enthusiasm, "You know the saying *Three talkers create a tiger out of air*? If blood is coming out of ears and eyes and even fingernails—and rumors of death in one night are blown through the city, you can be sure that rumors will spread faster than wildfire," he said.

Madam looked from one of us to the other. "I certainly know the story of the foolish king who listened to the evil courtiers, though his trusted counselor had warned him to be wary of ill counsel by one or by many, and I think I follow you. And I am quite willing to sacrifice myself in truth or in falsehood, if it will save my son and the innocent people of the island. But will a ruse be sufficient to turn them away from invasion? For their arrival can be regarded as little else."

"If Cousin Siarti is as afraid of poison and mysterious illness as she was when I was young, it will."

Madam accepted this, commenting, "I wonder if there is no more suspicious person in the world than one who has grown up haunted by an atmosphere of poisonings and secret stranglings. I would never claim this to be an auspicious thing, but if she does have this fear, then there is no danger of the imperials losing face, for surely she will turn away so there is no implication that we turned them away."

I said, "That is the idea. But for it to be successful, no one must know the truth outside of our few selves."

She nodded slowly. "I will not tell my son anything but to have faith. For his grief must be unfeigned, to convince the imperial spies infesting the island. I understand that this will be cruel, but far crueler is the prospect of Cloud Terrace laid waste by imperial decree. Can you make me appear dead without killing me? Are you a healer?"

"No, I am not. But I trained for a time with Grandfather Healer—"

At this, Falcon Minsa bent to whisper to her mistress, whose face cleared. "You know of this man? Ay, that is promising."

On said, "With the application of some terrible-looking symptoms at the same time as horrifying rumors spreading, your coffin will be sealed at once. Your Falcons can ensure that you come out and some rocks go in before the sealing. After which the entire island will go into mourning."

"Which is a *very* inauspicious time for weddings, even more than Hungry Ghost Month," Madam said with a little nod of understanding. "I cannot bring myself to lie outright to my son, but if I leave him a letter not to burn incense to me, but to offer it in secret to his father, I think he will know what I mean." She sighed. "I don't believe it is a permanent solution, but it would at least give him time to figure out what to do next."

On cocked his head, as in the distance, thumber rumbled. "If only this weather would persist, it would help greatly in creating an atmosphere of curses and demons," he added. "But how to make a live person seem dead even to physicians, Ren, that's up to you."

"Ren?" Madam repeated, glancing from him to me.

Why not admit to everything? "I have been living as Pangolin Ren," I admitted.

Madam looked startled. "The girl who blasted the reef with fire?"

On grinned as I blushed. It seemed every time I heard a reference to that story, it grew in the telling. Just like the false tiger roaming the streets in the counselor's parable! "The very one." He chortled.

Rather than explain, I said, "You Falcon masters surely are adept at the meridian freeze."

At this Minsa clasped her hands and bowed.

"Then…all you need is a charm to smother the sound of the heart beating long enough for the physician to pronounce the person dead. If we could find some Essence paper, I could make the talisman—"

There was an exchange of glances, then Madam said, "I believe there is some very old Essence paper in the library upstairs, left from an ancestor who was an Essence healer. But does not Essence paper lose virtue over time?"

"No, it actually accrues it," I explained. "With several talismans, you could create several 'dead'—"

"You make the talismans. Leave the victims to me," On said.

Madam turned to her chief Falcon, who said, "And her grace's part may be safely left to me."

SEVEN

The dragon banners snap in ghost wind, shaking off the sky;
Red-rimmed and wailing, victims will flee, leaving the dead to lie.
Hidden, hidden, the truth rises high above the clouds;
Far away, the imperial throne trembles under distant thunder.

"Influence," On had said.

As we made our way back to the inn, lightning flaring over the western mountains, On observed, "That was far better than I dared to hope. Why do you look glum?"

"Because it might go wrong. Because of the way she had explained away her beloved son's profiting off the slave trade, laying it at the father's feet."

On said, "She's a mother. What do you expect?"

I had to agree, remembering what Granny Zim said about her own wastrel son. I did understand filial piety — it was a vital part of civilization — but as yet I had no concept of the ferocious love of mother for child. Even for an erring charge. And yet, who could be more fierce than a mother who sees her child doing wrong?

I muttered, "I wonder if Huyun Shandek has ever looked into any of the faces of the victims he profits from."

"He might look, but see only dirt, grime, and misery, and think that that is their fate, and comfort himself with the reflection that they were surely serpents, or villains, in a past life. But!" On uttered a hollow, positively sinister laugh. "Just wait, O distinguished and admired Governor Duke Huyun Shandek. I don't need your mother to shame you."

"Oh?" I asked, the word nearly lost as lurid lightning briefly underlit broken clouds in the west, and thunder crashed nearer.

"My next play is going to be about that very practice. And *how* it's going to sting him. Though I use a lot of old poetry, and it's set in the time of high hats and long beards, everyone will know who's meant for the pompous donkey that thinks he's everyone's hero, while he tears children from their families to be sold for his golden throne."

"How can you arrange that and not end up in prison?"

"Because it'll be the hermit who wrote it," On said cheerily. "And I'll see to it that several playhouses manage to get a copy, then they can compete for who dares to put it on. That's why I don't mind so much about the *Duel of the Scholars* being interrupted, as it must be, by your plague, a day after its success. Already there have to be copies going in every direction, and my fame carried with them. But, Pangolin Ren, while I have to accomplish weeks of a whisper campaign in a day —"

"I know. I must get word to Dinek," I said. "I'll do that now. I know where her room is at the Chart."

We parted. Despite my pose of assurance, it seemed impossible that so flimsy a ruse could actually be made to turn away the imperials — even though the initial idea had been my own.

The rain struck, sudden and hard, amid a crash of thunder as I rode Sagacious Blade down the street to the Celestial Chart. The noise was so loud that I had to repeatedly bang at Dinek's window until a flare of light in her room indicated a lamp lit. She pushed her window out a sliver, then shoved it wide when she saw me. I tumbled inside, clumsy as I shivered. As a puddle spread around my feet, I told her what had happened as fast as I could.

She bit her lips and paced in a circle as she listened. At the end, she tugged on her sleep-frowzy braid, then said, "I told you I think we've been forbidden to leave. Discouraged against leaving, to put it more exactly. But no one wants to say so directly. Which means orders from..." She glanced upward, pointing a finger meaning *on high*. "I loved staying here, but not anymore. Not if we can't get a tea run because of the whim of someone I've never even met. The others are ready to go, too. If only Fan would get back!" She rubbed her knuckles absently against her underlip, then said, "There's another problem, and that's getting the ship past the patrols."

"I have a way to blur the ship, but I don't know if it'll work during the day," I said. "Especially if they are looking. Actually, two ways. But they are new, and there is no way to practice."

"I'll warn everyone to be ready to run. They're all gallant wanderers. Avoiding political trouble is inevitable. Doesn't matter who it's caused by."

"You're being very kind," I said. "When the problem is not someone else. It is I. Once again."

"No, it's the duke. The locals all love him, but if what you say is true about his solution to refugees, I think the sooner we leave, the better. I can row everyone out one at a time. Three go, two come back with a big bag. Two go and two come back, but then the same two go and one comes back for things forgotten. Ayep will make his grandsons swim to a boat, and they can climb in and lie at the bottom—we did that in Three Sharks Harbor. I told you about that. We'll get everyone there by nightfall whatever day you name."

I thanked her, giving her the gallant wanderer bow before I left. She flushed, her expression unhappy, and I knew she was thinking of Fan. And perhaps of Jai, who was developing into an excellent marine defender. Both were vital to *Pangolin*'s defense, but Fan was rooted in Dinek's heart.

I returned to the attic, changed out of wet clothes, lay down—and could not sleep at all as my mind tumbled over the same *what-ifs* all wearying night long.

The following day a great thunderstorm crashed overhead, obscuring the world with a roaring gray curtain of rain that flattened the water in the bay. There were few customers, mostly neighbors or friends of Ma Shao to bring the shocking gossip as it passed, as swift as lightning, up and down the street.

I had underestimated the inventive skills of the Xuan cousins and their trusted friends, I realized, as the dreadful news spread that beloved and respected Madam Duchess had taken sick at the play two days previously and was suddenly dead. And not only her…

"Dead?" Fia repeated, hands pressed to her heart.

Ma Shao's eyes were stark as she whispered to our tight circle in the kitchen, "That is the tragic part, for we have all loved her since she was a little girl. But the frightening part? It seems that plague demons rioted through the packed playhouse that night."

The Watcher said soberly, "That's what I heard from both

the ironmonger and the cobbler, that others were taken by the terrible plague. The number was jumping fast as each report came."

Ma Shao said, "Fia! Ren! Pull the street windows tight! Auntie Di swears she saw people running through the streets, screaming about the plague that got them. She told everyone on the street that the victims were *hurled*—" She flung her arms wide on the word. "—into a madness of fever and fire before they fell right down dead! I thought it might just be her usual exaggeration, but if… Ay! We're closing up. Better we earn nothing for a time than lose our lives altogether. And this on top of rumors of a princess coming to court our governor. What is she going to think of us? We'll have no face left at all…"

We had to put talismans up to ward sickness demons, and everyone in the house must walk in a zigzag, lest any present sickness demons had gotten in. I knew that the rumor was false, but I was as assiduous as the others, after all, how could it hurt?

As darkness fell, the Watcher, who had gone out to scout, came back to say, "The imperials have been sighted out beyond the reef. They're here, anchoring for the night."

As the others speculated about what the imperial princess would think about the plague rumors, I excused myself to go to the privy, obscured myself with my charm, and flew down to let Dinek know: TONIGHT.

I finally was able to get away after a hurried supper. I ran up to the third floor, where I then had to outwait my two attic-mates. Luckily chickens and laundry are inexorable in their demands, and both girls had risen before dawn, as always. They went to sleep early, freeing me to puzzle over a proper leave-taking from the Shaos. Finally I chose not to burden them with any letter. I suspected that if the *Pangolin* did manage to evade both the Huyun patrols and the imperials, the duke would be back to interview the Shao family, as well as people at the Celestial Chart. The less they knew the better; and Falcons came and went all the time. At least here at the Three Kingfishers, they were Falcons, and they would be able to fall back on the Falcons if he turned vindictive. Though I did not think he would. He was too careful of his reputation.

I packed my things up, noting that my carryall was heavier than it had ever been with my five tunics, as well as my hoarded pouch of earnings. I wore the dark blue gallant wanderer tunic, which was a very deep blue woven with forest-green bamboo stalks. It was sober and respectable seen during the day, but at night it shrouded me as well as assassin's black.

All day the weather had been unsettled as summer storms passed. After the sun set, I waited for a band of rain to roar past, thunder grumbling to the north. When it left the fresh-washed city in musical drips, I opened the window, glanced back once, sensing that this part of my life had ended, and then I set my feet to my blade, charmed myself to be unnoticed, and flew silently up over the empty street, and out above the bay.

I still hated being up in the air, though I was now used to it. I knew where the *Pangolin* lay, bobbing on the choppy water: the anchor had been eased up. Not the tiniest lamp had been lit—which would be instantly seen by the harbor patrol. And they were out in force, because, from high up, I could see the imperials outside the bay, ranged in a daunting array as they lay motionless on the water.

I turned my back on them for now, and drifted down to the deck of the *Pangolin*. I had learned to glide to a stop without the sword clanking the way it had when I'd begun to practice flying it. I picked it up, and I even bent over as I made my way with quiet step to the galley, for I had seen a patrol boat rowing silently in our direction.

I found the crew by the sound of their breathing. It was ink-dark in there. I set my carryall and harness down inside the door, backed out, and with only the sword, noticed that it took a lot less effort to pull Essence for my flight.

I waited until the patrol boat had passed and was well on its way toward the east, then I began to flying around the hull, laying on the charm for obscuring the ship.

When I finished that, I landed to recover a bit, and then, from the rail, I began the charm for creating fog. At first I performed it over and over as I stood there, for it took great effort to perform spells and guide my blade. Presently I sensed a living being at my side, and found Dinek's familiar silhouette barely limned against the darkness.

Dinek put a hand over mine to stop me from speaking and whispered against my ear, "Softly. Vapor carries sounds. Tell me when we can set sail."

She leaned next to me, watching as wisps of vapor rose from

the water and began to drift on the air, apparently vanishing. Over and over I performed the charm, until my mouth was dry and tiny lights glittered at the edge of my vision. I longed for sunlight and warmth, but there was none; it began to rain again.

At first the rain dissipated the vapor, and I could have wept, believing I'd have to begin again. But Granny Zim spoke, "Listen to your teacher, my Bu."

In my foggy stated of exhaustion, I had forgotten that I always, *always* had more to learn. That night would sear the truth of it into my soul: I bowed my head, resting my brow on the damp, rough rail, and sank into memory, where once again I visited Auntie Breeze, my name for that wonderful woman who had delighted in all the living creatures of the world.

She laughed, her face turned toward the sky — it was a spring day in her memory — as she chortled, wove her hands in the air, plucking Essence in great handfuls from the turbulent warmth of the clouds, and cast it out to gather moisture. *Take Essence from the lightning, you who've affinity for fire! It will sustain you. And enable you to sense the coming thunder. There are some of us who can even bring the weather, but I would never do that! Remember your first lesson, every action has consequences. Your storm here might cause a terrible drought for the next island…*

I opened my eyes, aimed my face into the warm rain, pulled a vast stream of heat from that summer storm, and scattered the moisture out to sea. Slow, soft whorls of vapor spun away, curling around the neighboring ships until the hulls and masts blurred, then vanished.

The Essence filled me as well. I knew this semblance of strength was as temporary as the fog I'd created, but it was there.

I whispered to Dinek, "Go."

And she pattered away on bare feet to get her crew to raise the sails.

I waited where I was, feeling the Essence now a steady stream, carried by the warmer air currents that I'd brought down to mix with the water. The fog thickened, surging in the slow wind.

Dinek was right, I soon discovered. By some trick of air and water, voices seemed to speak directly below me, but in a brief flaw in the fog, I caught the splash of an oar some fifty paces away.

And, as familiar as childhood, the accent of the imperial island reached my ears as a man muttered, "…waiting for ten years…?"

"Those were imperial orders." The other voice lowered, also spoken in the accent of my home island. "All I heard was *fleet commander.*"

I couldn't hear any more than that—as the direction of the voices moved not shoreward, but out toward the open sea. At first I tried to place those voices among those of the greens I'd heard, until my tired mind recognized the obvious: these were not greens. They had to be imperial scouts, or spies. They were using the fog to get back to the imperial fleet.

I was also sure that there wasn't a thing I could do, and yet the impulse to follow them—to spy on the spies—was so strong that I laid Sagacious Blade down, stepped, and rose into the air. My movement sent more whorls of fog spiraling to either side, spattering quietly against hulls and diffusing into vaporous components as I passed unnoticed by.

I rose up and up, until suddenly my fog lay below, a soft gray blanket that obscured the entire bay except for the tips of very tall masts here and there, and the dimly perceived grace of the temple roof on the eastern promontory.

I followed the two rowing, unnoticed above them. Their talk was intermittent, and low-voiced, so that I could not catch but a word now and then: *plague. Coffin. How many dead?* They seemed to be unsure of that, arguing briefly, their voices rising, then falling again as they reached the open sea, and the waters were rougher.

They did not speak until they were hailed by scout boats; there was an exchange of pass phrases, and then I guess a badge or token had to be inspected as one of the patrollers barked, "I know *you,* Owl-Eye Bin, but who's this other?"

"I was sent by his imperial majesty ten years ago, may his spirit find peace. My orders were to remain until summoned to return, or until imperial forces under the dragon banner arrived."

"Go on, go on, you'll be the Fleet Master's problem. And let me warn you, if he doesn't like you, it'll be over the side with you, with or without a knife in your ribs."

I had circled slowly above three times while this went on. I took advantage of that to renew the obscuring charm over myself. I was very soon glad I had, for out of the vapors emerged an enormous tower ship, hung with imperial banners, and streamers with protective talismans worked on them. I took in that enormous ship, my heart sinking at the sight of the cannon, and the catapult. Uncounted soldiers and sailors moved purposefully about the ship, or stood as sentries. Cloud Terrace could be reduced to rubble by this ship alone. How many others were out there hidden in my mist?

At least no one thought to look up at the sky, from which intermittent rain still fell, as the two spies were hauled up to the deck, then began climbing up the stairs.

I'd seen enough. Huyun Shandek's guess was right: this was no wedding entourage fit for a princess, it was an invasion with the wedding as an excuse. Either the duke permitted them to come into the island, in which case they would occupy it and do what they wanted—Xianti, with the higher rank, could not be gainsaid—or they resisted, which meant rebellion.

There was no possible good outcome, whoever won. It would be the ordinary people paying the price with life and livelihood. People like the Xuan cousins. The Shaos. The ironmonger's little girl.

I was going to turn away and fly back to the *Pangolin*, driven by a sense of profound defeat, when the two spies reached the top level, with its elaborately carved window frames, the windows pushed wide to let in the damp, sultry air. Central, a door with golden dragons carved in it.

That door was abruptly thrust open, and out walked a tall, thin figure, clad in glorious gilt armor with a great dragon on the breast.

It was Cousin Xianti.

EIGHT

Be wary of those, she learned,
Who can only admire what they cut down.
There is always some reason to fell the great oak —
There were termites! The great hall's beam is weak!
But once its shade and branches
Harbored phoenixes.
And now there is only air.

SICK WITH DREAD AND defeat, I knew I had to stay. Even if I was discovered. Which would be just, for this disaster was *my fault.*

Oh, I had truly believed I meant well when I warned Xianti to leave, but I'd let my hatred of him shape the message, which had denied him face just as surely as if I'd slapped him before the dragon throne. I could have made up any sort of lie. Or better, sent in Jai with a message, because I knew what Xianti was like! What possible outcome would there be except his slavering for retribution?

But there is no going back, only forward, and I had to hear the consequences of my total lack of foresight. I had to find a way to avert it, or give my worthless life in trying.

Cousin Xianti frowned down as the two spies dropped to the wet decking, foreheads pressed to the wood. In the torchlight, the bony contours of his face shifted, highlighted into exaggeration. To my eyes he looked ten years meaner than he had nearly four years ago when I'd last seen him in daylight — I did not regard our brief encounter at that Tiger Eye Bay inn a moon or two ago, as there had only been weak starlight.

"Come inside," he demanded, and stalked inside again, red cloak swinging. The door was left wide open. He threw himself into the fleet commander's chair as the two knelt before him. "Who are you?"

The elder of the two spies woodenly offered his explanation, after which Xianti uttered a crack of laughter. "Grandfather did lay long plans, didn't he?"

The spy seemed to know better than to answer. He knelt beside the other, both with their gazes on the planks beneath their wet knees.

Xianti went on, "And what have you learned in your ten years?"

"My observations have been confined to Cloud Terrace, save for a single journey to the east end of the island." The spy then uttered a long string of numbers, representing ships, soldiers, sailors, guards under the magistrate, and other types of military facts and figures.

Xianti listened, then uttered that crowing laugh of his. "They outnumber us, but not by much. But it doesn't sound as if their defenses will withstand us long, ha ha! Once we get the wedding alliance party sent, we can…"

Though I was outside, and a little above, I could see inside very clearly, as they had all the windows pushed out to horizontal, to let in as much breeze as was permitted in the damp, sultry air. Xianti lounged, the various commanders and captains standing to either side, heads bowed.

The two exchanged glances, and Xianti saw it. He interrupted himself. "What is it, Bin, what's *your* report? What's the truth of the plague banners we saw before the sun set? And mourning banners, too? I think the plague is just a ruse," Xianti scoffed, "though the fleet commander here insisted we anchor for the night. I always thought Huyun Shandek was a coward."

In a wooden voice that still managed to insinuate the obsequiousness that was a necessity for survival around that family, the spy described the living theater that On and his player co-conspirators had fashioned. And it did sound terrifying. People with blood streaming from eyes and ears running wild, to collapse in the street — to be quickly tossed onto stretchers by figures in green guard clothing, with thick kerchiefs tied over their noses.

"Carried off to the cold houses to be burned at once," the spy finished. "While up at the palace, they're chanting sutras for the soul of Madam Dowager Duchess."

"They're mourning his *mother?* Did the physicians see her?"

"They did. The rot had already set in, and they were choking. They closed the coffin very quickly," the spy said.

Xianti grunted, then straightened up from his lounging post to frown out the window, toward the island. My heart thundered, though his profile was to me. I was so tired, and I had to concentrate to keep a steady flow of Essence for Sagacious Blade.

Xianti got up and paced back and forth so that his long red cape flared out, and the kneeling spies had to wiggle and scoot this way and that to avoid fouling that flapping fabric. He stamped a couple of times in his fine decorated boots with the toes turned up, tassels dancing at his belt and sword hilt, then with the smirk that I'd hated since childhood, said, "We'll soon give them a lot more to be mourning, won't we?" He uttered that laugh, and the waiting line of commanders echoed it dutifully and mirthlessly.

He turned abruptly. "I want the troop ship holds full of these Mountain Peony islanders by the middle of Phoenix eighth month. We need to get them trained by the turn of the year if I'm to annihilate Whale Haven while that rat Yiuti thinks he's safe for the winter."

Whale Haven! Koi's voice echoed in mind, *Once we arrive at Whale Haven…*

"Pass the order to ready the landing boats —"

"Not quite yet."

I knew that sticky-sweet voice. A sting like poison burned my nerves.

At first I only saw her celestial blue outer robe with its long, floor-sweeping train. It was embroidered with peonies and hummingbirds. Then an elaborate knotted hairstyle, well-studded with golden hairpins with jewels and dangles glittering in the torchlight. The hair firmly covered her ears, and when she emerged between two of the military commanders, I looked into Siarti's face.

Like her brother, her features harshened when side-lit, the soft contours of ill-temper exaggerated into furrows. But then she turned, and her face was young again, expertly made up, smooth and expressionless in its courtly semblance of beauty.

"What, Sister?" Xianti demanded.

Siarti folded her hands, her voice that poisonously sweet tone that had never failed to make me shudder. "I said, not. Quite. Yet. Though I am merely a woman, may I remind you that it is *my* marriage we are arranging, and imperial uncle promised that I would be a part of all negotiations..."

"Out," Xianti barked at the listeners, hand sweeping in dismissal.

The spies rose to their feet and everyone, from fleet master down, hastily bowed themselves out.

I was very tired of hovering by then, but there was no chance I was going to miss what these two said. As the navy people and the scouts descended the stairs, I brought myself slowly to light on the balcony, intensely aware of all those alert sentries below. Though I could fly away, at a single command Xianti could have them shooting their crossbows at the sky. And even if they didn't see me, all it would take is one among the hundreds of lethal bolts to drop me.

Not certain if my blur might still reflect light, I bent slowly to pick up Sagacious Blade without letting it clank or clatter. When no one cried out, I stepped to the structure between the window frames carved with acanthus and bamboo fronds, as inside, Siarti confronted her brother.

He threw himself back in the command chair. She stood before him, all that costly fabric crushed as she crossed her arms tightly over her chest, the meek, modest pose gone. "Elder Brother, I still do not trust you," she snapped, the honey-sweet tone gone.

"Siarti, this is the emperor's orders—"

"*You* married Second Sister off to that braying donkey Nua Li. Imperial uncle never gave him a second thought."

"Tiger Li is loyal to *me*," Xianti retorted. "He wanted an imperial wife as his reward for ridding us of Lan Louza. So neatly done, too. There is never evidence in a shipwreck. He could have asked for a lot more, which would have been much harder to scrape together."

"Easy for you to say. I notice *you* not marrying a common-born brute."

He shrugged. "It had to be her. Imperial Uncle still favors Taisa, or she'd have been the first out the door. There are no unmarried princesses over fifteen left."

"Nua Li is a *commoner*. His mother was a *hairdresser*."

"Tiger Li's a marquis now, and if he wins his next battle, he'll be a commandery prince."

"He wasn't born a prince," Siarti retorted.

Xianti smirked. "No, he comes from three generations of imperial guards. The toughest bulls in the yard. And it takes a stubborn bull to corral that snake Liarti. Isn't it a relief not to have to get a taster for every dish, and check your bed for scorpions? Admit it!"

"That was a matter for servants." Siarti waved her fan dismissively. "As if I would ever eat any dish without a taster after I turned five! Outside of Chuti, who deserved it, I think marrying any of us princesses to anyone below royalty is a terrible precedent for our prestige. Also, it just makes Liarti more sly. You know when she's not squabbling with that Nua Li, she's crying to Imperial Uncle, and we're not there to counter her lies. If this marriage fails, I do not want to return to discover her married title soaring above mine. She'll *never* stop parading it."

"If Huyun proves himself to be loyal and obedient, he can be a commandery prince," Xianti said carelessly. "As long as he's obedient." He muttered truculently, "Very obedient. Plotting against *me*. How he's going to regret that."

Siarti swept around in a circle. "You're distracting me. Xianti, do not send the wedding ship, or your conscript raiders. I refuse to be on the wedding ship if you send it, and there goes your pretense of imperial amity and alliance. I *won't* marry him now. Not with plague flags all over, and his mother dead, which means even if I don't catch it, I will be stuck wearing ugly mourning white and burning incense and writing sutras for a *year*. Longer, if he's as filial as they say. As for taking all the men off the island, what good is that if they are infested with plague, and end up passing it to everyone in your fleet?"

"And what will the world say? It will look as if we cowered away like beaten dogs," Xianti snarled. "No face left!"

"Not if you word it deftly. It'll be a *merit*, if we leave them to their year of mourning, and it'll be prudent to stay away until they get well rid of any plague. Huyun Shandek can't escape. He's the *governor*, and you already got that wolf General Ji Jiang to guard the back door. That was clever of you," she added in that insinuatingly honeyed tone. "You're the one in command, and everybody knows it. Let's go home. Keep Liarti from poisoning Imperial Uncle's ears, and leave this island to their mourning year. You can find more conscripts for your army somewhere else, somewhere not infected with plague. What about Kianti's island?"

"We need the men to mine for brimstone," Xianti muttered.

"There are other islands. Plenty of them. And once you've trounced that white-eyed rat Yiuti this winter, you'll be stronger when it's time to take the throne. But first, next year, I get a *proper* wedding with me in red and gold, and music, and a universal holiday declared—everything due to an imperial princess. *Then* I'll be in a position to help you against Imperial Uncle. I can't when I'm locked up in a temple choking on incense and mumbling prayers, and being afraid every day that one of my maids will drop dead of plague."

Xianti uttered a grunt, then muttered, "I don't know how to word it so that it's clearly our merit, and not a retreat."

"*I* do. Didn't I have to write out those lessons over and over a thousand-thousand times? I never thought those would be of the least use, but I'm glad now. I'll send my maids down to sort through the gifts and cull out the scrolls and incense holders and the like that could be sent as gifts of commiseration, and I can dictate a beautiful personal letter for Assistant Secretary Nai to write in the finest calligraphy from me to my husband-to-be, promising him a glorious meeting next year. I'll hint at the promotion to prince. Meanwhile, he'll surely have seen us out here. He knows what's coming if he's not obedient in the interim."

"That's true enough. Ayoh, have it your way. But I so looked forward to a fine fight. And, I wanted very badly to send scouts to hunt down that snake Renti."

Siarti snapped her fan and waved it. "I still don't believe that was Renti. She's as stupid as a rock, raised like a nun by that mother of hers. You did say it was dark. You surely saw some lowly wretch who looked like her."

"I told you she raved and cursed about her family. Why would some commoner off the street do that? No, that was Renti. What's more, that sword she carried had to be charmed, or how could it freeze me like that? She would never be able to do it. That's a beheading offense, right there. I need to get my hands on her—brandishing her in the prison will break Yanti at last. He'll kneel to me if I hold an axe to her scrawny neck. And once he swears, he will stick to it, and hate every day, ha ha. I can hardly *wait*."

"You can force him to the floor just as well when you capture Banti. I say, send an assassin to get rid of that noisome girl." Siarti shrugged. "As long as Old Gu doesn't find out."

"I don't want her throat cut. Too easy a death. She made me

lose face—you didn't see how everyone in that bay was laughing up their sleeves when I left." He slammed his hand on a table, sending dishes jumping.

"Then send back that spy Imperial Grandfather put there. If she's on Huyun Shandek's island, he'll find her. Or, here's an idea, let Huyun Shandek know that a perfect bride gift for me would be Renti, chained up in the hold of a prison boat. Better them doing the hunting than any of us—stepping on shore is madness when there's plague."

Xianti muttered, "I still think it's strange that the plague breaks out the very day we sight the island."

"Everyone knows plagues come suddenly, like lightning. The books are full of tales—one day a village is fine, the next they're burying everyone. And *nobody* kills their own mother for a ruse. What could be more inauspicious?" Siarti flung out her arms, her sleeves rippling down to the floor. "Let's get away entirely before the plague demons decide to come floating over the water on the winds."

Xianti went to the other window and bellowed for the fleet master.

Snake! They called *me* a snake!

Ayah, I called him a snake, and a rat, but still, how I loathed them both, longing to send a flame of scorching heat in there to…

I caught myself, hard. It would be easy, so easy. And if I gave in, the next time would be easier.

"That is right, my Bu. That is right," Granny Zim said to me. "That road is there. You will always know it's there. You will have to choose over and over again not to step down it."

Fire and metal—Xianti and I shared that affinity, much as I hated knowing that. Siarti was fire and water, but still I recognized that we were more alike than I wanted to admit. Those two had long ago chosen that path. How to fight that instinct within me? I remembered standing on the ship with Second Brother, after the Journey to the Clouds. *Speak anger to the wind,* he'd taught me. I could not let it consume me, though it was as contagious as any plague.

And once I'd taken three long breaths, my temper dissipating like my fog was beginning to, I reminded myself that I had what I wanted.

Our ruse had worked.

NINE

When threat becomes a duty
Who stops to think of fame?

BELOW, THE DECK BECAME a hive of preparation for the retreat. I took the time to breathe deeply, scouring Essence from the thunderous clouds, and sped for shore. Because there was one pleasure I did not have to deny myself: making certain that Madam Duchess was in truth well, and telling her that the ruse had been successful.

I rose once again above the slowly churning fog, spotted the gleam of the temple roofs on the promontory, and used that as a guide. Skirting the fog, which filled the bay like a soft, silvery soup, I sped along, faster and faster, until the wind whistled through my clothes and hair, the latter coming loose from the hairpin, which fell away into the water. I shrugged off the exasperation. At least this rising wind had wakened me thoroughly.

I reached the outskirts of the city. The palace was easy to find by its triple-tiered roofs, and the gargoyles guarding each corner. I came from the east; as I passed the wing where the duke lived, I looked down at a hive of activity much like that I'd left on Xianti's flagship.

My eye caught on a messenger running in a straight line through all this activity, the two feathers sticking up stiffly from his hat clearing everyone out of the way.

"His grace, fetch his grace," this man cried hoarsely.

And when Huyun Shandek himself appeared on a balcony, I brought my blade to light directly above him, out of his sight, though not out of hearing. Instinct warned me that if anyone was to scan for me, it would be he.

"What is it?" he called down.

"My lord, Commander Nan has been overridden by the Defense Commander, who is going to kill all the plague victims and burn the building to the ground. He says that it's the only way to contain it before the imperials land."

"I issued orders about those plague victims. They are in the prison not as criminals, but to keep them from contaminating anyone else. I want my physicians to examine them first thing in the morning," Huyun Shandek said rather sharply. "Physician Mor is elderly, and I gave him permission to rest, and to consult the ancients for possible cures."

"With all respect, my lord, Defense Commander Qinak insists that we cannot effectively deal with two battle fronts, and..."

This was terrible! My glee over the success of my ruse withered to ash. I did not wait, but stepped back on the blade. It slid a little on the tiles. I heard Huyun Shandek say, "Did you hear something?" Then I was rising, and circled well around before flying down toward the magisterial buildings as fast as I could.

I knew where the prison lay. But what to do when I got there? No one would pay a girl of sixteen the least heed. If Commander Nan recognized me, would that be worse? Had I been declared a criminal?

Maybe, but in that case, I whispered to myself as I landed and wiped away the charm, they knew the reputation of my sword.

As guards turned my way, startled, I reached upward into the roiling heavens yet again, though by now it felt as if I scoured myself from the inside all the way down to my toes, and pulled down heat from the lightning I sensed out over the bay. Then I lit my sword and watched in satisfaction as flame shot toward the sky; lightning flared over the bay and thunder crashed.

The guards froze, some mid-step.

When the thunder died away, I raised my voice. "I am Pangolin Ren! And I have found the cure to the plague!"

Commander Nan ran out, guards at his heels, some with

drawn swords, though there was no intent in their stances. Only conflict, worry, question.

"Let me into the prison. I was taught by an Essence master, and I have the cure," I shouted—not quite a lie. That is, both things were true, just not related, but they were listening.

All faces turned with a snap toward the commander. Far, far in the back of my mind, I thought that someday that image might even be as hilarious as the absurdities I yelped, but right now I trembled from head to foot, my stomach churning sickly.

The commander gestured to the guard with the prison keys, and he entered—everyone following, but at a very prudent distance. They led me toward a clamor of voices, some sobbing. "We're better! We're better! It's only a day of sickness! Let me out! I'm sorry, I'm sorry."

Angry, despairing, terrified voices clashed—but in their center On stood, his patched robe grimy, his hair ruffled as if he'd been thrown to the ground and then hauled away by the hard grip of frightened guards. Which he had. This was the direct result of using a lie to create very real fear and terror.

"Open the door," I commanded, my voice a bleat in my ears.

The keys clashed. The door swung open, but behind me, the guards stood with swords at the ready.

I gestured flame along Sagacious Blade again as I cried, "I have the cure! Once I give you the cure, you will sleep, and waken healed!"

"Cure me first, cure me first," Xuan Suanek said, coming bravely forward. And it was bravery. For all she knew, I was going to use that fiery blade on her.

But her gaze was steady, with a little question. I waved the sword over her head, then snapped a little flame to the metal. Behind me, gasps and the scrapes of retreating steps. I made a warding gesture, then said, "You are now cured. You will sleep, and waken completely healed."

She slumped gracefully to the ground. And the rest—players all—took their cue from her. I needed to hurry. Surely someone was already running up to the palace, and I did not want to face Huyun Shandek.

I performed my false cure very quickly, fire flaring from the blade for each player. That was their cue to faint to the floor, which they all performed perfectly—and I believe with a profound sense of relief.

I left On for last. Once I'd made my mysterious pass over him, I blocked him from being seen from behind me, and I did the charm for blurring, hoping he would recognize it.

He did. Instead of going to the floor, he darted past the guards, who were watching my sword flame a bit brighter than before. I used the flame to make a slow, general pass around the entire cell, hoping it gave On time to get away. Then I cried, "Plague demons, begone! Beware the purifying flame!"

Then I turned to walk out, but staggered as vertigo nibbled at my balance. No, not now, not now, I told myself. I stood with my feet planted, forcing air into my lungs, and fighting back the glittering at the edges of my vision.

"I must go," I said, urgency returning in force.

"But the governor will have so many questions," one of the familiar greens said, his honest face bewildered.

"Not while the fire is still in me," I said, and there was no hiding the hoarseness of my voice. I added another flare of fire, and once again the guards stepped back.

They followed me to the outer court—just in time for me to come face to face with Huyun Shandek, with a host of his guards flanking him.

Commander Nan, that good-hearted and scrupulous man, rushed out and as he bowed to the duke, he said past him to a tough-looking man with two plumes in his flat-brimmed hat, "Defense Commander Qinak, the plague is cured. It was demon-caused, and the demons have been banished." He pointed to me.

Everyone's gaze went to the sword in my hand.

"Pangolin Ren," Huyun Shandek said. "It seems you found new charms for that sword?"

"I found an Essence expert," I said. And to forestall the obvious next question, "She's..." I waved up past the next street above us, carved into the great palisade as I mentally sought lightning to bolster my flagging strength.

"Another hermit," the duke said appreciatively. "I wish very much to be enlightened by this hermit. An interview that I trust will be graced by your presence, Pangolin Ren." Each time he said my name I thought I heard the subtlest emphasis, as if a truer name underlay. "So beneficial an outcome, and on our behalf. You are truly a remarkable individual."

I bowed, my heart in a frantic race against my ribs. His tone was so friendly, his countenance the same, and yet I could see his hand poised to gesture to those guards behind and before him. His pleasant voice sang warning through my meridians. Two steps on the part of those ready, eager guards and they would encircle me. In the heavens above, I sensed warmth and turbulence, but I needed lightning, thunder, and rain.

"I look forward to many fruitful conversations," he went on, as Commander Nan nodded in approval, and the guards all not only made little signs of agreement, but they clearly thought me singled out for the meritorious attention of their governor. If I froze him by a jab to the right meridians, they would attack me for certain.

Who knows what might have happened, had not my lightning chosen that moment to flash directly over the magisterial rooftop? Thunder shook the ground, and then rain struck in a cataract.

That startled everyone, giving me the instant I needed. I flung the blurring charm over myself and ran between the defense commander and his assistant, keeping wide of Huyun Shandek.

From there I bolted into the street, and from sheer habit turned toward the Three Kingfishers. But I didn't get far before a cold hand gripped my arm.

"It really works," On said, rain running down his face as lightning flashed again, farther east. "You just vanished, but I stared hard at the spot where you'd gone, and there you were."

Together we ducked under the awning of a boat repair shop. Its windows and door were shut up tight. "Why were you in there with them?" I asked. "I thought you were not going to be a corpse."

"I wasn't," he said, his gaze sliding away. "But the guards had orders… Ay, you saw. I thought, if this ruse condemns us, out of the fear we ourselves raised, then at least I could die with them. That was quick thinking on your part."

"Quick remembering," I said, aware that the heat of the storm was moving eastward, leaving a cold wind behind, which made me shiver. "Wasn't it the False Monk who tried that trick, 'healing' a disease he made up, and collecting gold for it, until Song Jiang compelled him to stop?"

"True, true." On looked up and down the street as greens searched in a slow line. "Where are the others?"

"If *Pangolin* made it out of the harbor, then it is sailing —"

"Search every house." That was Huyun Shandek, no more than two hundred paces away. "I very much fear that Pangolin Ren has fallen into the hands of a miscreant. Conduct her safely back."

A united shout rose into the rain.

In another distant flare of lightning, On gazed into my face, his pupils so wide that they left only a thin brown ring. He pointed upward, and held out his hands in unmistakable invitation.

Both of us? That was something to try when I was fully rested, safe, and with fire to draw on. But that storm was moving away fast.

The noise of greens diligently searching each shop and yard made me desperate. I laid the sword down, stepped on it, and On stepped behind me, poised lightly. I took his wrist, concentrated, scouring all the Essence I could find—and the sword rose, but hovered at knee height. I fought to keep it there, knowing that I could not go farther. My strength was failing.

Granny Zim said crisply, "Use this boy's Essence. The one you called Auntie Breeze taught you how."

I had already experienced shared and shaped Essence, completely unwittingly, when the eel-monk helped me drive a path through the reef outside the bay. I could lift and toss boulders—though while I was standing on the ground. And Auntie Breeze had shown me memories of Essence experts working together with geomancers, blending their Essence for the great bindings that kept devastating island quakes to gentle shakes. And I could sense On's Essence in a river, a storm. Water and air—those were On's affinities, and here we were, in the steady, cold rain, next to a sea. But to combine with another living person so intimately…

"Do it, my Bu," Granny Zim instructed. "This boy's affinities complement yours. Why do you wait?"

"I need your Essence," I whispered next to his ear.

"Anything," he breathed. "They are right next door! What do I do?"

What indeed?

"Leap," I said.

And he did, slinging one arm around my waist.

Warmth surged through me at his touch, giving me enough Essence to guide the sword upward just as a pair of greens tromped into the little yard. Their broad-brimmed hats kept the rain off, and also kept them from looking up, but I hastily sketched the diffusing charm over us both as we rose past the roof on Sagacious Blade.

I glanced back as Huyun Shandek neared our shelter, apparently heedless of the hard rain, though an attendant scurried about trying to hold an umbrella over his head. I shifted my gaze quickly lest he sense it and search the darkness. I guided us very close to the roof, almost touching, until he was well obscured by the building, and then I floated us down an alley and gradually up and up, until we rose over the bay.

"Ah," On sighed with sheer joy. "I get it. I see it!"

And we rushed skyward in a breathtaking arc. *He'd* mastered the art of flying a sword in scarcely the time it took to breathe—but then he had been practicing the rudiments all his life. All he'd lacked was the knack of drawing Essence. And this was his element, right here: air filled with rain, above the sea.

"How is this so easy now, when I tried and tried, with every sword in the armory," he shouted past my ear. "Is it you?"

"Us both." I could not risk more of an answer. I was too near my limits. We sped into the night as the storm rumbled and crashed its way toward the mountains behind us. And over there, to the east of us, spread a neatly spaced pattern of golden glows: the imperial fleet. They had turned aside, and in a slow, stately arc, were sailing southward.

I aimed us west.

And there was a ship, with lanterns fore and aft, as before.

"I don't know how to land," On commented on a breathless laugh.

I brought us down toward the *Pangolin*. Down, and down; the obscuring charm had already faded, I learned as the Hat brother on deck watch gave a shout, and crew members ran out from various doors.

We landed, I staggered, and Dinek exclaimed, "Are they coming?"

"No. The imperials are heading south. And we got away entirely—we just left Huyun Shandek. He doesn't know we're here. He thinks I'm somewhere on the island..." A sudden yawn caught me, so strong a yawn my knees tingled.

"When did you eat last? Or drink?" Dinek asked.

"I ... don't remember," I admitted. "I'm not hungry. Nor thirsty—I'm half-drowned."

"We're safe," Dinek shouted, drowning the questions being barked at me from all sides. "All the rest can wait until morning. Go rest, Ren."

I trudged toward the stairs to the upper floor, my thoughts not on my hunger, thirst, or the questions being barked at On from all sides. Or even on the near escape. It was solely on his touch as his hand lifted away from my waist.

TEN

Fallen blossoms, scattered at random,
don't see the passing of spring –
Just so, she did not see
The laughing glances of ardent youth.
Her gaze wandered past them
To cloudless skies…

BY THE TIME I'D flung off my sodden clothing, Hat Dove appeared with fresh tea and a steamed bun. I ate a few bites, drank, and tumbled into my bunk.

I have to lay down my brush now to laugh at myself. When I woke, did I think about what I'd overheard from my imperial cousins? Or revel in relief over the ruse that had actually succeeded? Or contemplate the danger I'd inadvertently brought to a lot of innocent players whose lives were balanced between what was real and what they used their arts to make real on the stage?

No. My mind was entirely occupied with the memory of On's arm around me, as my dreams had been filled with the flight through the summer sky with him pressed against me.

I sat up in my bunk. My ears strained to distinguish his voice from the calls back and forth among the crew, the clatter of the battens in the sails, and the wash-slap of seawater against the hull.

I mentioned earlier that occasionally my dawning

awareness of what hitherto I'd been ignorant reminded me of a familiar city as the sun comes up. First the night-shrouded buildings are limned with weak blue light, then, as the limb of the sun clears the horizon, it throws slanting rays of golden light to reveal hitherto hidden details of roof gargoyle and tile, treetop and birds.

So it was now. The mystery of the romance that I'd yawned impatiently past in the gallant wanderer tales, and the ardent tensions in First Brother and beautiful Cousin Arati when gaze met gaze, was no longer a puzzle. Though there had been no insinuation in that grip of On's arm, my physical self had responded with all the strength of fire to aromatic wood.

How was I supposed to negotiate this new awareness? Mother had never given me the slightest hint, except to caution that mere physical attraction was as evanescent as the moon's reflection on water, and that true regard was a matter best left to counsel before my future wedding. I had never wasted much thought on this future lesson. Not even to question why Mother's references to the duties of wife and mother differed so wildly from the yearnings of romance in the gallant wanderer tales and in popular songs.

There was no guarantee that On had felt anything within his tight grip but the rain-sodden fabric of my dark blue robe with the bamboo shoots, and perhaps the contours of my skinny ribs. Did I want him to?

I rose, and though usually I pulled on whatever of my clothing was cleanest, I actually rejected my favorite green, because of the reminder of Huyun Shandek's green and wheat. It was my blue tunic I pulled on. And I combed out my hair instead of jumbling it impatiently up into a gallant wanderer's tail, before tying my headband round my brow.

Then I started down the stairs toward the weather deck and the galley. Midway I picked On's voice out from the others, "…and she stood there like an avenging goddess with the sword in one hand, and her hair like dark flames in the wind, as Huyun Shandek devoured her with his eyes, and—"

It took a heartbeat or two to recognize myself in this dramatic description. And, hot with embarrassment, I exclaimed as I stumbled down the rest of the way, "There was no devouring! None!"

But all that did was elicit the very reaction I'd thought to ward: the others began to laugh. I ran to the galley, my face burning, to find those not on watch gathered around On, who sat cross-legged on the men's platform.

"What would you call it, then? Smoldering? Lingering?" His voice was so warm, with a ringing tone that one usually heard from singers. So different from Koi's voice, which was deeper, rougher.

The young Pangolins laughed as he mimicked a player on stage languishing. Even sober Hat Dove smiled. I think they laughed at the sheer unlikelihood of the suave governor swanning about like that.

"There was only glaring!"

The others—except for old Ayep—seemed to find that even funnier as On grinned at me, that fox-spirit grin that now ignited intense self-awareness as well as awareness of him. Since I did not know what to do with it, I turned away entirely, and went to get tea as well as a pancake.

"One pancake? One?" Dinek scolded, when I reappeared. "We left you three pancakes, and you must eat them all. You're too scrawny. Not good."

On said, "I told them our 'capture weapons with boats of straw' ruse. And about Madam." I still could not look at him—I was far too self-conscious.

Dinek said with much satisfaction, with a glance at Hat Dove, "I'd be a lot more frightened about how close your escape from him was—except there's the comforting thought of just how much trouble he's going to meet once his mother stops being dead for the imperial spies."

I said to my teacup, "She is a mother, so she will no doubt be kinder to him than he deserves. But I believe his unlimited funds are about to get a limit."

"He might be treated kindly by his mother," On gloated, "but you can be sure my new play will not make that error. He is going to be seeing himself as a donkey prancing across that stage."

"He won't put up with that," old Ayep said irascibly. "He'll shut the theater quick as lightning."

"If he does, it will only confirm that he's the donkey. And it will be twice as popular—elsewhere," On predicted. "After my success with the Scholars play, it will spread—as long as it gets off the island. In fact, I'd better begin writing it out again, while it's fresh in mind, so I can pass a copy along at our next stop."

Everyone then exchanged remarks at Huyun Shandek's expense until I'd eaten a pancake. Then On said, "But we've all been waiting to hear everything about your encounter with the imperial fleet."

I gazed out the window to the sea, memory flooding back. Then I exclaimed, "You know the worst of it? Those two vipers called *me* a snake!" And I recounted the entire conversation.

No one was laughing when I finished.

Dinek said after I stopped to drink tea, "What do you intend to do?"

She looked worried. It had always been easier to keep my secrets, and the plans they caused, to myself. But I was finally learning that it's not just myself who reaps the consequences. "I need to get a warning to my brother and Koi about Xianti's plans to attack them during winter."

"How? We cannot go back," Dinek said. "Where is Whale Haven? I'll have to consult my chart. I've never heard of it."

"My brother said it's roughly ten days north of Tiger Eye Bay."

Hat Dove pursed her lips. "How can you get word to them without risking our ship?"

"I think it should be easy, if we're sailing north. Didn't you say you wanted to make a tea run by going up to the tea islands? I'll try to send a message from every Falcon inn we find on our way. One message ought surely to get through."

"Yes, we can do that," Dinek said, as everyone hailed this idea with nods of fervent agreement.

It was only then that I saw that they were dreading my insistence that we sail for Whale Haven.

"Sending a message is the best plan," old Ayep muttered. "Because getting involved in imperial wars is as sure a death as jumping into a fire mountain."

I did not have to look at my shipmates to know that not a one wanted to find themselves caught between Xianti's forces and those of Grand Prince Yiulo. I didn't want to, either. But my fear stirred up my anxiousness on my brother's behalf.

That, at least, I could keep to myself. We were sailing northward, now, Mountain Peony Island sunk below the eastern horizon. I hoped never to see it again, though I'd miss Fia and others around the Three Kingfishers.

Dinek, whose sense of the passing hours was as trustworthy as a water clock, called the watch change. The two on night duty came in to get tea and pancakes before going off to sleep through the day, and the rest diligently trooped out to the deck for martial arts practice.

I went as usual to the back, where it felt good to let myself fall into the old rhythm without having to think about it. Sagacious Blade hummed in my hand, the sun was bright, the breeze cool, and no danger in sight. *Pangolin* was entirely alone on the sea.

Many poets yearn for their young days, saying that if only we'd had the wisdom to see how happy we were then, how carefree, when our heads were not frosted with snow! But it's not always that simple. I relished being free of Huyun Shandek's reach, and I rejoiced in each day that put more distance between me and the vindictive imperial crown prince and his sister, but I was anxious about getting what I knew to my brother, and I missed Koi and his steady presence. And I did not know what to do about my intense awareness of On, except to avoid him as much as is possible on a small floating vessel in the middle of the ocean where privacy is mostly illusion.

After a day in which he attempted to fly all the swords in the armory, and gave up — those swords did not have the charm that made flight possible, and Auntie Breeze had had no interest in charming weapons, so I did not know how to charm our weapons — he did his watch chores, and practiced, but he no longer sought me out, and indeed, his free time was spent in the cabin he shared with the two Hat brothers, writing out his play about the donkey duke.

I kept myself busy, either working to refine my forms or following Dinek around and learning what I could about navigation, specifically between islands. And what she knew of those islands. I was beginning, at last, to build a sense of the empire.

Busy as I was, I remained aware of On.

This state of unspoken tension persisted until our first stop. I was among those who'd drawn the first liberty. So was On, who had put on one of his student robes with the fine embroidery and worn, threadbare hems, his hair worn half up and half down in the manner of grown-up third and fourth and fifth sons of fine families who had little but their proud ancestries — he'd told us that it was expected among the scholars that such young masters who gathered at the sorts of tea houses or entertainment places would "sing for their supper," that is, entertain with poetry, stories, music, or Circle games, in exchange for wealthier students to treat them to meals. It was a splendid way not only to get sumptuous repasts that he could never afford on his own, but to hear all the latest rumor.

He lounged at the back of the boat with his eyes shut, to all appearances asleep, as our shipmates chattered about the best and cheapest inns. I was impatient to get onto land, to find the Falcon wing-marked inn.

I failed.

The Falcon inn that had been marked on Dinek's chart had been passed on to descendants who had turned it into a tea shop for wealthy travelers. They had nothing to do with gallant wanderers, they made that quite plain.

I tried to hide my profound disappointment. Nothing was said as we rowed back to the ship to take our turn on watch while the night crew got their liberty. On wore a new robe, embroidered beautifully with pine needles and dragonflies. From his silks drifted the aroma of expensive incense and perfumes.

But later that night, when he was at the helm, and I was assigned deck watch, once I'd put myself and Sagacious Blade through the entire run of forms, and went to get tea, he called, "Will you bring me some?"

He did not have to tend the helm since we were anchored. But the night was warm, the sky clouded over, pressing the humid air on us, and it was a relief not to be inside a room that was bound to be warmer, and stuffy.

I carried tea out to the bench Dinek had installed by the helm, which was bolted to the deck so that it could serve when we needed to tie the helm down during storms. He perched on the rail, unmoved by the drop into water if an errant wave caused the ship to pitch. I set his cup on the bench as he said, "Koi is in your heart, is that it?"

"What?" I exclaimed, thoroughly startled. Then heat singed my nerves as I said, "Why would you say that? Nobody is in my heart but my family."

"You were so very disappointed when you left *The Blue Robin.*"

"Because they are no longer a Falcon inn, which means that I can't get that warning to my brother," I said — too loud. As if defending myself. But I didn't have to defend myself.

"Your brother," he repeated. "Are you sure it's not Koi?"

"Why would it matter?" I asked. "Surely you're not about to raise an objection to my writing to him because Koi has gone back to being a servant."

"Not at all," On said, and pinched the skin between his brows. "I'm going about this wrong." He dropped his hands with a smack against his thighs. "Have you considered that the warning might be a waste of your effort? That they might know the imperial prince is coming? In fact, the grand prince might be waiting for them? Surely so experienced a commander as Grant Prince Lan Yiulo would have layers of scouts, traps, and the like, around his citadel."

"It's possible," I admitted. "But the way Xianti was talking, it seemed to me that he was looking forward to taking them by surprise. It might only be that he was going to attack during the new year festival."

On gave a slow nod at that. "Spring is the customary war season. And late spring at that, because early spring hasn't had time to put forth much in the way of food. Armies have to be fed. Have you considered that yon grand prince and his followers might not only expect an attack, but look forward to it?"

"Not my brother. Not Koi."

"I can't say anything to your brother, who is unknown to me."

"You're slandering Koi, then? Why?"

"Not slandering. I only met him the one day, remember. During that day, he beat me easily at everything but double sticks and fan, which I've practiced all my life. Seems to me he's chosen the warrior's path."

"The defender's path," I stated. "There is an enormous difference. If he wanted to fight to be fighting, he would be on the way to some duel, or competition, right now. Challenging other masters to prove he's the best. He has no interest in that. He told me himself."

"Ay, after he thrashed his way through us all, he spent the rest of that day talking to you. Then followed you to Tiger Eye Harbor. And then again when you went out to seek the firedragon fleet."

"And so?" I asked.

"And so if it's not war, could it be you who... Ay, how to word this?" He stretched out on the rail, nose pointed skyward, eyes closed.

"I scarcely know Koi," I said stiffly, though I was beginning to wonder what I felt about him. But that was not a subject that I wished to address out loud, to anyone, yet. At least not before I understood it myself.

"So it's just me you've taken against, then?" On asked, his voice as remote as if he spoke to those stars overhead. Except his eyes were closed.

"What?" I exclaimed—again. "I haven't taken against you."

"Really?" He sat up suddenly, eyes open. "Because from my perspective, ever since the night we rode the sword together, you've been avoiding me as if I've drenched myself in fish guts."

"I have not," I protested—thought, then said, "All right, I have. Not because I dislike you."

"Oh?"

What was the proper way to have such a conversation? Mother had never given me a hint. "I..." What to say? "I feel self-conscious," I admitted. "In a way I never have before."

"Oh?"

"That's it," I said.

He regarded me in silence, as I gazed back, my heart beating fast. Finally, he said slowly, "You don't want to do anything about it? Like, for instance, talk to me?" He added with rueful humor, "Or ask how *I* feel?"

"I..." A courtly compliment and evasion formed at my lips, but he had used no courtly language. "I think I was afraid to," I said finally.

"Why?" he asked, not at all aggressively, or demandingly, for if he had, that would have been our last such conversation.

"I don't know," I said, "Perhaps because of..." I was too embarrassed to admit to the intensity of my feelings, when he sat there, calm, cool, easy, on the stern rail of the *Pangolin*. "Because this situation is very new?"

"Then Koi is not in your heart? It certainly seemed that you are in his."

"No? Yes? I ... don't know?"

He put a hand to his eyes. "Right. You're fifteen and court-raised—"

"Sixteen," I corrected, from what I perceived at the time as a vast difference.

"Sixteen. Though at times, like yesterday when you faced that smiling serpent Huyun, surrounded by his armed men and calling to the lightning, you seemed more like sixteen hundred years old. But what I meant was, you didn't have the benefit of the Xuan cousins, five years older than I, and fifty years ahead in experience. Thank you, Ren, for telling me as much as you could." To my consternation, he slid off the rail to the deck and performed a full bow.

Then he hopped back up. "If you want to say more. I'm here." His tone changed. "And if you figure out the charm for swords, *please* don't forget me. Flying that sword was the best experience I ever had. I want to find my own sword, though maybe I won't be able to fly it. I remember you were doing the Essence work. That is, I sensed it. Somehow."

"I will." I held my hand up, palm toward him, in the gallant wanderer gesture for an agreement.

He laughed, raised his palm, and then we talked about forms, and it was easier, and after that I could look at him again. And found it just as agreeable, but that was a fire I stayed leery of.

ELEVEN

She knew the dragon prince's mood presaged winter.
In all imperial islands
None dared submit petitions for peace.
Hands cut brocade into strips,
Some for helmet mudguards,
Others to shield briny spray.

EVERYONE HAS THEIR EXPERTISE. A beggar knows the best spot, the best time of day, the best appeals, the best manner of supplication. Dinek, an accredited navigator who also captained a ship, had determined our position and chosen the best route in which to avoid most of the imperial fleets prowling the ways between the Inner Islands.

I asked her how long we could expect to take to get far enough north so that any message I sent by Falcons could the more quickly and reliably reach Whale Haven Island.

"It could be anywhere from ten to eighteen days. That side, the eastern edge of the empire, bordering as it does on the Great Sea, has a faster current this time of year, the summer-warm waters below the Jade Islands pushing north until they turn cold, at which time they push south again on the other side of the Great Sea. It's an enormous circle, such as you find when you empty a tub from a bunghole at the bottom, how the water will swirl and circle all on its own. So it is with ships."

"I take it that we're not to expect the same sort of current here along the Inner Islands?"

"Not at all," Dinek said. "Think of what a still pond looks like when the first few raindrops hit it. They ring out and intersect. It is so on this route—currents bump into the islands and intersect. That's before we get storms. Especially these summer storms." She looked skyward. "I smell thunder dragons in this one. It's going to be a blow."

It was.

We spent most of two days at our posts, being constantly battered by washes of rain slanting sideways, and mountain-sized waves, as we raced before a maddened wind full of howling demons. But the ship had been well reinforced. The water cascaded down the slanting deck and away, and Dinek listened to the clack of the battens, whose clatter sang different notes that only she seemed to hear. "Not yet," she kept shouting. "Not yet."

And then finally, "It's passing." Though it was still dark, the water dire.

But gradually the storm ended, and some of us dropped down where we were, and slept right there on deck.

When we woke, there were the inevitable repairs, while Dinek tried to determine where we'd been blown. "I'm afraid that we lost most of our westing, and all of our northward progress—and then some," she said, peering at the horizon, then at her precious chart, which had been wrapped in three layers, then stored in a box inside a trunk. "I wish I'd known it was coming before it was on us. I would have tucked us into a harbor, even if it was full of imperials."

She lived on deck until at last a blur appeared on the southern horizon, resolving into a bump. Dinek climbed up the highest mast, leaning out at a dangerous angle until she could make out the silhouette of the island.

When she finally matched its spiny mountain profile to the chart, she turned a grim face our way. "It looks like we were pushed all the way south to Benevolent Winds Island."

"Which boasts one of the three most important imperial naval bases," I said. "Because of the brimstone mines. My father's brother used to be governor. Now it's Xianti's twin."

"Helm over!" Dinek called. "Sun on your left shoulder: we're heading straight north as fast as we can."

Two days later, we'd restored the *Pangolin* to excellent shape, and had gone back to our regular routine as if the storm had never happened, when we sighted more island clusters, first mere dragon's teeth, then a pair of islands roughly the size of Crescent. There was the expected harbor that served the imperials.

Dinek said at breakfast, as we gave that island wide berth, "I know exactly where we are. We don't need to stop, thanks to our hold staying nicely watertight. We've plenty of stores. We can get fresh things two days farther—Auspicious Prosperity Harbor is smaller, but it's used by traders. And welcomes wanderers." She smiled at Dove. "The Hats have been established there for generations."

She turned to the Hat boys, who were—as usual—carrying on some kind of covert competition game with the Ayep boys. "You five, remember, not a word about where we've been or what happened. You never know who is listening."

No one likes to hear 'you ought to have' warnings akin to shutting the pen after the sheep have all escaped, but I ought to have paid attention to the way the five boys responded to Dinek's admonition. The Ayep boys, whose grandfather had been a governor in the navy for decades before leaving for the gallant wanderers when the previous emperor had taken the throne, gave short, respectful nods of assent, as did their irascible grandfather. The Hat boys—from well-known traders who dealt with imperials and gallant wanderers alike—agreed less formally, Bek with a silent nod and Tu with a muttered, "I know, I know, I know."

He might have known, but it seemed that didn't stop him from confiding the tale of our near miss with Governor Huyun and the imperials to one of his childhood friends, of course in the strictest confidence.

Dove politely extended an invitation to me to stay at the Hat house, and I just as politely turned her down. I was unknown to the family, and I did not want to create any sense of obligation, especially under the vexing circumstances of my living under a false name.

This harbor was old, with an entire street of inns and eateries. I found Falcon wings at The Swan Goose, and opted to stay there. After my usual first question and the usual answer— "No, I've never heard of a Falcon scrape called Peaches, sorry"—I even paid for a room to myself, so that I could concentrate on composing a letter to Koi without inviting the curious questions of friendly roommates.

I was in my little chamber that night, toiling over a letter that I was finding surprisingly difficult to write, when Dinek charged in. "We have to leave," she said, her dismay swirling in with the air from her sudden entrance. "Hat Tu seems to have blabbered about everything."

"What happened?"

"We're being chased. And Grandfather Hat Gan says we ought to assume the worst, that the imperials have at least one spy in this harbor, which might be small, but it is on a major trade route," Dinek said bluntly. "Thanks to Tu, there's probably a pigeon in the air right now, winging its way to the imperials. Oh, and to Huyun Shandek. Can you leave your task right now? Grandfather Hat wishes to apologize to your face."

Shock jolted me. My instinct to run now had to be squashed. I would not insult an elder by refusing to go, especially since he felt that his clan had committed a wrong against me. I would only worsen the grievance if I did not give them face.

"Do you have everything?" she asked.

As I was used to living out of my carryall, I had only to put on my harness and grab my stuff as we thundered down the stairs.

Dove was waiting below, her eyes reddened. Crying for family shame—or on her brother's behalf?

"What am I to expect?" I asked.

"At the very least, Tu will be kept home for at least a year," Dove said in a low, flat voice. Flatter than her customary manner. She was a person far more comfortable with numbers and the arrangement of impeccably logical proofs. "He'll spend some time among the children. That's if..." Her gaze flickered to me and away, her shoulders tight. "Grandfather is assigning Second-Cousin Da in his place."

It seemed that captains who wanted a Hat did not get to choose them.

The entire family was lined up in their ancestral hall, Tu on his knees, red-eyed and trembling.

When I entered, the grandfather led the entire family in a deep bow. I bowed back, then the grandfather said, "Here is the miscreant. This incompetent grandfather dares to entreat the benevolence of our esteemed guest..." I noticed he used no names. "And desire her to name his punishment. It will be carried out."

At that two husky Hat servants grounded long sticks of the sort I recognized with an inward jolt: family disciplinary rods. At the crack of those rods on the polished wooden floor, not only Tu but half the company started. From that I deduced that such extremity of punishment was rare, but not unknown.

With every heartbeat I longed to be safely at sea. If the imperials truly were on my trail, they could close off the harbor, and though I could probably escape, I knew Xianti was vindictive enough to take whatever he would claim to be my crime out on the Pangolins. But I could not wave off this dire situation, or this entire clan gathered here would lose face. I must preserve their dignity and question Tu, and it must be done correctly.

At least I had family models for that. At such formal inquiries in the ancestral hall, my parents had begun with establishing what we both knew, then delved into the why of it.

"Tu, did you hear Captain Dinek's orders about keeping silence?"

"Yes," he mumbled, soft as a kitten squeak.

"Tu, did you understand Captain Dinek when she gave the order not to discuss anyone's family, rank, or name of birth?"

"Yes."

"Can you explain why you chose to disobey those orders?"

"I didn't disobey," Tu said, and when one of the adults scowled and half-raised a hand, the grandfather shot a glance that way, and the adults stilled.

Tu writhed a little as he briefly met my gaze, then dropped his own. "That is, I only told Magua Tek because he's almost like a brother. He was," Tu corrected morosely. "He kept plenty of secrets when we were boys. He kept mine. I kept his. He liked stories about adventures. Especially if they're true. And he liked stories about..." A glance upward, not meeting my eyes. "Imperials. And what happened was so..."

As he piled on the superlatives, I sifted his words, and beyond his words, on that plane that is so hard to describe. I sensed no malice, or desire to profit other than the wish to be proximate to...

"To fame," Granny Zim said in her matter-of-fact way. "An entirely human wish."

"'Human' can mean so many things," I thought back. "Some bad, some even lethal."

"Being predictably human is not an excuse, but an observation," Granny Zim replied, unperturbed. "Your assessment matches mine."

That was what I'd hoped to hear.

I waited, curbing my growing impatience, as Tu rambled and backtracked through his sense of betrayal that his old friend could not even wait a single hour before bragging to his cronies among the rope-making apprentices, a lot of whom Tu didn't even know! He could not seem to see that the same motivation to talk about what he perceived as "great" events held for his friend, too.

"And, ayoh! If he wasn't going to be my friend anymore, he could have said," Tu finished in a voice of injury. "And he disobeyed, that is, I made him swear not to tell, and he swore on his ancestors, but he broke it, and I didn't swear on anything, but he gets away with blabbing—"

"No," the grandfather stated. "He will not. As his family will discover. But you and your offense is the subject here. This lacking grandparent begs pardon," he added with a bow toward me.

The chief fault, I saw, was mine, in living under a false name. The imperial prestige has been scrupulously guarded for centuries. Whatever we are as individuals, our dynastic reputation is as a dragon streaking across the sky from horizon to horizon. People fear, watch in awe, and then afterward mark that day with a white stone. Tu's wish to associate himself with "princess in disguise" lay behind his action.

I said, "I am still learning. My judgment might be at fault, in which case I seek instruction from the elders." Here, I raised my hands in the gallant wanderer bow toward the elders. "But what I see before me is a desire to associate with fame or reputation. Kanda teaches us that desires are not problematic in themselves, but pursuing them in a manner that ignores benevolence to the world and everyone in it is. Pursuing them in a way that shares joy with others is virtue."

I hoped with these words we'd safely shifted away from those terrible punishment rods.

A few of the adults whispered and shifted, then Grandfather Hat studied his miserable grandson, and said, "This errant elder presumes to beg our benevolent visitor to define virtue for one who so clearly has none."

Hat Tu's head turtled further into his shoulders.

I said to Tu, "Mana Ta defines the four elements of virtue as benevolence, righteousness, wisdom, and propriety."

—and then I had a suitable punishment—and an outcome that preserved face for this aggrieved family, that unfortunately would have to face any imperials who descended on them, searching for me.

"Tu, I am not going to further define the four elements of

virtue. When the *Pangolin* returns for you, I expect to find a written definition of each element, describing it in an example from your own life."

His head jerked up, though he was still crouched down. "You'll come back? For me?"

There was no trace of anger or resentment in him that I could see. But I didn't quite trust myself, as I had also not seen past Huyun Shandek's smiling eyes and kindly demeanor. "Granny Zim?" I asked inwardly.

"This boy is exactly what you see. You have just given him hope. Now give him a little face."

"You are too valuable a crew member for us not to come back for you," I said as sternly as I could. "But your family has decreed that you are to spend a little more time here for training, which will benefit not just you, but us as well."

I turned to the grandfather, whose forbidden aspect had eased only a trifle, but I had the sense that he approved.

The mother then came forward, bowing to me, her cheeks shiny with tears, and that broke the ranks, and the Hats surrounded us.

Over their voices, the grandfather asked, with immense dignity, if there was anything they could do for me. Though I was morally already in their debt, the only recourse was to verbally place myself in their debt. "Is there a chance that you could see a letter sent on its way to Whale Haven Island?" I asked.

The grandfather bowed. "We would be honored to be so trusted, and shall see it delivered, via our messenger hawks." He nodded to one of the young men among the Hats, who wore the heavy tunic and leather arm-cover of a hawk-master. He led me to an alcove where there was pen and paper.

Here, I hesitated only slightly; if the Hats were going to see my note delivered, then I need worry less about enemy eyes.

I remembered the code Koi had suggested, and wrote, *Please ask two to relay that…* We had not set a code for Xianti! But Koi would surely recognize: *…the viper intends to descend on the fox's lair by turn of year.*

That would have to do.

I signed it *Pangolin Ren*, sealed and addressed it to *Koi on Whale Haven Island*, and handed it to the waiting hawkmaster. We gave one another the gallant wanderer bow, and I was free.

Dove, that invaluable investigator who was better at delving for truth than at the Circle game of social give and take, knew her family well. "We must go now, before the pursuit catches up," she said to her mother.

That succeeded in prodding everyone into motion, and we were soon rowing to the *Pangolin*, surrounded by baskets of good things. Next to Dove, Bek sat with a huge young man of eighteen or nineteen who regarded me in silence.

Dinek pushed off, saying, "I'm so glad that On had ship duty. Now I won't have to search the entire harbor to find him. Why he won't stay at one place under one name is beyond me..."

Hat Bek and the enormous young man named Da began to row. He seemed to have twice Bek's strength—and Bek was a powerful rower. We managed to catch the last of the tide, and cleared the bay with no ships immediately in sight. I'd dreaded seeing the golden dragon banner marking a fleet.

We helped the Hats pull up the boat, and as Bek somewhat glumly took Da off to show him where he'd sleep, and Dove vanished to whatever her duty was, Dinek went straight to the helm.

I thought she was preoccupied with our getting away safely. As she was, but her silent mood did not alter over the next day or two. For myself, once we were safely on the sea, my own worries slipped largely from me. Though we had confirmed that there was pursuit, they had not caught us. Further, at last I'd been able to send off that warning—and I figured it had a better chance of actually reaching Whale Haven Island in time, which I'd not been so certain about if I'd had to rely on Falcons unknown to me to be willing to carry a message in that direction. Rather than some imperial spy pretending to be a Falcon. Because I was fairly certain that my secret—such as it was—was no longer any secret to those I wanted most not to discover my identity. It all hinged on Huyun Shandek having guessed. And having told the imperials.

But Dinek's mood did not change, and I often saw her at the rail, sweeping the horizons with her gaze.

I said nothing, for I had not been invited to intrude. Instead, I threw myself back into practice. It was good to return to seeds, forms, and martial arts sparring. On laughingly offered Eel form to me—the advanced fan fighting form that entertainment women used to deflect trouble, in trade for more of the Ze Bek style training from the long-ago master buried in the memories Granny Zim had shared with me.

"I thought you handled that deftly," he said in an

undervoice.

"I was just mimicking my mother," I replied, as we sparred and jabbed with our fans.

"I'd be terrified to meet her. Though Grandfather Hat was intimidating enough. Hat Gan. I've evolving a new role. Gan the adventurer. I just need some adventures for his play."

"I hope you get them—some time and place when I'm not there," I retorted.

I enjoyed fighting-fan practice once I was doing it, but I shied away from choosing to practice it unless it was offered, because it reminded me of Cray, who had begun teaching me when I was small. My heart still knotted whenever I thought of Cray, and that passionate conversation that I had never been intended to overhear. It was unsettling, to say the very least, to discover that one's very existence is an annoyance to another—even if one thought one was doing one's best toward all.

Hat Da proved to be formidably good at martial arts. He was unspeaking, or nearly. He had a habit of humming in his chest before he got as few words out as possible, and those with difficulty. The Ayep boys soon talked around him, but I was used to silent people, and I saw that he listened carefully.

Would I feel differently if I recognized omens before the event? That is a question for the gods, I expect. I understand that events that appear to be unrelated to us can turn out to be vitally important in our lives, though we did not foresee, or endeavor, to bring them about. And, conversely, sometimes what one might assume is a premonition might also be an awareness, below the level of thought, of another inevitable chain of events.

This is what I can claim: I tossed and turned for some days after we left the Hat clan. I kept waking, feeling as if a storm was about to descend. But the ship's noises were those of a normal spring night, the pitch and yaw, and the clatter of battens, those of a mild wind.

As soon as my window began to blue, I rose and dressed. And discovered On and Dinek speaking above me on the captain's level. They were already awake, though I knew that On had had a night shift.

Impelled by a sense of urgency, I ran up to join them. "Look," Dinek said, pointing eastward.

Spaced neatly, with the largest—no, the closest—mid center, the unmistakable triangles of ships.

"You are seeing a perfect hunt formation," On said conversationally. But I noticed that his hands were clasped so tightly behind his back that his knuckles had gone white.

Dinek had all our sails out. All she said was, "Now we shall discover if the Yim shipwrights are telling the truth, that anything they build or renovate is as fast, or faster, than anything the navy has."

The sun still lay below the horizon, but the summer sky was a pure blue, the strengthening light strong. It glowed in her face, strong enough to light the color of her eyes, revealing an unexpected amber component to them, with tiny hints of green, and though her face was more olive than the maple to mahogany of most of us, there were subtle undertones of those splotches that had been so distinct in the Cinnabar Princess's fish-pale skin.

Traders, I thought—unwilling to grapple with the evidence of pursuit—they must have ancestors among so many groups of people. Those subtle variations were like silent stories.

But I was not going to be able to indulge myself long.

On said, "Ren?"

And I began to understand the prompt behind the restless dreams as inescapable truth confronted me. Not so much the chase. I'd begun to expect that. I knew that Xianti was a champion grudge-holder. That and his resources as imperial crown prince meant he could send out an entire fleet, to chase down a single individual. Then there was Huyun Shandek, who might have orders reinforcing his determination to have that interview he so wanted.

The prompt was the cost to the others. And now I saw the true reason for Dinek's tensions. Ay, I could tell myself that she was sorely missing Fan, as each surge of the *Pangolin* carried us farther from Mountain Peony Island and that Falcon scrape up beyond Cloud Terrace, but here was the truth: if that ship caught up, everyone would pay the price of harboring a "criminal."

On said, "Ideas?"

He was in as much danger as I was. Or near. They were not looking for him specifically, but what if the truth came out?

I shook myself, to get rid of the extraneous thoughts, and looked around, then up. No rain in sight. Not a cloud. The water was lighting to the blue-green of a summer day. "If we could get rain, I could do the obscuring charm," I said. "But I am very certain it won't work while all eyes are targeting us."

On said, "We'll have to wait for night. If we can keep this distance, we can make it work, right?"

Dinek looked from one of us to the other as I said, "Yes." And then, hating the necessity, "As long as they don't have some sort of Essence master with them, who will be on the watch for such ruses."

Dinek gave a short nod, and as the sun's limb gleamed fiery gold, beginning the day, she said, "Our luck is our empty hold. They have to be full of warriors. We are not. As long as we get this favorable wind, they will not catch up."

It was so.

Ship chases are peculiar things. A chase on land is breathless, tiring, a wild dash with fractured impressions as one sifts for ways to shake the pursuit. A ship chase is slow and deliberate, relatively comfortable—if you discount the mounting dread.

All day we went about our usual routine, but in a state of tense alertness. Frequent gazes shot eastward, especially that morning, then gradually lessened as the state of the chase remained steady.

We ate, we tended the ship as duty required, we gathered for martial arts practice, from seeds and forms to sparring. We ate again at sundown, with the ships in more or less the same position. Dinek kept watching the sky; she studied every scrap of cloud with a frown, trying to wring from it a sign of how the wind might change.

Badly as I'd slept the previous night, I was wide awake when it was time for the night watch.

On had vanished, but reappeared after a short rest. He joined me, and said abruptly, "How likely is it that the Lans have a vault full of the charmed swords they've wrested from others over the years? Did they really destroy them? My uncle was always sure that they didn't, and that at least some emperors have elites even among the Emperor's Own."

"I can't say," was my answer. "But charms can fade if they are not renewed."

"I keep imagining a sky filled with armed warriors on swords descending on us," On commented. "I hate not being able to do anything but sit here. On land, I can at least become one of my many names and vanish in a crowd."

"I'm not worried about the sky filled with warriors. First, because I'm not that important to Xianti. I think if he had any, he'd save them to go after Yiuti. But I don't think he has any because he wouldn't trust anyone with skills he didn't, or maybe couldn't, learn."

On's gaze shifted eastward, to gauge yet again the distance between us and the pursuit, and I knew he had to be thinking, as I was, that we had enough danger right here on the surface of the world.

The night passed, the stars brilliantly clear overhead, the two moons entirely unobstructed in their small arcs at opposite ends of the world. We had passed Hungry Ghost Month, so the time in which there was no moon was slowly growing briefer.

Dawn brought the summer sun, hot and bright. This was coming into harvest time, when the skies could go for days, even weeks, without rain. We ran mostly west, Dinek adjusting slightly to avoid any islands, as they could block the wind, or create flurries of small winds, the way we do when we use a fan. Either of these could be disastrous for us.

The *Pangolin* was proving the worth of the shipbuilders who had improved it, and we stayed ahead of the pursuit. But for how long? Dinek seemed calm, but she had stopped talking to us, except for orders. I caught Ayep sometimes giving me considering looks from under frost-touched brows. And all the while I tried to go about doing my duty, practicing assiduously, but the awareness of myself as the cause of the danger the ship was in knotted me from heart to spleen.

I finally went to Dinek one night, as Ghost Moon dropped toward the sea ahead. "I think I have to go," I said—hoping that she would talk me out of it.

And I caught the relief—no more than a tiny sag of her jaw, and a sudden lowering of her eyelids—that she tried to hide.

I swallowed against the ache in my throat. "I have my map. Can you show me where we are?"

"I can." She unrolled my map, and, paying no attention to my tiny annotations, she swept her hand upward along the left, "This is a very, very general circle, you understand."

"The imperial wheel," I said. "within the dragon."

She nodded; I'd learned that the traders and the navy regarded the empire as a dragon shape.

I said, "I know that rice and silk and certain other trade goods come up from the south, and in turn, wheat and tea and other goods come from the north, going south. In the middle, though it's not truly the middle, is the imperial island, where all taxes come in. A bit like a wheel."

"True enough, in a general way," Dinek said. "The tea route can be seen as a circle within the circle. And, I suspect you did not know that gallant wanderers have their own pattern, but it goes this way…" She drew her finger in a zigzag around from southeast to west, and then up northeastward. "That is why one island will have several sects in its mountains, and the two islands closest on the north or south or east or west sides haven't even an inn. Falcons are within that pattern. Most gallant wanderer sects are. More or less. Ships do go all over, and then there is the matter of wars scattering everyone and everything, but my mother said that we all prefer what we know, which is why we have habits. Big ones, like routes, and small ones, like always eating a steamed bun right when the sun tops the neighbor's eave."

"I understand that," I said.

"Good. So, you'll find old gallant wanderers here … here … here… ay, and sometimes here, at Tortor, though that's mostly criminals, my mother said. It's treacherous landing. Very. The imperials can't establish a harbor there, so they ignore it." From the way her voice lowered, I sensed that this information was not shared widely. Which spoke of trust, but also I think it might have been a sort of apology for the relief she could not hide that I was taking myself away.

I looked down at the islands that Dinek had marked, then rolled my map again, put it within its silk cover, and then into its box.

"It's going to be a long journey for a sailboat," Dinek said when I was packed up. "But not impossible. Especially for you. If you have to abandon the boat, it is just a boat. We'll get another."

Whereas lives cannot be replaced. She didn't say it, but I felt it. Or maybe it was entirely my own conscience.

As it was, the best time was not far off. Everyone who was awake helped to get the sailboat readied as I walked around it, touching it repeatedly and murmuring the obscuring charm. The deck crew swung it over the side to be lowered to the sea, along with its mast and sail.

Dinek said, "I do wish there was a way to obscure *Pangolin* the way you did when we left Cloud Terrace."

"I wish I had Essence paper," I said. "It would be easy, then."

She looked up, startled. "We do."

"You do?"

Dinek flushed. I could see it in the light of the dimmed lamp. "My mother bought all kinds of talismans at the temple. I don't know if they actually function—I keep thinking of Aunt Lily, who hung talismans on every redbark tree outside every temple for two runs, in hopes of getting a fortune, but last I heard, she is living exactly as she always did."

"I don't know about those things," I said. "You'd have to talk to a diviner—one who is..." *Honest*. "...knows Essence matters. But this I know. If it is true Essence paper, I can write my charm on the back. It won't interfere with the charms on the other side, unless they are written to draw attention."

"No, they are all for warding storms, and good luck."

As the cook passed down packets of food, and finally one of our precious barrels of water, I stood above on the deck, summoning all the Essence I could reach, and made as many talismans as Dinek had paper.

I handed these to her, saying, "Don't use them unless you get a storm long enough for them to believe you could have broached, or the wind could have separated you. They know I have Essence, and they will look hard each morning, in which case the charm is useless."

"I know," she said tightly. "But it's a chance. And if they do see past the ruse, at least..." Her gaze shifted, and I finished silently, *At least I won't be there*. "At least we could say we thought they were pirates." Then, clutching those to her, she said, "It is benevolent of you. A true merit, going like this, when this is your ship."

"But it was never truly my ship. If it belongs to anyone, outside of those slavers we took it from, it belongs to us all," I said. "Like the fortress that belonged to Jong Siang and all his 110 heroes, after they took it from oppressive villains."

Dinek clasped her hands fervently in the gallant wanderer bow, and I bowed back, saying, "I know that my proximity is a danger to you all. It is merely practical to leave." And, my throat tight with the tears I would not shed, I hefted Sagacious Blade and my carryall, and let myself down the side—into the boat where On was busy setting up the mast and sail.

When he was done, he straightened up, then went to the helm. "Aren't you going back up?" I asked, as above me, a row of faces waited for him to leap back to the rail.

"And let Huyun Shandek catch up with me for the donkey-duke play? You know by now it has to be all over Cloud Terrace," he finished with a distinct tone of relish.

No one looked surprised at On's sudden decision to go with me. They were too used to his butterfly ways.

"It really is hard to see you," Hat Bek commented from

above, as he cast off the line holding the sailboat to the side of the *Pangolin*. "If I turn my head, and look over there a little, I can't see you at all."

With that, On let the sail fall. It caught the gentle wind and the distance between us and the *Pangolin* began to widen.

TWELVE

She learned that in darkness shared,
the wild storm becomes
a flowered wind — and lightning an orchid candle…

ONCE WE WERE A safe distance from the *Pangolin*, On said, "They're not looking for me, but I can't risk falling into their hands. If I'm seen by any of the surviving imperial generals, one is sure to recognize me. My nanny used to say that I'm my grandfather born again."

"We can't risk it," I agreed. "Uncle Koza would either use you or kill you outright. Xianti as well. My thought is, with you and me gone, Dinek can now turn in any direction. And when they catch up — and they're bound to if they stick to her like a shadow, unless she can lose the pursuit long enough to hang the talismans — she can say they are on a tea run. And that I was left behind at Cloud Terrace. There won't be any need to treat them as criminals without my criminal self present."

"Which is why I never told them my name."

"I suppose I ought not to have told them who *I* am. Except that would not keep them out of danger. Xianti sees everyone who doesn't serve him as rebels and criminals. Me, a criminal," I muttered. "When he is the very embodiment of evil intent."

"He would never see himself that way," On predicted.

"No, because he and Siarti truly believe that their imperial blood places them above the law, instead of their living as examples of law, as my parents believed. As do I."

"Living examples of the law," On repeated slowly. "I feel a poem coming on. No, another play. It's a shame that you weren't born a prince. If you were to raise your banner among these other princes, I would follow you all the way to the dragon throne."

I flushed hot in the darkness, because even though he was laughing, his words lightly spoken, there was an ardency that I could sense in his undertone. It was not merely the attraction between us, though that was as inescapable as the soft, summer night air. It was the ring of conviction in his voice.

I did not know what to do with that, except to turn toward a side of the matter that was familiar, and I said with indignation, "Why should I have to be a prince, supposing I *was* right? Cannot a princess be right? Is not my brain sufficient, even though my physical form is this one, instead of that one? If we were all mere brains, without these bodies, then the throne would belong to the best suited. There would be no immediate ban of half the world because of a lack of beard."

"You forgot the other important form: imperial blood," he corrected, and laughed. "As for your idea of existing as mere brains, I reject it utterly. Life would not be nearly as much fun if there were not girls and boys. Ay! But I agree, I agree, please do not draw that sword. I agree about brains being the best claim to rule. So, you want to be empress?"

"Of course not!" I sighed. "But if there were to be another empress, Mother would make the best one. Not merely on the phoenix throne, that is, as consort."

"I know. Sage Empress in the very oldest sense—as they claim for Suanek."

"Yes! A sage empress. And likewise my father would make a sage emperor. It's not just me saying that as a filial daughter. I suspect the entire court believes—"

On suddenly raised a hand, alert and still as a creature of the air, listening. His hearing had to be more acute than mine, for I heard nothing. I turned, to discover that the pursuit was a lot closer than I'd assumed they would be. Lights twinkled, marking each ship.

We sat in silence during the slowest chase ever. The fleet was moving incrementally faster than we were, them going west as we floated northward.

Presently he dropped his voice to a whisper. "I don't think we'll drift through the middle of them, but we might be heard if we speak aloud."

Though we had been sailing by starlight, I quickly sketched the obscuring charm over the both of us, and over all our things inside the boat. Slowly—inexorably—the northernmost of the pursuing ships passed a mere two hundred paces south of us. Voices floated over the water now and then. Not many, as it was very late—last Turtle hour, or first Tiger. A laugh, and "Come, come, come!" a sound often heard before toasts.

On leaned over the side, as if that would bring him closer, squinting to make out the banners. I did the same, but the darkness leached them of color. All I made out was the form of a dragon on one, but that was to be expected. We still could not tell if these were all Xianti's, or Huyun Shandek's, or even a mix of the same.

They clearly did not expect any encounters out in the wide-open sea. The ships gradually drew apart. After they had passed into the west, blurring against the horizon, we both relaxed.

I looked around the inky ocean before pulling a tongue of flame from the stars, enough to light a lamp. The boat was much like the boat of the old wine merchant that Cray, Granny Ou, and Koi and I sailed down the river with. Hers had been a raft, not a boat, but the two vessels had the same sort of a tent affair that gave scant shelter. Into this we'd pushed our supplies and belongings. I leaned against my carryall, saying, "I just realized, I don't really like being in the ocean. I do it because I must. I don't understand Dinek at all. She actually relishes those storms."

"Certainly," he said. "It's a battle. Some relish a battle. Fighting against the elements to stay alive is a clean war." He leaned back, one hand carelessly on the helm. "When we reach land. Disguises, you think? Ought we to trade clothes? That was what I did when I first escaped my uncle. I had nothing but what I wore. It was Xuan Wuyang's idea to trade clothes. And it worked."

I was tempted to try his idea. I rather liked the idea of going as ragged-hemmed Scholar Someone, On's favorite guise besides On Lu the writer of satiric plays. "Alas, it will only work in places there are no imperials," I said. "And then, what use is it?"

"Why?"

"Because when I'm dressed as a boy, I look like my brother." And I explained about the encounter with Tiger Li's bullies before Koi and I ended up captured by the slavers.

"No disguise, then," On said. "Do you play an instrument? No one looks at musicians, unless they are very good."

"I never learned."

"I could teach you some common airs on the flute. It'll take me only a few moments to make a bamboo flute, once we land. There's bamboo everywhere. The good thing about the flute is, when you get the knack of fingering, and how to breathe across the hole, you can play anything."

I had to laugh. "So says someone with an affinity for air."

Though I'd negated all On's suggestions, his mood remained sunny. He did not seem to mind at all that the two of us were alone in the middle of the ocean. He charitably offered me the first sleep watch, as I'd never tended helm before, and it would be easier to show me come morning.

I took him up on it, and wrapped up in my cloak. I slept immediately, but found it increasingly more difficult to stay asleep, until a surge of cold water poured over me and shocked me awake.

I sat upright, gasping, to find On with one arm straining to hold the helm steady, and the other hand clenched on the rope, as his entire body leaned away from the shuddering sail.

I grabbed for the rope.

"You're awake? I was just about to..."

His words were lost as a green wave swelled off our bow, and we began to ride up it, then crested it, water foaming to either side. Off to the south, I could see morning sky, though an odd, aqua shade that was not reassuring. But that was preferable to the north, which was a threatening grayish green.

"That's the direction we're going." I had to raise my voice. "Should we turn aside?"

He lifted a shoulder. "The winds can change at any time. We need to meet the waves head on. If we let them come alongside, they will tip us over for certain."

I held onto the rope until my hands began to burn. My palms had become callused after all my sword practice, but even so, I knew I could not hold long, and so I wrapped the rope around one of my legs, which pulled mercilessly. I wrapped my hands in my sodden cloak and then grabbed the humming-taut rope once again, mostly as a guide.

Lightning flared, thunder crashed, and that gray-green sky moved inexorably over us, a terrible chariot drawn by millions of demon wind-steeds.

On was using his entire body to keep the helm steady as we

climbed, rushed down, climbed, rushed down, now and then doused with splashes of seawater. He laughed once or twice, as lightning branched overhead, and thunder rumbled and crashed.

There's always my sword, there's always my sword, I told myself as the waves steadily grew. Our things began to slide and he stuck out a foot to block them, still laughing. Was he ever afraid, I wondered amid my own sick dread as our entire boat tilted at an impossible angle. With a breath-snatching surge we crested the wave and raced down amid the foam, and I knew that in these winds riding my sword would only get me more tumbled about in the air if I flew.

Around me the boat shuddered and creaked. Wood floats, but that would not aid us if it was wrenched to pieces. "You know what to do," Granny Zim said, her voice behind my ear just discernable. "You know what to do!"

Back memory hurled me to my secret spot up above the Three Kingfishers, when I drew on Essence to lift boulders. Could I hold the boat together? But where was my Essence? The sun had gone until morning, and there was no fire in all that great sea. Even the stars had drowned.

I turned to On, whose wide eyes reflected the lightning, his teeth bared in a ferocious grin. As if he tried to hold the ship together by sheer will.

What had I done? "Give me your Essence!" I shouted, but the words were immediately snatched away.

He turned his head, saw my desperately held out hand, and though his entire body was braced, taut as the ropes, he wound one arm more tightly around the arm of the helm and then reached.

Our hands met, and Essence rushed inward, a flood as strong as the wind and the sea. He couldn't control it, but I could.

I snapped an invisible net around us the way Auntie Breeze had taught me to imagine a host of invisible hands lifting that boulder in the secret grove. At once the strained wood groaned less, and though the waves still towered, and the wind screamed, we rode a little easier. Lighter. The sail, bolstered, caught enough of that wind to send us skimming freely up, down, and even — I am very certain I did not dream it — into the air, once, twice, from wave crest to wave crest.

Time seemed to stop as the air and water elements around us shrieked and boomed, until at last the storm began to pass northeastward, chased by a strong wind out of the south. We rode that wind, scudding over the surface of the ocean, which was now a startling blue in strong morning light. At one point the choppy waves rippled in strange patterns, and On cried, "Look."

I turned my head, gazing at the water — which had gone the deep inky blue of a night ocean. For two, three, four long breaths I gazed down, the hairs at the back of my neck prickling — then abruptly the inky shade passed.

"What was *that?*" I gasped.

"My guess is a kraken," On said breathlessly. He had begun to loosen his death grip on the helm. "Curious, maybe? But not curious enough to surface and throw us end over end, thank all the gods."

My terror had only begun to recede. But wonder was there, the ant admiring the tiger. I could not possibly comprehend the shape of so enormous a creature's life.

When it had passed, the wind seemed to go with it, leaving us floating once more in smaller seas, the sail curving gently.

On lifted his hands from the helm. I saw blood streaked across his palms. I gave a start, then saw that my own hands had also been scraped raw. He wrung his fingers, his smile slanting as he said, "Ay-y-y, the salt hurts."

I nodded, my body thumping down into the boat as if I'd become a puppet with its strings cut. Then On plopped next to me, one hand gently taking one of mine. He looked from my scored palm to my face. To my lips, as he smiled with such unrestrained joy at our having survived. It was not the self-satisfied glee of an easy life of triumphs, it was an eyes-raised, tears glimmering smile with a hint of the pains we had shared together.

My full heart overflowed at the sight of those tears, and it seemed natural when he extended his arms in mute appeal to lean into them. For an unmeasured time we clung to one another, both vibrating with exhaustion and with the rising tide of another, more urgent emotion that swiftly replaced the relief and affection consequent to surviving near death.

But a deeper, older instinct caught at me, and when his face neared mine for a kiss, I turned my cheek.

He loosened the grip that had tightened around me, and he peered into my face. I did not even have the right words, I was so new to these feelings, and to this situation, sitting entirely alone in the middle of the sea with an ardent young man.

But the Xuan cousins had taught him well, and he—in spite of his airy nature—had compassion enough to listen. He let me go, and patted my shoulder as I sustained a sharp, conflicted sense of …regret. I knew that all I had to do was reach for him, and he'd be ready. But did I truly want to embark down that path with him, and accept all the consequences?

Granny Zim was utterly silent.

My own cautious nature insisted, *not yet, not yet.*

And so he said, "We're both tired, but I don't think we ought to lower the sail. We're too low on water for a halt. We can trade watches—you can sleep first."

I was far too tired to protest. Everything was wet, of course, but the sun was hot. I lay down, and though now my shoulder pressed against his ankle, the awkwardness of forced proximity—something very new to me, outside of the practice field—had vanished. The boat was simply too small.

He woke me when the wind began to strengthen. He used his salty, stiff cloak to tie the helm into place as I put together a scant meal of dried fish and rice balls wrapped in grape leaves. A dipper of water each was all we allowed ourselves. Then I tended helm and sail while he slept.

And that was the pattern for the next two days. During the times when we both were awake, On asked a stream of questions about how Essence worked, and because we were alone on the ocean, where no one could see us, we experimented with Sagacious Blade.

Though Granny Zim did not speak to On, the sword permitted him to ride it. He struggled at first with the difficulties of conscious reaching for Essence. His gift was so like the air, coming in bursts. He could not call fire, even at noon, with the sun baking right down on us. But here, on the water, with clouds above, he was able to summon enough Essence to fly. Quickly—far more quickly than I had—he mastered the art of flying a sword, swooping easily up over the mast and then around and around us, and finally out over the sea, until I lost sight of him, and only heard his laughter floating behind on the wind.

Meanwhile, there was no escaping wind and weather, which did what it pleased with us. I taught him what I could, and he regaled me with stories and poetry—so much poetry—as I leaned against his legs, or he against mine when it was my watch, which felt as natural as the wind and the sun. He said I was always warm, which made me laugh. I had not realized until then that it took a cold, wet wind to chill me, though I disliked being wet and chilled.

Our barrel of water was below the quarter mark when at last an island jutted on the horizon. We began to watch for other craft, as I renewed the obscuring charm. Late in the day, I was able to match the island's silhouette on the map.

"It's got a navy harbor on the south coast," I said, scratching my salty scalp. "It looks like a distance of several days' travel overland."

"And a day by sea," On said. "How's our water?"

"Getting stale—we'll have to begin boiling it, but we could make it to the next island, which Dinek marked as a gallant wanderer stop. No, it's probably too close."

On leaned over and stared for a while at the map, blinking. "If I'm right, the patrol pattern for the imperial harbor will be like this. They won't go to these others, unless called to them. Remember that they're spread thin."

I rolled the map, saying, "It takes men to conscript men."

"Exactly. And they are likely to have already swept up all the men off these small islands. The gallant wanderers included."

Being even more sparing with our stale water, we bypassed the imperial harbor and made it to the gallant wanderer island, expecting to find mostly women and children and the elderly. Braced for imperials scouring for more conscripts.

Mindful of this last, we kept off-shore until nightfall, then drifted in on a late tide toward the inlet frequented by gallant wanderers, according to Dinek's marks. We found two boats already in residence, both pulled up under leafy tallow trees overhanging the shoreline on either side of a small stream. One was a rowboat, the other a sailboat about half again as long as ours. We collapsed the sail, unstopped the mast, and then pulled our boat as far up under the leafy canopy as we could, then dragged some brush to cover it.

"Good sign," On commented as he slid his barbed fans into his sleeves, his fighting sticks into his carryall, and then slung that over his shoulder. "If these are gallant wanderers, they're sure to know where the cheapest bath can be had."

I hailed this idea with approval as we trod upstream, and we both bent to drink our fill. The mild headache I'd experienced over the past day or so eased almost immediately as we set out up a narrow path from the inlet.

We rounded a hill with a mossy wall covered with bright trumpet creepers still blooming, and caught the scent of pomegranate blossoms on the somnolent summer air. So still it was, not even birds singing; I was so overjoyed to be on land again that it did not occur to me that it was odd to be so very still, before we came suddenly on the remains of a burned cottage. That wall back there was ages old, but this damage was new. The singe of wood smoke overpowered the pomegranate blossoms, and made me sneeze.

On's quick glance quieted me. He opened his lips to speak, but I was already in motion, throwing the obscuring charm over us both. That burned cottage could be the result of any number of causes, but now the blanket of quiet seemed threatening.

He shifted his carryall so that his double sticks were in reach, and my right hand was loose, ready to grab Sagacious Blade, as we pushed on. There were others newly arrived—those boats back there were evidence of that. The brush covering them had been almost as fresh as the tallow branches we'd broken off to spread over the stern of our boat.

A little farther on and we reached another cottage, this one round, the clay tiles plain. The cottage, glimpsed from between walls, was all closed up. Unusual in the heat of a summer morning.

The path wound around another small hill covered over with rows of vegetables, then we encountered two more domiciles, equally closed up tight. Eventually we reached the center of a tiny village—everything except a large, rambling inn and teahouse closed and silent. From this inn rose men's voices. Drunk, this early in the day?

On made as if to enter, but I was instantly wary, only hearing male voices. He checked after a step or two, then looked back in question. I stood beside one of the windows and peered around the edge. Men, mostly young or at least youngish, sprawled around a table, with a number of empty wine jars scattered about. A gray-haired woman appeared, hefting a tray of more wine jars. Her face was lowered.

One of the men bawled something at her in one of the southern dialects. She started, nearly dropping the tray, then set it down and scurried away, the man roaring mostly unintelligible words, except for "rice!"

We walked on until once again we'd reached the path leading away. Then we stopped. "Bandits?" I said—at the time, I believed it to be a perspicacious remark. "They don't look like gallant wanderers."

"Deserters," On said.

"How do you know that?"

"Those swords stashed in the corner behind them? Those are the swords issued to front liners in the army. Their boots as well. Only that one with the accent had older boots, decorated like a captain's. My guess is, he led and they followed. Most of them don't look any older than twenty. Conscripts, probably."

I saw again that grandmother starting, her somber face. That was fear. "I want to fix it, if we can."

On's hand caressed the top of his carryall. "Shall we split up, nose around, count how many there are? Meet back here and make a plan?"

I refreshed the charm over us, and we parted. As I walked, for the first time, I considered what made people into bandits. The obvious, easy answer was a child deemed bad or incorrigible, in trouble more than out of it, until he gets sent off to prison or the mines. Or the army. Or the lowest, roughest types of drudgery, if you were a girl. Were these men here all wicked, or did the emperor's forced conscription make them wicked?

I could not answer, but I was mulling this question when I rounded an umbrella tree, and nearby ran into a tall, husky boy. I dived to the side, as the boy frowned and looked around. I tripped over a hidden root. He whipped around—and he saw me at the same moment I exclaimed, "Jai?"

"Ren?"

"Are you alone?" I asked quickly.

"Yes, I—ay! You mean … I came with Koi and Fan," Jai said.

"*Koi? He's here?*"

"He's here."

THIRTEEN

A clear stream laughs over a fall,
Casts rainbows in the scented air.
Green bamboo thick as well as deep
gently shades a mountain path:
The golden phoenix lingers...

"THEY'RE..." HE WAVED IN another direction.

"But I thought he was with my brother!"

"He was," Jai said. "He turned up the day before we left the scrape. Two days. Said that your brother sent him to protect you. Since he was safe in a fortress for the winter."

I thought of my message, and flinched. Would it even reach Second Brother now? It was easy to imagine the honest Hat messenger turning around and leaving on discovering that Koi had gone.

Jai added, "How did you end up here? Or were you searching for us at the same time we were searching for you?"

"You were looking for me?"

"We've been chasing after you since we left the scrape. Chasing and being chased. We've stayed ahead of them, though there were at least three different pursuits. That we know of. You really must have stuck a straw right up that tiger's nose," he added admiringly. "The Falcons told us to try certain islands, ones where Falcons and martial experts go, and here you are."

"Let's find Koi," I said, though I knew there was nothing to be done about that warning, now gone completely astray.

"He and Fan are trying to find the girls. I guess they're hiding," Jai said as he led me back in the direction he'd come, up a goat trail.

"Girls?"

"Yes. One of the grandmas said that the marauders showed up, burned down a house, then the captain killed two men. Right there. Neither armed. One was a grandpa. The other was blind, so the conscript parties didn't want him. Then they made their demands, that the young women have to choose one of them to marry. Then he gets to move right into their house. There aren't any defenders. The men got taken by the emperor—ay, you know how it is."

"Ay! I know," I said, furious.

"Fan wants to kill them all. But she said to make sure the girls are safe before we lay into these rats. They're trying to find them."

I knew how to do that. Koi was here? Impossible, yet here was Jai, taller than before, and as solid as life. I laughed as I pulled Sagacious Blade, dashed the charm over me, and took to the air, leaving Jai blinking up at the sky from below.

I circled around, remembering those lessons on scouting from the days in the Falcon scrape on the imperial island: begin with a tight circle, and gradually spiral outward.

As I widened my circle, I gained height so that I could look down at the hills up behind the tiny village. It was on my fifth circuit that I caught sight of movement. There was Koi! He and Fan paced along a path, then Fan shouted, "Come on out! We're really here to help!"

I turned my head—ah, clustered around a cave covered by hanging vines stood girls our age, looking terrified. I glanced back. I hadn't known those brigands for deserters, and neither would these girls. To them, Fan and Koi, equally husky and bristling with weapons, would look just as threatening.

It was time to intervene. I glanced down at myself, hoping I would not appear equally threatening. I'd put on my green robe, and my hair was in its usual high tail, hanging free down my back. It would have to do. I waved away the charm, and flew over the girls' cave, shouting, "Any brigands who dare to attack shall have to deal with me!"

Faces turned upward. Mouths opened. I flew down slowly, so it wouldn't look like an attack, and when I stepped on the ground, I sheathed Sagacious Blade with a quick movement.

"I'm here to help," I said to the leading girl, who seemed to have more courage than the rest. "And the two you can hear on the path below? I know them. They are Falcon defenders."

"Falcons," said a woman of thirty or so, pushing past the girls. She held a baby tightly in her arms. "Hear that? Falcons!"

Drawn no doubt by the voices, Koi and Fan appeared, crashing past a clump of locust trees. The girls pressed back until Fan dashed toward me. "Ren!" She enveloped me in a crushing hug. "We've been chasing after you for weeks! You wouldn't believe the legends arising about you. Pangolin Ren banishes the imperial invaders. Pangolin Ren calls down lightning from the sky to cure the plague!"

I scarcely heard all that, for my gaze had gone to Koi, who stood behind Fan, a tentative smile on his somber face.

I said to him, "I'm so very glad to see you…" No, now was not the time to mention the missed communication.

Koi blushed a fiery red, and at that, the bolder of the girls came forward, most going to him, their fear giving way to appreciation for a handsome young martial expert who was not on the attack.

The woman turned to me. "Pangolin Ren," she said on a note of question.

Rather than get mired in explanations about myself, I said, "Can you tell me what happened here?"

"Just before harvest the Year of the Horse, the army came to take all the men," she explained. "We've done all right on our own—few outsiders know about us, other than wanderers now and then—until these showed up ten days ago, demanding food, drink, and then when they got drunk, wives. Their idea is to take our *houses*, too." She flushed with indignation.

"*My* idea is to give them a feast and poison them all," the boldest girl declared.

"Ay, so unlucky," another said. "Once the first one takes sick, they'll know, and they'll turn on us with those swords."

"And what if one of the little ones sneaks poisonous food, thinking it a snack?" someone else put in.

"We add the venom to the wine, of course…"

Leaving them arguing among themselves, I turned to Koi and Fan.

"How did you get here?" Koi asked.

"Is Dinek with you?" Fan asked eagerly, then the brightness dimmed from her face when I gave a quick explanation.

Koi said, "You and On are alone, then?"

"We are. Koi, I overheard Xianti saying he plans to attack Whale Haven by New Year's Two Moons. He was slavering about it! I sent a message to you, but it seems you were already on the way to Mountain Peony. Do you think Second Brother will read it anyway?"

Koi blinked a couple of times, then gave his head a quick shake. "I don't know. Maybe. But Ren, they know the imperial prince is aware of their retreat. That is, they assume that spies have found that much out. They've planned for it. The Grand Prince chose that island specifically for the way the land lies, enabling several deceptions. His favorite is the Empty Fort strategy."

On had guessed that much.

"That's what I wanted to prevent," I cried. "No fighting *at all*. I sent a message so that there would be time for them all to go somewhere else..."

Koi shook his head. "Isn't going to happen. You say the imperial crown prince was slavering. I believe you. I know that look of his. But Ren, Yiuti is slavering just as hotly. And so are his boys. Most of them. Not all—your brother for one. His cousin Oraiti. A couple of others."

My eyes stung. "What good is reluctance? They could be killed just the same. It's so *senseless*." I scowled. "I'll have to go—"

Fan said, "Without a fleet of your own, you'll never make it. Finding help will be difficult, if anyone suspects who you are. And why would a girl with a sword who looks very much like the drawing of the wanted princess need to borrow a sail craft? So many questions. Though people might be in secret sympathy, the warnings were dire: anyone caught providing aid and shelter will be executed to the third generation. Villages entire."

Koi looked away from my expression, which must have reflected the helpless desolation I could not hide. He said, "If it helps, they won't be caught by surprise, though they expect an attack in spring. They have watchers posted far out, and there is no hiding an invading fleet of warships."

The voices behind us had stopped, and a row of round eyes regarded us.

I got hold of myself. "Let's go meet up with On, and collect Jai. Tell me about your adventures on the way."

With an admonishment to stay hidden to the girls, we trod back down the path as Fan and Koi—mostly Fan—related their history. I had forgotten how very quiet Koi was, after On's waterfall of chatter and poetry. It was so deeply comforting to pace side by side with him, listening to the low rumble of his voice as Fan regaled us with chases and close calls.

The gist: news about the dowager duchess's fake death reached the scrape within hours after the events. Because the duchess's Falcon companions had pigeons, the Falcons at the scrape learned at once that the plague was a ruse, but as more news arrived, each report more alarming—the imperial prince demanding a search for me, and so on—Fan, Jai, and the newly-arrived Koi decided that they ought to leave before the duke turned his eyes toward the Falcon scrape.

They nearly did not make it. Huyun Shandek's fury at being duped (and, I hope, his mother's demands about the slave trade once she was awake) made itself manifest in orders that no one was to enter or leave the island without permission, supposedly to keep the plague from spreading.

But Fan, Jai, and Koi were strong, and experienced with rowboats, which were easily overlooked. As the little islands dotting the sea between Mountain Peony and Ji Jiang's Tiger Islands were scattered within hours of hard rowing, they made it to Tiger Eye Bay—where they were captured. Ji Jiang himself interrogated them, and, hearing their story, remembered my warning. Saying that he owed me a debt, he smuggled them onto an innocuous trade ship going north.

From there, they were in constant motion, twice nearly falling into the imperials' hands. Xianti had sent general orders to lay me by the heels—my crime? The possession of a charmed sword, as well as my blood relation with criminals.

"Though that part came up rarely, and not without rolling of eyes," Koi said with grim satisfaction. "Your father is so well spoken-of that no one who knows his name regards him as a criminal. As for the accusations against you, everywhere they searched, stories about you spread, until it seemed that Pangolin Ren, the princess who cured plague by calling lightning down with a charmed sword, was regarded as a hero."

"Princess?"

"Governor Huyun revealed your name," Koi said. "The Falcons told us that he was ordered by the imperial crown prince to produce you, preferably alive, and your true name as well as a drawing was furnished. The governor saw to it that all these were in turn handed to his searchers."

"And the imperials have their own, as I said," Fan added from Koi's other side. "I saw your image on the Wanted walls on one island. But someone seems to be secretly on your side. It might even be someone among the duke's own people who got the stories going about you curing the plague, and the rest. From there the stories spread, the way stories do."

"The conscription raids have been fierce. Everyone everywhere is afraid that one or another of the warring princes will choose their island as a battleground," Koi finished.

"One or *another?*" I queried. "You make it sound like more than two. I thought the main contenders were Xianti, in his uncle's name, and Yiuti and his grandfather." And On would have a claim, but I knew that he at least was striving mightily to stay out of this fight.

"Prince Guiza is also out there," Koi said. "At first he was imprisoned. But the emperor didn't quite dare to kill him."

"The Ye family are such staunch supporters of the throne," I said. "Still?"

"Yes. Their relations hold several important ministries, and it's said that the emperor cherishes them much, for they get him the funds he so desperately needs. And Fourteenth Consort Ye was very popular in court, you'll probably remember."

"I do," I said. "I take it the Perfect Guiza was released?" That nickname, the Perfect Guiza, had been a disparaging term used by Siarti and Liarti, but it had fallen into general use because Guiza—actually an uncle, as he was the emperor's youngest son, one of the generation ahead of mine, but he had insisted on us calling him Cousin—really was the ideal imperial prince. The handsomest of us, smart, diligent, scholarly, and fond of music, especially the guqin.

"Yes. Word is, he was the Perfect Guiza in prison. All he did was play music and study. The ministers sent a flood of memorials on his behalf. Probably to get him and his influence away from court, the emperor gave him a command, and sent him north to request fresh conscripts from the independents. Prince Guiza took his mother with him, which no one expected. She not only left behind copies of the emperor's dying will— with the imperial seal—that stated he appointed Prince Guiza to follow him in favor of his two elder sons, she has been swearing to it up and down the coast, including at Benevolent Winds, where Kianti hosted them. Guiza's force, made up of Ye's defensive guard, has sworn to obey the former emperor's last command."

I shivered despite the warm air. "When the tiger fights the boar, it's the ants who get trampled."

"Exactly," Fan said.

I tried to shake off the mood. "There's nothing any of us can do about the warring princes. But we can do something right here."

Fan nodded firmly. "Between the five of us, we can take down those rats eating up the harvest stores in that inn. I'm in the mood for a good fight."

"Let me talk to them first," I said.

"Why?" Fan asked. "A surprise attack seems the best solution. We'd be on them before they were even aware."

"It's the word 'wives'," I said, struggling to express a nascent idea. It stemmed from my realization that my blithe assumption that brigands were all villains, worthy only of death, had been too easy. And I explained what On had said about deserters, finishing, "Would we blame someone for running away from Xianti's war? No. We'd run, too. Whatever their motivation, I suspect a lot of the younger ones followed that captain. From what we heard, it was only he who drew blood. They could have slaughtered everyone if they'd wanted. Who would have stopped them? No, I want to talk to them. If they attack me, or threaten me, then we can go from there."

Fan shrugged. "I still don't see it, but then I grew up in a guard post. I know how fast men can turn bad, if a bad leader lets them loose."

"If Ren wants to talk first, then we can wait," Koi said.

And so it was I who walked into the inn alone, Sagacious Blade sheathed but within ready reach.

The air was thick with the odors of sweaty men, rich food, and wine. Drunk they were, but not so far that they missed my entrance. I swept my gaze over them fast, seeing bemusement, question, anticipation here and there as eyes raked down my form, and wariness in the red-eyed captain. He alone had his sword propped against the table, though most of the others had stashed theirs in the corner where On had first seen them.

"I am here on behalf of the villagers," I said, raising my voice.

"You can be my wife," one boy about Koi's age said, and followed that with kissing noises.

That was met with raucous laughter. Fan had said, "When the men in the garrison got rowdy, they always responded to threat."

So I pulled Sagacious Blade, and in a heartbeat lit it with fire, then slammed it down on the table in front of that captain, hard enough to make the dishes jump.

At once sparks scattered everywhere, but before they could dig in and grow, I waved the fire into nonexistence.

The company froze into silence.

I said, "Tell me why I shouldn't gut every one of you right here and now."

In that moment, still caught in their shock at my action, they could believe I could do it. I saw that in their faces, their instinctive recoil.

Voices rose around me, protesting, gabbling justifications — and threats. That especially from the captain.

There is no use in retailing it all. It took a bit of time, but we learned that the young ones were indeed conscripts, most from three long years of wearying toil. They'd seen an opportunity to slink away from a hot attack on the grand prince's last fortress, previous to Whale Haven — it was the ancestral estate of his deceased wife.

"There was a storm. We got out unseen. We were going to go home," one of the youngest said. "Dress as fishers. Get back to our families."

"My wife was in child," another put in. "We'd married at Spring Festival that year. Now I've got a son or daughter somewhere, I've never seen. Unless the king of the underworld has got them," he muttered.

"That's right," another said. "We heard that our villages are dust, our families gone."

"So we're here to start over again," another said. "It's reasonable! I'm a good farmer."

"And I make tile. Everyone needs roof tiles," put in the biggest.

The captain sneered, "Why are you rabbits trying to justify yourselves to this girl? She's one girl! She can pick among us, or better, we'll auction her off — her and the sword."

And here was the clear influence that had got all these others to follow.

I said to the others, "What would you like to do? If you did not have this man trying to make you into brigands?"

Some uttered protests, and a few looked abashed. The rest looked uneasy. Uncertain. The captain and the two sitting at either side of him muttered curses as the captain half stood.

But Fan's warnings rang in my ears, and I was ready. He did not even bother reaching for his weapon, he was so certain I couldn't fight. I drew Sagacious Blade, evaded his lunging hands, and touched the point of the blade to that heart-center acupoint, sending Essence into it. He jolted, freezing as still as a sculpture.

The rest stared in shock. The two on either side of the captain stood, met my gaze, their eyes going from me to richly gleaming, scaled Sagacious Blade—and they both slowly sat down, one licking his lips.

"I want to go home," said the youngest of the followers. At a closer glance, he seemed maybe a year or so older than I— probably taken at fourteen or so. "But there is no home, they say." He glared at me with a mixture of accusation and grief.

"Your accent is familiar. You come from the imperial island, do you not?" I asked.

"I do. Two Lotus Pools Village, Kanda's Peace Prefecture."

"And I!" three others spoke up.

"Isn't that on the other side of the valley from Four Cranes Prefecture? I thought so. I am fairly certain where your sisters and mothers and wives are," I said. "The imperial crown prince looked the other way as General Nua Li and his company permitted slavers to take most of them. I know where a few sheltered after their escape, and I know who has the records of where the rest were taken," I added, thinking grimly of Huyun Shandek. Perhaps his mother could wrest that shameful list from him.

"But what use is that unless someone can get them away? We can't," the young one said, waving his hand in a circle toward the others and himself. "That's why I wanted to start over. We landed here. Thought it was fate, putting us on a new path. Since we never did anything wrong to get us here."

"That's right," many of the others spoke up, angry and aggrieved.

"I promise, on my true name, that your wives and mothers and sisters are not forgotten. Nor are you."

"What is your name?" the youngest asked, more accusatory than not.

"Pangolin Ren," I said, from habit—and then, because the truth was out anyway, thanks to Huyun Shandek—"That is, I am living as Pangolin Ren now, but I am Princess Lan Renti."

"A princess," said one, and clumsily dropped out of his chair to the floor, one knee down, fist to heat. "If you speak true, I'll fight for you."

"I honor your words," I said, making the gallant wanderer bow. "But I don't want innocent blood shed. And I think you are innocent, for you did not start this war. You did not want it. I know I have this sword. And as you see, I can use it. But I don't want to use it to kill. You have been in the army. You've seen who suffers the most in fighting. I'm trying to find another way to stop the imperial crown prince's wars, and to restore our peaceful lives from before."

There was a stirring, and one muttered, "I wish I could believe that," as the ardent-souled one got back into his chair, head bent.

Who could blame them for their wariness? One of the first lessons in Circle was that a force requires a force of the same size, or larger, to counter it.

On entered then, saying loyally, "If anyone can find a way, it will Pangolin Ren. She did chase off the imperial prince from invading Mountain Peony Island. Not by fighting, but by wit." He tapped his head. "Isn't that better, when everyone gets to eat, drink, and enjoy another day, instead of lying in the dirt before their time, their families weeping tears above them as they light incense?"

At that the drunken men, who I suspect just needed direction, gave a cheer, and then everyone was talking.

I will not describe the remainder. Suffice it to say that I went around to each of them, with Sagacious Blade at hand, and Granny Zim heard only two liars. By this time, I had noticed that my instincts had become better, whether through her guidance or just experience. The eye and ear often catch small things before the mind does.

For the most part, they wanted to live lives of peace once more. Their captain did not. He was full of rage once the acupressure wore off, and though at first he tried to baffle me with professions of loyalty, I knew he was lying by the force beneath his apologetic whine, by the way his gaze shifted between my eyes as if evaluating my reactions, and by the tension in his shoulders and hands, even before Granny Zim said so. I said, as I had with the two liars, "Why are you lying to me?"

The other two had promptly backed down, not questioning how I knew, but he lunged at me. Foxy On had his blades out in a flash and the man stilled. The only thing he respected was a killing weapon.

Koi solved the problem by offering him the chance to fight for his life. I could not bear to watch, I was so worried for Koi.

The captain lost in three fast exchanges, Koi's last blow

mercifully fast.

Once he was buried, the other two crept away in the night—stealing the scout ship that they had taken when they deserted from the emperor's force. From there, their fates are unknown, but I suspect they fell into the hands of the imperials chasing after me. The possession of a stolen scout ship would be difficult to explain.

As we all walked away, Koi turned to me. "The imperials are coming. We don't know how close they are behind us."

Fan agreed. "They could easily come ashore in the night, and we'd waken with swords at our necks."

The five of us withdrew to talk over what we ought to do. That is, when to leave, and for where?

This conversation swiftly became a debate, as I'd often noticed among gallant wanderers. Everyone had to be heard, even if only to repeat what was said before. That was Jai. Koi spoke the least, but On countered everything he said with a quotation, until Koi stopped speaking altogether. Then Fan and Jai argued about Jai's having to test everything, and finally Fan and On debated various islands, until they settled on Tortor—which Koi, and Fan, had suggested at the outset.

Before we gathered with the deserters and islanders for a last meal, Koi said to me, "You're frowning. You don't want to go to Tortor? Why didn't you speak up?"

"Because I did not want to add to the noise. That decision took five times longer than it ought to have. Ten, if I count in all the times people repeated themselves."

"It's the Falcon way. Maybe other sects, too. Ones without a master they've sworn to," he corrected, and then he eyed me, as our steps slowed. "You would rather go back to the ways of court?"

On glanced back at us, but then Fan addressed him, and he went on ahead as I considered what to say. "It's ritual, but so orderly..."

As soon as I said that, I remembered how excruciating it was, morning after morning, listening to the dowager empress tell us what we thought of the weather. Then those with the proper seniority had to thank her, and to compliment her on her cleverness and wisdom. This is after beginning the morning by exclaiming over her beauty and how she looked younger every day. "Ayoh! It was orderly in part because only those with rank could speak."

"It was much the same with certain of the elders, when

Second Young Master had to attend on them," Koi said, a tremor of laughter making his deep voice husky. The sound caused in me the exact same twinge of heat within my vitals as On could raise by his smile, by the right quotation, even by an especially graceful movement. "You miss order, is that it?"

"Yes, but even that is conditional. I've never been to court, of course, but from what Father said, everyone knows how to shape their point, how to defer, to respond, and ayoh! Most especially how to speak without repeating themselves."

"Training," Koi observed. "Not always heeded. Even in court?"

"You saw court in session?"

"Not saw. But the Chief Censor sometimes took Second Young Master to sit against the wall so that he could learn. We servants stood outside the screens, in case we were needed to fetch things. We could hear just fine."

"In the imperial palace, there is always the emperor, or empress. I guess it's the same wherever there is hierarchy. If that person is wise, such as in a school, then their leadership in conversation is the idea. What we read about in Kanda's conversations. But in truth?"

Koi lifted a shoulder. "Everybody wants to be heard," he said, echoing my earlier thought.

"It's the tension between the two. Hierarchy that ideally permits orderly exchange, and the gallant wanderer way, where everybody has to talk and talk and talk."

His laugh was no more than a breath, and we joined the others. Over that dinner, the deserters swore to defend rather than attack, and to return to Kanda's laws of civilization that they had been raised with. I tried to remind them that these were truly upheld by day to day decisions. By everyone. Civilization was not merely a matter of princes giving orders from faraway thrones. But I was afraid that the words of a girl were little more than the chirp of birds.

FOURTEEN

In youth, she observed,
The distance between those gripped by passion
Can be measured in silk-slippered steps
Or a single gaze,
While the distance between hearts
Is ten thousand days.

"LET'S GO NOW," FAN said, after we waved to the departing former deserters. Except for one, the tile maker, who decided to stay, as he had no family to search for. He and a widow had taken a tentative liking to one another. She had offered to rent him a room, and it was easy to see what was going to happen there.

The villagers had given the rest a fisher craft that had belonged to one family whose men had been taken, and the boat had been sitting in a tiny inlet ever since. The searchers set sail, having been provided with some stores by the villagers. We told them everything we knew about Mountain Peony Island, including directions to the Snow Crane temple that had taken in the rescued refugees. Surely the monks knew where their refugees had gone, and these in turn might be able to give the seekers some clues, if they turned out not to be the families the men sought.

Fan added earnestly. "We don't want to risk endangering these villagers after freeing them."

The grateful women generously offered us stores, but these we adamantly refused except for some vegetables, knowing that the deserters had eaten into a lot of their winter stores.

We walked down the trail to where we'd left our boats.

"Where to?" I asked, when we got there.

Koi and Fan said at the same moment, "Tortor."

Jai chucked his belongings into the larger boat, and began dragging the shrubbery away as Fan looked doubtfully at the small boat that On and I had lived on. "We were crowded with three," she said. "Ours was built for two fishers, dragging their catch in the sea behind the boat."

Koi made a motion toward the smaller craft. "I can handle that," he said to me.

Fan turned to me. "Ren, if you don't want to go cramped up in that bathtub, you can sail with me and Jai." She threw her things into the larger boat, then helped Jai to clear the last of the camouflage, leaving us to sort out who was going where.

On stepped to my side. "We're used to this one." He smiled from me to Koi.

I sensed question from Koi, and another kind of question from On. But I was not certain—nor did I know what to do about it. "Used to it," I mumbled awkwardly, put my things in the stern, and reached for our nearly empty barrel of stale water. "I'm going to fill this," I said to the air between the two boys.

On was right on my heels. He began to push the boat into the water. I sensed Koi rather than saw or heard him turn toward the bigger boat, as I went upstream where the water trickled clear.

And to Tortor, that mysterious island of escaped criminals, convicts, martial artists, and others, we set sail. There was no privacy for any of us during that journey, but everyone was determined, or willing, to make the best of it.

On had managed to pick up a piece of bamboo, which he spent a day and a night carving into a flute. Then, for several days during which the wind died, leaving us floating in soft summer airs, we entertained ourselves with singing songs, and listening to him play.

He was not very advanced as a player—enough to carry a melody. At first everyone listened to everything, but by the third day, people began to get choosy. After a popular tragic song about seeking missing beloveds and wandering alone and in grief, during which Fan sat with locked jaw and the set shoulder of endurance, Jai said, "I'm tired of those woe, woe,

woe, my loooove is gone, woe, woe, woe ones. How about giving us 'The Battle of the Wine Jugs' again?"

On said, "No more tragedy." Which left out a surprising number of songs.

The next setback occurred after an especially lively one about a duel between two of the dashing scholars in his play. "I like that one," Jai exclaimed. "Play it again. What were the words again?"

"They're stupid," Fan said, eyeing him in challenge.

Jai scowled. "Why?"

"Because that girl is stupid. If she wants one of those boys, well, she ought to take a knife to the other one, the one trying to get her to kiss him."

"But she's a timid scholar's daughter," On protested. "Everybody expects her to be timid as a butterfly. It's a given character."

"Given means you always know what's going to happen."

"Exactly. That's part of the fun, watching it all play out as you expect," On said.

"Pah! You write me a play where the girl does her own duels, and I'll pay down money to watch," Fan said in disgust—and then looked over the water at me. "What say you, Ren?"

On flashed a smile over the water at the other boat, but not at Fan. His bright, challenging gaze locked on Koi. Who never said anything about the music.

The song stirred up my old feelings of helpless anger on behalf of my beautiful cousin Lan Arati—who was probably the best example of a graceful, timid, good girl as you could ever find in real life. Married off summarily to a scarred general twice her age in spite of her love for my brother. And his for her. An ending which would still have included my brother's betrothed, for that had been settled when they were babies. "I don't see why she shouldn't have *both* of them," I burst out. "It's always the boys who collect consorts and lovers and wives like anyone else collects hairpins. I think it is time for the girls to get their chance."

On collapsed back on his bench laughing. He kept laughing from time to time between songs, though he wouldn't say why.

Koi never did say anything.

Then the next night, Koi called over, "Who wants to play Circle?"

"Did you find a board?" On sounded incredulous.

Koi tapped his head, and said to me, "Playing without a

board was something your brother did to pass the time during those long days when he had to kneel in the Hall of Ancestors during punishments. He didn't think the ancestors would mind—some of them had to be like him, or how would he have inherited his lamentable nature?"

That sounded exactly like something Banti would say! I was intrigued, and a little saddened. Another thing my brother had never told me, just how much he'd tried to bend his nature toward what would please our parents. But he'd always managed to find a way to happiness. That was the admirable thing about him, and if Banti could play Circle without a board at the age of ten, surely I could at sixteen.

"I'll play," I called back.

And lost. Lost again. Lost again, and again, and again.

Sometimes, when the sea was calm, Koi and Jai sparred in the narrow bow, their footing precise. Occasionally On leaped over to join them.

I practiced flying every day, and occasionally landed on the bigger boat, when Fan wished to compare our chartlike maps. But I always came back to Circle. I was not used to losing.

Koi never attempted the smaller boat.

We were well into ninth month when we neared that mysterious island, marked on the map with solid, dense forest. We had been skirting smaller islands, avoiding all naval harbors, our two small boats wearing fishing nets draped over the side, and empty fish-barrels stacked in bow and stern. We wore straw hats on deck, as fishers did, hiding our headbands. The hats were a torment when we first set sail, but as the storm season gave way to colder winds, I was glad of mine to keep my ears warm, as the constant cold winds were keen and sharp.

We reached Tortor without incident, then sailed slowly around it. The map—which was fast becoming a kind of chart as I amended it—did not lie about its inhospitable aspect. There was no inlet. The coast all the way round was rocky and treacherous, white water everywhere, but the real dangers of course were those rocks below the surface that could puncture craft like ours. I was glad that we'd soon be on land. The longer I was at sea, the more I longed to be quit of it.

On and I in our smaller craft followed their bigger boat as we began a circuit of the islands. I assumed that Fan, as the most experienced at sea, was looking for a good landing place. But there was none that I could see. All that coast was treacherous, with dense forest growing right up to the rocky shore. On pointed out two streams emptying into the seawater, from little waterfalls, which meant we could empty the last of our stale water.

We passed a number of anchored ships. A couple of them looked quite old and neglected, as if they had floated there a very long time, but others were newer. I was watching Fan for clues, and noticed her gaze assessing these grimly. I could not tell if she was reading something in their long-neglected state, or if she was disappointed at not finding the *Pangolin* here. I myself was aware of regret; though the chance had been slim, I'd hoped to find our ship awaiting us.

Finally Fan gave out a short, "Hah!"

Lai loosened their sail so that we could slide up beside them. Fan cupped her hands around her mouth, shouting, "Wing sign on that old trader there."

She pointed, as Jai blinked skyward, and Koi watched us impassively from the helm. His gaze was not on me, but behind me, and I became aware of On standing close behind my shoulder as I swung about and shaded my hand against the sun-splashes winking brightly from the water. There it was. I would never have noticed that innocuous wing sign carved into the hull of the old trader, left side of the stern.

"Land here?" Fan called.

We agreed.

On and I had no rowboat, of course. We shipped our slender mast and collapsed our sail. Then we drifted in as close as we could, using the oars to fend off rocks, until we were able to toss our scant remaining supplies and our carryalls to a large, flat boulder that protruded over the water.

The others unloaded their things into a rowboat after anchoring their craft. It took all five of us to haul the rowboat up onto the shore, where we covered it with pine boughs. Then we distributed all the baskets, sacks, and jugs between us, and began toiling our way up an incline as we looked around for the Falcons who belonged to that trader. But all I heard was the sough of the wind in the tall pines, and the shrill clack of chattering birds.

I was going to ask if the others wanted me to scout from

above the treetops when On halted, hand up. Then he shook his head, and dropped his hand. We kept going, everyone alert. Though nothing had changed, the peace I'd imagined had vanished, replaced by a sinister silence.

Then On stopped again, and this time he pointed down. Everyone looked at the pine duff, undisturbed by humans for who knows how long, then I noticed the subtle rumble of the earth, as of many feet pounding it not so very far away.

Siss!

Zip!

Arrows.

"Target practice?" Jai asked. He seemed a little disappointed at this guess.

Fan scowled, then shook her head. A heartbeat later, a distant angry shout corroborated her guess — and then without warning, the shrubs rustled and the hunters were among us.

I had only a chance to glimpse Falcon headbands on two runners before a third staggered and then dropped, three arrows in him, from shoulder to thigh.

The front runner was tall and spare, her head down as her long braids swung. The other ran lightly. No, she skimmed over the duff, barely disturbing it, her crimson face an oval, and her hair the black that sheens silvery in diffuse light. On turned completely around as he tracked her, his lips parted, an expression on his face that over the past summer days had been reserved entirely for me. Jealousy flashed through all my meridians, to be chased right out by a pulse of laughter. I knew his nature, probably better than anyone alive, for I could read affinities. There was no stopping a stream, or capturing air.

Then she blinked at Fan's headband, and huffed hoarsely, "Pirates."

And the pursuit was on us.

I dropped my cargo of rice and carefully-wrapped tea, pulling Sagacious Blade, as Fan and Koi charged into the midst of the pursuers, staff and sword whirling. Right behind them was On, his blades a wicked flicker. The pursuit outnumbered us, but they were winded, and we'd caught them by surprise. They had been driving their quarry toward the sea.

We killed or injured the pirates, then, suddenly, the forest was quiet.

The first Falcon had been leaning down, hands on her knees as she fought for breath. She looked up then, and I sustained a shock.

"Cray?"

"Cray?" Koi exclaimed right after me.

You must remember how Cray, Koi, and I had traveled away from my first Falcon scrape, in company with Granny Ou, a relation on Mother's side to Cray and me both. Cray was my distant cousin, though that had not kept her from resenting me utterly for Sagacious Blade having chosen me.

Koi exclaimed, "Cray! Sun!"

I remembered Sun from my first scrape, on the imperial island. The other girls in my cottage had said that her father was a crane. Her eyes were the dark brown of cranes' eyes, and her crane nature was very evident as she spoke. "Koi," she said, her voice light. "You are most welcome. All of you. Ren, I scarcely recognized you. Actually, I didn't recognize you, but I remember that sword!"

I turned toward Cray, sick with apprehension, to discover her coming toward me. Then, to my utter astonishment, she made a low bow, hands clasped tightly. "Ren, I'm so ashamed."

"Cray," I said, my wits entirely blown. "I thought—that is, I ought not to have been eavesdropping." Because I had been. She had not intended for me to hear that confession to Granny Ou.

Cray bowed a second time, saying, "Did not my mother often warn me that I ought not to speak words that the world could not hear? But I was too angry, too selfish in the worst way." She shook her head. "Ayoh, and did not Grandmother scold me, making me embroider 'One moment of patience is better than a thousand days of regret' on my undershirts after we discovered you and Koi gone, utterly vanished? She laid the blame for that at my feet, and I knew it must be true. I searched for three days, even going to the cold house to look at the dead, but you had gone without a trace. I've apologized to you a thousand-thousand times in imagined conversations ever since," Cray said, and bowed a third time. "Please forgive me."

"There's nothing to forgive. Most of what you said was not wrong. As for Sagacious Blade…" I made a motion toward the sword, but she misinterpreted the gesture.

"No! Please. If it really talks, I know exactly what it will say. I'm afraid to hear again how wrong I was."

"Not wrong, but angry," Granny Zim commented to me. "That girl has a good heart, but she was so self-righteous in her anger. I do not hear it now."

Nor did I, but I decided not to translate that. Cray was still talking. "…and I've been striving to be a better person. But that does nothing toward my moral debt to you. Is there anything I can do? Ask anything."

"All right," I said. "Please answer a question."

She bowed again, head down. Shoulders braced.

"Where is Peaches?"

She looked up at that, so startled she actually met my gaze instead of staring at the toes of my shoes.

"Peaches," I repeated. "I know I remembered it right. You and Granny Ou talked about us going to Peaches. We did try to go there. Or, we meant to before the slavers got us."

"Slavers," she gasped, going very pale.

"Ay, it's all right! As you can see, we got away. But we asked at so many Falcon inns, and no one had ever heard of a Falcon scrape named Peaches."

Sun was laughing, a bright fall of sound, as Cray said, "That's because there is no scrape called Peaches. Peaches — Suanek's Peaches, though we were in the habit of just saying Peaches — is the family farm, behind the village, where Falcons — ayoh, I feel worse and worse."

Sun danced about, laughing. "*You* are the Pangolin Ren we've been hearing surprising stories about, are you not?"

Koi spoke up, rescuing me from increasing awkwardness. "All that can be explained later. What should we do about these?" He pointed back at the two or three pirates groaning and twisting on the ground. All seriously injured.

"Leave them." Cray's voice flattened. "I don't know which will be worse, the other Falcons catching up, or their own kind finding that they didn't succeed in killing us."

"And him?" Fai asked, stopping before the man killed by three arrows. "Is he a Falcon?"

Cray and Sun both shook their heads. "He's a scout for the Iron Fist Brethren," Cray said. "He was in the midst of telling us how stupid we were to enter this island, and that we ought to leave, when the pirates charged us."

Sun sighed. "He did try to shield us — until he saw that we were as fast at running as he was." Under her breath, she added softly, "Actually, I'm faster."

"But he was a larger target," Cray said tightly. "The Iron Fists will probably want to honor him in their way."

"At least we can show our respect by laying him out properly," Fan suggested, and this was done before we picked up our things again, dropped at the beginning of the fight.

"We can help carry things," Sun added, snatching up a bag

of precious rice.

The two led us up to a ridge and then along a narrow path into the dense forest, as the mix of trees gave way to bamboo, and then to oak, cypress, and near a stream to jujube and plum, as well as the ubiquitous pine.

When the path crossed an even narrower path, Cray said, "Don't go that way. It leads to Three Ghosts."

"Real ghosts?" Jai asked, hand scrabbling for his sword.

Cray turned a glance his way. "No. Some say the hills are demon-infested, and others that a there's a hideous hermit there, who will send wild boars to attack you. If the hermit doesn't attack you outright."

"Won't boars attack anyway?" Koi asked noncommittally. "Is that not in their nature?"

"I'm telling you what we learned when we came," Cray said.

I caught up with Cray as we walked on, and said, "I am very glad to learn that you and Granny Ou escaped being seized by those slavers. I take it you made it successfully to Peaceable Breezes Harbor. Did you see my grandfather?"

"I'm sorry to say no. We did not dare to call on Governor Gu, as we both felt rightly to blame for losing you, but we found a silk trader related to the Ou family and sailed north with them."

"Did you hear any news there?"

"Only that the emperor was sending the new crown prince to punish rebel islands and princes, meaning Grand Prince Yiulo. We heard rumblings about Governor Gu readying to march south, but when we left, the horns and drums were still. We took that as a sign that Madam and the Chief Censor were still alive."

Though that was very old news by now, I still thanked her.

She went on, "Once I got Granny Ou safely home, I went back south, and ended up at Benevolence Scrape on Hundred-Day Tree Island, where I met up with Sun."

I gazed at her in surprise. Hundred-Day Tree was a poetic name for myrtle, a tree I loved. But did it not grow mainly in the warmer rice islands? She seemed to be watching me obliquely, for she asked a trifle diffidently, "Did this one not explain well?"

"Only my wonder that myrtle can be found so far north."

"It only grows on the slopes facing the summer sun, and is much cultivated by the temple there," Cray explained. "Sun and I trained there, until all the wars broke out. Some Falcons showed up as refugees from islands under attack, and the idea was raised to retreat to Tortor, which the imperials ignore. We came, but when we landed, a colony on the east side warned us that pirates had invaded earlier in summer, chased by the Iron Fist Brethren, who had a mission to get rid of the pirates and make the island safe for martial artists. I think the Iron Fist sect had an idea of establishing a place where everyone could come for competitions."

We were all alert as we walked, but though once or twice we heard distant shouts that might have been the echoes of squawking birds, we came across no one before we arrived abruptly at a camp tucked into a fold between two rocky ridges. At the top of this fold a trickle of water splashed. Tents marked both sides, old habit separating women on the west from men on the east.

"The pirates have been on the far side of the island, where the big caves are. Master Ferig thinks they have their loot stashed there. This is the smaller of our two camps," Cray explained. "Sun and I have been staying in this one. If you look down, you'll see rocky juts wide enough for a bedroll. The elders prefer more space. They're about sixty paces that way, in another crevasse."

I scarcely heard as I waited for a chance to speak to Koi. I caught a glance from him toward On and me before he began picking his way along the steep, rocky wall, away from any of the other ledges.

I followed. "Wait," I said.

He turned. "I was just going to lay out my bedroll and grab my stuff to wash before the sun sets."

"I know. I'm going to do the same. But why so far from the rest of us?"

He looked away, then back. "Aren't you going to go be with On?"

"No," I said. "He likes windy spots. I don't."

He said nothing, then straightened up, and dropped his bedroll and sword on the ledge where he stood. Then he hooked his thumb through his carryall, and followed me down the jagged path and along the stream until we found a good spot with boulders to lay out things to dry.

I knelt in the shallow water. It felt good on my salt-stiff clothes. I picked up a smooth round rock, and pulled out my laundry. A whoosh of stale, sweaty, briny air hit me in the face before I plunged it all into the water then began to beat the dirt out.

Koi was doing the same a couple of paces away. "You two were very close on that plank of a boat," Koi muttered to the shirt he was pounding.

I smothered a laugh. He seemed far too uncomfortable to share laughter. "We were," I said.

"Were?"

"Were, are."

He looked uncomfortable, but there was that tension in his hands that seemed to mean that this awkward conversation mattered. He muttered something, out of which I only caught the word, "Sun."

I smothered a laugh that was partly awkwardness, but partly sheer amusement. "Ay, he's going to flirt with her."

Koi glanced up at that, bewilderment in his face.

I said, "She's pure water in affinity, though it seems she's somehow also a creature of the air. He's a mix of air and water affinities. Fox and crane. Two of a kind in affinity, and complementary in natural form."

"That's ... what you want?" Koi looked away again.

"It just is," I said. "I think. I do know that trying to change someone's nature is like trying to flatten a mountain with a spoon. We were close on the boat, and I was so very glad, because to sail on a plank with someone you can only tolerate would be terrible. Wouldn't it?" That was as close as I could come to trying to resolve my own feelings. Everything was as chaotic as the fire-mountain I sensed beneath us.

Koi whooshed out his breath and turned away to spread the shirt on a rock. "It's true," he finally said. "It's true. And you did say before you left your brother on Yiuti's ship you wanted a string of lovers. But..."

"But what?"

"It seems like inviting trouble to begin with someone who is already faithless."

"Can't someone be faithful to more than one person?" I asked. It seemed vital to ask a question that had lain in my secret heart, one I'd not thought I would ever air.

Koi lifted his head, hands still as he squinted up at the trees. "I never thought of it that way," he said finally. "It does seem the wanderer way."

"Anyway, On is ... a lot of people," I said, trying to explain, but that seemed to bewilder Koi more. Then his brows met. "Do you mean, a liar?"

"No! Not at *all*. I think it's part of being a poet." Or maybe it was part of having to outrun his uncle's hunters for years—but I could not say that. I decided to change a subject I still didn't really understand, and which had veered dangerously close to the secret On had yet to reveal to anyone in our group besides me. "It's all guesses. I don't know enough yet. I don't have any experience of my own. But it reminds me. I've been longing to ask about Second Brother."

"There is little to say," Koi murmured as we kept pounding and wringing. And I heard relief in his voice. "He was glad to have me on the ship journey, but we both saw how Yiuti's servants resented me. When we reached Whale Haven, he took me aside to say that he knew my—my loyalties were divided between him and you. He said he was safe. But you were out in the world, with only that flying sword. Which someone might try to take away at any time. He said I must go and protect you. I tried to convince him that the sword looked after itself. And that if you had wanted protection, you would have said. But to Banti, you will always be Little Sister."

"He sees all girls as little sisters, doesn't he?" I offered, thinking myself at last on the path out of childhood.

"Did I hear Banti's name? You found him?" Footsteps chuffed toward us.

There was Cray, her attention unwavering on Koi.

Koi flicked a glance between me and Cray, and said, "He's fine. With Yiuti. No, truly, he's fine. It's a princely fortress. All the comforts. He even has a lover, and—"

"A lover!" Cray exclaimed. "Banti?"

I heard my assured *he sees all girls as little sisters*, and reddened as I smacked that unoffending cloth. So much for my comprehension! Ayah, even in the gallant wanderer tales, brothers didn't show that side of themselves to their sisters.

But neither Cray nor Koi paid me any heed in that moment. Koi said, "The fortress is full of pretty girls waving fans and wearing perfume, and bringing fruits and things. Those are the daughters and sisters of the guards, or the merchants. And there are many servants." As Cray still looked surprised, he added a bit defensively, "Nobody makes them come. They just come. The grand prince says that wherever rich and pretty flowers grow, the butterflies are sure to flock, and even if they aren't so pretty, the butterflies will land on them anyway and make them think they're pretty."

Cray said stiffly, "It's worse for girls. All those worthless scholars crowding around. I just didn't think he'd become one

of *those*. But then, I always thought that Yiuti would ruin him."
She turned her back and walked away.

Belatedly—oh, far too late to be of the least use—I finally
understood that poor Cray had kept my Second Brother secretly
in her heart all this time. Or to be more precise, she'd kept an
image of Banti now rather outdated. But Cray was a very loyal
person, to whom faithfulness was important, and I suspected
that now that she had discovered that Banti had a someone, she
was going to chop that old image right out along with the
cabbages she was cutting up.

Koi turned back to me, and I said, "He's so like the rest of
the boys, thinking he had to protect me by deciding for me
what's in my best interest."

"That's how we were taught," Koi said, shrugging. "I think
he feels guilty. Unfilial. For having left the way he did. And
when Yiuti joked him about needing more personal servants
than any of the other boys had, I knew there might be trouble.
So I left before it could happen. Glad I did," he added, with a
brief, searching glance.

"I'm glad you did, too," I said, reddening again, and then
shifted the subject. I told him about everything that had happened to me on Mountain Peony, right up to sending the message
through the Hats.

"That was another thing," he said at the end. "I promised to
write to you, and I was reasonably certain you would return to
Cloud Terrace, but how to send it to you? There were no gallant
wanderers at Whale Haven. And no one there was willing to
carry a note for me. But Banti said—"

I never got to hear what my brother said as the crash of
approach brought all our attention. We scrambled for weapons,
leaving the washing spread over the rocks, as a party of Falcons
returned, some bearing nasty wounds. Those had to be dealt
with, a recounting of the skirmishing shared, and more plans
laid for patrols and scouting.

Cray and Sun began fixing a meal, which we newcomers
helped with as we could. I was able to give them fire, so they
did not have to struggle with raising sparks in that wet
environment,

After the food was eaten, there was the inevitable martial
arts assessment. Fan and Koi were hailed as experts, and I was
the least experienced as a warrior, but they welcomed my healer
training. Even though it, too, was inexperienced at best, the
senior Falcon, Master Ferig, said I was still better than any of

them.

As a result, I was assigned to camp tending, trading off with Cray and Sun, who were also scouts. I thought about offering to scout from above, but hesitated. The forest was far too thick for easy flying, but more importantly, I had not told Cray that I knew how to fly on my sword; though there was now peace between us, I was still concerned that Sagacious Blade might be a sore subject for her.

FIFTEEN

*Those three sunlit and shadowed slopes
to her, were the tension between east and west,
young and old.
Battle or game? She asks the mists
that float like smoke over their noiseless contest.*

TWO DAYS PASSED, LARGELY with me left alone to tend camp. I was able thus to soak in the hot spring by myself, getting clean at last, and while my hair hung loose, drying, I also beat the dirt out of my bedroll, and aired it until it smelled of sunshine.

I was glad I did. Two days later the sunny sky clouded over, and tough, wiry Master Ferig declared that it was time to construct a roof over the crevasses, making these temporary camps less temporary.

There was plenty of wood everywhere, which enabled us to lay beams across the higher ground. Then it was a matter of foraging for autumn-dry water reed, tying it into bundles, then layering enough of these to create a roof. Then we lugged flattish rocks from the stream bed to keep the roof from blowing away in the first autumn storm to rumble over the island. Now the warm air from the hot spring had only the narrow wall at the mouth of the crevasse to escape to, and though this rough shelter would have been intolerable in the heat of summer, it was warm and welcome as bad weather set in, the rain with an icy sting that was an omen for the winter to come.

We finished barely in time; the first of ten days of storms closed in as we were laying the last rocks. I sat on my narrow ledge, my hands throbbing from wrestling with water reeds, but I was aware of a sense of contentment, mostly in the sight of the rain sheeting down over the edge of our roof into the tumbling stream below, as from the other side of the crevasse, On spun out poem after poem, speaking them to the air.

> *Wild geese fly down to a stream of pale reed*
> *The rain is our fourth wall*
> *As the bright rocky peak darkens*
> *And the summer sun sinks in autumn's dusk.*
> *Ay! The cicadas chatter, hidden*
> *Chatter and hide like us, like us.*

Is his poetry good or bad? Such distinctions have little meaning when the birth of a poem is tied so vividly to memories and emotions of another time and place. I still hear those words spoken in his voice as he sat cross-legged on a rock, peeling lychee nuts as he composed.

This record will bear scarce mention of the seldom seen older Falcons. They had scant interest in On and me, with our Pangolin headbands. They were heroes to the Falcons, and their deeds are remembered by Falcons. And not just them, as On collected many of their deeds told over wintry firesides, and folded them into the many adventure plays he was beginning to invent.

Sun and Cray were on the way to becoming experts in Eel form, and Cray seemed determined to pay off her imagined debt by teaching me. This martial arts style had been devised specifically for nuns, back in the days of writing on sticks. The Falcons had added their own emendations, with such lethal additions as fans that flung poison needles, as well as the fans with thin barbs in the sticks. At least all the basic stances, and shifts in balance, were familiar. All I was really learning was new and more difficult forms and combinations.

As was Falcon custom, we practiced rain or shine, though Master Ferig did call us out between the worst deluges, at least. Outside of practice we huddled for warmth in our camp, cultivating in our individual ways. Sometimes I pressed Koi to play Circle in mind, though I continued to lose. It seemed either I could picture the entire board—the empire—or else I could remember the sequences of moves in one area, but then I'd lose the rest. Frustrated with my own limitations, I asked for game after game, though I suspect he lost interest long before I'd give up.

Then I would furiously revisit Essence lessons. I had better success there. And when I was done with that, I found it soothing to imagine myself back in our warm, clean palace, as First Brother read aloud to me, then quoted what he had memorized, and I coached him from the scrolls he had neatly copied from Father's exquisite hand.

Sometimes I could hear First Brother's steady voice over the splat, splat, splat of rain on our makeshift roof: *Cultivating through Virtue requires the ruler to extend benevolence from freeing an ox from the slaughter to preventing wars that make people suffer. There are three prerequisites for extension: an environment that meets people's basic physical needs, ethical education, and individual effort.*

Only a handful of people, Mana Ta had argued, have the strength of character to "have a constant heart" in the face of physical deprivation. I was beginning to learn the truth of that through experience, as the weather steadily got colder and wetter, and the pirates seemed unending in their determination to exterminate everyone on the island but themselves. And not always that. When they squabbled with each other, invariably they left corpses for the roaming Falcons to find. They didn't bother to bury even their brethren decently, and it was far too easy to imagine forlorn ghosts wandering those dim, chill, vaporous forests.

On the eleventh day, when the lowering autumnal sun reappeared, Master Ferig called the experts together to make a wide patrol.

Cray was ready, as always. She leaped up and vanished. Koi and Jai were right after, and then On, who was batting mud from the hem of his winter robe.

To my surprise, Sun lingered, and then turned to me with a smile. "Ren. Is there something between you and On?"

Being a good-hearted soul, she did not laugh, or even smile knowingly as my face flamed. "I don't know," I said.

"Then the two of you are not sharing clouds and flowers?"

"I'm not ready for that," I said.

Sun nodded, then paused. "Nor even with that handsome and silent Koi? He only looks at you, you know."

"We are friends," I said.

"Lovers come and go like summer birds. But no one ever has enough friends," she replied, and ran to catch up with the others.

After that I wondered from time to time what might be going on during all those long patrols—and then reined my mind to cultivation, as a handful of days passed.

It was between Sky Wishes Day (which we could not celebrate, as lanterns would surely bring the enemy) and the eleventh month when the first snow dusted the ground. This was earlier than I was used to. Everyone's breath clouded as once again they assembled for a sweep, and ran off, weapons jingling. Only this day, Sun and On, the most fleet of the runners, arrived back breathless, to say, "Pirate raid!"

"Heading for the hermit," Sun added. "They seem to think there might be treasure there. We need to warn the hermit, but we have been warned of traps. So we must go in pairs, in case something happens to one."

"No, let me go," I said. "I can fly on Sagacious Blade."

"You can fly?" Sun asked. "You did *not* tell us that."

"This is an island full of trees," I said, not looking at Cray. "Not good for flying during the day. Impossible at night."

On stayed quiet, as Sun looked worried. "It's too dangerous. That hermit is not just reputed to be ugly, he's also cruel."

"Has anyone actually seen him?" I asked, remembering Cray's words about commanding boars to attack. So unlikely!

"Not for years and years, we were told," Sun reported. "But he's killed people who tried to scale that hill. There are grave markers at the beginning of the trail. As a warning."

"Pirates are likely to take those as provocation," On remarked. "Ren, let me go. You know I can fly the sword."

"Over water, where your Essence naturally draws," I said. "I worry about you trying to draw Essence up above rocky land, and the steam of a fire mountain."

On hesitated. He had enough failed experiments behind him to see the sense of that, and I said, "I'll be careful. I'll also obscure myself. Surely there are no traps in the air. I'll go till I see a domicile, shout the warning, and leave."

They accepted that as reasonable.

"Be careful," Sun said, On echoing her as the others caught up I stepped on Sagacious Blade and threw the obscuring charm over myself before they could see me and interfere. At last I had a mission, even if a brief one.

I rose swiftly above the unaware heads of the Falcons. Once I moved away from the clear air above our rocky crevasse and its spring, I entered the dense canopy of trees and had to slow. This was extraordinarily hard, as I could not ride a wind current, and had to draw on mostly my own Essence. There was little fire to use, except for the weakening sun. But I had to stay in that moist, diffuse air as I did not know the island at all, and must follow that winding path that I'd only trod once. Why hadn't I gone exploring? Because preparing meals took a great deal of time when one was alone. Because I disliked mud, and being dripped on. It was easier to stay in that camp, my mind cutting free as my hands chopped, or ground, or mixed, or shaped.

But the excitement of a task, and the awareness that I might spy creeping pirates, sparked my willingness to expend Essence. I remained confident that even if I spotted pirates, they would not look up.

At last the hills that formed the hermit's high lair emerged as a shadow in the slivers between the trees, and then, quite suddenly, I emerged from the stand of pine and now I could see three very rocky hills.

There was a narrow goat path, grown-over and neglected. And there were the grave markers, mossy and overgrown. Was the hermit even alive? Either he had gone to the underworld, or else he was self-sufficient on that precipitous height, for he certainly did not use the path regularly, judging by the brambles overgrowing it, and the rivulets that cut deep across it.

I rose higher, sailing around towering rocks sculpted by fierce winds off the sea. I glimpsed a kind of cup valley between two rocky cliffs, on which rows of harvested vegetables and herbs had recently been bedded down for winter with leaves mulched with compost, from which a pungent aroma rose. Someone definitely lived up there.

I slowed, scanning for a domicile — and then jolted to a stop, caught in some kind of weird net. I could not see it, but I could feel it. When I moved, it stung my meridians. I stilled, frightened by the weird, cold numbness left by the stings.

"So," a thin, heavily accented voice accused. "One of you thieves found a way up here, eh? You're going to regret it."

A shrouded figure emerged from a cavern overhung by streamers of wisteria and String-of-Arrows plants, cultivated to act as a door.

I could not move, but at least I could speak. "I came to warn you," I cried. "Pirates are attacking this end of the island. We think they are trying to come up here in search of treasure."

The figure cackled, a high sound that made me realize the hermit was less likely a "he" than a "she."

"Treasure." She spat the word. "No doubt they think of cold metal and a lot of sparkly stones as treasure. Useless! They would not know treasure if it bit them."

"That's all I came for," I said. "To warn you. Please let me go. I'll not disturb you again."

The figure's hood dropped back as she squinted up at me. "Eh, a half-grown girl."

At the same time as she raked me from my headband to my worn shoes, I stared down into a wrinkled face that at first I took for sickly with a disease, framed by flyaway white hair. But I had seen that "disease" before — it was nothing but the splotches of an easterner, called freckles, against fish-pale skin. Unsightly perhaps, but entirely natural in those people. I remembered the Cinnabar Princess, that mysterious figure who played that beautiful armonia that sounded like silver hammers on crystal, and who had apparently healed my First Brother as much as she was able. Along with healing others of Xianti's victims.

"You've seen my kind before," the hermit observed.

"Yes," I said.

"Eh, you might as well come down." *Downward mayhap go you*, were her actual words, in an accent thicker than bean paste. That is to convey an idea of her archaic, difficult speech in the imperial tongue.

She made a quick sign, whispering under her breath. I sensed a spurt of Essence, fashioned differently than I was used to. It seemed woven, somehow. I was able to lower myself to the broad terrace before her plant-draped cavern, but I still could not move.

I watched in surprise as she went into the cave, then emerged with a round cushion-shaped object, which she cast on the ground. She dropped onto it with a grunt, neatly crossed her legs beneath her voluminous, ragged-edged robe, and then, to my absolute astonishment, she gestured and rose into the air on this cushion. With another quick gesture, she blurred herself.

I found it difficult to track her. At best I could follow the blur if I gazed a little to one side, as she and her flying cushion raised itself upward, and then vanished sedately around a rock formation.

I was left there on her terrace as chickens clucked and pecked here and there, and a trio of baby goats blinked at me from one side. At the far end of the terrace sat another gravestone, but this one was well tended, with drying flowers atop it.

One of the baby goats began hopping back and forth between rocks, joined by the others. They were so adorable—I watched them in delight until a flicker on the edge of my vision distracted me, and the hermit was back.

She wiped away the obscuring charm with a gesture, then said, "You spoke true. But the locals have just accounted for most. Two evaded them, but fell into my traps. I released them in time for your soot-hairs to find."

Soot-hairs? I realized she meant us, the people of the Empire of the Thousand Islands. A term equivalent to our calling the easterners cinnabar, on account of *their* hair color.

She then released me from the ward that had restrained me, saying, "You're free to go. Or you can stay. Tell me about yourself. Unlike these other barbarians, you seem to be trained in rudimentary magic."

"Magic?"

"Essence. All the same. Different languages. And some different approaches."

I did not have to stay, but at those few words about magic and Essence and languages, my curiosity bloomed. I bowed gallant-wanderer style, introduced myself, then pointed at her cushion. "What is that? Is it common in the east?"

"We call them windrunners. Though they don't actually run—you'd be blown right off. They're common on some islands. Where they are not altogether forbidden."

"Forbidden by kings. For the military?"

She grunted a laugh. "Fast you are, walla! It's the easiest way to dominate a populace, when the military has them but no one else. They are not easy to make."

"Charmed swords have been forbidden here dynasties ago."

"I know. Or I would have been shot down when I was first exiled. No one here thinks to look up, though I was told it was different in the past."

"Exiled!" I exclaimed, scarcely hearing the rest.

"An exile has to go somewhere, doth not she? Who would go among barbarians else?" She added, wryly, "You westerners call us barbarians. Ay! Human nature. So predictable."

Not knowing what else to say, I murmured, "I am sorry to hear that you were exiled from your home. I know a little of what that is like."

"So? You are a thumb or two young for wandering the world on your own. But then so many your age insist." She said that, peering into my face, and whatever she saw made her own expression alter. "I was exiled because I was too talented, and too brash about it. When you refuse kings, this is what happens—if you aren't killed first. I would have been, had I not been part of the royal Namath Family. It would have tarnished our regal reputation."

"It was an emperor's son who sought to destroy my family," I said. "I escaped."

She grunted again, then said, as hard drops of cold rain began to fall, "Come inside. Do you like spiced goat's milk? Of course you don't. None of you people know what's good, ha ha." She cackled.

Again, it was curiosity that drew me to follow her within. The cavern was an odd shape, neatly swept out. A bed had been put against one wall, and near it, a rack of carefully wrapped scrolls. A clothes trunk lay adjacent to that, and the other side of the cave was where she cooked and ate. A pungent aroma I could not identify wafted from a side-tunnel or cave. She said, "I was about to turn my cheese. I'd better do it before I forget. Then I'll warm the milk."

"Cheese?" I queried. "May this ignorant one ask what is that?"

"You can smell my precious cheese wheel, can't you?" She laughed. "It will taste good the winter after this, I assure you. Come along."

I had to hold my breath, as the smell was very strong, but it was not like rot. It was more like very strong goat, with a hint of astringent thistle. I was glad she did not ask me to sample it. Goat milk I'd had a few times in the scrape. It was drinkable.

She used cinnamon in the goat milk, which I'd only tasted in medicine if my head was stuffed, or smelled in perfumes and incense. To it she added monk fruit, which made it sweet. Very odd, though she consumed it with the curled lips of something tasting delicious. I was glad the cup she gave me was tiny, and I held my breath as I gulped it down in order to be a good guest.

Meanwhile, she said, "You are an exile within your own empire, then? Ay, I've heard enough of trouble between islands. So had we it, so had we. I, Namath Dhak, came to this one precisely because your overscrupulous navy leaves it well alone."

"It is not my navy," I said.

She cocked an eyebrow at me. "I've heard a little about the latest emperor." Hermit Namath shook her head. "Occasionally all one can do is wait for them to expend themselves. Another will come along, no doubt."

I thought of Xianti, conspiring behind Uncle Koza's back, and said, "A worse one."

She cackled. "I can't say that, at least. The queen regent, now queen, is a good one. People prosper under such. But will the generations to come learn, or take her enlightenment for granted?"

"This one means no disrespect in asking if your having a good ruler now means that you can go back?" I asked.

The hermit's smile vanished as she stared down into the little cup in her wrinkled hands. "No," she said finally. "Yes. I could. But why? My home is gone. All those I knew are gone, or old. There is nothing to go back to, except perhaps distrust. Walla, walla, as we say. I will finish out my life here, among my little friends who do not speak, but keep me company, along with my ghost friends." She pointed to the racks of scrolls, and then glanced out at the gravestone on the terrace.

"Ma-aa-aa-aa," a goat complained from the terrace, and she laughed.

"May I ask if you command the animals? The boars, in specific?"

She scowled. "Who can command a vile old boar? Or worse, a young one? Piglets are so amiable when small, but then they turn irritable. Driven by lust, so like so many men," she said, turned her head, and went, "Pah! Pah!" as if spitting. "I had to plant wards to keep them from finding their way up here to root in my garden and go after my chickens and goats." She pointed at me. "You used the sight-warding spell. You know magic? Ah, that is, as you say it here, you study Essence matters?"

"I do," I said.

"You've a life like mine, and so young?" Hermit Namath asked, shaking her head. "Study hard. See a problem that you can fix. But which a king doesn't want fixed. Refuse to use your skills for his purpose—and find yourself condemned."

That was of course not at all how my life had gone so far, but I was not ready to tell her anything about Sagacious Blade, even though Granny Zim was silent.

The chickens set up a squawk, and I caught a very distant shout, "Ren!"

"Ay!" I stood up. "My companions are worried. I was supposed to just tell you about those pirates."

The hermit eyed me, then said, "If you want to return, I will not ward you. You're made me curious, young one."

I hesitated, my gaze going to those scrolls. Were any in our language? I missed reading. But… "Those gravestones down at the foot of this hill," I said doubtfully. There was no polite way to ask about those.

She looked away. "Two of those are brigands from two ships before this. My beloved killed them before he died of his wounds." She glanced at the gravestone. "The third, I had to kill myself, before he could kill me, for a treasure I do not even have. I was younger and stronger then. I leave them there to dissuade."

Then she wasn't preying on random visitors? I didn't feel that she was lying, and Granny Zim continued to say nothing, so I bowed, and said, "Thank you. I will return," and went out. At the other end of the terrace, I drew my sword and took flight.

I soon spotted Cray, On, and Koi at three different turns in the paths below, called to them, and we all returned to our camp.

SIXTEEN

She was the lodestone
Beckoned to the long needle…

IT WAS ON WHO insisted I return to visit Hermit Namath Dhak—because of the windrunner cushion. He wanted me to learn the Essence charms for his sword. Or for a cushion, or anything else he could fly on.

This despite Master Ferig saying practically, "Not on this island. What's the use of it?" He indicated me with a callused, scarred hand. "Pangolin Ren here, the least experienced of us, understood it would be useless to scout for pirates from the air. You're sure to kill yourself by hitting an unseen branch, strangle yourself on one of the many vines—or you'll have to go above the tree canopy, in which case all you'll see will be the tops of trees."

"And get dizzy," another of the older Falcons put in, who explained to us that she had tried a flying sword in her youth. She put up her palms. "Never again, even if by some miracle I could master enough Essence to keep it in the air longer than a leap."

"In history, before the emperors interfered, flying swords were only common in sects who practiced Essence as well as martial skills," the master finished.

Though the others lost interest, On didn't—until I came back from my second visit to report that I hadn't nearly enough expertise for a charm that complicated.

"The cushions are bound to the affinities of the owner," I explained to him. "That, she told me, takes a long time to perform. And then there is renewing what she called the spells, or the Essence."

"But the sword isn't bound to you," he protested. "I flew it."

"Exactly. It's a different sort of charm. I think her beloved was an Essence scholar from our empire. He was the one who taught her something about our Essence matters, once she learned our language. She explained that it involves binding all five elements to the metal. I could learn to bind fire, but that alone would just melt the sword. I'd have to study a lot longer to make a sword fly."

"But you said you were able to lift a boulder."

"Yes. Lift, as in move it. I can't fly a boulder across the island. And I have terrible trouble with water. Even more with air. However, there is one solace that I can offer you: the windrunners move very slowly." And at On's looked of disappointment—for I'd seen how he loved swooping about the sky while standing on the sword, as fast as he could go—I pointed at the pile of paper sitting on my bedding. "Another: she gave me that paper."

On leaped across the crevasse to my little ledge, as usual without a glance at the steep and rocky drop below. He touched a sheet. "It's good paper. The best, made from the silkworm tree. And hemp, and rice. She gave that to you?"

"She gets a trunk once a season, she said. Mostly books and scrolls, but also paper and ink. She says she can no longer write in winter. Her hands are too stiff, and she has no one to translate for."

On picked up the paper as carefully as if picking up a newborn kitten. "Ink, I can make. There's bark and ash everywhere. But paper..."

"On!" one of the Falcons called from above. "You're on scout duty!"

On sprang lightly back to his own ledge, gently laid the paper down, then with another spring, he vanished up to the surface, and away.

That left me to read the book Hermit Namath had loaned me, a testament written by that queen she'd mentioned, who woke up not long before her sixteenth birthday, surrounded by guards and ministers as they took her to the throne. That was the day, she said in the first line, she crossed from child to adult.

I read intermittently over the following days, between the unending and arduous cooking chores. As it got colder, and wetter, living in this way became a constant chore.

That was the problem, the wet. I seldom felt cold unless I was wet. And wet was difficult to escape now. Unfortunately, the hot spring had diminished to a trickle; now I understood why no one had made any permanent dwelling here. Washing clothes became a miserable chore, especially as they froze before they dried. At least I could call fire to light wet wood, so we always had a fire—with me adding Essence to prolong its burning.

There was a reason for houses, I told myself, trying to laugh myself out of what could very well turn to misery. I would not permit that. I had my freedom. I was alive, with my wits, and the constant companionship and wisdom of Granny Zim in Sagacious Blade. I had On, and Koi. Cray and I had come to an understanding. Sun and Fan were my friends. I was rich in luck.

Even so, waking to ice crystals around my blanket from my own breath made me remember those refugees in the imperial city so long ago, coming to stand in line for a single steamed bun. After which they had to go off to find the most rudimentary shelter when the temples were overflowing.

I continued to read the stiff, sometimes incomprehensible words of this princess turned queen at an age younger than I. It was not a true journal, of course. A much-copied text by a monarch was bound to be stiffened with laudatory language as well as layers of admonition about the virtues easterners held precious, but even so, between the long, earnest lessons, there were glimpses of a girl not unlike me. I found myself absorbed in what she thought she must do first. What others thought she must do. How she did them.

As I washed and chopped and cooked, and kept water on the boil constantly through the day, I also continued to think about refugees. I wanted a world in which there were no refugees. It was maddening that wars created refugees, when there was plenty of room for all. Could be plenty to eat. Could be plenty to do.

It snowed again.

This time, the snow was still there the following day. The stream below was now a tiny trickle under a thin layer of ice, which I had to break in order to fetch a bucket of water.

"I think this is winter," Cray said as I passed tea around to the seven of us in our crevasse-camp.

Everyone was warming their hands between tiny sips. Bathing was reduced to a quick wash, under layers of clothes. They commented, or cursed, or joked, according to their habit. Koi said nothing. His habit. Until I went up to slog through the mushy snow and mud to collect firewood.

He followed me. "I hope winter has set in," he said with satisfaction.

"You want a long winter? Living outside?" I asked.

"It's Banti," he said softly, and at the mention of my brother's name, I forget my wet, grimy hem slapping at my ankles. "I was not going to say anything. No use in two worrying."

"Say anything about what?" I asked.

"The reason the grand prince chose Whale Haven is because it's situated in a conjunction of current and winds that causes the bays to freeze. As long as winter settles in by double-eleven, it means by New Year's Week, no one is coming or going."

"You mean, the island will be surrounded by ice by New Year's Two Moons?"

"I think it likely, judging by our weather. It's barely the first of eleventh month, and winter is definitely here. Things will be icy soon. If it's icy here, it's icy there. Even princes cannot fight the ice and expect to win."

"So whether or not Second Brother read my letter won't matter, if this cold winter reaches there," I said, my heart easing. "Ay! I hope so."

"Whale Haven being somewhat farther north than we are, it's fairly certain that if we have winter, they surely have it," he said, his somber expression much lightened, and together we brought back enough wood so that I would not have to go out for a day or two. "That will keep them secure until spring next year."

A few days after that, the Falcon patrollers came back, indistinguishable from one another with snow caked all over them, to announce that the last of the pirates had vanished, along with their ship. The Falcons had met up with the surviving settlement on the west coast, who disclosed that they, too, had found no pirates anywhere.

"We still must scout," Master Ferig warned. "They might come sneaking back under cover of a storm. We all must remain vigilant."

I went back to visit Hermit Namath Dhak to report this news, and to return the book.

"Good," she said. "Thank you for telling me. We can enjoy the respite until the next shipful arrives. In my experience it's been every ten years or so."

"The Falcons seem to want to establish a more permanent camp on this island, so that there is always someone on the watch for pirates."

"I hope they do. Now, what did you think of our cinnabar queen?"

I had to laugh within me at her use of the term 'cinnabar' we so thoughtlessly spoke. "It was difficult to read, as there were so many references I did not understand. But I did appreciate her determination to survive, and then to counter the forces who wished to remove her. And the ones who tried to use her. I wished the book covered more than one year. But you say she is still ruling, though she had no military knowledge?"

"Cannot women rule by their wits?" the hermit asked, misinterpreting my exclamation of wonder. "Don't you have a saying that the clever fox exploits the tiger's might? Though we've had famous women generals."

I thought back to our previous emperor, briefly glimpsed when I was a child. I didn't think he could have ridden a horse or a chariot. But that was irrelevant. "We have one or two famous women war leaders as well, though no generals that I know of." Mother would not have wanted me reading about such. "But *I* believe they ought *not* to be war leaders. No one should be," I added.

"At your great age," Hermit Namath retorted, laughing. "No, I am at fault. It was I who gave you her serene majesty's first volume, to prove that sometimes young women are called upon to act where usually we turn to the older and wiser heads. I ought not to scoff about your age. Especially as you and I are grasshoppers on the same rope. Another of your delightful sayings that my beloved was fond of."

She reminisced a little more about her queen, and then, as the icy wind was rising, bringing in another storm, I quickly left. I was adept at the journey between her domicile and our camp by now, but that did not make it safe. I had to fight hard to keep the wind from smashing me into a tree.

When I got back to camp, I discovered that the others were all there. Sun and Cray had taken over preparing a meal.

"Did you learn any new Essence charms?" On called over to me. He had not given up hoping for a flying sword of his own.

I shook my head, and because we had another long, icy-cold

winter night ahead—it was already dark, and the hour was probably no later than last horse—I repeated the conversation.

"Ayah," On exclaimed. "Ruling by wit and not might. So much written on that for scholars to stuff their heads with for the Imperial Examination, yet how often do we get it?"

Cray said, "I can still remember hearing the young masters reciting Kanda at length about how the ruler must be aware of the first virtue."

Sun called up from the fire pit, where she was carefully carving off another sliver from a tea brick, "Which is? Count your money?"

On leaned over and addressed her. "This is *Kanda* writing, not an emperor. Kanda teaches that for us, the study of Principle, nature, and fate as revealed through the medium of the heavenly bodies is a *single* study, which leads to comprehension of right and wrong."

Koi looked up from his ledge where he sat cross-legged, cleaning his weapons. "My young master had to write that one a hundred times once. I wrote fifty of them."

"I remember that," Cray said. "I offered to do the other fifty, but he insisted he must, for he'd be expected to remember it. Did it all stick in your head, Koi?"

Koi's thick brows met as he considered, then he put back his head and quoted, "To gain the knowledge to rule well and wisely, the ruler must perceive the fundamental truth in things, and to perceive that, he must both study and experience life as lived by his subjects."

"Any listening emperors are welcome to come scrub and chop these garlic chives," Sun called.

"Any listening emperors, or would-be emperors, would be too busy sending assassins to spit us," On joked.

Koi waited with his usual calm patience, then finished, "'Only when investigation has been practiced long enough can it become possible to comprehend truth. And then the pursuit of truth leads to virtue.' Ayah! I did remember it all.'"

"Except that 'truth' can look like a plum to one and an apple to another, yet both are fruits," I said.

"Very well, then define your 'principle,'" On retorted. "Be wiser than Kanda. I dare you."

"I can't. But I can quote Mana Ta, who had the diviner's answer to every problem. 'Principle governs the five elements. The balance of male and female, east and west. It commands all things created in the universe. They all have Essence but Essence has no shape or shadow. In that it is like a natural law unchanging and powerful…'"

"Enough, enough. I ought to know better than to challenge you," On said, falling back with his palms out.

"Good, because we need more firewood for tomorrow, and it takes all night now to dry out," Cray stated, and I secretly rejoiced in this evidence that Cray and I were a good way toward the parity we both so wanted. Maybe one day I'd even be less self-conscious.

"Going," I said, reaching for my harness.

On started up, but Koi said, as he sheathed his sword, "I'll go with you. Let's get enough for a couple of days. I smell snow on the wind."

I was going to tell On he was welcome, too, but Fan had pulled on her coat. "I'll help." She had gone very silent of late, and I sensed that she needed to be busy.

The three of us set out, as the low winter sun emerged briefly between clouds. For the space of a breath or two, our three shadows lay in an archway of light between the elongated shadows of trees, the ground glistening in a thin covering of ice.

Koi gave Fan a considering glance, then turned to me. "I don't remember you studying Mana Ta," Koi said to me as our footsteps crunch, crunch, crunched.

"I didn't. Then. Except when coaching First Brother before he took the Imperial Examination. It was at Mountain Peony, when On brought me schoolboy books. I discovered that all those many, many readings lay in memory, without comprehension. But once I began reading those books On brought, it all came back. Familiar, and now so clear. 'The river of time runs eternal, balanced between the vast heavens and fathomless earth. I must overcome all boundaries, between sun and stars, moons and sun, mountains and seas, so that the mysteries of heaven become clear as air…'"

Fan spoke up from my other side. "What is that actually saying? Seems a river of words."

"It *is* a river of words," I told her, laughing. "But it's about balance."

"Balance," she said, on an exhaled breath.

And because we had a long walk ahead, for we'd long since scoured all fallen wood close by, I went on, hoping she would at least be soothed by this river, "Everything must be in balance. Our ancestral halls with parasol trees on the west side of the temple, and redbark on the east. Dark and light. Male and female."

Fan snorted at that. "What *is* male and female, really? The Iron Fist boys never acknowledge when I beat them, except to say that I ought to have been born a boy. Or that I am half-boy, and don't know it. Which I am not, and I very well know it."

"Only you can decide that," I responded, remembering what Mother said on the subject—when she spoke about graywings, many of whom were firm about being neither the one nor the other. And then I thought about On when he was Sister Oriole, as coy and demure and flirty as the most coy and demure and flirty of the entertainment dancers.

"The Chief Censor used to reserve judgment about the mysteries of divination," Koi said, with another considering glance toward Fan. "All he'd say—and he repeated it to both young masters—was…ay! 'Prognostications attempt to impose order. Books of predictions tag particular days through the year, illustrating them with a local adage. For example, for the third day of the third month, if you hear the sound of frogs croaking before noon, crops at higher elevations will ripen. Whereas if you hear the croaking after noon, crops at lower elevations will ripen. Great cold almost always falls in the twelfth Ghost Moon month, whereas lesser cold falls often in the eleventh Ghost Moon month…"

He faltered there, and I continued, the school manual before my eye, "'When either falls midway through both Phoenix moon month and Ghost Moon month, wind or snow occurring on that day will signal losses to domestic fowl and livestock.'"

"One of my friends among the graywings, who was always consulting a diviner, said that these prognostications are based on experience," Koi admitted. He so seldom spoke of his family that I listened closely. "Insisted the diviner who uses them correctly will find that it is accurate in predicting flood or drought and disaster or good fortune."

Fan was listening. All this talk did seem successful in penetrating that fog of melancholy she tried to hide. She said, "Look there! A fallen log. I've got the axe." She brandished it. "I want first crack at it. Ay, we all crave order, and to know what lies around the corner. I would vow to be a donkey for the next ten lives, serving any diviner who could tell me truthfully if Dinek is well, and where she and the *Pangolin* are. But I suppose that's too direct for all that demon and ghost nonsense."

"Are you saying it's all false?" I asked. "That the world of demons, and the order of the heavens, is perceived incorrectly?"

"I've never *seen* any of it," Fan said, as I began gathering up fallen twigs and small branches.

"I have," I said. "Further, I've read accounts, very old ones, of strange sights and unexplained events, found in distant regions, high mountains, and hidden realm of spirits. The wise ones of old insist that these afford a glimpse of the hierarchy from Heaven to monarch, to land, and air, and the connection between all realms visible and invisible."

Crack! The axe bit into the fallen wood. "*That's* what I believe in," Fan said. "I can see it. I can feel it. I can smell it. And my own two hands can order it." Crack!

I saw in her profile that the melancholy still befogged her heart, and so I tried to divert her. "Here's something that Hermit Namath Dhak said about the easterners, that though she'd never seen a ghost, everyone insists they exist. They are so certain, that the word has a purpose in their culture. They give all leftover food to their living ghosts, that is, to the old people who retire by going to their hometown, putting on white clothing, and declaring themselves dead. Once they are ghosts, they no longer own anything, but family and villagers take care of them for the rest of their days. No one smart fails to do so, for that is inauspicious. They will all become a ghost of some sort, sooner or later."

Fan was diverted for the space of a few breaths, but then I saw that I had chosen an unlucky subject, for her mind settled on ghosts, and she was back to worry about Dinek.

The walk back was much the same, and after that, Koi and On and I tried to divert her as the weather steadily worsened. Cray and Sun, perceiving at last what quiet Fan had kept to herself, did their best to help.

On, of course, had an unlimited fund of poetry to fling at any who would listen. I continued to pester patient Koi for mental Circle games (which I lost). And occasionally Cray remembered lessons that my brothers and I had had to study and repeat until we had them perfectly, and offered them for discussion. I had always thought the servants free of that toil, but of course they were not if they were on duty, standing silently within hearing.

I must pause here to add that though our intent was to keep ourselves occupied during those long, dark, cold days, as well as to bring Fan out of her melancholy, these conversations were stirring my own mind.

I am trying to show the steps toward the decision I was

about to make.

It was Cray who spoke up on the last day of the Year of the Dolphin, as the two boys debated Mana Ta on the powers of the ruler, "Madam taught us that power, to remain in balance, must be free to run in its circles. Large, small, interlocked, all contributing to the great circle: the south trades with the north, the north trades with the south. The east and west gains from the traffic of both. And contributes."

I went to sleep that night dreaming of Circle games, my mother's hand my opponent, but sometimes that hand lengthened and strengthened, and it was Second Brother playing, then On, and when he altered into Huyun Shandek, I woke myself up.

That evening, the winter sky lit silvery with both moons touching in New Year's Two Moons. We could only honor a few of the usual customs as we symbolically swept out the Year of the Dolphin, and brought in the Year of the Dog, a salute to steadfast loyalty—quite an irony, considering the fractured empire. We did our best for a feast—the patrollers were able to bring down one of those big, mean boars. No one had incense, but we had set up a simple altar, and I prayed that the Cinnabar Princess Vaha was still looking out for my family, and that Banti was sitting snug in Whale Haven as Xianti fumed uselessly, warded by ice, outside of it.

First I took a portion of the boar up to Hermit Namath Dhak. She offered me some of her cheese, which she had just broached. I turned that down but accepted a cup of her fermented goat milk, which had a strong and not unpleasant tang. Over that, after we toasted one another, she described how, as a girl, they release hosts of birds when the two moons met. The birds were to carry the smoke of incense and prayers straight to heaven to help carry the year's souls over for rebirth.

The weather was already worsening when I returned, so cold from the wind buffeting me that I had to sit right over the fire. I smelled the singe of the thick fabric of my robe as Sun made another batch of tea. We then had our feast, singing many of the old songs.

What would have happened if we had been staying in a

comfortable house, with plenty of distractions, instead of holed up in a crevasse?

Many were the jokes, or the chin-lifted comments about Falcon hardiness, but I kept thinking of the long winter ahead. "Am I the only one who hates this?" I asked Granny Zim silently as I burrowed into my grimy, damp blankets. "Are they lying about being comfortable? About enjoying the challenge?"

"If some lie, it's merely the lie of pride," she said.

To distract myself, I reviewed old lessons, and when Koi and I went to get firewood on the first day of the Year of the Dog, we reminisced about palace life, before the trouble.

While it was a comfort to share memories of warmer, easier days, once I was alone, my mind threw itself to that unknown island where Second Brother might be. Had winter ice repelled Xianti until spring? Koi was the only one who had seen the bay at Whale Haven. The fourth day, we could not sweep, of course. Nor could the Falcons patrol as a blizzard roared and whistled around us. We sat in our camp, and Koi sketched Whale Haven out on one of On's precious pieces of paper. The three of us sat over it and discussed various likelihoods.

"The best outcome is only temporary," I said finally, looking into their smoke-smudged faces as the fire leaped below. "If Xianti withdrew, and I hope you're right about that, On, he'll be back in spring. And surely he's left watchers for any movement on the grand prince's part."

On nodded. "It's a siege without having to mount a siege. 'Your best weapon is no weapon.'"

"Except Xianti won't allow for a peaceful surrender," Koi said, low-voiced.

"I *wish* I could get there," I said. "But even if I could get there on our bigger boat, what could I do? My grand uncle would clap me into a pretty room, throw silk robes in, and try to marry me off to some ally. He wouldn't listen to me."

"Not unless he had to. If you brought power equal to his power," On commented, carefully folding up the paper with the drawing on it. I knew there would soon be a play, or poems, on the back of it. "Then he'd have to."

"Where would I find a shipful of gold?" I laughed, watching my breath cloud. "Too bad the pirates are gone. I could have asked them where to find it."

"You already know the answer," Koi said, as if I'd been serious. "Steal it."

On flickered his fingers as if waving a fan. "Gold. Allies. If you had a trunk of flying swords. Power comes in so many forms."

"But he only sees it in military terms," I grumped, biting down on my irritation. I knew he was not wrong. "It's time for me to soak the vegetables so I can peel them," I said, and climbed down to our cooking area.

The next day, I had to go fetch firewood. I looked around for Koi, but he was over with the older Falcons, scrapping against the masters, kicking up clots of brown, mushy snow. From what I could see, he was not losing—the masters were hard-pressed against him. The pulse of pride I felt in him surprised me.

Sun had just returned from scrapping, her cheeks glowing with exertion. She glanced at Koi, then to On, at that moment sitting cross-legged on his ledge, brush working away on a poem. He'd taken to wearing his hair in braids, which he then bound up, but one had slipped over his forehead.

"He's very pretty in a sweat," Sun remarked in an under-voice to me, grinning.

I laughed because she expected it, but beyond her shoulder, On—quick as a hummingbird—was watching me, not her, a question in his lifted brows.

These were swift waters.

I said, "I've got to get going." I pointed to my firewood basket.

"I'll help," Sun said. "No patrol today. Master Ferig said it's a swamp. If the pirates have come back, they're welcome to it."

On then leaped to the surface, snagging our other basket. "Another pair of hands."

These baskets were deep, woven to slip over the shoulders, so I left Sagacious Blade behind when I gathered firewood.

On said, "I've been trying to think of a way to make a Circle board. Not just for you, Ren," he added. "For us all. It's the carving of the markers that puzzles me. At least three of us play, I know. The others could learn."

On explained to Sun why we couldn't just pick up stones, and dye half with ash—"It's the balance, you see, it has to look the same from either side."

I stopped with a squelch in the icy slush. "Balance."

The two paused, staring at me with twin expressions of surprise. As if I'd lost my wits.

Maybe I had. "I've been looking at it from the wrong side," I exclaimed. "Turn the board around."

"What board, Ren?" Sun asked.

"Board," On prompted, metaphor being so much a part of his life. "Being?"

"I keep worrying at getting to Whale Haven, though I know that… Ay! I've said that, a thousand times already. Balance, influence can be levers just as strong as gold. What if I were to go to the source?"

"Of?" Sun asked.

"You mean, the Lans' ancestral island?" On asked.

"Yes. See if this makes sense. The Lan island was traditionally the source of family wealth and influence. Islands, actually, though the large one is most important. I could go to them for help."

"Do you know them?" Sun asked practically.

"Not really," I had to admit. "I did meet my cousin once, but I was very small."

On said skeptically, "Also, surely that rabbit of an emperor is wise enough not to eat next to his own warren." And at Sun's bewildered expression, "He's surely showered promotions and tax-exemptions on his own family. Won't they be enthusiastically on his side?"

"That might have been at first," I said. "But equally it is said that that the skin is nearer than the shirt. And who's more selfish about his own skin than Xianti? On our imperial uncle's behalf right now… Everyone knows he's desperate for conscripts…"

I thought back to when I was a child, and my brothers got called away to help entertain our distant cousin Lan Kandati, visiting court with his father Lan Louza, the Prince of Lan Island. How had that gone? Father had pointed out how proud he was of our distant cousins and how loyal they were—and he'd given one of his rare entertainments. But I had not been permitted to see our cousin, whom my brothers had had to entertain…

"Koi will know," I said, and bolted forward, not missing the amused looks Sun and On exchanged.

"Quite mad," On said.

They industriously helped me to fill the baskets and lug them back. By then the practice was over, and Koi was on his ledge, drinking tea.

"Koi," I said, too impatient to climb down—I called Sagacious Blade to me, and used it to glide to his ledge. "Do you remember when the Prince of Lan Island came to swear before the emperor, after his father died, and he brought our cousin Kandati? Didn't he make friends with my brothers after being picked on by Xianti and his followers?"

Koi said, "Xianti scorned Young Master Kandati for his accent, for his clothes, for his outland ways. That was before he discovered Kandati was short-sighted, and loosed his pack on him with a series of cruel tricks. Liarti was a willing participant in those, I remember. All three of them called him a little girl for adopting the kittens of a cat Xianti shot off a wall, meaning to impress him."

"I have it now," I exclaimed. "That's when Banti brought in Shadow and Bandit. I had not known Xianti liked to shoot at cats."

"Banti said not to tell you. The grand duke would not permit Young Master Kandati to take them on the ship back to Lan, because he already had so many pets at home. Why?"

"Because," I said, "I'm going to Lan and talk to Kandati on my brother's behalf. See if he can get his father to cut off support to Xianti. But that means sailing right away, before spring. Today!"

SEVENTEEN

"AM I WRONG, GRANNY ZIM?"

She said, "Ayah, now you are at last beginning to draw on the lake of talent you have been given by the gods! Keep your heart from poison of greed and hate, and I am by your side, my Bu."

Bolstered by this voice the others could not hear—and some, I think, did not believe truly existed—I turned to face the others' objections.

And objections there were.

As expected, everyone had reasons why this was an idea doomed to fail. *It was so far away*—yes, but at least the great summer and autumnal dragon storms were over until next summer. Snow storms would not stir the seas nearly so high. But there were other objections. So many.

Didn't I remember that Lan Banti was an outlaw?

I reminded them that I could get away if I had to, but I remembered how much Kandati hated Xianti. I maintained stoutly that I believed he'd at least get his father to listen to me due to our shared blood.

And what if Lan Louza disregards shared blood?

I'd go as an envoy from Grand Prince Yiuti. Yes, I knew it was a lie, but wouldn't the grand prince want an alliance if it was offered? Even Xianti had heeded the rules about envoys, twice this year, in my experience. Once when he waited at Ji Jiang's Tiger Eye Bay for that "peace conference," and once when he sent envoys ahead to tell Huyun Shandek that his arrival with Siarti was imminent.

What if the Lans turn me in despite the rules governing envoys?

Koi said at last, in that slow, measured way of his, "This is what I remember about them, their loyalty. That suggests to me that your esteemed relations prize order and tradition, even if your cousin still dislikes the imperial crown prince. Who *is* the imperial crown prince."

"Will they like it when they hear that Xianti is plotting against his imperial uncle?"

Koi opened his hands. "I can't answer that. I think the likeliest outcome will be that you'll be escorted to a fine room and kept for your own safety, just as you expect to be treated if you go to Imperial Grand Prince Yiulo."

I was looking down at my forearms that strained against my grimy sleeves, then over at On, and I said, daring him to argue, "Then I'll go as my brother."

"What?" Sun gasped, and On smothered a laugh.

I spoke firmly. "Cousin Kandati hasn't seen Banti since they were boys. Everyone says I look like him. Koi, I *do* look like him. Remember when that horrible Tiger Li thought I was Banti? And I wasn't even wearing a disguise!"

On crowed. "This might be a mad idea, but it sounds like fun! I insist on going with you."

"Do." My heart was thundering, but I hid it. "I expect you to coach me." And to them all, "I know it's a long journey, especially if I don't stay but a day. It'll be cold and wet, but I'm cold and wet here. There's no use toiling in the cold and wet while accomplishing nothing. I just want to find out if my uncle from our ancestral land truly supports Xianti's wars. Perhaps he can use his influence to talk the emperor into freeing my family. Lan could be a safe haven for them. Banti, too. If my uncle is against me, I'll leave."

That decided my steadfast mountain. "I'm coming, too," Koi said, low in his chest. "For such a long journey, you'll need backup. That will be me."

"And me," Jai spoke up, glowering as if expecting argument. "There's no pirates left here. It's boring!" He shot a guilty look in the direction of the camp of the elders, but as always, if anyone heard, they paid us no heed.

"You'll need a servant," Cray said practically, color stealing into her cheeks. "As well as extra protection. I will be that person."

Fan glanced up. "Lan lies to the southwest, does it not?"

I nodded.

She said, "I'll guide you as far as the westmost Falcon island that intersects with the Inner Island tea run. That's the most likely place to find the *Pangolin*, or maybe a message. From there you'll go straight south. You won't need me at the helm for that."

"Thank you," I said.

Sun sighed, then shrugged. "I'll go with you. If you all leave, I'll be the youngest, which means the tasks no one else wants. And Jai is right in that our mission has been completed."

That agreed, no one wanted to linger. We decided to set out at first light in the morning, which would give us daylight for crossing the island to where our boats lay. "It'll take another day to chop them out of the ice," Sun predicted.

"If there's ice, I can take care of that," I said, calling a flame to hand, then extinguishing it. Despite the sources of heat being winter-distant, my own Essence stirred at the prospect of an action I felt was right and true.

But first I must call upon Hermit Namath Dhak, to take proper leave. Despite clumpy snow falling, I sailed up the trail, aware that it was for the last time.

She was deep within her cave. Not sure of the etiquette when there is no door to knock upon, I called from outside the hanging vines.

She soon appeared, buried in furs and blankets. "Young Renti," she exclaimed.

"I came to say my farewell," I said, putting my hands together and performing a full court bow. It felt natural, though I'd been suppressing that instinct now for four years, almost five.

"Farewell? Come within, come within."

I explained quickly. She listened with an inscrutable expression, and at the end, she nodded slowly three times, a pensive, bobbing almost-bow, then muttered, "Walla walla walla! What must be must be: it is written that the old are never ready to give up the world before the young become eager to take it into their own hands. I, to my regret, was certainly one. You will do better than I, I feel certain, for you have learnt to listen, and I in my pride never would until it was too late."

She shuffled over to her trunk, then reached down into it. She brought up something small, wrapped in silk, and brought it to me, and then, to my surprise, offered it with both hands. "My beloved gave it to me when we married ourselves under the two moons, long, long ago. I kept it against need to leave this island, but now I feel certain I never will. Take it," she urged, and when I stood there uncertainly, "Is this not correct, you offer a gift with both hands?"

I extended my hands, but looked at her in question. "A gift? I beg pardon, this uncouth and reprehensible one did not think to bring a farewell gift for you —"

"We both know you don't have anything over in that camp of yours besides dirt," she said, pressing the silken thing onto my palms. It was surprisingly heavy. Her eyes gleamed with unshed tears as she said huskily, "Somehow, I believe that our fates have crossed to a purpose. If you are to discover my dear sister alive, will you remember me to her?"

"Your sister?"

"She was forced to marry your Imperial Grand Prince Lan Miluo. The fierce general who won the war, but who showed us mercy. I regret that my foolishness happened before she was out of childhood, so she would barely remember me. The last scrap of news that came my way, she was still alive, and she had a daughter, named Vaha. I hoped she might teach that child our ways."

The Cinnabar Princess! Hermit Namath Dhak had told me at the outset that she was related to the easterners' royal family, but I had been hesitant to bring up bad memories. "I know her," I said. "That is," I corrected quickly, "I've seen her. Never spoke to her. I was too young, and too insignificant, to be included in imperial family gatherings, except at the proper distance. But she has a wonderful reputation. For healing. And music."

"I wish I'd asked before," the hermit said. "I was reticent. It seemed you, like me, have some painful memories, and I thought surely you'd know little. Tell me now, tell me now."

"It truly is very little."

I told her what I knew. She listened silently, and though her head was bowed I think I saw the gleam of tears. But the wind was beginning to moan around the towering rocks, and she shooed me off. I bowed myself out.

When I got back to camp, I remembered the silken object clutched in my hand. It was a tael of pure gold.

EIGHTEEN

KOI WAS THE FIRST to point out that though Xianti, and Huyun Shandek, had searchers all over the northeast for Pangolin Ren, they were very unlikely to think that I would go in the opposite direction. That was what caused him to agree to this mad plan.

We rose early, made our bows to the elders, saying that we were going to venture on now that the pirates were gone. In gallant wanderer fashion, the elders accepted that; the pirates were gone, and wanderers wander.

I kept to myself my relief to see the last of that muddy, frozen spot. We were back on board our two boats by evening the next day, with what remained of our stores. On—full of laughter and poetry—saw to it that he and I were on the same boat, as before; when Cray and Sun stood uncertainly on the shore, looking from one group to the other, Cray said, "I'll go in the small one." She added, "We can always change between boats, can't we? If we sail together?"

Sun's eyes turned in question to On, who shrugged. I did not attempt to understand the unspoken communication between them as Sun shrugged back, and that was how it was.

"We have to be sparing with our stores. Which means a stop fairly soon," Fan pointed out, having ignored all this silent interaction as she pondered her map from the bow of the rowboat. Jai and Koi picked up the oars and sent them bumping over the small gray wavelets to the larger boat, then came back for On, Cray, and me.

For a time, we were all busy sweeping the detritus from the boats as best we could. The larger boat had a tiny hold that slept two, though I was told no one could sit up without crouching over. The rowboat, secured on the deck, could with a cover over it sleep a third.

Fan picked up the map again, looking uncertain. "Here's my fear. If any of us, looking the way we do now, turn up with a gold piece like that, the first thing any cautious merchant will assume is that we stole it."

"Ay, we ought to try where gallant wanderers are welcome."

"Who is the most respectable-looking among us?" Sun asked, eyeing us all anew. "Koi, I'm afraid that right now you look like a pirate captain."

True, honest Koi blushed to the ears as he raised the sail.

"On, you look like a thief, or a young master fallen in with a bad crowd."

"If I clean myself up?" On paused in raising our own sail, with my help.

"Perhaps."

Sun's eyes shifted to me. "When you draw yourself up like that, Ren, you are probably the most formidable. Not in the martial way. Jai and Koi both look like martial experts."

"Which we are," Jai gloated, tapping his fist against his broadening chest. If only his voice hadn't squeaked on that last word! But no one laughed.

Sun went on, "Fan, you look martial as well. Cray and I just look like refugees. No, it must be either Ren or On."

"It has to be me," On said. "Once I get myself cleaned up I can be a loafing young master, a role I have played many times. The advantage is that they will not remember me, or at least as myself, whereas Ren, whether you like it or not, your face is memorable."

I had not seen myself in a mirror for so long I had to take that on faith. They were the ones who saw my face. Not I, who merely wore it.

The slow, icy wind caught the sails, and we set sail for Suanek's Mercy, a small island known for its great temple. "We won't be able to trade our gold there, of course," Fan told us.

"The monks don't keep belongings, and the food will be vegetarian, but we can at least get water, and more than that, wash our things and get clean."

Everyone liked that idea—and so it was. These were not fighting monks, so we had to leave all weapons on our boats, but the two days we spent in the temple were very peaceful, with animals wandering in and out—including a young tiger. I had never realized that these splendid beasts were so huge. It was clear that this temple was very old, centuries at least, if the animals were that accustomed to living among humans.

"We can't go straight south," Fan said when we headed back to the boat, our things and ourselves clean again. "There are two naval bases before Te Gar, which has an enormous garrison."

"That is tempting fate," On agreed.

"If we go west, then south, we'll touch at Little Otters, which is the home of the Golden Blade sect, according to the chart."

Sun said, "My mother has relations among the Eel sect there. They've enclaves of the Boxwood Brethren, and the Ki are now there, too. They have competitions once each season. I say that because we might make it by Fire Wishes Festival, in which case there will be all kinds of booths selling everything."

"Can I compete?" Jai asked eagerly.

"If there's a competition," I said, hiding my reluctance. I did not know if the sense of urgency within me was the invisible command of fate, or simply the desire to be about my plan.

We found ourselves among several small craft when we neared the Otter Islands, so we knew we had not overshot the festival. Jai was delighted—and stood at the bow of the larger boat, working through his forms in a challenging way, for all to see. He was not the only one—on other boats and on a ship, martial artists exhibited their skills in spite of the icy weather.

I was glad to see a lot of makeshift booths and tents lined along the shore, the hills behind smooth and white from a coating of newly fallen snow. "If we can't find lodging, we can try the Eels," Sun said before we disembarked. "The women, that is."

"We can sleep on the boat," Koi said to Jai.

On only smiled, and I could almost see him contemplating which of his roles would net him comfortable lodging, for free.

He said to me, once we were ashore, "You only have the single tael, correct?"

"You know I spent the last of my earnings getting supplies before we reached Tortor. I believe I know how to shop wisely.

First I have to change the gold. I know better than to trust a merchant I want to purchase goods from for that. I see the sign for a money-changer, over there."

"That's a good start."

"From there I know what to do."

"Without being remembered?"

I sighed. "Please, O esteemed and benevolent teacher, instruct this ignorant and foolish—"

He snapped a fan open. In winter! But there it was, decorated with beautifully painted plum blossoms, and I knew that he was being either a roaming young master, or he was evolving some new role. "First. You take the time to look at everything. Second, when you mark likely sellers, buy one thing here, one there. Nothing all at once, unless you want them to remember you. If it turns out one has most of what you want, come back when a different seller is behind the table—they usually trade off, just as everywhere else."

This was excellent advice, and my impatience to get the buying over with dissipated. "Anything else?"

"Yes. The more finished the product, the more it costs. If you're willing to do your own sewing and embroidery—"

"I know that much. I planned to do my own sewing."

"Then you'll be able to afford twice as much."

And that is what we did.

As for the competitions, there were several rings, with duels going on at the same time. People bought hot food of various sorts, and brought it to watch.

Jai pressed Koi to join him in signing up. Cray surprised me by also signing up, Fan right behind her. Sun said she'd watch— but she changed her mind when it turned out the single inn only had floor space left, for which they were charging a swingeing amount. She and Fan went to the Eel enclave, and then came back with a few other young women. "They want you to compete as well," she said to Cray, and in an undervoice, "as the best of them are on the road. They can't look bad before the Brethren! If we do well, we're sure to get a room and maybe a meal for all four of us." She laughed silently.

As I knew that they were superlative at Eel form, there was a very good chance our lodgings would be taken care of.

On signed up for double stick, then said to me, "I'm number 187, and they're not even in the sixties yet. I've a suggestion. If you are really going to pretend to be your brother, you'll need coaching. Why not practice here, where no one knows either of you? See if you can get ordinary people to treat you like a boy instead of a girl?"

"But I haven't bought anything yet."

"You can wear my clean tunic. You're not that much shorter than I."

"I'll have to do some adjusting first," I protested, blushing as I indicated my bosom, which would need to be flattened.

To my surprise, he said, "If you move well, no one is going to notice in these loose, thick winter clothes. Just pull it on as an extra layer."

This we did, and the coaching ensued. I expected to lengthen my strides, but I did not expect to be told to shift my point of balance from hips to shoulders. That brought back those early dance lessons, in which I was taught that the center of balance was my hips. I'd assumed that true of everyone, without really noticing it wasn't. Men and women, complements and contrasts, itself a balance, to which he retorted with a cascade of poetry about the Golden Point of Balance in the world of material things.

When we got a meal, he had me copy his movements. Generalizing severely, men move their arms elbows out. Shoulders open. They try to be bigger, taking more space. Women keep elbows in, trying to be smaller. Conscious now of the small ways in which hands handle dishes, I was annoyed to discover that I still had not shed court manners when eating.

There is little to be said about the purchases, after which I kept an eye on what sorts of things some of the rich young men favored in their embroidery. I purchased plenty of silk thread, and then it was time for the competition. On—as usual—had signed up under yet a new name.

Cray won bout after bout in the fan competition, finally ceding a respectable third place to a short, fast woman of about thirty. This woman moved like an adventurer—but On was right. Her balance point was her hips.

Jai had signed up for all weapons. He got turfed out with halberd, but made it respectably far in the sword competition, easily the most popular sport. Koi calmly faced expert after expert, and ended up at the top of the day's competition, which meant he was supposed to return the following day—the actual festival day—in order to duel against the experts in other weapons. Sun did even better than Cray, which surprised me. The best were Fan and Koi, no surprise.

On won his double-stick match, but didn't go back again. "I

know how good I am," he said to me privately, before he took off for his own purposes, leaving me to wander about. "Practice!" he exhorted me before going off after a strolling party of wealthy-looking young masters with fine cloaks and long, loose hair.

I had never before paid attention to the speculative subtleties of eye to eye except to watch for threat. I'd never flirted. Now I became conscious of the silent assessment always going on as pairs and threes and larger groups met, chatted, and parted. Talked, laughed, ate, drank, danced. If I concentrated on my walk and demeanor, I won speculative looks from girls. And boys, too, some of those puzzled. I tried to shift my arms the way On had demonstrated, and if those looking for girls to flirt with faded away, triumph leaped within me.

I slowly gained confidence, trying to be bigger — to claim more than my share of space. It was lucky that for four years I had already been trying to break the training of tiny silent court steps. For the most part I was successful, especially as the sun dropped behind the hills, though too much of that caught the eye of some whose attitude made it clear they were looking for competition — if not trouble.

That night, Sun achieved for us girls a room at the Eel conclave. I used On's tunic as a pattern as I carefully cut out the silk I'd bought, one the blue of a summer dawn, the other a more sober but very showy lavender. That one I intended to make even more showy by embroidering green dragonflies and intertwined peonies, in white, deep blue, and crimson.

I assumed that On had lodged with the boys, but the next day, when we all met, having eaten and made what purchases we wished (I'd shared out a string of a hundred moons to each), everyone was there but On.

"The tide is about to turn," Fan stated the obvious as she faced us. "As soon as you collect On, Jai, you know how to navigate. It'll be easy — the winds ought to take you straight down to Lan."

She glanced at each of us, clearly torn between going with us and staying, but as her eyes strayed toward the competition ring, I saw the decision in her face. She'd stay because there were Falcons among the gallant wanderers, because she might hear a scrap of something about Dinek and the Pangolins, and that was where her heart lay.

"Thank you for all you've done," I began.

She interrupted, saying roughly, "When it gets to the

gratitude, I'm gone. I trust we meet again. May the gods watch over you."

A quick clasp of her hands in a bow, then she hitched her things over her shoulder and strode off toward the competition rings, leaving everyone staring after her.

Jai misinterpreted those looks. "If we're staying, Koi can go against the masters," Jai said, not hiding his eagerness.

Koi said only, "We're missing On—"

There was a rustle among strollers, and On appeared at a run, tassels dancing. "I'm ready," he said. And to me, with a flourish of triumph, "Look what I won for you."

He held out a gorgeous man's fan with a long crimson tassel hanging down. There was also a cord for decorating a sword sheath, tied in the longevity knot with a long, expensive tassel. I had not even thought about such accessories. "Won two poetry contests," he proclaimed.

"And nearly missed our tide," Jai said, but without heat.

NINETEEN

She looks out over the ranks of purple robes, of scarlet, of green,
The hard-earned hats with wisdom-tassels.
She asks if they contemplate
Not the Why but the When of the Great Phoenix who reminded her of
humble Ys:
There was nobody poorer, nobody purer.

THREE STORMS OVERTOOK US, but like most winter storms, they came out of the north and thus sped us on our way. Snow gave way to sleet, and then to rain, as we began to glimpse plane trees again. We were coming into rice lands, welcome to us all. During that time, we experienced a shift among the boats' occupants, with me going to the larger boat so that I could huddle in the cramped space below the deck to do my embroidery.

With this taking up my concentration, I told Koi that I was giving up on Circle without a board. "If you change your mind, I'm here," was all he said. I was profoundly disappointed in myself, but I had to accept my limits. My many limits.

Cray and On both helped me sew. As the fabric and silk began to transform into the clothes of our various roles, we raced over gray waters under gray skies. We stopped again for supplies, and On spotted on a tray a handsome hair clasp of the sort a modest prince might wear while traveling. He traded a jeweled earring for it—an earring I didn't even know he had, as

I had never seen his On Lu role among the stylish young nobles of a city. But I remembered his brother's jade that he kept hidden in his clothes. He must have more such treasures. Now, one fewer.

Then back to the journey, until one night my dreams filled with a golden effulgence bright as daylight. The dream was so vivid that I could see the morning sun limning a stray hair on Koi's forehead, and catching in the threads of his worn gray tunic. Beyond him, Sun gazed upward, glowing in silver light as a flock of snow-white cranes wheeled above her head, calling down. In the midst of them, glowing golden like the sun at dawn, a phoenix drifted, long tail feathers rippling slowly like the sea grass below us.

There you are, the phoenix said to me. *You are the one they follow willingly. Need you my granddaughter?*

In my dream, I stepped on Sagacious Blade, and the warmth of Essence radiated from the phoenix, drawing me over the tranquil, lucent waters. The world had stilled as I floated between sea and sky, the dawning sun's heat on my back. *It is not her quest*, I said to the phoenix. *But I won't decide for her. It's important to me that any who come with me come of their own will.*

Her father desires her to learn the ways of the cranes before she settles her feet on her mother's path or takes to wing in the skies.

I scarcely knew Sun. I did remember the rumors of those days in the scrape above the imperial city, when the other girls said that her father was reputed to be a crane. Demon was always the next word, an easy word for the uncanny. But I was already aware that the unseen world was as vital, and as natural, a part of the universe as the world of the five human senses.

I reflected. Sun was not interested in my self-appointed task. She was with us for the company, for the adventure. But that was for her to say, and so I told the phoenix.

There will be an island, the phoenix responded. *Land.*

It was a command, but the tender authority of a grand-mother, and not of a demon or god. That is, there was no threat in it. The phoenix flew toward the morning stars still dimly glimmering, and I was asleep again.

I woke to the memory of that dream just before true dawn. It had been so intensely vivid, so lucid, that I was certain it had been real in some sense. I crawled up onto the deck, reaching gratefully for the tea we kept on the boil for all the watches. Fan, who was ready to sleep after a night watch, yawned.

I said, "We have to go west."

"West?" Jai repeated doubtfully. There was no sign of any island save a few dragons teeth behind us, to the northeast. "Why?"

"Can you just set the sail and helm?" I said, not wanting to say that I'd been given a command in a dream. "Only for the day."

He shrugged, clearly too tired to debate, and after angling sail and helm properly for me, so I'd only have to tend them, he went to sleep. On, on the small boat, saw the change in direction, and followed, and we headed into such flat water our wake rilled out slowly. The wind was barely a breeze, yet we moved steadily, until a jut on the western horizon turned into a small island whose single great cone of a mountain smoked lazily. I sensed the molten rock below, surrounding a young dragon in its slumber. 'Young' I write, but it's impossible to measure their age in human terms. I only knew that it would stir, and fly, soon—though that soon might be a year, five years, or five hundred years.

The morning sun had risen by then, revealing no village. There was only a simple pagoda. As we neared, I could see that before it stood a wind-smoothed statue so very old that its contours were mere hints of a motherly form: Ys, the goddess of the common people. Ys, who had fashioned the first humans out of clay, and gave them fire, and rice, and wool to weave into clothing. Atop the statue a golden gleam, as if something reflected the radiance of the morning sun.

Around this pagoda and statue flew thousands and thousands of birds. Some hopped and flitted close to water and sand, poking for food. The middle layer was the largest, a swarm in great, dizzying circles. Then a third layer very high up, motionless against the sky as they drifted on currents.

This was a sacred place.

Out of the mass of birds a formation flew, distinct long-winged shapes that resolved into not the common cranes with black necks and heads, who dwelt on mountain tops, but those with white throats and silver heads.

The cacophony of screeches, caws, shrill whistles, and squawks had woken the night watch sleepers. Everyone was on deck on both boats, looking upward.

"Papa," Sun exclaimed, eyeing the foremost bird. "Just another year?"

The cranes circled.

Her shoulders slumped, but she did not seem desolated. She said to Cray, "It was fun partnering with you. But I did promise, once I turned eighteen. If I can, I'll find you. I really like being a Falcon. And you are so fun," she called to On, who clasped his hands to her.

She stooped to pick up her carryall. "It's gonna be so cold," she muttered, and stepped to the rail.

"We can row you," Koi said.

"I'll still have to get wet," she replied. "Look at that long beach. The rowboat will ground long before we can get to dry sand."

"I'll take you," I said. "It's only a short distance."

I could see she was going to protest, then she looked at the water, and agreed. "Just don't drop me," she muttered. "Please."

"It's all right," I said. "I flew On once before, and I didn't drop him."

I easily took her to the shore. As we approached, most of the birds took flight in a thunder of wings, scolding in protest. Some remained, ignoring us. I set her down before the statue, which I saw was not bespattered, though birds are messy creatures. Perhaps they knew to avoid it, or perhaps it had simply been washed clean by wind and rain. Though I had no incense, I knelt to bow three times.

When I rose, I blinked up at the phoenix sitting atop the statue. This was a real phoenix, as rare as a qilin. She was gold, but other shades gleamed subtly in the pure light of morning: palest cream in the soft feathers of her underside, rose-gold along her wings, a hint of blue in the long curling feathers that crowned her head and swept in a graceful arc over her back.

Was she there on the statue of Ys to remind me not to forget the humble creatures of the world, those without voice, those without power? That lesson had burned itself into my brain when I was aboard the slave ship, among the refugees. Or was there a promise in the liminality of the unseen world I sensed around me? Or was she merely flying by, utterly indifferent to human affairs?

Time would tell. I had to get back to the ship, and Sun was already walking away, almost obscured by cranes. Whatever was to happen next was apparently not for the eyes of other humans.

I stepped on Sagacious Blade and rose into the air slowly, so as not to frighten the birds. Sun half-turned, and called to me,

"Thank you, Ren. Be kind to On, will you, when you're ready? He needs it more than he will ever say."

I clasped my hands to her in promise, flew across the water and landed on the boat.

We set sail again. That eerie windless current that did not shake the battens brought us out again, to where the northern bluster caught the sail, and we glided out to sea.

TWENTY

WE TALKED ABOUT ROLES. Koi and Cray knew the rules governing servant behavior, of course, having spent their childhoods in the imperial palace. As a bodyguard, Jai needed only to maintain silence — hardest of all lessons, perhaps — and to remember to bow.

On said he would remain with the boats. After all, someone had to, he reasoned. I was skeptical about this, but said nothing because of who he was, and the somewhat distant danger of chance recognition, for during our many conversations while sailing together, I'd learned that his paternal grandmother's twin had been sent to the ancestral Lan island as a bride when she was sixteen. Though On did not know if she was even alive, if any of her servants still lived, they might see his beloved grandfather in his face.

"I've been wondering this past year or so if it was that distant marriage between our families that caused the emperor to look for an excuse to massacre my clan?" On muttered to me a few days before we landed; the two of us were alone on the smaller boat as I practiced being Banti.

I was going to deny this, then remembered that horrible story about the monk who sold the emperor a poisoned elixir to bring sons, resulting in barrenness for most of the men of the imperial family.

"It's a possibility," I had to admit. I told him that sordid story, adding at the end, "I can believe that if he thought that there would be no more Lan sons through Lan fathers, and that someone in court might think of looking to the Kwais for a male heir, he would make such an order in secret."

Again, there was the question: what about sons from daughters? Were not Lan daughters' sons equally Lans? Ayah, we knew they were. And furthermore the lawmakers also knew. In cases of old and venerable families having no sons to tend the ancestral graves, it was legal to make matrilocal marriages, bringing a son in to marry a daughter of the house, so that the matrilocal husband's son would inherit and carry on the name. But as was true back to ancient history, the lawmakers — all men — were preoccupied solely with sons begetting sons.

I said nothing further about his refusing to be part of the landing party, given how good he was at disguise. My suspicion was that he wanted to be free to spy about. And if he did, surely it would be to our benefit. I could trust him for that.

Then I got back to practice. I had to make my adopted movements as natural as I could. Beginning with wearing my sword at my sash, dangling maddeningly unless I kept a hand on the hilt, or clapped it by my forearm against my side. On assured me that boys had to practice with that as well.

Bolstered by the others assuring me from the other boat that I looked like Banti (Fan and Jai saying only that I looked like a youth), I worked hard at it as I helped tend the boat. Take the rope as a boy would. Sit on the bench with knees apart, forearm on a thigh, as a boy would. Take the cup elbow out as a boy would. If I had to tip my head, move my head and shoulders as one.

A hunted prince is not expected to turn up with an army at his back. Indeed, few would welcome such. However, even a hunted prince is expected to arrive as a prince, and not a beggar, which means an entourage. I now had Koi and Cray as servants in gray, but wearing the side-split robes, trousers, and boots, of defense-trained servants, and Jai was to be a bodyguard. Though we now had scarcely two silvers' worth of small coins left of Hermit Namath's bounty, we presented a respectable — but not threatening — face as we sailed along Lan's long coast toward the main harbor. Which, like Benevolent Winds' main harbor, faced east, and not south.

Being in fishing boats, we were not expected to fly banners. I'd prepared a white flag just in case, but no one paid us any heed as we anchored unexpectedly close to the main wharfs. At first this surprised me, given that this was the main harbor of a huge, powerful island. But once we'd rowed the short distance to the wharf and had a chance to look around, we saw that there was less trade than one would expect.

This impression did not alter as we walked up toward the city's East Wall, I wearing my fine new lavender outer robe with the dragonflies, which I'd finished embroidering only that morning.

The gates stood open. The guards looked us over, largely with disinterest. We advanced up the main thoroughfare, and I gained an impression of general shabbiness: the unswept street, broken roof ornaments and missing tiles stuffed with detritus, here and there faded door couplets that at a glance seemed to go back a year or even two, every couplet an earnest wish for prosperity and peace.

About half the tea shops and eateries were closed. In the few we saw open, no delicious smells emerged; it seemed that people were just drinking tea, not eating. From the pinched faces of many of the laborers on the street, it appeared that few were eating enough. Indeed street vendors were rare, and those we saw all seemed to be selling steamed sweet potatoes or grilled fish.

A bit farther on, and the hanging banners from the lamppost were the white of mourning, ragged-edged as happens in the second year or infrequent third year. The only things that saved this vista from dreariness were the plane trees growing in clusters, bamboo and apricot blooming, and the water dishes at street corners for passing dogs and other animals.

Despite these dishes, the air of neglect caused Cray to whisper under her breath, "Not good. Not good."

Who had died? The others left it to me to speak or not speak. I decided to save all questions for my interview, as there was enough tension in the air, in addition to the general dilapidation, to cause me to suspect that asking anything was certain to make someone wonder who was asking and why.

People did not seem to be chatting on that street. Going about business, yes. But idlers, children playing about, oldsters sitting on benches with their tea—all these signs of ease were missing, and could not be entirely laid to winter, as the air was hazy but fine, coldest in the shadows, this far south. The street meandered in an arc so that the palace could be laid out properly, entrance to the south. We reached the outer gates to the palace, and this time we were stopped. "Your business?" said the right-hand guard, whose spear was in his left.

"Envoy." I spoke my first word as Lan Banti while holding out the small white banner I'd sewed with the grand prince's crimson firedragon in the corner.

The guard raked us over with his eyes, and Granny Zim said, "It's your youth that will get you by. The indifference I hear is close to despair, as well as long-endured pain." I saw then that the guard's hanging right hand was an empty sleeve from the elbow down.

The other guard had all his limbs, but I spotted a walking stick in the shadows between some ornamental carving in the stone archway. This was not at all a good sign in gate guards, who are customarily burly and intimidating.

"Envoys," he repeated after a wait during which a fly buzzed about our heads. "Go through."

We did, stepping around an undisturbed pile of horse droppings, a thing I would have thought unheard of at the entrance to a prince's palace. When we reached the palace itself, guards barred our way. These guards wore a different aspect, more threatening. No one was maimed, though I did see scars here and there.

Koi, the most intimidating of us, stepped forward, sketching the briefest salute, and said woodenly, "My young master is here to speak to the heir to Prince Lan of the ancestral Lan Island."

"Weapons here," one barked.

I hated leaving Sagacious Blade behind. Though I knew I could call her to me, and I also knew that Granny Zim could hear me, she would not be able to hear anyone I spoke to unless the conversation was in her proximity. She could only hear them through me, which means she must hear through my limitations. Thus I'd be cut off from her vital assessing for truth in this knife-blade-balance situation. But those hard eyes from all four guards made it clear that to take a step over the threshold while armed was to invite exactly the sort of situation I wanted to avoid.

I unhooked Sagacious Blade from my sash. The others followed me, and then a tall, thin graywing emerged from the shadows. What little was visible of his hair around the distinctive hat with the wings extending to either side was gray, his earlobes pendulous.

The graywing bowed. His voice was light though he was so tall, almost a whisper as he said, "Might this lowly Steward Plumflower be honored with the esteemed name of the visitor?"

As he spoke, his gaze searched among us, coming back to me twice, three times. I barely caught the hitch of breath that meant he'd recognized my family features. Since he'd recognized me, I said as if I'd intended to all along, "This insignificant one is Lan Banti, cousin to Prince Kandati, heir to the Grand Prince of Lan."

Steward Plumflower bowed very low. "This unhappy one is desolated to inform the esteemed relation of our grand prince that perhaps there is news that did not reach northwards? The Prince of Lan was lost in a shipwreck...?"

I was startled enough to exclaim, "You mean Cousin Kandati is now ruling?" My voice came out too loud, but sharp rather than high. I had to rein myself back into court habit.

Graywing Plumflower bowed assent. And that explained the mourning banners in the city.

Another graywing turned up, one hand emerging from his sleeves long enough to make a sign too brief to catch, and Graywing Plumflower said, "If the esteemed visitor will honor us by coming this way..."

We left our weapons.

Any hope that the interview would take place close by was summarily squashed. No outer hall for us. Which might be a good thing. Fewer witnesses, I told myself as we were led through the public building and out to a very fine garden still bedded for winter, except for blossoming dogwood and wintersweet. I concentrated on my stride, heels striking first, not the smooth court gate achieved by walking on the balls of my feet. The ring of my bootheels on the stone flags reassured me as I tried to radiate a confidence I not feel.

On the other side of the arched bridge lay the private buildings and side-yards. The graywing took us into the main hall, to a study paneled in fine boxwood, with silken hangings depicting orchid blossoms of all the seasons. A model house stood in one corner, lifelike to the tiny guardians on the roof corners. A cat face or two peered out through open windows, then vanished at our attention.

Behind an enormous desk sat a slight figure, testaments

stacked to either side. He held a crystal piece up to his eyes with one hand as the other opened the testaments.

Behind him, to the right, stood a general in armor, with a golden dragon worked into the breastplate. His eyes flicked over us all before we'd taken two steps into the room, but he did not move.

The young man at the desk started up as he dropped the crystal piece. "Who…"

"You remember me, Cousin? Banti? Second son of Lan Kaiza?" I prompted.

Kandati snatched up the crystal, and for a moment a huge eye peered at me, flattened and enlarged. He stopped when he saw Koi, and I saw complete recognition there, and the quick flare of a smile before he smoothed his face.

Koi stood head bowed, a posture it pained me to see him in.

Kandati dropped the crystal piece again. "I thought you looked familiar, Cousin Banti." His gaze flicked sideways toward the general, his entire body stiff, then he said, "Permit me the honor to introduce Left General of the Dragon Circle Zoa Huek. Left General Zoa, my cousin Lan Banti. For the sake of filial piety, for we are still in mourning for our respective relations, I will overlook, ah, questions of status in favor of heeding the … the treaty-defined period for envoys."

In other words, no one was to arrest us for three days. But his tone was tentative, more plea than command.

Ayah! We'd talked enough about this, though being presented with the real situation did make my heart bang hard against my ribs. I strove to assume some of my brother's breezy manner as I said, "Most kind, most kind. What a long journey! Do not ask how tired of I am of boats. And fish!"

"I can promise hot meals and a dry bed that isn't heaving on waves. Though we are not as sumptuous as we've been in the past, I remember how much you liked onion pancakes in the past, and pickled peppers."

"I still like onion pancakes," I said, and we then lurched awkwardly forward in a falsely cheery conversation about our last meeting, and the fine repasts Kandati had shared with me during that visit. I did not neglect to mention the cats he'd had to leave behind, venerable animals now, but very much alive — when last I saw. He asked after them by name and I assured him of their wellbeing, reflecting that palace cats are very good at looking out for themselves.

During that chatter I noted Kandati's tension. I noted the

general standing there, listening, watching. I did not remember his name—no surprise there—but Koi might know something of him, to be discussed as soon as we were alone.

When the subject of Kandati's visit to the imperial island had been thoroughly thrashed out, he stole the most furtive of glances in the general's direction, then cleared his throat. "And so, Banti, you're here as an envoy? For…"

"Grand Prince Yiulo, with whom I had been staying since I left the imperial city," I said. And, completely speciously, "He had a message that I was to speak to your much-respected and esteemed father, but I am sorry to see that I have come too late."

The general spoke for the first time, before Kandati could. "What is the message?"

We had talked this out, too. "Ayah, he is old and tired, and wishes to die in peace and accord with his family. He asked me to come invite his old and trusted distant nephew to unite with him in approaching our imperial relation, Emperor Koza to make peace with all the family." We had decided that as false messages go, this one would cause the least harm.

At the mention of the emperor, everyone clasped hands, gesturing eastward instead of southward, a reminder of how very far we had sailed.

"That … is laudable," Kandati said, his eyes shifting. He was clearly struggling for something to say.

I continued as smoothly as possible, "Which I trust we can speak about over the next three days?" And I faked a yawn, then begged pardon.

"Yes, yes, of course," Kandati said.

At that moment a door opened, and in walked a girl around my age. She was as plump as a steamed bun, her face round as an apple, her undyed mourning elaborate, unlike the simple robes of the two servants at her heels. That meant she was a person of consequence. She, like the two maids, carried a tray bearing fine porcelain. The maids carried snacks. A trio of gray cats trotted at their heels, tails high.

"My dear husband," she said in a high trill. "Here I am! I'm so sorry to be late—you know the distance from the kitchen—some snacks, though this time of year we've—here, permit this lowly wife to pour out some—get down off the desk, Rain! Thistle!"

Here, after the rush of words, and flapping her sleeves at dish-sniffing cats, she looked expectantly. Kandati stiffly introduced us, his voice self-conscious as he said the words 'my wife,' then her name, Shu Min.

"You are newly married? Congratulations! I wish you many years of happiness and progeny." I spoke the traditional words as Shu Min began to set out the cups, fussing unnecessarily as she set them just so. She reminded me of a twittering bird as she carried on a sort of broken conversation under her breath, never quite finishing a sentence, and fussing softly at the two half-grown kittens intent on getting to the snacks.

"My father desired to see us wed before he sailed to the imperial city," Kandati said. "Though I know we were considered young. But we've always known it was to happen."

Shu Min looked up from pouring the tea, and beamed at me. "I've lived here ever since I was ten. My dearest Madam thought I ought to get used to—oh, oh, oh, I spilled *again!*" Her voice rose as she looked in dismay at my cup. "I never seem to get it— you must not think Madam to blame for my mistakes—she shows me over and over…" Still twittering, Shu Min bustled up to my side, mopping busily, her sleeves fluttering and flapping, one getting into the spilled tea. The cats, undeterred by her flapping and gentle scolding, were not proof against spilled liquid, and took off for the door.

Then she backed away, twittering more and apologizing for being so clumsy and stupid as she set out the cups for Kandati and the general. Once they had tea, she shooed the maids out, backing herself as she mopped at her stained sleeve—then at the door, she turned to exclaim, "Ayah, I nearly forgot, husband. I was to say, Graywing Lavender waits outside to take your esteemed guest to a room to—that is, I ought to say that a meal will be served on the hour—vegetarian, you know, while we're mourning—but I assure you there will at least be *no fish!*" On this triumphant, shrill note she made her exit.

I glanced at the general, whose tightened mouth did not quite hide his disdain, as Kandati blushed deeply. He said self-consciously to me, "Banti, if you'd like to withdraw, I can summon Lavender. I'll finish things here, and we can chat more over dinner?"

I assented, Kandati called, "Lavender!" the door opened, and in glided a graywing as short at Plumflower had been tall. "Show Prince Banti to a room so he can rest. Banti, I'll send a servant when we dine," Kandati said.

I clasped my hands, and we started out, that shrill *no fish* still echoing in my ears. Why would she say that? Then I remembered my blathering at the start of the conversation, about how the journey had been tiring and I was sick of fish. The obvious struck me—of course we were listened to by unseen others. That was always the way in a palace. At the very least, servants stood by, waiting for orders.

And surely she'd know that Banti would know that. Unless it was a general warning… About the room I was shortly to be in?

We traveled to the guest wing, and outside the door, Graywing Lavender bowed, saying softly, "I am ordered to conduct your personal guard to comfortable quarters with our household guard."

This was no more than we'd planned for. Koi and Cray were dressed as my personal servants, she for my clothes and he for me, and we watched Jai go off with Lavender—his orders being to listen to guard talk.

My heart lifted when I discovered that the guest suite I was given lay on the ground floor. That meant a tile bath with fresh, hot water, because most palaces were built over thermal springs. The rest of the suite was clean, full of old furnishings carefully mended, the screens traditional in theme. The windows were a little open. For cats? Two silent servants stood by, in mourning. With my back to them, I gave the old gardener's sign for silence, and danger. Koi did not so much as blink.

I sent both servants off with orders for hot tea and snacks. These I would put outside the window for On—if cats could come in, food could go out—and then we quickly took turns bathing the salt water from our clothes and ourselves. I gave Cray my clothes to hang with hers to dry, because the servants would of course be snooping, and we did not yet know to whom they would report.

The cats provided a suitable subject for talk. Mother had never permitted any animals in the living areas of the palace. We'd had to go out to the yard to play with them, and given how busy I'd been kept, my time with my brothers' pets had been limited. It startled me to see cats coming and going everywhere, but the servants seemed to regard cleaning up after them, and seeing that water dishes were fresh, as part of their duties.

A servant came to get me when a distant gong crashed.

The entire family was at dinner, which included several elderly women. My eye was drawn immediately to the grandmother, first in rank. Aged she was, but she wore the older style of headdress with an air of fashion. It suited her face, in which I saw a resemblance to On in the shape of her forehead, and in her mobile mouth. On Kandati's side, there was only one elderly uncle, him, and me. It was odd to sit on the men's side, a bit as if I looked in a mirror reflection of the customary imperial dining hall.

The food might have been considered poor by court standards, but after weeks of boiled cabbage, cooked and dried fish, and little else save wild garlic and the rare, hoarded pepper for flavor, it was the height of luxury for me. Glutinous rice balls! Dumplings! Though not many of each. There were exactly two onion pancakes at my place—and I noticed everyone else had one.

Otherwise the atmosphere was tedious and tense both, an unlikely and thoroughly unwelcome combination. I had plenty of time to scold myself for this dangerous blunder. What could I have realistically expected to accomplish? Kandati was nervous the entire time, and his wife chattered strings of broken phrases in that irritatingly shrill voice. At first I amused myself counting up every time she finished a sentence, while paying no attention to what she was saying, but that soon palled. Very soon.

I practiced my role as Banti, and responded with courtly politesse, every utterance praise, until Kandati said, "I apologize for the lack of entertainment."

"Not to be expected during mourning," I replied, bowing. Was I free? Except when would we be able to talk?

No, *if* we'd be able...

"If you would care to accompany me to the ancestral hall for the mourning ritual, I know my esteemed and lamented father would appreciate the honor. After which, my mother, aunts, and Min like to hear sutras."

What could I do but bow and accept? Glad that my place as the youngest, and a girl, had been to kneel directly behind Second Brother Banti, I knew exactly how he would behave— how he'd bow, and to what degree. Servants tenderly led the grandmother off, along with the oldest aunts, leaving two aunts, Kandati's mother, and Min to follow us, heads down, the servants behind them.

Kandati poured out wine before the altar, lit three incense sticks, and made nine full forehead-to-the-floor bows. Then it was my turn. After me, the women, in rank order.

Then Steward Plumflower conducted us to a windowless side chamber, where often coffins were set. It smelled of mourning incense. Here, tea things had been put out, the kettle boiling on a warmer. I saw the other graywing, Lavender, standing respectfully with a long scroll in hand. Further, there was a table on which paper had been placed, with inkstones and brushes.

Shu Min was there, fluttering about, apologizing and disclaiming and explaining in a tangle of words that during their nightly ritual, when Kandati was moved to write sutras, it was her privilege to grind the ink for him.

Steward Plumflower closed the door—with himself outside it—Graywing Lavender opened the scroll and began to read sutras in a mellifluous voice.

And Shu Min put her finger to her lips, gesturing me to the table next to Kandati.

Who was writing.

He pointed to the paper, on which I read: *Did you say anything in the guest suite?*

He handed me the writing brush. Surprised, I wrote: *Nothing but talk about baths.*

Kandati and Shu Min exchanged triumphant looks, and I knew that indeed, that comment about fish had had the import I'd guessed at!

Kandati scribbled, *What happened in the imperial palace? Father said that if your father truly turned criminal and rebel, then everyone in the empire was guilty. It was one reason why he wanted to go to the emperor himself, to plead before the throne. Was Xianti behind it?*

I thought back to my brief meeting with Banti aboard Yiuti's flagship. He had explained quickly what had happened that horrible day when my family was arrested. It had been Banti they came for first—that I remembered well, as I'd gone to seek him.

He'd explained to me that when he discovered the imperial guards coming to arrest him for something Yiuti had done, he went straight to Yiuti—who took Banti to his grandfather, the only person powerful enough to act. Any other friend he hid with would suffer for it.

Imperial highness Grand-Uncle Yiulo had swept them away from the palace, and thence the imperial island. Banti had not known about Father and Mother and First Brother being arrested until they landed at one of the grand prince's palaces up north, whence they caught up with news by virtue of the grand prince's own pigeons.

I was not permitted to go back to the imperial palace (I wrote, as

Kandati and Shu Min read over my shoulder). *Imperial highness Grand-Uncle Yiulo pointed out that there was nothing I could do but join the family in prison, which he deemed more unfilial than staying free and working to defeat Xianti. Ministers' sons joined us in hiding. They agreed — all their fathers sent them to safety. My cousin Oraiti, too. But there is a stalemate, and I've come to you.*

Then there began, in writing, a quick, scrawled conversation as Graywing Lavender droned on and on for the benefit of any listening ears outside, and the ladies sat listening or sewing. Each time a piece of paper was filled, Shu Min twisted it up, and fed it by bits into the fire beneath the tea kettle. Heavy incense burned at various places around the room, covering the smell.

I can remember entire conversations, but not that disjointed cascade of scratches and scribbles.

Here is what I learned: Kandati's father, Prince Lan Louza, who'd remained scrupulously loyal despite the steady increase in taxes and other demands under the previous emperor, endured two years under Emperor Koza, having had the taxes doubled twice, and the conscript requirements raised twice — the age extended down to thirteen-year-olds, reason given: to be trained for two years before being put in the field. But the few severely wounded men who returned bore with their scars and missing limbs the grim tidings that boys were being sent to fight before they were ready.

Kandati protested that the Lans had prided themselves on supporting the imperial branch of the family. It was their honor to serve as the emperor's wellspring. But that well was running dry.

Prince Louza first tried writing to my father after word came of Emperor Koza's ascent to the dragon throne. When word came back that Father had been arrested, that shocked the Lans. Prince Louza wrote to several trusted ministers, and while those ships made their way from one end of the empire to the other, he dealt with affairs, including the joyful event of his son's wedding. Then he took ship, intending to plead his case before Koza.

Silence for nearly a year, then word came back — brought by Left General Zoa Huek of the Dragon Circle — that the Prince of Lan had died along with all passengers and crew in a shipwreck a week outside of the imperial island. No, they had been missed by the naval patrols due to a storm. All they found was wreckage floating, and rumor of pirates.

Pirates, that close to the imperial island? Who would dare?

That was one of many questions unanswered. General Zoa came as advisor to the young prince, his considerable force took over the palace—and its severely diminished defense—and every order must be seen by the general. His servants moved into the palace to serve, but they soon discovered that everything they said and did got reported.

Zoa did nothing directly, but certain people vanished, never to be heard from again.

The Lans' only defense was certain loyal servants who found out by painstaking care who the spies were. The family's only time for communication was this ritual each evening, something they'd stumbled on after those first agonized weeks of true grieving. Kandati and Shu Min did not even have the privacy of the bedroom, as an imperial-palace-trained personal servant was on night duty, a gift from the emperor himself. Listening to every word.

General Zoa despised Shu Min, who promptly became more stupid, thus gaining a limited amount of freedom. She tried to get a message to her own family, until Zoa's people killed all their birds.

Kandati's eyes reddened when he wrote that: *They killed our birds. The family had raised them for generations. They not only flew to places all over the island, they knew each of us — we all had the task of feeding and caring for them from the time we were small.*

Shu Min took the brush for the first and only time. I noticed her wrist bone protruding from the worn hem of her sleeve, and realized that she ought to have been much rounder, for she had broad bones. Though she did not look thin next to Kandati, she was too meager for her proper size.

Her eyelids glimmered with tears as she wrote in emphatic strokes: *Every day mothers come to me, saying that the family has to sell their children into service in order to get them fed. Yet all we hear from the imperial island is, it's never enough, we are hoarding, we are disloyal. I pray they become vipers in their new life, and will come and bite Zoa in the night.* After which husband and wife exchanged sad smiles as she burned that, too.

Kandati was bound by invisible fetters. He could do nothing, command nothing, save household matters and to an extent the household guard, veterans all. He could try to give orders, but unless Zoa endorsed them, they were as whispers to the wind.

It seemed a hopeless situation. Had I pushed us into a thousand pains and ten thousand punishments? No! I refused to acknowledge defeat. If I was not actually in prison, I could act. I must act.

Lavender was reaching the end of the sutras. It was time to part for the night.

I scribbled a last question:

What would you do if you could?

The answer was immediate: *Turn to the Prince of Ran, who commands the entire western fleet against the encroachments of the westerners.*

Shu Min read that and turned to me with her hands clasped in prayer, before she burned that paper, too. I watched the ink catch fire a heartbeat before the paper, so that the words appeared to be written in gold fire.

Then it was gone, the sutras finished, and husband and wife straightened up, thumbing their eyes dry. We filed out in rank order, bowed once more before our ancestors, and I headed back to the guest suite, absently stooping now and then to pet a cat or two in case I was watched.

TWENTY-ONE

She told the ragged scholar:
There is no demon to blame, no inauspicious fate —
When a dragon scorns what he has,
He is enslaved by what he desires.

WHEN I GOT TO the guest suite, I tapped my lips and my ears, and Cray and Koi nodded. Then I chattered aloud about cats, and how incredibly boring it was to have to sit through an evening of sutras, but no one could say that Cousin Kandati was not filial, for he and his family observed the prayers every night.

While I blabbered, I searched the rooms for pen, ink, and paper — to find none.

"Ayah, I could sleep for a month," I declared. I looked between the two, and mimed going out the window on the sword, then pointed at Koi. He blanched — he clearly did not like the idea of flying on a sword. Cray gestured that she would remain, moving between the rooms as if she were the three of us.

Koi looked stolid as I called Sagacious Blade to me. Then I moved to the window and cautiously glanced out for sentries or listening ears. There was nothing but the empty snack plates. No, not empty. The curls of lychee peels lay on them. But there had been no lychee on those snack plates. That had to be On — and if I was right, I wouldn't have to search.

I gestured to Koi, then cast the obscuring charm over us both before climbing out the window. Koi followed, and I laid the sword on the tiles, stepped on it, and gestured Koi to step behind me and hold on.

He did, cautiously. Tentatively. And whoosh, there it was, that fire of proximity. I'd sometimes found myself wanting to touch his jawline. His crow-wing hair, to see if it was as soft as it looked. To feel the strength and contours of his arm. To trace the little dip between his collarbones. I'd suppressed those flares of curiosity. Sun had said he looked after me, but there were so very many layers to the mysteries of attraction. What if I got very close and he recoiled? Living next to someone whose touch repelled one would be torment.

He held me lightly, and my Essence flared. I floated us up and his grip tightened, then—I could feel the effort he made—he consciously loosened it again, settling his balance as a martial expert does.

The lychee peels were indeed no accident. It took only one circle to find the next pair, and so on, following the path On had made over the complicated roofs. Sentries were posted here and there, some alert, but no one looking upward toward the cloudy sky.

We found him crouched over the kitchen, whose roof was warm from the cookery going on below. And there were no sentries anywhere about. I set us down a few paces from On, and banished the obscuring charm. On gave a start, then grinned at us as we joined him, crouching down.

"Was that your first flight?" he asked Koi. "How'd you like it?"

Koi grunted.

On's smile, barely visible from reflected torches on the distant wall, vanished. "They smashed our boats right before sunset."

I winced. "I thought they might decide to send pigeons—"

"Oh, that happened about ten breaths after the lot of you walked into the palace. My guess is, when they heard your name."

Koi's hands tightened to fists on his knees, but all he said was, "We expected that."

"Any other bad news?" I asked.

"Yes. They've got Jai in prison. Ay, not true prison, though I expect that's going to happen whenever the commander gives the word. Who is the commander? Anyone either of you know?"

"Not I," I said.

Koi dipped his head in a short nod. "Don't know him. Know *of* him. Part of Emperor Koza's old imperial guard inner detail. Commanded the shore patrol when young, Gui told me." And to On, "Gui was a household man, a Falcon."

"Then Zoa is another imperial guard raised to command," On murmured. "He'll be loyal to Koza, who's no doubt handing out wealth and promotions to this man's family."

I gave them a brief summary of what I'd learned in that mourning room. I finished, "I think Kandati would like nothing better than to aid us, but he's powerless."

"The Prince of Ran..." Koi repeated. "Ran is one of the old military families. Most of whom the former emperor either killed, promoted into governorships on distant islands no one ever visits, or forced into civilian life."

I remembered something that Father and First Brother had talked about, half-heard, and utterly incomprehensible at the time. "He was so popular with his regiments that the emperor had to pile on the promotions."

"And shift him firmly to civilian life by making him a prince, and renaming the island for his family. While still keeping him on duty protecting the western border islands," Koi murmured.

I should have thought of him before, but my childhood prejudice had kept me from considering him, except as the husband forced on Cousin Arati. Ay! I was learning. Too slowly. Far too slowly. "Kandati's right. We need to go there next."

Both boys looked at me. "The defense on Ran will be far more formidable than it is here."

"I'll go alone, then," I said. And when both made movements to protest, I added, letting my impatience free, "But we still have to get out of here. On. Is there a window where Jai is?"

"Yes, but it's barely big enough for his head to fit through — assuming he can climb that high."

"But you can get to it?"

"I can. With a little difficulty... No, I can."

"Then tell him to claim he's got terrible diarrhea, and he needs the privy. And when he goes in, he's to put on a talisman I'm going to make, and I'll teach you the sign to teach him."

"When?"

I scowled down at the roof tiles, colorless in the darkness. "We need to find some sort of craft..."

"Already did that," On said. "As soon as they smashed our

boats, I figured you'd want something to escape in. I've marked out several possible vessels."

Koi's tight expression eased and he nodded with approval as I breathed, "That's excellent." I was so very glad that I'd mastered the charm for hiding boats! "Come back to the guest wing in an hour. I'll have the talismans ready, one to Jai, the rest to the boat we are going to steal."

On regarded me doubtfully. "Do you have Essence paper?"

"Yes—Dinek let me keep the last of the papers her mother gave her. She said she had no use for them. They got wet at Tortor, but the Essence is undisturbed."

"We're going to disappear without a trace?" Koi asked.

I turned to him. "We are. That is, if we are careful they won't find us. But there has to be a false trail, must there not? Or Kandati and his family and servants will be blamed."

Koi sat back a little—he'd been thinking the same thing. "Then … when?"

"We have three days, according to tradition. It seems that Zoa is traditional. Or he must be under strict orders to maintain the forms, or else he would have gotten rid of Kandati altogether and taken over as prince. Who would stop him, if no communication is going out except to the imperial island? I think he'll be issuing orders to arrest us the moment we leave the palace two days from now."

"We can all see Mt. Lir." On waved impatiently at all these obvious things. "When is Jai to have his stomach trouble?"

"Tomorrow night, when the family goes in to the ancestral altar. Zoa will thus have them accounted for, including the two graywings who are clearly in support of the Lans. You and Cray vanish out over the roof while the search for Jai is going on."

On chuckled. "Guard the stump while the rabbit slips away? Wicked! They can only blame themselves, if Lan Kandati and his family is closed off chanting sutras."

"You've until dinner tomorrow to select a boat and get the talismans laid over it."

Koi looked down at his fists, then said, "If anything goes wrong, Cray and I won't have our weapons."

"I think I can lift some," On said. "While the search is going on."

"We have to get away without notice," I said. "We can perhaps leave one coin somewhere, as if someone among Zoa's own searchers took a bribe to spirit us away. That means we need a route of retreat."

On gave a theatrical sigh. "Ayoh! I did want to get my new wanderer Brother Gan some adventures, didn't I?"

Whether as himself or Brother Gan, On kept his promise. And the others were well practiced in evasion skills. I used up every scrap of the rather grubby paper Dinek had left with me, but the result saw us safely out of Kandati's palace, and sailing very slowly between naval vessels the next night, as rain fell.

Cray had sent the guest room servants to fetch snacks for me, and then sent them out again for fresh towels preparatory to a bath that I never took. She thoughtfully wrapped up the snacks, sure that we were going to be on very short rations indeed once we left Lan.

We did have to fight every instinct to put up the sails and catch the wind driving an early spring rain across the bay, but we could not risk the vessels with naval people on them seeing a sudden wake with no boat or ship to make it.

To distract myself I rescinded my petulant command to Koi to never bring up Circle without a board again. It gave me something to throw my mind at besides Zoa's ships—some of whom we passed within biscuit-tossing distance—and what to do when we got to Ran, and my sense of failure on Kandati's behalf. I knew rationally that his and his family's plight was not my problem to solve, but I had seen their faces, and I had seen the relative poverty and the bleakness of their situation. And that was their reward for generations of self-denying loyalty?

Ironically, it must have been the days away from my frustrated attempts that enabled me to suddenly see the entire board and the 361 island-points within it. I shut my eyes, and there were Koi's boats advancing, and here were my supply lines, and my strong islands and my weak…

And for the first time, I looked up, my vision swimming, as I said, "I won. I truly won."

"Look," Koi said, arm out wide.

The last patrol had dwindled behind us. We were advancing out to sea before running parallel to the coast as we headed north. "I believe we can safely make a wake now," On observed. He and Jai leaped to pull the sails all the way up and tie them taut.

Then we explored our new vessel, no longer afraid of making noise. On was justifiably proud of his theft. It wasn't just that it was fast, and weatherly, but it also had been loaded with supplies preparatory to some journey that it would never take. Even Jai, who was furious that he'd spent his entire time locked up alone—except when Zoa's people had begun a careful interrogation under the pretense of bringing meals—which meant there was no chance to overhear some crucial bit of information that was going to enable us to...

"To what?" On asked, laughing.

Jai scowled. "I don't know. It's you two who have to pull the snake from its hole," he said to Koi and me. "With your too-talented and clever 'West-five-in-four-down.' At least have the decency to steal a Circle board if you're going to keep that up forever."

"Never mind," Koi said, clapping him on the shoulder. "You stuck to what we worked out?"

"Over and over again," Jai muttered. "I'm a sword for hire you found on Te Gar, outside the garrison, I don't know where you two came from, you don't tell me anything. That's what I said. Over and over." He now had time to inspect the scout ship with more leisurely attention, and in a different voice, observed, "This is a good vessel. Fast. But it's going to take all five of us to sail it once we get out of the lee of this island."

Now that the worry was over, tiredness settled over me like a soft, smothering blanket. "Let's each trade off getting a watch of rest while we can."

The scout was made for a minimum crew of eight, twelve if it needed defenders. Beneath the deck were four bunks and a tiny galley.

I tried to sooth my still-galloping brain by gazing out the open air hole at layer after layer of brown rice terraces filled with straw-hatted farmers stooping over the mud, busy planting. Row after row, terrace after terrace. It was beautiful, seen from a distance, how the terraces followed the contours of round hills and inlets along the rivers coming down from the distant mountains. But weren't there too many?

Sleep almost came, almost came, until I sat upright, staring intently. There was definitely something wrong: every terrace was being planted. From early childhood I'd chanted Kanda's lessons about the orderly world, including the three/four rule. Each year one of every four terraces would be left fallow. Two, when the granaries were full, so that the land-spirits had time to replenish them.

But I could not fix that, I told myself. And it was only after I turned my head away that I was able to sleep at last, waking to Phoenix Moon off the bow, the island a large hump off to the left.

I discovered Koi sitting alone at the stern, one hand on the rudder, the sails tied down. I got some tea, poured two cups, and brought him one. He took it with thanks, and I said, "You can sleep now. I can tend the rudder."

"I slept a little earlier." He looked at me with an air of question, and my mind shot back to those two flights on Sagacious Blade—now tucked below with my carryall. I felt the question he did not give voice to.

All I said was, "Ready for some more Circle."

He laughed under his breath. "White or black?"

That set the pattern for that journey, with occasional interruptions by spring storms, and by patrols.

Our first patrol caught us by surprise, a frightening jolt. It was lucky that Jai spotted them before the sun went down, as they began lighting lamps. Tiny lights twinkled straight north, which meant we lay bow on, not quite visible to them yet, as we had not lit lamps.

I had just enough time to move along the boat in haste, beginning at the bow, to shroud us with the obscuring spell. We proceeded softly and quietly to the east of them so that we would not create a silhouette in the twilight, and after that, each morning after dawn I flew scouting circles from above.

Thus I was able to survey the islands we passed. In going north, we discovered that the change in season had worked its way down in our wake during our trip south. Now, sailing northwest, we passed islands that had burst into bloom. Anywhere we passed close enough to see land, invariably it was filled with conical straw hats bobbing over planting.

When Phoenix Moon began to wax again, I realized that I had turned seventeen somewhere in the past days. Siarti was now twenty. Had she summoned all the court daughters to celebrate her birthday, as she always had as a child? Probably. One benefit of being declared a criminal was that I would never again have to think about a gift for her. Though I suspect that she had held those gatherings not for the gifts—she who would order anything she wanted, at any time—but as a way of drawing all attention away from the dowager empress and the empress solely to her, so that she could favor or scorn us as she wished.

I shrugged her image away as our ship plunged toward the great isle of Ran. Koi and I played Circle now and then, until I was certain that my ability to grasp the board had become a part of my mental assessment, and not a fluke happening once and never again. Winning was no long the matter of urgency it had been when I was struggling so futilely against my own brain. Now I could regard the game the way I always had, as a method for playing around with different ideas in trade and trade consequence. Koi's and my wins and losses were about even.

On played flute for us, Jai largely served as captain, and Cray quietly took over the cooking, having learned to adapt the needs of meals to any kind of situation. This was a Falcon attribute, but her own urgency was in keeping martial skills honed. It was she, and not Koi, who called us to practice on the bow each day.

Between spring rains, I made a daily flight from above, looking for imperial patrols. This was the season of two and three and five-day steady rains, sky, air, and water layers of slate gray. I refused to fly in that weather, though On was content to. He usually returned admitting he couldn't see anything, but he just liked flying. That was fine. If we couldn't see much past the immediate space ahead, then no one could see us.

These things and our discussions of plans in various possible circumstances kept us well-occupied until suddenly—before I was ready—the rain cleared one morning, revealing a line of ships in the distance, moving toward an island whose profile matched the drawing on my map:

Ran.

TWENTY-TWO

They met on the Phoenix Bridge
While the sound of the drum invoked the gods.
Do you truly want them to listen?
Power can be hot as flame
And burn the heart.

"DO YOU THINK THAT'S Xianti?"

"This far from the imperial island?" Koi asked. "No. That's not nearly a large enough fleet. He's always going to want to outnumber an enemy several times over."

"They aren't in battle formation anyway," On said, peering under his hand. "Might be a Ran patrol returning, though if they are, they're really sloppy. Maybe the rain out that way is fog, and they lost their stations. Anyway, since Ran is near the western ocean, they probably patrol in convoys."

All this was no more than I was thinking, once I recovered from the initial jolt. "Here's an idea," I said. "Let's not try the capital harbor at all. We would never be able to explain disembarking from an invisible ship, or sailing in under the emperor's golden dragon and having to name our commander, fleet, and orders."

We cruised along the coast outside Ran's capital bay until we spotted a likely little cove with overhanging willows and bright red pomegranate blossoms on the hillock above. A couple of other craft were anchored there—there were numerous boats along the shore—but there was no guard, and those boats looked like fishers and pleasure boats.

Our plan was to walk in through the back gate and assess the situation. Including finding a popular inn, preferably with a waiter or innkeeper with a tongue faster than six aunts and twelve grandmothers. We'd meet where we parted when drum or gong or bell rang first dragon, compare what news we'd gleaned, and plan from there.

It was sensible—but when we actually reached the back gate, our plan galloped over the broken bridge of reality, straight into the churning waters of events that we'd been isolated from.

The city looked prosperous, but the atmosphere was fervid. Knots of people stood around talking. Each person's voice differs, yet a crowd can produce a common pitch: angry, uproarious, awed, shocked. This tone was excitement, but with an undertone of fear, with many glances cast back toward the bay on the other side of some gentle hills.

We tried walking close to some of these gossip knots, but when people saw strangers approaching, they broke up and went about their business. As we made our way onto a main thoroughfare, I saw military pairs walking about, hands to weapons. They wore golden dragon emblems, but their tunics were edged with deep blue, not the crimson of the empire. Ran's own guard.

"I'm going to take a look at the bay," I said.

"You sure you want to risk that?" Cray asked me.

"Who is going to recognize me at this end of the empire?" I asked. Then I thought of gentle, retiring, beautiful Cousin Arati, married off summarily to the Prince of Ran nearly five years ago in spite of her love for my eldest brother. But she would be locked up in a high-walled harem, surely. I hesitated, wanting to know how she was doing, as I had been fond of her and her chatty sister, Chuti. So timid and retiring a person would not be able to aid us. Better not to risk recognition.

The five of us parted at an intersection with a bronze dragon water clock at its center, easy to find again. I walked on, concentrating on my stride. Since I'd seen no warriors in imperial crimson and gold, I did not obscure myself, which meant I did not have to constantly dodge around people, very maddening in crowds as thick as I found here.

It felt good to walk with confidence. After all my worry, Kandati's family had accepted me as Banti, though I think he was a little puzzled by me, compared to his instant recognition of Koi, who had grown a head and shoulders since Kandati had seen him last.

"People see what they expect to see," On had repeated. "Didn't you accept me as Oriole when you saw me on stage?"

True! With his words echoing in my ears, I walked with Banti's gait as I peered ahead, toward the top of the ridge that paralleled the bay. My stomach rumbled when I passed through wafting fragrances of street vendors' delicious foods, nearly irresistible after a winter of a diet even monks and nuns would find stringent. We each had a small handful of coinage — enough for a roasted sweet potato and some tea. Later, I scolded my empty stomach.

And then I forgot my hunger when I topped a small ridge and found myself overlooking a wide bay. The last of that fleet was still coming in. At first it looked like some of them had grown thousands of spines. No! They were studded with arrows! Many were marred by scorching, and a few were missing a mast, or had holes stove into the hulls. I realized with horror that this fleet was limping in after a hard battle.

My gaze shifted to the boardwalk, where patrols of Ran guards waved swords and spears to clear off wharf workers and gawkers. From the water, rowboats full of wounded and dead were being brought in. More Ran guards jogged in orderly lines from the direction of the guard towers at either end of the bay, spreading out to intercept those rowboats. They carried the covered dead in one direction and the wounded in another.

Who were these dead and wounded? I peered under my hand against the dazzling morning sun, scanning the banners. Golden imperial dragon against white, edged with silver. Ye? But not Ye. That golden dragon with five toes that only the imperial family could use — that had to be Prince Guiza's banner. The Ye clan were powerful northerners, well respected, counting many ministers among them.

I could not say I knew Guiza or he knew me, for our encounters in the imperial palace had always been in company with the entire family. But he would know Banti well.

I cast a wary eye about, but did not see the prince, or an entourage that would accompany a prince.

I proceeded cautiously, my eye drawn by two shamans who made their way through the crowd, one in a Ghost Moon mask and the other in a Phoenix Moon mask. People parted respectfully, some making the signs of the moon gods as the shamans passed, both wearing voluminous robes covered in long streamers with charms written on each.

They began to dance among the dead, shaking rattles and dispersing incense over the bodies to help guide souls once their physical selves had been burned and returned to the earth. Yes, before a temple on an isolated hill a fire licked against the sky. And here was a steady, solemn procession carrying the dead one by one, once they'd been blessed.

At the other end of the cleared space, sailors and guards alike were bringing stretcher after stretcher of wounded, as physicians and medics began to move among them. Not nearly enough of them.

Was there something I could do? My healer training had barely covered the fundamentals, but I did understand many concepts. Specifically, I could draw the heat of burn pain. I pushed past onlookers, and headed for the line of guards keeping the crowd back.

When I approached, a tired-looking boy in Ran blue waved me off.

"I can help," I said.

"You're a physician?" he asked doubtfully, eyeing me.

"I had some training. Essence training, too. I—"

"Essence training?" a graying physician said from behind. "What can you do?"

"I can bandage, but slowly. Mostly, I can use Essence to alleviate pain from fire."

"Put him to work." Then someone hailed the physician, who bustled away.

"Burns are being put over here," the young guard said.

I cut around the rows of sufferers. The burn victims were easy to find by the stink of burned flesh on the spring air. A physician straightened from a stoop to address me in a low voice. "The prince gave permission to use our precious one-hundred-year Longevity Herb salve, but the pain is too great for most of these to tolerate touch. If you can ease them enough so we can apply the salve..."

Already cloths had been laid over the faces of some sufferers, who had surrendered a life to painful to bear; I chose a man who writhed slowly, in agony at the touch of the breeze on his burned scalp, neck, and all down his right arm. I used the warmth of the spring sun toasting my shoulders to draw the heat caused by his pain. The man's contorted face gradually eased, and his eyes cleared as the ferocious pain receded enough for him to breathe deeply. "Ay! It barely hurts! I'm healed —" he began.

"You are not healed," I said quickly. "I can't do that. I'm only easing the pain, and it won't last forever. I'm sorry."

"That's right." This new, deep voice belonged to an old physician with a long silvery beard as he knelt down. "But it ought to last long enough for us to get our precious salve onto the burns, which *will* help start you toward healing. You lie flat, my boy. Let me get this salve on your burns, and wrap them. This is the prince's own salve — it costs more than you'll earn in a lifetime. But it will reknit your flesh. You're not to move or touch it until the scabbing takes hold."

The fetid air filled with the fresh scent rising from the purple salve the physician carefully spread on the burns. I noted how it sank in immediately, spreading a glistening coat over the ravaged flesh, before a light bandage was wrapped around the wounds to keep the salve from drying out.

A physician's apprentice followed next, with a jug of poppy-laced elixir and a dipper.

I moved from victim to victim, until the sun had jumped to the other end of the sky, and all the burns had been loosely wrapped, the sufferers filled with elixir. Tents were being set up to keep the sun off their faces, with open sides to permit the sweet air to blow away the noisome smells.

By the time I'd reached the last one, a gunner whose cannon had burst and pocked him with terrible metal gouges, I was relying solely on the sun's Essence to call the metal pieces out from his flesh, one by one, before I eased the pain.

Then I sat back on my haunches, weary and dizzy, but filled with the satisfaction of accomplishment. Only then did I notice a trio of physicians' apprentices looking at me intently. "Can you teach me that?" one asked.

"You draw the Essence," I said, as hunger and thirst reawakened in me. "Any Essence skilled healer can teach..." A violent yawn seized me.

"Ren." There was Koi. "Have you had a chance to eat?"

"No," I said, surprised to see him. "What are you doing here?"

Someone called, and the physicians' apprentices hastened away. Koi turned back to me. "I saw you heading for the most dangerous part of the city, and decided to scan, and provide backup if you wanted it. There's a vendor selling steamed buns right over —"

"Renti?"

I looked past Koi to one of the people moving among the wounded — and stared into Cousin Arati's astonished face. She was as beautiful as ever. Moreso, in spite of a blood-smeared apron thrown over a fine robe, her crow's wing black hair coming loose from its golden pins.

"No." Doubt puckered her brow as she eyed me.

"Banti," I said, deepening my voice as much as I could, and squaring my shoulders. "Cousin Arati. Forgive my awkward lack of politeness." I forced out the words, thinking desperately, how was it possible she was *here?* She had really changed in these intervening years!

"You have not changed at all," she said to me, still eyeing me as she approached. The guards around us saluted with a kind of fervor that said a lot about how they regarded the young Princess of Ran, and parted to let her join me.

Then she saw Koi, and there was the eyebrow-lift of instant recognition. I was glad he was there. She would have seen Koi with Second Brother as a regular occurrence.

"Cousin Banti," she said to me in a welcoming voice. "I want to thank you most gratefully for your aid! The physicians insist that we are finished here. They will come around with healers' soup, and to tend the more physical needs, once they finish setting up these tents. Come away. You look rather pale."

"This unworthy cousin must not trouble you," I said, looking in appeal at Koi.

Who spoke with quiet authority, which servants never used, "Second Young Master will be fine once he gets something to eat. He tends to forget such things."

Arati gave him an absent smile as she beckoned to someone beyond the guards keeping a crowd of gawkers at a distance. "I'm so very glad that you are alive, Banti. And not with Cousin Yanti in prison. He used to forget to eat, too, I remember. Studying through days and nights. It seems to be a family trait."

We passed the barrier of guards. The crowd of gawkers bowed. They made a solid wall except where the guards had cleared a space to a waiting cart, and I saw that it was impossible to leave without drawing even more attention.

Heartened by her instant acceptance of me as Banti, I followed her, and we got into a beautifully decorated cart in shades of blue and peach and green. Perforce Koi had to walk alongside it with Arati's two maidservants, as Arati sat back with a quiet sigh. Then she leaned toward me. "How did you escape Xianti's claws? Chuti writes me such terrible news, I can scarcely bear to unseal her letters."

Drained as I was, and light-headed with hunger, I remembered my pose—lounging back, knees apart, over feet. Fist on one knee, holding Sagacious Blade in place on my leg, other elbow out.

I gave her an even briefer recounting of Banti's story than I'd prepared for Kandati. She listened closely, then said, "I understand Great-Uncle Yiulo sending you to Ran to seek alliance. My husband has been expecting one or another of the rebelling princes to turn up sooner or later. He's certainly received many, many exhortations about Grand Prince Yiulo, Cousin Yiuti, and you, from Imperial Uncle Koza."

I sat forward. "What does the Prince of Ran respond to the emperor?"

She waved her fan tiredly. "How can he respond, but with obedience? Ymek has returned the same answer each time: that his orders from Imperial Grandfather were to guard the border, and leave the rest of the empire to him."

"Though the rest of the empire is full of wolves and rats— the worst of them Uncle Koza and Cousin Xianti?"

"He never met Xianti, and knows him only as the legitimate imperial crown prince. Further, Uncle Koza wearing the dragon robe and bearing the imperial seal of our ancestors, sworn to by the court, acknowledges him as Heaven's Chosen. Ymek says that he cannot break a promise made on his ancestors' graves only for rumors full of sighing winds and calling crows."

"Then you don't know how desperate Lan is? Our cousin Lan Kandati is controlled by General Zoa. The land is on the verge of famine from being overworked. People are selling off daughters right and left in order to pay taxes—figuring it is the best way to save them from starving to death. I saw the land, and heard about the cost to the people of Lan from Cousin Kandati. I just came from there."

Arati regarded me steadily, her eyes glistening. "I don't know anything at all," she said softly. "I sometimes overhear Ymek saying that General Zoa's communications are all about how loyal Lan is peaceful and thriving."

"Loyal, absolutely. Thriving, absolutely not. I was just there. As for seeing things, you said that Cousin Chuti writes to you of terrible things. I am assuming she gave you and the prince the details, perhaps eyewitness account, of my family being hauled off to prison on a specious charge?"

Arati looked away. "Ymek cannot regard my excellent sister's letters as military reports. This ignorant one has come to understand that any decision he makes outside of obeying Imperial Grandfather's orders would be seen as an act of treachery and rebellion, and that would involve many lives."

These diplomatic words were not completely wrong. Action outside of orders, even investigation, might rouse Uncle Koza, who had inherited his father's suspicion. And while I'd known Cousin Chuti, she'd been fond of gossip as well as exaggeration. I doubted her letters were in any way like a military report. But they would still be eyewitness accounts. I suspected that if it had been a man writing gossip, the prince would have taken it more seriously.

"I understand." I bowed, forcing down my ire. I could not even claim to have seen my family taken away, as Banti had not witnessed it—he had not found out for months. Grand Uncle Yiuti had seen to that. "Is Cousin Chuti still in the imperial city?" I asked.

"Ayoh, she is indeed." Arati's face brightened into her beautiful smile. "Between the counsel of Grand Uncle Miluo, and Consort Ye's influence, they convinced Imperial Uncle Koza to marry Chuti to First Secretary Ze's son. This was right before Uncle Koza and Xianti could start awarding princesses to their new generals. She and Ze Abaz are quite happy together."

The cart halted in a beautiful courtyard full of spring blossoms.

A maid entered with soundless steps and stood at a distance, eyes down, hands crossed before her. I'd been raised to consider maids as furniture until I had need of one, but now I wondered at the mind behind those lowered eyes, the character hidden behind the meek pose.

Arati beckoned, the maid approached, bowed to us both, then Arati murmured quick words before the maid withdrew in a backward glide.

She turned to me as we walked inside her private suite, another maid trailing. "I asked them to set you up in one of the family guest chambers," Arati said, and indicated the second maid. "Dandelion here will take you to retire and rest a little. I must visit my children, who have not seen me all day, and then venture to explain things to Ymek on your behalf, if you will permit this unworthy cousin to try."

I was about to protest that I could speak for myself. But then I remembered that Banti had even more of a price on his head than I did. While I'd been prepared to face this new bridge of knives, I could see in Arati's thinned smile and the set of her shoulders that she had appointed herself the task to serve as intermediary. I must trust her to do it.

TWENTY-THREE

The Sage Empress said:
Even when a thunder of dragon banners shakes the world,
The Spring Sun still turns the duckweed green.

KOI WAS WAITING FOR me, having been taken ahead of the slow cart.

"I brushed your blue robe. The rest is being laundered. And, ah… In case we spend the night."

I looked at him tiredly. "Spend the night?"

"There is a servant's room well apart from the guest chamber," he said quickly, pointing. "Looks comfortable."

"Servant's room?" I repeated blankly. Of course there would be a servant's room! Then I caught the meaning: two beds, well separated.

I smothered a laugh, for ignorant as I still was, I suspected by the color along his cheekbones that his thoughts, anyway, had gone in the direction of where we ought to sleep.

Warmth coursed through me as well as laughter and a froth of affection. Dear Koi! As with On, I was so tempted to close the distance and reach for his hand, but again I hesitated before treading the first step down that path. The idea was exhilarating, perhaps too much so. What did I fear? That this wild, beguiling path would beckon me to run, and forget all else? There was enough in song and story about that, and now that the feelings had begun to waken, I understood. A little.

The press of urgency steadied me. I thanked him for making my lavender and dragonfly robe ready, and undid my hair as I quickly outlined the conversation with Arati. At once a waft of brine and sweat offended my nose. "I'd better bathe, and be ready if he summons me," I finished.

"There's tea on the way, and snacks," he said, as I ducked into the far chamber.

I bathed quickly, my stomach cavernously empty. When I emerged, I fingered my wet hair hastily up, my eyes going straight to the plate of rice balls, tender bamboo shoots, cooked with chestnuts and grilled fish, and taro cakes.

"Come," I said to Koi. "No one is here, so we needn't pretend our roles. Let's eat."

He sat down with me, and between the two of us, we'd just cleaned all the serving dishes when the summons came, which caused me to suspect that the Prince of Ran was exactly as aware of the urgency of the situation as I was. And, being no coward, he was going to confront it like a warrior riding to face the enemy attack.

I leaped up and was going to run out, but Koi dismissed the messenger, then grabbed my arm. "Not like that," he said.

"Like what? This is my only clean robe—"

"Sit down."

"Oh."

I sat, and he pulled out the hair clasp I'd thrust on the top of my head without looking. For the first time in many years, I felt someone's fingers in my hair. My young maids had learned a soothing stroke when I was small. I'd missed that, many times, over the years, an unspoken wish. Gallant wanderers did not have personal servants. They combed and arranged their own hair. But Koi's patient hands touching my head and combing my hair up into a proper topknot gave me shivers deep in my belly. I could have curled up and slept—except for the vital sense of urgency that awakened once again that awareness of proximity.

As soon as he was done, I gabbled thanks and bolted out the door, to find the servant waiting.

"Lead on," I barked, and was relieved to discover that this palace was a warren of buildings, courtyards and gardens. I was able to settle my thoughts by the time we reached the main hall's interview chamber.

The Prince of Ran was not as old as I remembered. That is, I'd recollected a rough-looking, scarred military man who could have been any age between forty and fifty, a wild beard hiding most of his face. But the beard was now neatly trimmed, his hair braided up into its pear-edged hair clasp, and he wore a splendid robe of twilight blue silk embroidered with eagles against clouds, and along the hem, lotus floating among reeds. The scars were still there, and the sun lines at the corners of his eyes, but his countenance was not my father's generation. My estimate of his age dropped down to between thirty and forty.

He made a quick, abrupt bow, which I returned, careful to mimic the way he used his hands and arms.

"Welcome, Young Prince," he said, his voice deep and gruff. "I want first of all to thank you on behalf of my imperial physicians and medics. They all praised your abilities, insisting that it would have been impossible to treat many of the worst burn victims. You undoubtedly saved lives."

"I was glad to help."

"It seems that you've been putting your time away from the imperial island to very good use, learning Essence healing."

"I am only a beginner," I said truthfully.

He grunted, eyeing me. Then he said abruptly, "You will have to forgive an uncouth military man. Though my wife has done her best introduce me to the niceties of civilian life..." His voice warmed on the words *my wife*. "...I am still a Ran, which until now has meant generations of military upbringing."

I bowed again.

His eyes narrowed. "Ay, but you seem a lot younger than I'd expected."

"I look that way," I said, striving to sound tough and abrupt. "Everyone says it. But I've seen what I've seen, to be specific, Lan Island is nearing famine. Disabled veterans guarding the gates. Streets unswept. The prince's family eating like monks."

"Still in mourning, is what I heard," the prince replied. "Otherwise communications with Zoa claim no difficulties."

I bit back an exclamation about wolves and rats and evil winds. This man was used to dealing with military reports. Eyewitness details. Specific. I said as neutrally as possible, "Perhaps, in the martial sense. I make no claims there. I've no interest in wars beyond preventing them. But, mourning or not, planting four out of four? Everywhere along the coast from the capital bay north."

Did he understand what four and four meant to the rice farmers? I did not think General Zoa did, or perhaps he was too secure of his position to care what anyone passing by would see:

overplanting, the surest invitation to famine. Or perhaps orders had superseded sense. In the short term, planting every field would provide needed supplies to the hungry army. But for how long?

He sent a sharp look my way. "Four and four?" He repeated. "All the rice farms, right there, in view?"

I bowed assent.

"There was a time when I did not know what that meant. Ayah! Perhaps Lan will need aid. But that is a matter for the emperor to decide." He seemed to hesitate, then said, "Come, come, come."

He led the way from the spare-looking interview chamber to a room even more sparsely furnished, the only wall hanging an enormous, beautifully painted map of the empire. If that was not every island painted on that expanse that had to be twenty full paces wide, then the tiny clusters were symbolic, but the big islands looked accurate as far as I could tell.

More importantly, he had all naval bases labeled in red, with tiny markers that I guessed were for fleets, and in green ink, trade centers. Tea. Wheat. Rice. Silk. Brimstone. Hemp. Many other important commodities were represented by different colors. It was the map I had yearned to see, and had tried in my clumsy, ignorant way to make — and there it was.

The Prince of Ran stood before it, hands clasped behind him. "Nearly five years of orders from Emperor Koza, in recent years especially warning me against the wiles of evil, grasping, demon-ridden princes whom I was to guard against. And now, in one day, I've two turning up. My diviners seem to have missed any omens," he finished with fine irony, turning my way.

Was this a warning? I thought of Sagacious Blade back in that guest chamber, with Koi guarding it. I had an escape nearly ready to hand, but my heart still thumped hard.

"Young Prince Guiza has roused, last I heard," the Prince of Ran continued. "At least he remained unconscious long enough for them to sew his scalp back on without him feeling the pain of it. You … you were not with him when these bannerless pirates," he said with fine irony, "who used our weapons and tactics, attacked him as he was crossing between his ancestral islands?" He reached up to tap the two most northern of the three huge plains islands — immediately noticeable because of those rare flat expanses.

The northerners historically formed their society around

horse travel, I knew—most of us had Mantai ancestors, and had learnt some of the traditional Jun songs. As I studied that map, I could see why horses might be necessary. I also remembered that these ancestors had had no navy, having scant interest in conquering clusters of small islands on which they could not ride their horses without difficulty.

And I saw immediately the thrust of Xianti's viciousness—he would not want to invade those islands to fight horse warriors in his conscript raids unless he had an enormous army, sure to win. "Right where the Ye and their allied clans are most easily attacked, by water," I muttered.

"You see that, do you?"

"Isn't it obvious?" Then I recollected his comment about omens, and the oblique question: were we in any way connected with Cousin Guiza's plans?

I turned from the map. "I did not know Cousin Guiza was coming to Ran until we spotted his ships approaching the bay. As I said, I came up from my own ancestral island at Lan."

"Sent by that wily fox Lan Yiulo, no doubt," the Prince of Ran said—not without some approval. "Of course he'd seek allies, and even though I am sworn to refuse him, I'm glad he's decided to do that within the empire."

Then he glanced in my direction, hesitating. Was he about to explain? My mind flashed back to On and Koi bent over our grubby, wrinkled map with me in our sodden camp, and On saying, *My uncle was determined to take Mountain Peony because possessing it, and Tiger Islands, would give him the best staging point for ventures into the east as well as south. The easterners would see that as a position of strength. I really believe he was going to try to negotiate an alliance with them to help him attack the imperial capital...*

"Grand Uncle Yiulo would not use a wolf to attack a snake," I said. For Koi had been definite about that—Grand Prince Yiulo had not needed my brother and the other ministers' sons to argue against the idea of approaching the easterners to join his war against Emperor Koza. Wild Grand Uncle Yiulo was, but not wild enough to invite foreigners in.

The Prince of Ran pursed his lips. "Mmm. I must admit to a certain amount of relief to hear this. I respect his imperial highness greatly. He was a loyal and brave captain during my young years, when I was a company commander under Grand Prince Miluo during our trouble with the easterners. But I was wondering if they, in their turn, might see their defeat back then as an excuse to meddle here."

"Their queen is too sensible, from what I have learned," I said, remembering my discussions with the Hermit Namath. And what I'd read in that book of the queen's exhortations, based on a journal she'd written when she was my age. "She won't want to risk the silk trade, is my guess."

As I spoke, my hungry gaze roamed over that beautiful map, taking in the shape of the eastern edge of the empire, and Tiger Islands jutting into the Great Sea. That was right where a massive current swooped in a long circle across the ocean to the easterners' two main islands. Now a lot of what Hermit Namath had said about the troubles made a lot of sense. I could see why trouble with the easterners often started or ended there.

Silk trade… Was there a way to use that considerable trade, with its significant tax stream, as an influence on the emperor to curtail Xianti—

"How old *are* you?" the Prince of Ran asked abruptly, startling me. Then he actually reddened, and bowed. "Forgive this blundering warrior. I know better than to ask that of anyone who has put their hair up." He indicated his topknot. "But it's true, you sound much older than you look." He turned his attention to the map. "If you're right about eastern prudence, that relieves me on the emperor's behalf. Ay! The most pressing matter is the two of you princes. Beginning with what you want."

"I came to beg for aid for Lan," I said. "I've done that. As for what I want in the larger sense, it is some agreement that will cause the emperor to stop forced conscription, to begin with, then to ease the taxes to support it. And to order Xianti to stop attacking our own people. Again." I glanced at the Ye island on the map. "But I wanted to ask you not to attack our own people. Even if the emperor asks. Actually, if Xianti starts issuing orders—"

He raised a hand. "Let's be specific. I realize it'll be weeks before the emperor finds out about the two of you turning up, and I trust you'll be about whatever it is you intend to do long before then. I don't fear retribution—the emperor knows I'm too strong for that. I'm also his wall between us and the prowling wolves of the west, who, as it's said in these islands, don't make but take. It's important for the westerners to see my warships cruise north every two years, flexing our muscles. However, the emperor must protect his prestige, so I'll have to—"

The far door opened, and Arati walked in, wearing floating

layers of silk, her glossy hair elaborately done up in a headdress of gold with pearls, and tiny dangles by her ears, winking with brilliants. She led a tottering child by one hand, and a maid followed, carrying another child. "Thank the gods my cousins showed up on the eve of Spring Festival. Can you not declare a day or two of amnesty for the sake of my family?"

"I was just saying that I'm going to need to justify my harboring Prince Banti," the Prince of Ran said, as she joined him. He did not admonish her for intruding in "men's" affairs. A quick private smile passed between them, and he bent to kiss the baby, and to ruffle his hand over the head of the toddler. "Amnesty for the holiday will do. After all, Young Prince Guiza has no charges against his name. And I've received no orders concerning him. If you slip away during the festival, say, and leave with him, it will save my face, but more importantly, it will save the emperor's face before court. Amnesty for a festival day, yes, yes. You won't mind adding slipping parole to all your other crimes?"

I knew that Second Brother would find that more hilarious than not, and agreed. "May this ignorant one put a question?" I asked. They both turned to me, and when the Prince of Ran opened his hand in invitation, I said, "The fight Cousin Guiza's fleet lost was against bannerless ships? Was anyone recognized among these pirates?"

The two of them exchanged glances.

The Prince of Ran said slowly, "Young Prince Guiza was brought in unconscious, and though I'm told he's awake and aware, we've yet to speak."

Arati said firmly, "He did not see Xianti."

Ah. Then my guess was right. An easy guess.

The Prince of Ran added, "But the two I questioned earlier insisted they recognized a former imperial guard in one of the commanders. Though he was dressed like a northerner. I'm hoping that after a good night of rest, and medicine, Prince Guiza will be willing to talk to me. To us," Prince of Ran amended, clasping his hands in my direction. "I trust he can furnish an eyewitness account of events in the imperial capital these past few years."

"If this wife may offer a humble reminder: it is nearly time for dinner. The Dowager Princess is on her way," Arati spoke.

"We can safely leave the emperor to his distant affairs," the Prince of Ran observed mildly, "but Heaven preserve us from the thunder of dragons if we keep my mother from her dinner.

Prince Banti, I invite you to join our family meal, such as it is. I cannot promise the sumptuousness of court banquets…" He went on politely, and I just as politely disclaimed as we proceeded to a dining room.

Once again I was seated on the men's side, in the guest of honor spot, ahead of some older men who appeared to be the husbands of a pair of aunts. On the women's side, the Dowager Princess of Ran presided, with Arati below her, and the aunts below that. The old woman with white hair eyed me from pouchy eyes, then said, after the food had been served and the welcome toasts drunk, "I am only an ignorant old woman used to the military life, and I know nothing of men's affairs. I say *nothing* about this prince who seems to be attacking everyone like a snake in the wall, but I must wonder if his mother can hold up her head at such behavior."

I would not dare to say that his mother was far worse. As it turned out, I did not need to. After unburdening herself of this "nothing" the dowager princess gave Arati a triumphant look, winning a quick smile in return. I strongly suspected that the dowager princess knew very well what the empress had been like.

The conversation turned general, marked by many toasts. I only sipped, unlike that sharp-eyed old princess, who seemed to relish her cups of wine.

It was after I'd emptied one cup, to the princess's tenth, when she looked across at me. "This old, witless mother might be slow, but like the turtle in the saying, she arrives at her destination. *I* know now who you are. You are the second son of the Imperial Censor, young Lan Kaiza."

It seemed strange to hear Father referred to as 'young' as well as hearing his given name. Not even Mother used that in our hearing.

"…who everyone still praises," the dowager princess stated. "What is it that censors teach their young? Not two weeks ago we received news that your sister, in the guise of a wanderer, cured a very lethal form of plague on one of the big eastern islands. The governor's mother had been pronounced dead, but the coffin lid had broken in a stroke of lightning, and it turned out she lived."

"Oh?" I said, plunged into sudden discomfort.

"You did not know? But if you had, you would provide a proper escort, yes? She seems to be traveling about in ways I would never permit a daughter of mine, though what we hear of her doings is a catalogue of merits. The governor's lady was said to be in a coma, like that boy upstairs. But she woke on the first day of this year, right after the governor led the ritual in the Hall of Ancestors."

"Let us toast her happy recovery," Arati said smoothly. "And also the merit of the one who cured her."

That done, the dowager princess had a point and she was determined to make it. "That is a good girl, but it would be better to find her a good man and get her married off. See to it, when you find her. That is the duty of a brother when the parents are unable. Prison…so reprehensible…"

The Prince of Ran shot a glance toward Arati, who gave a tiny nod, and then signaled surreptitiously to the maid standing behind the dowager princess. The wine cup before the dowager princess was removed, and tea put in its place. That did not stop the dowager princess from offering muttered opinions, usually prefaced by *I say nothing about… but.*

The meal came to a close after some talk about Spring Festival plans, after which the Prince of Ran invited me to join him and a few of his captains for some games in his own chambers.

We proceeded to the royal wing, where there were musicians ready to play in the background. A Circle board sat on a table, and there were some other games. Arati appeared, bringing tea, her maid carrying a tray of snacks.

The Prince of Ran gestured toward me, and began to introduce the captains when the door opened and a messenger entered. Though he was dressed in servant livery, he had all the bearing of a military aide as he moved to the Prince of Ran's side and whispered.

The prince looked up, his genial expression hardened to inscrutability. "Ayah! Was there a triple comet in the sky, beyond the clouds? Come along, young Prince Banti. It seems my prediction was wrong. I'm afraid we're going to have to disturb your cousin right now."

I had to concentrate on lengthening my stride as we hastened from that room across to another wing. I realized belatedly that this was a men's wing of the palace. I had been given a guest house standing separate, with its own little courtyard. I forgot that when we reached a chamber with two Ye guards before it, as well as a guard in blue.

They opened the door, and we went in. The Prince of Ran led us straight to the bed against the far wall, where Cousin

Guiza sat up, half his head bandaged. He squinted at us, clearly trying to see past a thunderous headache.

The Prince of Ran bent over the bed. "I'm glad you're awake. Listen, an envoy just arrived, sent by the Grand Prince Yiulo, who says that a fleet flying the banner of the imperial crown prince is on its way, probably arriving tomorrow night, depending on this storm moving in—they'll be sailing straight into it. The envoy's down at my command desk, giving details to Commander Ryu. He'll be brought up here anon, but I would like to put a couple of questions to you. Can you speak?"

"I can," Cousin Guiza said. He was nearly paper pale, but even that wretched color, and with half his head and face bandaged, he was still handsome—still the Perfect Guiza I remembered, except with all the boy gone, and faint shadow on lip and chin.

"Why did he attack you? What have you done to cause it?"

"Nothing," Cousin Guiza whispered. "Nothing. In both meanings. I have visited islands as ordered, to find that they have met the demands of the law. I did not investigate further."

"I understand. You were ordered to find conscripts, and you found none. But that is not a reason to attack you, unless it were proved you were deliberately disobeying orders."

"Yes. I was crossing islands. West. They came bannerless out of nowhere…"

"We know that much," the Prince of Ran said gently. "He could have commandeered your fleet, except I suspect it was too small for him to trouble over it. He wanted a fight. I would even go so far as to say he expected to annihilate you all, so many against so few. Why is he determined to kill you? Do you know?"

"My mother swears. She was there. When Father Emperor died. He had a will. Already writ. Put his seal to it. Two graywings. Mother. Witnessed. Both graywings disappeared … the next day. Another saw one … being carried out. Wrapped in cloth … Mother went to Uncle Miluo. My brothers and Xianti … did not dare. Break into his house. They put me in prison."

His low voice had lost all its force, and it was clear how much it pained him to speak. He drew a shuddering breath, and a servant sprang forward to offer some medicine. Guiza drank that, sighed, then forced out more words. "In the will. I was to inherit. Testaments…memorials…charges. First Brother Koza. Never heir. Sent me … to fetch conscripts. I took Mother…" He shut his eyes, and reached toward the servant. "Willow. Tell him."

Willow bowed toward the Prince of Ran, and in a voice devoid of emotion, said, "This unworthy, ignorant one will try to explain, however poorly, that his imperial highness Prince Guiza stayed at Ye, and then at relations, checking the records, to discover that the islands had been meeting the requirements. He did not search for more young men, but crossed the island visiting, until a missive arrived from Grand Prince Yiulo requesting an alliance against the emperor. Her highness the Princess of Ye convinced Prince Guiza to inspect the islands north of Ran as an excuse to sail here to consult you. He insisted on sending her imperial highness to safety, then we departed from Ye. Then this attack."

"Xianti…" Guiza whispered. "Wants me dead…"

The Prince of Ran glanced my way. "Did the grand prince say anything to you about this prospective alliance, Prince Banti?" He frowned. "Why didn't he send you to Prince Guiza?"

I was spared having to think of a lie when the door opened, and following a servant entered a scruffy-looking young man. I gazed in astonishment at those familiar blunt features, the broad mouth that had been pressed in a line, but at the sight of me rounded in astonishment.

"Cousin Oraiti," I said voicelessly at the same time he exclaimed, "I *didn't* hear wrong. But I left Banti in Whale Haven. He couldn't possibly — is that you, Cousin Renti?"

Every eye turned to me.

TWENTY-FOUR

She believed that to use what's given you
Is the way to heavenly harmony,
Freeing your soul beyond the blue clouds.
Twist your nature and
Lose the high mountain vision of Truth.

"RENTI?" GUIZA STRUGGLED TO straighten up. "But she's … a little girl."

The Prince of Ran swung his head back and forth between us.

Oraiti said, with his usual good humor, "She was a little girl five years ago. And even then I wouldn't say she was *little*. You're quite tall, Cousin! I swear before all the gods and demons you've grown even more since that last glimpse, aboard Yiuti's vessel, and you do look somewhat like Banti! But why are you dressed that way?"

The Prince of Ran let out a bellow of a laugh, startling everyone. "I thought he — she — was just very young."

"I'm seventeen," I protested.

He laughed again. "And I was right! You *are* young. I wish my mother hadn't drunk so much at dinner. When she discovers this masquerade, she will shout the place down in disappointment for having missed catching it." He chuckled, thumbed his eyes, then said, "My sister ran away and joined the army. Did really well, too, until she turned fifteen, and, ah, got found out.

That throat was never going to grow a neck knuckle."

Cousin Oraiti turned huge eyes to me. "Banti said you vanished from the ship because of some thief with Essence who sneaked up without us noticing and took you away, but I never believed it, even if Yiuti did. Banti was always laughing behind his fan when he said it. How did you get off that ship? No, was that really you down at Mountain Peony, calling down lightning to cure a plague?"

"Curing plague is not a matter for beginners," the Prince of Ran interjected.

All my lies were coming right back at me. As was just. My only defense was that my motives had been righteous each time. But lies are like a very sticky web that spins bigger and bigger, until it swallows the spider that spins it.

With that thought in mind, I squared my shoulders, held out my hand, and called Sagacious Blade. She smacked into my hand, causing everyone to jump.

"With this." I slid two fingers down the blade, bringing up a lick of flame. Then I doused it as everyone jumped. "There was no plague," I added. "It was a ruse to keep Xianti from invading Mountain Peony in order to gut its populace for his wars. Against no enemies, against no pirates. Against *us*."

The Prince of Ran said briskly, "Bringing us back to our original dilemma. From my perspective, the only one with a crime attached to his name is Prince Banti—no, there was something more recent about Princess Renti under a disguised name, I remember now. But that search was confined to the east."

"Here is what happened," I said, and gave them a fast summary. I said to Oraiti at the end, "That's why I came to warn Cousin Yiuti about Huyun Shandek's plot. And last spring, when Xianti turned up at Harvest Time with his invasion army disguised as a wedding party, I overheard him talking to Siarti about his plans to attack Whale Haven at New Year's Two Moons."

They stirred at this prospective sacrilege against the empire's most important ritual—a celebration and a plea to Heaven for peace and plenty. I finished, "Because he needs enough of an army to take and hold the throne. He *said* it. I *heard* it."

At this, the captain who had brought Cousin Oraiti stirred, sending a glance at his prince. When he was given a nod of permission, he turned to me. "I trust your highness will forgive this ignorant warrior for a stupid question, but how was it possible for you to overhear this conversation? Was his imperial highness the crown prince talking to you?"

"No. I was eavesdropping on him. He was in the commander's cabin on the top floor of the fleet's warship."

"He let you listen?" Cousin Oraiti asked. "I remember how much he liked to brag, but…"

"He did not know I was there," I said. "I did it in this manner."

I drew my sword, dropped it, stepped, and rose in the air before it could even hit the ground, so practiced was I. I only rose to waist height, as I did not want to brain myself on the ceiling, then I thought, no more lies, and threw the obscuring charm over myself.

Every one of them blinked, heads turning slightly, gazes shifting, but they brought me back into focus almost immediately. Though one or two had that slightly squinty look of a person trying to see past a smear. This was the best proof I'd ever had of the effectiveness of that charm.

"I…see," the Prince of Ran said.

Cousin Oraiti said, "Banti kept making strange comments about where you had been wandering. I think I understand some of them now. Though he doesn't know the extent of … what you've learned?"

"He does not," I said.

"Can you waft young Guiza here to safety?" the Prince of Ran asked.

"I could fly him a short distance, but he'd have to be standing," I said. "It seems to me that's only for an emergency escape. Not a solution."

"This is true," the Prince of Ran said. To me. Even though he now knew I was a girl. He was addressing me as part of this conference.

Intensely aware of this change — for *all* of us — I exhorted myself not to ruin it by angry rants against Xianti. That devastated fleet out there was as much evidence as anyone needed.

"I can insist on hosting you safely here," the Prince of Ran said slowly. "He's not mad enough to launch an attack here, in my citadel. Not unless he has a far larger fleet than I believe."

Here Oraiti repeated numbers and types of warships.

"He chased me *here*," Guiza whispered from the bed. "Wants me dead."

"We know he considers himself above the law," I said, as I mentally rearranged my Circle board. "But if he's coming with your defensive arrows plucked from his hull, and his banners up, then at least he shows he's aware that law exists."

"Yes," the Prince of Ran said. "It's easy enough to predict. He will order me, in the name of the emperor, to surrender Prince Guiza. And if I don't, he can declare me a rebel, subject to confiscation of my ships and men."

"I can't be here," Cousin Guiza whispered. "I can't let him get me again. I know he will use me to get at my mother before killing me. He'll kill her for revealing Father Emperor's will."

I turned to Cousin Oraiti. "I came here in a ship I stole from Lan pretending to be an envoy from Grand Prince Yiulo, the idea being an alliance to convince the emperor to stop the attacks. But you actually were sent as an envoy. Is there any chance Grand Uncle Yiulo actually wants peace?"

"Yes. No. Yes," Oraiti said, wiping his sleeve over his forehead. "Peace after he removes the emperor from the throne. Grand Uncle Yiulo sent me to try to talk Guiza into backing him. At least come talk to him! He promised that if Guiza came to him, he could leave again freely, whatever was decided. I'm sure he'd extend the same to you."

"I am not sure of that at all. You heard Yiuti aboard the ship. He wanted to stuff me in a cabin to keep me safe. His grandfather is certain to think the same way."

"At least he would never surrender you to Xianti." Cousin Oraiti sighed. "Anyway, I'll finish up. It's short enough. I got to Ye to see what we first thought were pirates, attacking the smaller Ye fleet. But the grand prince only gave me a seahawk with one cannon, which would be spitting on a forest fire. There was no taking them on. We hauled wind and slunk off. A storm came up. We rode that out, no lights, couldn't navigate. When morning came, we headed west—and sighted them on the horizon. We didn't dare go near, but from what we could make out, they were anchored, busy repairing damage. Make it look like they weren't the attackers, maybe?"

He paused, but no one encouraged him to develop on this obvious guess, so he cleared his throat and finished, "We figured Cousin Guiza might be heading to Ran."

"We can't sail now," Guiza whispered hoarsely, struggling up and wincing badly. "We'll smash right into them."

"Yes," the Prince of Ran said to him. "I can try to impound your ships—including the stolen one, to hide your traces—but there's really nothing I can do if he commandeers them. And likewise your men. *And* you." At this Guiza struggled, and the Prince of Ran held up his hand. "About your people, I can, and will, hide their numbers. We will begin by putting the hale ones in blue, and sending them to patrol the countryside with my regulars. We can show him those with the worst wounds. The funeral fires are still going—he will see the smoke first thing on his arrival tomorrow." He finished on a hard note. "We'll simply double their numbers in our report. It was bad enough."

Oraiti turned to me. "How *did* you get here? Fly on that thing?"

"No, I have a small party of trusted friends. Do you remember Koi?"

Cousin Oraiti brightened. "Banti will be glad that he found you. He sent him to you. There was trouble with Yiuti's—ayoh, never mind that. My mission is over, I guess. I'd better leave while I can."

I turned to the Prince of Ran. "How about if I take Prince Guiza away? Cousin Oraiti, if we can go on your seahawk, I can use my Essence talismans to hide it. Even if we cross their path, they won't see us."

"One seahawk, one cannon," the Prince of Ran said. "I hate to send the three of you off with only the protection of Essence charms." He looked dubious.

"Either we need a fleet his size, or none," I said. And for Guiza's sake, as he was looking painfully distraught, "But as long as you have Essence paper, I truly can make charms to hide a seahawk. I've already successfully obscured a trader that size. I don't want a fleet, because I don't want more funeral fires burning caused by our people fighting each other just because of one mad prince."

Oraiti sighed. "I don't understand how anyone could follow him. He was always mean."

"I imagine some like the rewards. Others like fighting. Still others think that that is the order of things. Might as well be on the winning side." The Prince of Ran bowed toward me, a military bow, fist to his heart. "But now we're idly speculating while the water clock is dripping. I relinquish them to your protection, princess."

It's difficult to express how much those words gratified me—and how swiftly the doubts then came, storm clouds after the sun. But I was determined to walk out of there looking as if I knew what to do. Because I would know what to do, if not right away. At least, I told myself as I left the Prince of Ran walking down a hall as he uttered a string of commands to his people, they didn't know immediately what to do either. Except run. And yet we did seem to have a kind of alliance implied.

Is this how influence works, I wondered as I raced back to the guest chamber. Not suddenly, like the aftermath of battle. Or imperial edict. But gradually, agreement here, trust there. If so, it was no different than we Pangolins agreeing together on where to go, and what to do. Each of their opinions matter, just as happened here.

I paused in the courtyard, aware that this guest court was surrounded by garden. Isolated. Perhaps for guests so exalted that they required a courtyard of their own, not on the men's or women's side. But I was no exalted guest, with an entourage, banners, and the like. Then I remembered that Arati had insisted on going before me to introduce me to the Prince of Ran.

She knew, I thought to myself. She knew, but didn't tell anyone.

I opened the door, to find Koi in the act of pouring tea. On sat in the open window, half in and half out.

"On," I exclaimed with relief. "Do you know where Jai and Cray are?"

"I do. I just found Koi here, and was telling him which inn they're at."

"We have to leave," I said abruptly. "Xianti is arriving with a fleet."

On shuddered dramatically. "Say no more. You can give us the entire story when we reach our ship. We are taking our ship?"

"No, we're back to a seahawk, with Guiza, Oraiti, and their servants."

"Extra stores?"

There was a quick tap at the door, and Arati entered.

Koi bowed to her, and said to me, "I'll pack our things."

"My clothes," I mourned. "They have to be sopping wet. Ay, can't be helped."

Arati said, "I can get you anything you want. For that matter, what can we give you besides medicine and bandages for Guiza?"

Koi poked his head back in from the bedroom. "I can provide a list."

Arati waved her maid toward Koi. "Get that list," she instructed, and drew me outside into the pretty little courtyard and the cool night air.

I said, without any courtly delicacy, "You knew I wasn't Banti."

"I knew almost from the moment I laid eyes on you," she said in a passionate undertone. "Who would know your family's features better than I? But you had helped the healers, and I'd heard such things about you, and I thought, if you had to be a boy, there must be truth in the report of First Brother Xianti chasing you."

She lifted her head, headdress dangles dancing, her beautiful profile turned toward the stars. "I was lucky. I was married off to a good man. Though I was not in love with Ymek, I came to love him. He waited for me—that's one of the many reasons why I love him. That desperate fire in my heart for Yanti burned itself out after a year of mourning, and I am, I think, much happier with Ymek than I would have been with Yanti, even if the crimes against him had not happened. He is so … possessed by duty, there would have been little time for me, I suspect. Chuti is also lucky. But Kuiza was not. Nor any of my cousins on Mother's side. And the little twins? They are eleven now. If Xianti decides in three years to marry them off as a reward to some brute who trampled and burned an island into submission, who will stop him?"

"I want to stop him," I said. "I intend to. Without more wars." I hissed in my breath, steadying my voice. "It seems that best alternative to him is Cousin Guiza."

"Ymek thinks so, too."

"I intend to talk to Cousin Guiza. See what his vision for restoring the empire is, and convince him if I can to protect people like your little sisters. This—and no more selling of women—has been my goal all along. I don't know Cousin Guiza, but he has to be more sensible than Cousin Xianti. And Cousin Yiuti."

"Thank you," Arati said. "Thank you. Let me show you my thanks by personally overseeing what you might need."

Arati was true to her word.

A plain but comfortable cart, well-guarded, trundled toward Oraiti's seahawk in the cool predawn hour. On its arrival, the seahawk had been directed to an outer wharf, out of the way. Consequently no one was around to see us, save early morning wharf workers. My carryall was now stuffed with fine clothing, including several exquisite robes for women of the sort I had not worn since I was twelve. And not even then, for Mother had always preferred sensible over decorative. Golden hairpins and gems for finger and throat lay in a beautiful carved box.

When I'd protested, Arati pushed the box back into my hands. "Most of those were Mother's. I don't wear them because of the reminders of unhappy days. I only saved the ones that Mother made herself, and Chuti. As for gems and jewels, Ymek takes great pleasure in giving me such things. More than one person will ever need in a lifetime. Take them." She studied me earnestly. "I realize you were raised to modestly disregard such things as beauty. I remember well how Siarti despised your esteemed mother for it. But you are growing to be so handsome, good cousin! More than that, striking. You might need to armor yourself with your appearance. And Ymek agrees that when the time comes for you to become Lan Renti again, you must dress like a princess."

Cray had volunteered to carry all that, but she had a far more important task: she was entrusted with a pair of the Prince of Ran's trained pigeons. As we walked down to the wharf, Cray rubbed her eyes once, then admitted to me, low-voiced, that the bird trainer had kept her for all those scant hours of the night half with instructions not only on the care and feeding of the birds, but how to train them to know her. "I'm to repeat my name before feeding them from my hand," she said. "If I am diligent, Bird-Master Mi promised that the birds would be able to find me if sent to 'Cray'."

"How?" I asked. "I understand them finding the same location, even the same nest, though they fly so far from winter to spring and back again. But persons move around!"

"He could not explain it, but he said that they are the descendants of too many generations to count. The Ran people hold contests for the birds—who can fly farthest, who can find the right target, and so on. He swore the birds are proud of themselves when they do well."

"I hope we have plenty of whatever seeds they like best."

"We do."

Arati's and Guiza's servants carefully saw him deposited in an airy room off the galley. Guiza, of course, weakly protested that he was fine, and we ought not to trouble over him. Once he was settled, his servant Willow brought a last object, long and awkwardly shaped. A guqin, I realized.

Willow must have seen my curiosity even in the dim light, for he bowed to me, then murmured, "He will truly need it."

He bowed again, clutched the instrument to his heart, and went into the chamber. Cray passed by on her way to take the birds to the top, where she and I had been assigned next to one another. "What kind of emperor will Cousin Guiza make?" I wondered.

Cray glanced after the guqin. "From my experience, he was a lot like First Young Master, except music was his solace, then studies. It seems he has not changed in that."

"No one is more dutiful than First Brother, except for Father and Mother. At any rate, he ought to be far better than Xianti."

"Anyone on this ship would be," On commented, joining us. "Down to the deck sweepers; as we say, you can't teach a pig to write poetry. I'll carry the feed, if you want to handle the cages."

Cray relinquished the feed jars as the crew let down the sail, and I got busy affixing talismans around the rail.

We then sailed off toward the rising sun.

TWENTY-FIVE

Her phoenix headdress chimed as she bent
To hear the snow-head speak:
Those cold hands when small
Grasped my sleeve and patted the wooden horse
When large, only touched reins or hilt.
Why do I weep?
Not for him — he cannot hear.
I weep for his unborn sons
As the old wooden horse burns to ash.

I GAVE THE PRINCE of Lan no destination. What he did not know could not be wrested from him. He'd looked over my companions, ignoring On and Cray completely, then gave an approving nod at Koi, now equipped with his sword again. Respecting a martial aspect, as one would assume from the product of generations of military forefathers.

Force respects force. I could argue against it all I wanted, but the truth is there in human nature. I could summon my own semblance of force. I did not have to use it.

I did not regret revealing Sagacious Blade, my Essence training, and flight. I was done with lies.

We sailed a wide circle south through that day. After the sun reached the highest heaven I went around renewing the charms. I was glad I did, for just as the sun began its descent, we caught sight of Xianti's fleet in perfect formation, standing west toward

Ran.

We then turned sail and helm toward the north.

I found Oraiti in conversation with the gunner. Having grown up on an island mainly valued for its brimstone, Oraiti was knowledgeable on the subject. This seahawk, built for speed, only carried the one cannon; even one more would slow it.

When Oraiti saw me waiting, he turned away, and I cornered him for news of my brother. When Koi had been in Whale Haven, he'd been confined to the servants' areas, but Oraiti had spent a lot of time with Banti, and gained a better sense of his mind these days. Oraiti described appreciatively some of the jokes and pranks Banti dreamed up for the entertainment of Cousin Yiuti and the ministers' sons, and it occurred to me that some of what drew me to On was that same ability to find the laughter in a fraught situation. "I was never one for brains," Oraiti said. "I would never sit the Imperial Examination. And expect to pass, that is. But even I could see that whenever Banti got Yiuti laughing, he'd halt his latest revenge rant."

"Is that the reason Grand-Uncle Yiulo sent you to Cousin Guiza and not my brother?"

"Banti doesn't want to leave. I think because he needs to hear whatever news that comes. He can be holding a gambling party, or riding out on a picnic, or sitting at one of the pleasure houses, but if a pigeon is sighted he's *always* there, steadfast as Mt. Lir. A reminder of the promise his imperial highness made about freeing your family first thing, if he's able to take the imperial capital."

That sounded like Banti. In his own way, he had as steadfast a will as First Brother, as Father and Mother.

As I had.

Cousin Guiza slept all through that day. Midway through the night, Willow came upstairs. It was Cray who woke me, whispering that Guiza's pulse was slowing dangerously.

I had been sleeping in my clothes for so long I thought nothing of running downstairs barefoot, my hair lying in tangles down my back. I dropped by Guiza's bedside and took his cold hand in mine. Not even a twitch.

I threw myself into that other sense—and discovered Guiza's Essence stuttering. Shock flashed through me. I delved down into my Essence lessons, though Auntie Breeze had not been a healer. But words from Grandfather Healer whispered in memory, mixing with those Essence memories, and I reached deep within, or behind, the purely physical realm, which was nearly overwhelmed with unrelenting pain. Warding the pain was a familiar task; it was the bolstering of blood vessels that I attempted now, to halt the seepage of blood into his brain

It took many tries, during which I was vaguely aware of water appearing at my elbow. Tea. Buns. Guiza tossed on the bed wearily, sometimes whispering what sounded like names. So many names.

"Is he going mad?" someone unfamiliar whispered, breaking my concentration. One of the crew members? "What's his whispering?"

"Hush." That was Cray. "If it gives him ease, why not?"

I sank back into the mysterious space between the physical and the soul. Grandfather Healer had said that pain was the front line of battle to defend the body. Unfortunately, pain has no brain. No will. It can only intensify, until its warning overwhelms the sufferer.

I had to keep walling pain off, and only then could I slowly curtail further damage. Meridians, veins, arteries, bone and muscle now went about their slow repairs.

Finally I sensed vital physical processes gradually shifting from shock, and the stutter smoothed to a weak but steady pulse as the tentative bonds held. Slowly I withdrew, and withdrew, until I found my cramped body sunk beside a bed, my legs cramping, and the motion of the ship merciless as it clawed at my balance.

When I was at last able to part my sense of self from Guiza's, I opened gritty eyes to find Cray and Willow side by side, one holding medicinal tea, the other a half-eaten bun.

I sat back on my heels as Willow soaked a tiny bit of bun in the medicine, and gently tried to ease it past Guiza's lips. The prince stirred, then obediently ate the little bit of food. Sighs of relief sounded behind me—crew members. Guiza roused enough to drink a few sips of medicine, then lay back, his crackled lips moving as he whispered … more names.

"Ren?" that was Koi. "Is he well enough for you to leave him and get some rest?"

I tried to speak, but my voice came out a croak. It took an effort to moisten my lips. Swallow. "He can't bear the ship movement. He's alive, but if we stay on this ship, we will not make it to Ye, much less all the way to the east. He won't truly recover until he's on land."

Cray said, "We've talked about that. We've convinced Oraiti to avoid all imperial harbors. The best place to stop is Hundred-Trees Island. If we put them in gallant wanderer clothes, no one will know who they are. We can lose ourselves among all the sects who regularly stop there."

I nodded, then embarked on the long, long journey up to my own sleeping space, where I forced down food and drink, then flopped onto the bed.

And slept.

I woke briefly to the sound of a flute, and again to the melodic strains of a guqin.

When I woke for the final time, I emerged on the deck for the first time in what felt like forever. I blinked against the fierce sunlight, and found Koi and Jai sparring at the bow, as Cray worked at unpicking the stitching holding the crimson firedragon to the banner. "Who took care of my things while I was with Guiza? That was you, Cray? With the tea and food? I owe you nine times nine bows."

She reddened. "No bowing. You said it yourself," she said, her fingers touching her Falcon headband, of which she was so proud.

I said to her, "Those bows are in my heart." She blushed and declaimed, then I said, "How far are we from Benevolence Scrape?"

Jai pointed. "The captain said if this wind stays with us, we could be there in three days. We're already past some of the islands."

He unfolded our grubby, battered map to indicate the swarm of islands that Hundred-Trees was part of. Now I recognized that this swarm was roughly midway between the two main routes of the great trade routes, or as Dinek—northern born—called them, the tea runs. As I looked at the islands, I wondered idly if southerners called the two routes silk runs.

I realized On was not there, then recognized the soft sound of his flute playing. It came from Guiza's chamber. I went in to discovery Guiza lying, pale and thin, his gaze fixed on On, who sat cross-legged on the deck, playing. As always, his playing was not expert, but executed with great spirit. Judging by the relaxed almost-smile on serious Guiza's wan face, though he was accounted an expert, he was clearly diverted.

On looked up and grinned at me. Then he kept on playing; while Cray and I had altered the grand prince's banner, trimming the firedragon into a pangolin, then we dyed the whole with thinned ink. The banner looked dirty and battered by the time we reached Hundred-Trees Island.

There along low hills grew the famous myrtles, bursting into leaf. We sailed past a sizable trade city on the main bay, and headed for the Falcon scrape, which had its own much smaller bay on the east end of the island. We succeeded in landing well before any of the big storms could be expected to blow out of the northwest.

Cray directed the captain where to anchor.

The captain, one of Grand Prince Yiulo's men, had ordered his crew to alter their dress to gallant wanderer robes and headbands. But they were still under his orders, so Koi, Cray, On, and I held no conversations in the crew's hearing about our further plans. Grand Prince Yiulo was not our enemy, but he could not be regarded as an ally.

We rowed ashore, Guiza carried on a stretcher. Though it was midway through the night, Cray knew where to go. We roused the household of the Falcons' Guesthouse staff.

The next morning, we all got a chance to bathe, and I met Cray and On in the Guesthouse courtyard, away from listening ears in the dining area. I said, "I think that Guiza is better off right here, at least until he's a bit stronger."

On said, "Do *you* need to stay?"

"I … I do. I need to know what he will say to Oraiti to take back to Grand Prince Yiulo. I want to understand him, if he is to be the next emperor. I hope he will listen to my ideas."

I expected argument, but got none. On lifted a shoulder. "If I'm not needed here, I'll travel between the scrape and the town. There's a celebrated playhouse, and I not only finished writing out *The Donkey Duke*, but I've begun on the dashing adventures of Hero Gan."

I eyed him. "Won't *The Donkey Duke* be like a beacon to those chasing us, if anyone talks about it?"

"Oh, never fear. I will make certain that gossip insists it's the latest thing from the imperial island. Also, the copy I made is going to go east with Oraiti. I'm going to write it out again for the locals. I have to establish myself anyway—I figure on Midsummer being a perfect time for it to appear in both places.

We might be long gone by then. No beacon!"

Koi then emerged from the front building, hair still wet. "The gods are smiling on us. They say the scrape buildings are so full that they could set up as an inn, except gallant wanderers never have coin to actually pay. A couple of taels of the gold the Prince of Ran gave us brought smiles to all the faces. I arranged Guiza's stay with Master Durxu, who offered to send for a physician to examine him."

"Master Durxu?" I asked.

"One of the Four Masters governing the scrape. He let me see the list of Falcons, in case we knew any to stay with." Then Koi grinned broadly, an expression rarely seen in his face. It struck me yet again how handsome he was. Or was that only to me? Those well-spaced eyes framed by such strong bones, that chin with the dimple that I wanted to put my finger to. Ay, I'd seen other girls' glances linger as he walked by. "There's more," he said, breaking my thoughts.

"Yes?"

"There's something I think you ought to see first."

In surprise, we followed him into the front, which smelled enticingly of spicy noodles cooked with crab. Koi did not stop, but dodged around tables, with us in his wake like a string of ducklings. He led us downhill toward the bay, then paused. We could see a good part of the bay. I squinted against the bright morning sun at the ships rolling slowly on the water, masts inscribing lazy circles against the sky....

On's eyes widened as we took in familiar scrollwork on the flat bow. "Is that the *Pangolin*?" Then he laughed. "Dinek is never going to let me forget this. She's always accusing me of turning up randomly."

"That's because you do," I said.

"I need to find out where they are. I can't resist walking by as they come out their door, ha ha!"

I might quickly say right here that the scrape was laid out like most empire buildings, where possible with a north-south orientation, and when not, east-west. They all had their small courts, but central was a large grassy area where training and contests were held. The outer fields were cultivated, and we were told that every household was expected to contribute labor, which included vegetable tending, organized through the Guesthouse. I remembered my first scrape had been run the same way: I'd learned enough by now to understand that scrapes were organized roughly the same way that they had been when nuns began the Falcons.

On waved off breakfast—all they had was porridge, but plenty of that—running off as soon as he found someone who told him where the Pangolins were staying as a group. "I'll see if they've got room," he called back.

The others dispersed in various directions, and Oraiti beckoned me back out into the courtyard garden.

"Prince Guiza promised me a letter to the grand prince," he explained, and gave me a troubled glance. "You know, your brother will expect me to bring you along, or at least to find out why you won't come. I know he's going to grill me over a fire for not bringing you."

"I can't support the grand prince's plan for invading the imperial capital in order to take the throne," I said. "Not that he would listen to me. I also don't want to be tucked away for my own safety. I've learned to take care of myself."

"Yes, I can attest to that," Oraiti said, nodding emphatically. "And so I'll tell Banti."

TWENTY-SIX

…Victory in war is but
Another funeral ceremony…

ORAITI LEFT TO TELL the captain of the seahawk that he was staying for a few days, and I went off in search of the others.

I passed around the perimeter of the grassy field, on which Falcons were busy doing seeds and forms. There were a lot of them out there. Mostly men, it seemed. Men and teenage boys. All in very straight rows. It reminded me of the one time I'd seen the imperial guard exercising, and less like a scrape, whose rougher lines were designated by skill level so that the less experienced would have good examples before them. The imperial guard had been rigid in their sameness, acting as one — a tool in the hand of their commander

On ran lightly up. "I found the Pangolins. What's more, they found Fan. Or she found them."

"How? Where?"

"She'd sailed with some of those Eels, and at each stop, put her name on the list of those hiring as protection for traders, knowing that Dinek always checks those lists whenever she stops at a Falcon inn. Third island along, Fan was right upstairs. Come! They're waiting to see you. Koi's already been coopted over there." He pointed across the field to where the highly skilled martial artists were leading the lines in doing seeds and forms, Koi among them.

Dinek and Fan sat side by side on the same bench as if they would never be parted again, both faces beaming as On and I entered. Fan had a bandaged ankle, which explained why she was not out in the field with Koi.

"And there you are, Ren," Dinek exclaimed.

"What happened to you and the *Pangolin*?"

"We did not have to use those talismans you made. I have them carefully stowed in a cedar box," Dinek said. "We ran until a storm overtook us. When it passed, we saw their scouts, flying green banners."

"Huyun Shendak's pursuit," I said. "Better than Xianti, though not by much. He really is determined."

"Ayoh, he did get orders from Xianti, you told us yourself," Dinek replied. "We decided to stop at the next harbor. They followed us in, they came over, I pretended I hadn't been aware of the chase, they asked about you, I acted surprised and said, *Didn't Pangolin Ren stay on the island?* Which isn't yes or no. One of them nosed around, and they left. Then we…"

What followed was a long and tangled tale concerning a trade run, taking passengers north, then joining a tea convoy through the winter. They were on their way back, stopping at harbors friendly to Falcons, when they met up with Fan, who was recovering from defending a tea convoy against sea marauders. "From the looks of 'em, I'd say they were army deserters. I leaped over to their stolen fisher to chase the boarders, just to trip over a bucket on their deck," she exclaimed, laughing at herself. "But we chased 'em off, ha ha. All they got for their effort was knocks and pains."

The Pangolins decided to finish the winter out on Hundred-Trees Island, and figure out their next destination when spring had warmed the northern world.

"We weren't sure if we ought to look for you or not," Dinek finished. "We did make a promise to return to Auspicious Prosperity Harbor to retrieve Tu Hat. I know they will have made him write out an entire scroll on the virtues. We were going to leave here at the turn of Phoenix Moon sixth month, but I was afraid you might not make it."

That promise had been in my mind now and then ever since we'd left the Hats almost a year ago. I'd considered sixth month's full moon as a marker. Once I reached it, I ought to have a better idea about freeing my parents. But I was beginning to discover that being sure that an entire year will furnish the time to figure out solving a problem was false comfort. That year had spun away, and though much had happened, I was no closer to a solution to rescuing my parents. Indeed, I seemed to be doing everything else but rescuing them, and it was difficult not to feel unfilial.

But that was not Dinek's problem. "I've not forgotten. Sailing at the turn of sixth month is a good plan." Then I asked about everyone, and once Dinek had told me something of each, learned that the Pangolins had saved bedroll space for us. "The scrape has never been so crowded, that's what they told us," she said. "Ayep thinks that a lot of these newcomers are deserters, young as they are."

Fan said, "As long as they don't steal, or attack anyone, that's how a lot of wanderers start." She shrugged.

"I'm surprised to see a Falcon scrape this close to a town," I said. "The one on Mountain Peony—which I never saw—was weeks away, and my first scrape, we had to turn into a sheep farm when the imperials were coming. Though that was for the conscription. I guess conscription isn't as much a worry deep in these islands?"

Dinek said, "There's usually no need for secrecy or disguise. Gallant wanderers just disappear if they must. They own little, which makes it easy. I think the earliest Falcons were all nuns, and they preferred isolation."

Fan said, "Cray told me this scrape was once a fighting sect. It was so large that the town grew up alongside it. But they split up. Most left, and the Falcons took it over. The town since then always depended on the enclave for defense the rare time pirates or suchlike turned up."

"All right, that makes sense. But with these many roaming deserters, or displaced men, turning up, won't that eventually be a problem?"

Fan—child of a garrison—shrugged again. She had spent all her young years among military men, so she was not daunted at the number here. She chuckled. "From the sound of it, the imperials are too stretched out to burrow through all these islands in search of a few here, a few there. Anyway, I expect the masters will be glad of Koi."

According to her, Koi and Jai had chucked their things into the boys' side, and gone straight out to the field. Cray had chucked her things onto the girls' side, but instead of going to the field, she'd taken her pigeons to the roof to work with them. The pigeons were a reminder that I had yet to send a message off to the Prince of Ran. Which brought my mind back to my sober, serious Cousin Guiza.

I must have glanced back in that direction, for On, standing by while he munched pickled radishes and newly harvested and peeled lychees from a tiny bowl, said, "You decided to go east with Lan Oraiti?"

"No," I said. "Right now, I want to see how Cousin Guiza is."

He popped the rest of the radishes in his mouth, tucked the lychees into his sleeve pocket. "I'll walk you back to the Guesthouse." And fell in step beside me, sniffing appreciatively at the wild mustard and lavender that grew alongside the path.

When we left the dwellings behind, he said, "Have you considered what Oraiti is going to be telling your brother, and the grand prince, about your exploits?"

I had, yes. But I was determined not to worry about what I could not control. "He'll say what he's going to say. It doesn't change anything. Not for me."

"Ayoh! Have you considered that what others think about you might change?"

"What makes you say that?" I glanced at him suspiciously.

"Because that grand-uncle of yours might decide to try to marry you off to his precious grandson."

I laughed. "That can't happen. Yiuti and I are cousins."

"Five generations apart," On said with a shrug, and popped another lychee into his mouth. "One generation away from the prospect of inter-clan marriage. Often practiced in clans with long and venerable histories, to keep the name strong. He might want to prevent you from marrying Guiza."

"Guiza is my *uncle's* generation," I exclaimed, scandalized. "He just prefers very strongly that among us we address him as Cousin, not Uncle. I think it was a way to appease Xianti when we were all young, not that much ever did; as Cousin, we did not have to defer to him, except of course before the elders. But we all would know we are from two different generations. The idea is disgusting."

"It's happened before," On said. "Have you *looked* at dynastic history? I remember getting you several books."

"Not the marriages," I said. "I was reading for the balance of trade. In any case, no one beside my parents can arrange a marriage for me that I will accept. It's for Cousin Guiza to negotiate an alliance with Grand Prince Yiulo, if he decides to inherit the throne his father left to him. Nothing to do with me. This is a useless subject. I'd rather talk about the birds. Cray thinks she's very nearly got them trained to come back to her."

On stopped to stare at me. "You think the Prince of Ran is going to back Prince Guiza?"

"Yes. Now that the Prince of Ran has seen Xianti himself. And, I trust, discovered what Xianti and the emperor have done to loyal Lan between them."

"What would you do if you could negotiate an alliance?" On asked, and tossed the last lychee nut into the air before ducking under it to catch it in his mouth.

"It's useless to think about that, except to laugh at the sheer arrogance. As anyone would do at the idea of me, a girl and outlawed, assuming she could negotiate anything. But I can and I will talk to those who do the negotiating. My mother always discussed my father's cases with him. He relied on her. I'm hoping that Cousin Guiza will listen to me."

"Talk to him about…?"

"To form an alliance strong enough to get my imperial uncle to stop the raids, and bring the empire back to peace. And if he can do that, disinherit Xianti. Who isn't his son, after all. I trust he will consider it, at least, once he finds out that Xianti is planning to attack him…"

"How would you—or Prince Guiza—get word to him? And be believed," On added.

"That's the problem," I admitted. "But first I need to understand Guiza's mind."

"All right. Here's my request: while you are talking Prince Guiza into rearranging the empire, I would very much like to ride your sword into the town, and start on getting *The Donkey Duke* on its way to fame."

"You can't fly Sagacious Blade over land, you already know that."

"I was thinking of flying out over the water, around the two peninsulas, as rain is coming in. land as far up the beach as I can. Will the sword let me?"

I closed my eyes and asked Granny Zim, who said, "You have already chosen this young Bu of steadfast heart to share the sword."

Steadfast heart! And yet, though On would no doubt be flirting with any handsome young scholar or pretty dancer he encountered, I knew that he truly was steadfast in the ways that mattered.

I pulled the sword free from my harness, sheath included, and held her out with both hands. He laid his hands briefly, lightly, over my fingers, and his gaze met mine, warm and fleeting. It was comforting as well as enticing, how well we understood one another.

He gripped the sword in one hand and we continued to walk toward the Guesthouse, for he would not be able to fly until he was right along the water's edge. A leap out over the waves, and he would find the Essence to draw on between rain and wind and water.

When we reached the Guesthouse, he followed me into Cousin Guiza's chamber. My still-weak uncle was sitting up in bed with a lap desk before him. His gaze met mine as he smiled. There was gratitude and appreciation in that smile, but not a hint of the warmth that brightened his entire countenance when On walked in behind me. Oh!

"Are you a bit better now that you're on solid ground? You look a bit better," On said with careless cheer.

"I'm well," Guiza said softly—as always. "I must thank you for your trouble aboard the ship. The both of you," he added, addressing me.

We both demurred, me reflecting ruefully that of the two of us, I'd put in the far greater amount of labor, but here was evidence yet again that passion had its own standard of measure.

Willow appeared then, kind and patient, more tooth than chin in appearance. He carried a bowl, spoon, and tea with medicine, by the sharp herbal scent. Guiza tried to wave the tray away, not wanting to commit the error of eating before us. I quickly said, "I'll be back. I was going to take a look at the bay, and On here has errands to execute."

Some of the joy faded from Guiza's face, but he accepted that with his customary grave politeness, and On and I left.

On seemed to be musing as we paced to the shoreline. Drops of rain began to patter on us, around us. I watched him depart into the silvery sheets of spring rain, then I retreated back up to the Guesthouse, where I found Willow taking away the remains of the meal.

Willow bowed, then murmured, "If this one may be permitted to speak—"

There was no use in trying to break Willow's carefully inculcated habits of a lifetime, and I did not try to get him not to bow to me. I indicated permission with the old court gesture.

"—he is eating again. But will not lie down."

"Let me see what I can do," I said, though I had no authority over Guiza.

I knocked on the half-open door, then entered to find him having been bathed and dressed in fresh clothes, his hair knotted properly once again. He was in the process of carefully inscribing a name and a sutra on the thin paper that was usually used only for lanterns.

Then I spied a stack of bamboo strips in a basket, clearly just arrived, and I said, "You are making lanterns for...?" The day for Water Wish lanterns floated either on a river or in the air had passed weeks ago.

"Mourning," Cousin Guiza said.

I saw that a number of papers had already been inscribed, and a substantial stack awaited him. Then I saw the significance. The feverish whispering while he was struggling to hold onto his own life had been to commit to memory the list of all those who had died in Xianti's attack on his fleet.

"May I help?" I asked.

"Your kindnesses continue to heap higher than Mt. Lir," he said, his brush unerring. "But I must write each one. However, as yet I haven't recovered the strength to bend the withies."

"I can do that," I said. "My brothers taught me how to make lamps when I was small. I don't think it's an art one forgets."

Nevertheless it took a couple of tries to get the frame properly sturdy, but once I completed one, the second was easier. I considered bringing up the matters on my mind, but he was looking so pale and determined that I decided to wait.

Indeed, he inscribed another ten or fifteen, then had to lie down, so I took an armload of bamboo and went back to the Pangolin House, where the others offered to help me, once I'd explained.

Three days passed, during which Koi was firmly established among the martial experts, and Fan took off the ankle bandage, insisting she was fine—though she limped toward the end of the day.

Koi took me aside the last night and said, "The situation with a lot of the newcomers, maybe most, is like what we found at that island of widows and women where we met up. None of them will admit it outright, but they're all deserters, yanked from their homes for the conscription. Most didn't know one end of a sword from another until subjected to bad training, abuse—the stories are grim. Too many, especially the young ones, seized from home at fourteen, are one step from brigandage."

"Because that's been their training ever since leaving home," I said. "Fighting, fighting, fighting."

"Yes. The Four Masters are willing to take them in as long as they are willing to listen. The Falcons might be able to put them on a path to a better life."

Martial training in the mornings, then scrape tasks after the midday meal—unlike a martial sect, which honed its fighting skills all day every day. "Maybe some of them will want to go back to their family skills," I said, then remembered Xianti, determined on commanding the empire's largest army.

"Except they can't," Koi said, voicing my thought.

"Yet," I muttered. Another thing to discuss with Guiza.

Cousin Guiza rapidly got better. He was determined to stay on his self-appointed task—and On's visits were rarer and shorter now that Guiza was recovering. On helped us build frames, and continued to fly Sagacious Blade to the town. The odd thing was, if I paused to concentrate, I could sense how far away she was.

The ninth day dawned clear and cool. By now I'd formed a habit of going to do forms with the others, but when it came time for scrapping, I departed for the Guesthouse to help Guiza. On always helped at the Pangolin house, not at the Guesthouse, and I believe Guiza was too reticent, and too scrupulous, to ask after him.

There was quite a number of lantern frames stacked neatly in the yard, with so many more to be done, a spirit-lowering thought when one considered that each name represented a life cut short before its proper time. But everything comes to an end, the sages say, and so it was here: on that day, I arrived with the latest load of frames, to discover that Willow had finished the rest, and Guiza was now painting the last sutras.

He laid his brush down and said to me, "If the stars are out tonight, will you return and set them off with me?"

Surprised that he had not asked On, I said, "I will." Then I understood that in his mind, this was a Ye duty, secondarily a Lan duty, and I was the closest Lan to hand.

I returned to the Guesthouse that night, having put on my finest robe, a new one that Arati had given me. It was a man's robe, woven of silk the pale, pale shade of Ghost Moon in summer, embroidered with silver, three-toed water dragons and lotus blossoms. It, unlike the gorgeous women's robes she had given me, was suitable for a mourning ritual.

We went out to the roof, where Willow and the household

had brought up all the lamps. They covered the entire roof.

Willow and I brought Guiza the lamps, and he lit them by a candle, then bowed, whispering a sutra for their souls.

It took a long time to set each aloft, but again, all things come to an end. Phoenix Moon had crossed a good part of the sky, and on the other horizon, Ghost Moon was beginning its arc, when the last lamp rose to join its brethren.

We stood on the roof gazing up at the many fiery glows against the vault of stars in the highest heaven. He watched the lamps rise until they had to be crossing to that unknown realm, and then he said, his gaze still upward, "You and On Lu are the only persons who did not try to divert me from this task, or admonish me by saying that a future emperor must harden his heart to the loss of lives in carrying out his will. I will do my duty. But I do not *ever* want to harden my heart," he added with sudden vehemence.

"That is exactly how I feel," I exclaimed.

He glanced aside. "To that, I suspect, many will say that is how a woman ought to feel. And I can only answer that if women are truly born with peace in their hearts, unlike us, then how to explain Siarti and especially Liarti?"

"Angry," I said. "Very angry."

Guiza stilled at that. "Yes. The invisible poison." He sighed. "I will do my duty. And it is a duty I do not want. I am not fitted for. But how many are? I know it is unfilial to observe that Father Emperor was ... will never be listed among the great emperors, and yet he was Heaven's Chosen, by all the signs and omens available. Now, the future is not clear, though my mother insists that it must be, that I am the only legal heir. I don't want to fight for the throne. But for peace I will strive to obey the will of both my parents."

"Filial duty," I said, amazed that he was answering some of my questions, and without my having to ask.

"Dealing with Xianti is like swallowing a fly—disgusting whether it's alive or dead. However we meet will be equally repellent. But that will be my first task, and I cannot get past the conviction that he will not listen to reasoning, that it will take war to overthrow him."

"Maybe not," I said. "Do you think it's possible to form a great enough alliance—the Prince of Ran, and Cousin Kandati, as well as your Ye clan and their allies, and perhaps the grand prince—to influence the emperor?"

"He will not give up his throne."

"I know that. My thought was, to influence him to stop Xianti's conscript raids, and to agree on peace in the empire? If there is peace, there will be no need for the world's largest army. And if he does that, the next step is to pressure him to disinherit Xianti. Especially if he finds out that Xianti is conspiring against him."

"It *sounds* reasonable, though I don't know if my imperial brother Koza would believe you even if you stood before him and recounted every word of that conspiracy. Xianti would be certain to lie in his own defense. You grew up in the imperial palace. You know what Xianti's like. It was always violence that relieved his feelings. If he hasn't a war to fight, he'll find one. And his followers, those with a taste for war, will go with him. Whether for rewards, or for the glory of it. And it looks like glory, deceptively like glory."

His troubled voice dropped low, almost dreamy. "My first sight of it was much like this, tonight." He raised both hands toward the dwindling glimmers of golden light. "It was when Xianti launched his attack. There was no communication. No warning. The trebuchets were first. From our perspective, the air filled with fiery glows. At first we thought it was sky lamps, but to celebrate what? It was burning oil casks, arcing ever so slowly upward through the air. Beautiful. Until they struck, and then there were the screams, and the smashes, and the chaos of fighting the fires as his bannerless ships advanced. Then began the rain of metal death. Over the noise of fire and screams, death by arrow came suddenly, unseen. Unheard, except for the hiss of one passing near. That was before his warriors boarded."

He passed a hand over his face. "I fought, as I've been trained to fight. I was always praised for my precision, for my speed. Training in war was important to my northern ancestors, and so I was diligent. That was one of the reasons why Xianti hated me. He had always to be first."

"I remember that."

"I fought because one has to. What could be more unfilial than to die before one's parents? I fought until the rage-madness came on me, pain and anger enough to drive my arm and a thirst for blood I never thought I had in me. I passed out, woke, half-blind with what I thought was my hair hanging in my eyes, and fought more, and I heard praise all around me for my strength, my wild hacking into others' flesh."

I tried to hide a shudder, but he did not notice.

"In those moments they weren't people to me, just targets,

only they came apart in smears of blood and noises I will never get out of my head, instead of being wooden posts, the targets I was used to. When I fainted again, I woke in Arati's palace, dreaming of the dying eyes of those I struck down, most half-trained boys no older than I am. Before we left, Arati told me the wounded among Xianti's boys begged to stay in Ran. One said, they were told it would be easy, we were cowards, and they would be blooded men. Warriors, glorious warriors, though many were barely fifteen. Killing, they were told, defines a man."

He extended his hand toward the sky. "I don't even know the names of those we killed. I only know the names of my own dead. Men? They are nothing now, except heart wounds and memories to their parents. Brothers. Wives. Sisters. Children."

His hand dropped. "I'll do my duty, and many will continue to praise me for my bravery in battle, and to tell me that a good emperor learns to wall his heart against the knowledge that lives are spent by his orders. *That is the cost he must pay to sit in the dragon throne.*" His voice dropped to that vehement whisper that raised the hairs on the back of my neck.

"I don't believe that," I said.

"What don't you believe?" He turned to face me.

"That that cost is inevitable. That it's unavoidable. I want to believe there's another way. I keep trying to find it, a way to bring enough influence to bear so that the emperor must listen."

Guiza sighed. "I don't think he'd listen even to you, though everyone claims that you're half-demon, half-god." He gave me a brief, wintry smile.

"If I thought he'd listen to me, I'd go back home, and risk everything to speak to him. But I know he would look right through me, seeing only a girl. And that's why the necessity to build a strong alliance."

Guiza glanced away. "Yes. Though, were you not a girl, I believe more strongly with each day that it is you, and not I, who ought to be leading this alliance. You've the same education I have. More. Though On Lu had the kindness to play to me while the unrelenting pain in my head was making me insane, I know that it was you who saved my life."

"That was merely beginning healers' lessons. And beginner Essence lessons, combined together. Don't overthink it. What I want most is an end to the fighting. The emperor does not see the effects, there in his peaceful palace."

"And even if he did, he will be assured by his flatterers that such is historical. Tradition. I wonder what it will take to dismantle the tradition of the emperor answering every problem, or suspected problem, with force. I don't want to be praised and flattered into becoming … oh, not like Xianti. He's always been half-mad, but I think back to the punishments and scorn he endured as a boy in order to force him to be the best, to think himself the best, and I can find at least a little pity within me. But that's part of the tradition that emperors must be trained in the ways of war. Those traditions are inextricably bound up with all our rituals. With the dignity and awe of the dragon throne — which must be preserved, or how can one rule at all?"

He turned away, passing his hand over his face again before pressing his fingers gently to the bandage near his left eye, then he glanced up. "They are now in the realm of the gods."

We went back down so that he could rest. He said before we parted that he would begin composing a letter for the grand prince on the morrow. It might take him some days.

I said what was necessary, and departed, but my heart was sorely knotted. I did not need Sagacious Blade with me to be sure of Guiza's utter sincerity. And I understood the weight of tradition. All his scholarship — all *our* scholarship — was the river shaping our direction, inexorable as a flood.

But we can build canals to stem floods, I said to myself. We build dams against drought and famine. He is reasonable, and thoughtful, and surely he can find another way? If he can't, he will listen to counsel?

And yet, as he'd toiled with the lamps, then spoke, it was always to me, and never once did he seem to think of asking for the thoughts of faithful Willow, right there by his side. Because Willow was just a servant.

TWENTY-SEVEN

GUIZA FINISHED HIS LETTER for Grand Prince Yiulo, and it was time to let the Prince of Ran know that Guiza was recovered enough to sail home. Cray rolled my short note into a tight little scroll, and fitted it into the small phial on the bird's leg. She then tossed the bird into the sky and it flapped up and out over the sea, and away.

The other pigeon perched on top of the cage, shifting from foot to foot as it pecked at the little tray of seeds she'd put out. Then she turned to me, saying, "I'm pretty sure that she knows me enough to reach me again. Especially if we return here after fetching Hat Tu, now that she's familiar with this scrape."

"I marvel still at the birds' understanding."

"We know that many animals have senses far superior to ours. Like dogs and their noses. And how cats see ghosts," Cray said.

Cray was fast becoming a bird-master. It would be wrong to say that her growing interest in training messenger birds arose out of her closeness to the Benevolence bird-master. She had too practical a nature for that. But it wasn't until I saw them doing seeds and forms together one morning that I perceived how close they were.

Tall, rangy, with curly dark brown hair always escaping its topknot, Bird-Master Zi Tian was a friendly, patient soul, who had enthusiastically taught Cray a lot about birds on her earlier stay at this scrape. Her willingness to take charge of the birds the Prince of Ran offered arose from her familiarity.

Bird-Master Zi, I learned from Fan, approved of Cray's excellent work with the two pigeons, and demonstrated his trust by giving her squabs from a nesting pair. "We won't see much of her while they're training," Fan predicted.

Cray, so reticent about personal matters, said little beyond, "We might have four birds by the end of summer."

Whether these would be for the benefit of Pangolins or Falcons, Cray didn't say, nor did I ask. I was not certain what my plans were going to be once we returned from fetching Hat Tu. And once those plans *were* in place, whether or not the Pangolins would want to be a part of them. Dinek was emphatically against being mired in imperial matters — as were most wanderers.

She was not alone in that. And here was I, professing to be a gallant wanderer, and yet, because of my identity — and my determination to find a way to free my parents from unwarranted imprisonment — I kept being drawn back to imperial affairs, because they were tied into family affairs. Ayoh, that, and I could not bear to remain silent in the face of injustice.

I contemplated these matters over the next days, as the weather warmed steadily. We had missed Kraken Boat Festival by two days, but I was secretly glad. It always reminded me of making the Journey to the Cloud Empire with my family, the last festival we had spent together. Soon would be the fifth anniversary of the day Xianti destroyed all our peace. Five years, and I was still no closer to freeing my family from the imperial prison.

I kept my turmoil to myself, though sometimes I caught long gazes from Cray and Koi, who had to be recollecting the terror of that day, and the days immediately after. But we did not discuss it; perhaps they waited for me to bring it up, for it was my family who had suffered. What would be the use?

At least Guiza was recovering his strength, with the burden of his self-appointed mourning ritual done. He was often found on the Guesthouse roof, playing his guqin, the sound of which carried on the soft evening air.

One night On, who'd stayed in the scrape to practice forms with us, answered with his flute. The two instruments blended beautifully, but after a time—too soon—On brought an especially compelling melody to a close and said softly, "Best I can do."

"Play some more," someone called from one of the other houses.

"How about something merry!" came a fainter shout from farther away.

"That last one was especially fine," I said, matching his low tone as the night was once again quiet. "But it was..." *Poignant* was the word I wanted, though I did not know it then. "Sad."

On and I had been sitting on the rooftop; he glanced toward the golden light from the Guesthouse windows up there on the hill. I glanced, too, but saw no movement behind Guiza's window.

"You didn't recognize any of those songs, did you." It was not even a question. At my admitting ignorance, On said, "That was a conversation without having to use words. Painful enough as it was."

I considered the unspoken yearning in the guqin's voice, and said, inadequately, "Ah."

"On the ship, Willow said he likes music, and he was in so much torment. I was the only one who played an instrument, so I thought, why not."

"Music seems to be a way for him to express his heart without risking," I guessed.

"Yes. But there are also different natures in the matter of, ah, call it ardor. You've often used the term affinities. You and I, didn't you say we're like the air, never staying in one place?"

"Your affinities are mostly air and water. Mine, mostly fire and metal."

He lifted a shoulder. "Fire is like air, when it comes to passion. Whereas your Koi, and Prince Guiza, their ardor is like trees. Once it puts down roots, there's no moving it."

"Koi and I haven't ... *done* anything!"

"That doesn't mean the passion is not there." He grinned. "Those Eels who came through a few days ago? Handsome girls, every one. All ages. Gave him plenty of attention. Hints. He was as kind as a monk. Whereas someone that pretty gives me the eye, and ayoh! Clouds and flowers, rainbow, sun, and then away. I hate hurting Guiza. It's like kicking a qilin."

I said, feeling it was time for him to be teased instead of teasing, "He's handsome, even with that terrible scar. And the kindness is as deep as his bones, that much I remember from the imperial palace days. He's also extremely wealthy. That's before we can, I hope, get him on the dragon throne. You would make quite a beguiling imperial consort..."

On put up his hand in warding. And again, I knew that he was more steadfast than he liked people to believe. "No tree-hearts. Not even for wealth and thrones."

I laughed at him, and left him on the roof to watch Phoenix Moon in its ride across the sky.

The morning of the anniversary of my family's downfall, Koi walked out to the field with me. I caught a glance from him and I knew that he was remembering, too.

Koi knew me well enough to avoid well-meant words of assurance, for which I was very grateful. "We've got so many newcomers that I've been pulled in to help the masters. Cray's due over at the bird-master's, something about her new pair. She usually takes the young Falcons through the fan forms. Why don't you offer?"

"Me? But I'm a beginner myself," I exclaimed.

"No," he said, unwavering as always. "You think of yourself as a beginner. But you can defend yourself if you have to. You just don't like sparring."

"These things are all true," I said. "But Master Kuin is better." That was the white-haired master, spare of form, who floated through the fan forms—but when she sped up, those steel fangs cut through wood. She was one of the Four.

"Yes. She's needed with all these newcomers," Koi said, and lowered his voice. "As individuals, they are ordinary people. The wanderer way is to preserve that sense."

"Rather than form them back into an army?" I guessed.

"Right. I'm told that Master Durxu, the sword expert, dealt last month with a pack of predators who thought this scrape might make an instant army once they took over. Word spread, and these turning up now seem to be less set on fighting and grabbing. But this many newcomers..." He shrugged, permitting me to finish the thought.

I did, which led eventually to the imperial island. And the possible idea that I'd been struggling with ever since that Cray's pigeon had flown off toward Ran, "After we get Hat Tu. I'm going back to the imperial capital."

"Ren…"

"I know how to hide," I said quickly, as people began lining up and shaking out arms and legs preparatory to beginning seeds and forms.

"You can't travel as a boy."

"I know that. No boy over ten is safe from being grabbed by Xianti's conscript gangs, anymore. Although it seems to me he's losing them as fast as he's gaining them."

"The monks can run but the temple remains," Koi said under his breath.

"Exactly. Which is Xianti's problem. Or rather, Uncle Koza's problem," I said. "And no, I won't try to confront the emperor, though I might try to find a way to get the word to him about Xianti's plans. My goal is to find out, for myself, exactly how my family is guarded. Their welfare. To get there, a girl with a basket and an apron traveling with, or behind, a caravan of traders is nearly invisible."

"And then what?" Koi asked.

"I'd have to see…"

Koi stopped, and put his hands on my shoulders. "Ren. And then what?"

I'd been looking around the field as I spoke. People were still streaming in. Mostly boys and men. At his touch I startled, gazed up into his face, and put my hand to his chest. His fingers twitched minutely, as if he expected me to shove him away. But I closed my eyes, feeling the steady thump of his heartbeat as his earth-deep calm steadied my conflagration of emotions.

"And then what?" he said, even lower. "I think you know what you will find. But there you'll be, still unable to act effectively, as you keep running."

"I'm not running."

"I think you are," he said. "Going to Lan turned out to be worthwhile. Going to Ran as well. But now?"

"I won't form an army," I said, quickly. And laughed. "How arrogant that sounds. How absurd? Even if I could!"

"No more absurd than Xianti thinking the entire world ought to bow down to him just because he wants it to."

Words about succession—birth—rose to my lips, but those could be said for me, too. Though I was not in the immediate line of descent from emperors, and moreover, I was not a man. *And* I had no desire whatever to sit on a throne, with all bowing before me.

"You could raise an army," he said, still calm. "All the components are right here." And then he named off, in quick succession, a succession of Circle points, causing me to depict the entire Circle board.

A barked laugh and some shoving caught our attention. One of the Falcon masters, a woman almost as large as Fan, walked through the middle of the rowdies. "Line up," she said.

Koi said to me, "Who would be better, Ren?" He walked off, and took up his place at the front of the rows of probably deserters.

I refused to contemplate that question, and loped over to Cray, who accepted my offer with an expression of relief.

She raced over toward the bird house, and I rounded up the children, who were running about playing tag. We did seeds and forms until the gong rang for sparring, but the small cluster of young Falcons below the age of twelve stayed instead of running off to be paired up with the other youngsters doing different weapons. A couple nudged each other, with sidled glances my way, then the oldest of them looked at me with owl eyes. "You're the one who flies on her sword."

It was very strange to have that secret out in the open. Also, freeing in an odd way. "I am."

"My uncle is a monk up at Dogleg," a girl stated. "They learn Essence and they can fly on their staffs."

The others ignored her. "Will you show us?" one asked.

"Will you *fly* us?"

"Let's see how well you do in your sparring. I'll watch and wait."

They were very diligent, their gazes coming occasionally back to me and to Sagacious Blade. I had to smother laughter from time to time, but when the gong rang for midday, they stayed as everyone else ran off.

I began by flying around them in a circle. Of course they demanded a ride. I took the largest onto the sword, but as soon as I rose in the air, he clutched at my hands holding him and croaked, "I think I'm going to..."

I set him down in haste. His eyes watered, but he managed not to lose his breakfast. The others eyed him doubtfully, but the girl with the monk uncle came forward. "I want to try!" I kept very low to the ground, barely clearing the tufts of grass here and there, as she grinned then squeaked, "Higher!"

I rose to head height. She, too, clutched my arm with fingers like pincers, but she did not want to be set down. "I want to learn! How can I learn?"

They were all young, their affinities like buds on a branch. Granny Zim said, "That girl's got air affinity."

I said to that child, "First you must learn Essence matters. Now, go get your meal, for work time will be soon!"

The others looked disappointed or resigned, except the girl, whose scowl was one of determination. And I knew she had heard that before.

TWENTY-EIGHT

Their eyes on the distant shore,
They sailed to keep concord.
Not seeing the kraken's shadow below —
It too kept concord.

KOI DID NOT LET me forget that discussion, though it led to no decisions. Instead, our chat over meals strayed into what constituted an army, how people formed crowds and crowds formed into armies. Sometimes the others joined in, most of these conversations taking place in the eating room below the two sleeping chambers.

The other Pangolins seemed to regard these conversations as the wanderer form of scholarly debate. It was fun to exchange stories and opinions, but if anyone began quoting anyone outside of Jong Siang of the 110 Outlaws — even the military sage Liad Il's *The Way of the Blade* — the Ayep boys and the two male Hat cousins would take off, muttering disparaging comments about scholars and schools.

Cray was largely silent, except to repeat, once, "You'll need communication."

Koi listened, but I could feel that question still floating in the air between us. It was up to me to answer, and I had no answer.

When On was there, he listened, watched, and invariably offered stories or songs that got everyone laughing.

The rest of the month sped by, the moons separating more

each night. Summer was on the way. Oraiti came over regularly to train with Cray so that he could receive messenger pigeons.

The physician pronounced Guiza well, and he, scrupulous and genuinely filial, told Oraiti that he needed to get back to his Ye relations to find out if his mother was still safe, and how many of his surviving followers had been smuggled out by the Prince of Ran, before he made further plans.

Oraiti ordered his seahawk readied. He and Cousin Guiza came to say farewell, speaking to us all, but Guiza's gaze rested on On, who stood with us, saying all the usual auspicious things—though I suspect not what Guiza probably wanted most to hear.

He sailed off with Oraiti.

I'd kept visiting him, but gave up trying to talk him into innovations. He was firm that his duty lay in preserving tradition, as everyone knew what to expect. Knew their place. Order was peace, and peace meant order. He'd scrupulously asked Cray for a target cloth soaked in specific herbs, which would draw the hawks that the Ye clan used for messages. From there they would refine a way for birds to find the way back and forth. I never listened after one session full of highly specific training terms.

Meanwhile, Dinek arranged ship things. In her own mysterious way, she determined the right day to leave, for she intended for us to arrive at Auspicious Prosperity Harbor on the precise day a year from when we'd left. "The Hats will be waiting," she predicted.

To that, the two Hat cousins agreed.

And so we set sail. On was excited about visiting Auspicious Prosperity Harbor's town, which the Hat enclave was on the edge of, as they had a splendid playhouse, and he'd left a copy of his *Five Scholars* play there last year. Cray came with us, saying that this was a perfect opportunity to get not only her Ran pigeon but her two new birds used to the *Pangolin*.

Spring had ripened all around us. As we passed through the smaller islands of the swarm, the heady scents of fruit trees drifted across the water, mixed with blossom and herbs. There were mostly small farms on these islands, built around a single mountain. Other islands were barren and rocky cones. A few were rounder at the top, covered with growing things. We were at the extreme southern edge of the tea growing islands.

We made our way eastward, snaking through these islands on a serpentine route seldom used by the imperials. It occurred to me that Hundred-Trees Island was truly in the center of the empire, though it was always said that that distinction lay solely with the imperial capital. Perhaps, if you ignored the Great Sea and included the far eastern islands, the imperial capital could be considered the center. But the empire had lost all its far holdings over recent centuries.

I'm sure that Xianti was anticipating the prospect of reconquering them.

But that would have to be after the empire was restored to peace. Now, with our military stretched so far thanks to Xianti rampaging all over the empire, there was no sight of any imperial ships as we sailed northeast. Dinek walked about with a smile; the ship was in excellent shape, Fan was back in her place at the bow, overseeing the crew and the martial practices, the weather brought only spring rains, and there were no threats.

We stopped twice for fresh vegetables, because we could; though I'd handed to Guiza and Oraiti all of the gold that the Prince of Ran had given us, as I felt it was their due, I kept Arati's donation for us.

At last we sighted what I thought of as the Hats' island, though it was in actuality under an imperial magistrate. But Dinek had told us last year that this magistrate, with an eye to general prosperity, did not interfere with gallant wanderers or traders.

As we drifted up on the tide, the hour was not long after midday. We saw that the usually busy pathway to the Hat enclave was empty. I began to suspect that Dinek had not been exaggerating when she'd predicted that the entire clan would be gathered formally. I ran back up to my cabin, and shucked my favorite green tunic, which was getting rather worn from all those vigorous beatings under the waterfall over winter.

It was time, I decided, to break out Arati's pretty robes. I even washed again, so that I would not get it sweaty, as the day was already quite humid under a glary haze that promised rain. Then I put on fresh underthings, a thin under robe meant for summer, and over it a robe of summer-sky blue, embroidered with bunches of pomegranate blossoms and hummingbirds with iridescent wings. After looking at my own embroidery for so long, I marveled at the excellence of those hummingbirds. The satin-stitching cleverly alternated not only colors but threads of silver so that when I moved, the wings and throats flashed with rainbow hues. I'd forgotten how beautiful true embroidery art could be.

She had given me a pair of soft indoor slippers. I eyed those. They were so fragile, embroidered in red and silver with blue edging. My rough gallant wanderer shoes, worn by boy or girl, and which had carried me from one end of the empire and back, looked dreadful under the fine silk. I'd have to walk carefully. At least the Hat enclave was not far.

As I pulled the slippers on, my hair, which I always wound up and jabbed with a practical hairpin, bobbled and—now impatient—I pulled it all down, and actually took the time to comb it out into smooth ribbons. I could feel the ship was merely drifting now, the sail having been let down. They would drop the anchor next. I pulled half my hair up into a topknot and put one of the gold hairpins through it—that would have to do, leaving the rest to hang down my back. I had never attempted the elaborate styles of young court women, and was not about to begin now.

When I ran down again to the deck, Dinek looked me over, and beamed with approval. My impatience vanished, and I was glad I had made the extra effort. Mother had always said that dress speaks as loudly as manners. Again, her words were being proved out.

On sauntered over, fan twirling. He wore rose pink, embroidered with blue-violet orchids and silver two-clawed water dragons. "We make a fine pair, do we not? Too bad you won't be entering the playhouse on my arm. My prestige would top the clouds." He bowed, fan spread.

I bowed back, consciously resuming court manners to manage my floating sleeves, and he said with a wince, "You're not planning to put your sword harness on over that silk?"

I looked down at myself. "Oh. I did not think of that."

"Let me take the sword," he pleaded.

"You can't be seen flying a sword, splendid as you'd look," I said. "This is still an imperial island, and though the magistrate is said to be friendly, he'd have to report a charmed sword that everyone saw."

"No, no, much as it makes me weep inside at the thought of the populace missing the splendid sight of me on the sword, I know I need to be unseen. I'm thinking of sparing my beautiful robe the dusty, sweaty walk down the main street. The playhouse overlooks the strand." He brushed at his glossy silk.

I laughed at his unrepentant vanity. "Who are you being?"

"Oh, gathering rumors and discussing plays is solely a

matter for On Lu," he declared. "I ought to get at least a couple of meals out of it, especially with a few new poems I've been saving up." He indicated an impressive yacht docked at the far wharf. "I suspect the play season is flourishing. Judging by the size of yon vessel, we've at least a party of very wealthy and idle young scholars in residence who ought to be good for a banquet or two, and the hot rice wine to go with it. I still have not experienced one of your wine canals! I mean to rectify that as soon as possible. Also, I must discover if *The Five Scholars* is a success." He coughed. "Or being done at all."

I had to laugh again, and surrendered Sagacious Blade to him. "There you go. I don't expect to need it while fetching Hat Tu. But don't go skylarking, just in case the Hats seem to require a flaming sword as part of our ceremony."

On's expression turned considering as he took the sword. "I wonder what would happen to me if I was out over the water and you had to call it to you. Would I drop into the drink?"

"I don't know," I said. "We'll have to experiment."

"Not today," he said firmly. "And *not* in these clothes. Just as well I can't fly over land. Or inside buildings! What if the sword tries to squash me into walls if you called it, and it doesn't know about doors? Think of the stains to my silk!"

"Come on, you two, stop preening," Dinek called from the other end of the ship. "The boat is down."

On stepped from habit between our cabin building and the weapons storage shed behind it, obscuring him from sight. I cast the obscuring spell over him and he blurred. I looked away, to find everyone waiting for me.

I jumped down into the boat, mindful of my sleeves and floating panels. Koi and Fan picked up the oars, and began to ply them as I glanced around the peaceful harbor. Not surprising to see a lot of trade ships about.

We reached the wharf, Fan tied off the rowboat, and we climbed to the quay and started toward the Hat enclave.

To my surprise, none of the young Hats ran out to greet us even when we reached their gate. This really was a formal situation. The original problem had not really warranted all this parade—a thought I did not give voice to.

Sure enough, the entire clan was gathered in their Hall of Ancestors. I approached Grandfather Hat Gan, who looked a little older and grayer than I remembered.

I bowed in the gallant wanderer manner in spite of my court robe, and said, "As promised, we've returned for Hat Tu."

Hat Tu was there, behind his grandfather. He came forward, his eyes red-rimmed, which sent unpleasant zings of shock through me. Had he been mistreated for an entire *year* over his desire to brag to his friend? It was the friend who had truly transgressed! No, he looked perfectly healthy, just very unhappy.

With shaking fingers, he opened a short scroll, and his voice bleated as he read out a composition that relied very heavily on the words of Mana Ta. At the end, he bowed and handed it to me, and I bowed back and said, "You've completed the task I set you. We welcome you back among the Pangolins."

At that there was a hiss and shuffle of many feet behind me, which surprised me, as the clan was standing shoulder to shoulder behind the grandfather.

I turned.

And snow chilled every nerve as I perceived a company of armed guards in green with white sashes having surrounded Dinek and Fan and especially Koi. Weapons bared. A heartbeat after, more greens appeared from behind doors at either side of the ancestral hall, flanking the Hat clan. All silent.

Then those many pairs of eyes flicked to a point behind me, and I turned once again, as Huyun Shandek strolled down the middle of his guards, immaculate as always, dressed in pure white. Not the rough, undyed fabrics of deep mourning, but exquisitely woven silk in the lotus blossom pattern, several layers, all in the white of the second year of formal mourning. A white sash circled his narrow waist, with a long white tasseled jade ornament the only color—bearing the wheat spike symbol of the Huyuns, the tassel depended from silk cord tied in the lotus knot.

"Your covenant has been duly kept with these traders," he said to me. "I respectfully request you to resume our interrupted conversation before I am obliged to comply with an imperial order." And he held up a scroll stamped with the red of an imperial seal, for all to see.

It kept everyone perfectly still, for no one was going to disobey an imperial edict.

I could call Sagacious Blade to me, of course—possibly even dumping poor On into the ocean. But then I'd been seen flying out on a charmed sword. Which would be two imperial edicts broken. Besides leaving the other Pangolins to their fate.

My gaze met Koi's across the expanse of the hall, his eyes unblinkingly resolute. He was merely waiting for a signal, and he and Fan would launch to the attack. They might even win against those greens, but that meant leaving dead and wounded people lying about, with more fighting beyond the door, no doubt.

No. It was time to use my wits. I gave my head the tiniest shake, and Koi stilled. Fan's shoulders eased.

I turned to Huyun Shandek. "Leave my shipmates here."

His lips twitched. "I would like to..." He tipped his head slightly at Fan's sword. She sheathed it, Huyun Shandek made a slight gesture, and the greens around Koi and Fan lifted their points, but they remained where they were, poised to act.

"Lead on," I sighed.

TWENTY-NINE

Mountain waters shot through with clear light —
Such is loyalty and friendship, she said.
Whereas the scorch of desire
Occludes as it burns.

THE GREENS PRESSED MY shipmates and the Hats back as I left the Hats' ancestral hall. I tried to control my shaking knees. I now deeply regretted having put on Arati's fine robe. It would be so very difficult to defend myself without getting tied up in my own silk.

At least I looked like Lan Renti again; I needed every scrap of confidence I could find. I straightened my spine, and mindful of On's advice about how boys are trained to assume command of the space around them, though I was no boy nor pretending to be one, I could — and I would — command the space around me to the best of my ability.

I walked head high, shoulders square, elbows out, confident strides, despite the tiny stitches in those soft indoor slippers straining. Though I suspected they would be ruined forever, I refused to skulk like a guilty and fearful victim. I was convinced that Huyun Shandek would enjoy that too much. I was going to walk like a princess, commanding all she surveys.

Huyun Shandek fell in step beside me, and his guards closed in around us.

During the time it had taken to walk up to the Hat enclave

and inside for that brief exchange, nine of the supposed traders in the bay lowered false banners and raised the green with the three tan wheat spikes, white streamers appended. Cannon appeared, having been covered by fishing nets or obscured by barrels.

Huyun Shandek led the way toward the wharf. "I don't see your charmed sword," he observed.

"I don't have it," I responded—knowing that if he sent someone to search the *Pangolin* (and indeed, he gestured toward some waiting guards, who jogged off toward a rowboat) he would not find it. Let him assume what he would.

He didn't speak again until we trod up the ramp onto the beautifully polished deck of the yacht. Which did not belong to an insouciant, rich young master at all. On and I had both been very wrong in our assumptions.

"This way." With a polite gesture, Huyun Shandek indicated the open doors to the main cabin.

My heart was thumping frantically, my thoughts racing. Inside the cabin there was fine furnishings, tasteful hangings depicting white cranes and snow-topped mountains and a pagoda, all acceptable decorations during mourning.

I entered, braced for the windows to be slammed and the door locked, but Huyun Shandek followed me in, and indicated the cushions on one side of a low table edged with a pattern of woven wheat stalks.

He doesn't know Sagacious Blade flies, was my first thought. Or else he'd surely be shoving me into some airless hole below the deck. Much was against me—including, I thought bitterly, my own stupidity in not foreseeing this possibility—but his unawareness of my ability to fly my sword was a very small point in my favor.

"I relied," he said, "on your good sense to avoid bloodshed. Behold. Not a drop spilled."

I wanted to retort that he could have saved himself the trouble and stayed home, but there was that imperial edict, which he now laid aside. It was a sobering reminder that Xianti had given him an imperial order.

A servant entered, bearing tea and snacks on a tray of beaten gold. She set it down and bowed out noiselessly, leaving Huyun Shandek to pour. He did it with an air, discommoded not a whit by the movement of the yacht as it set sail.

He poured one cup and set it before me. I sat unmoving, concentrating on commanding the space around me as he poured one for himself, then sipped. "It has been a long morning, awaiting your arrival. You are a very difficult individual to hold a conversation with."

I stared down at the little ripples in the tea as the yacht surged over the waves. My mind galloped ahead. Wrong we'd been to assume our safety when we had not seen any imperial flags, nor green ones, but that was done. I had to escape—but not too soon. The door was there. I had no doubt I could fling my tea in his face, dash through, and call my sword to me, but if I did that too soon, would all these ships go back to shore to attack the *Pangolin* with the excuse of recapturing me?

My mistake here had been assuming that just because his pursuers had been unsuccessful in chasing me that his scouts would be, too. It was now clear what had happened: some scout had caught the gossip after Hat Tu's friend blabbed about us. The Hats were well known all up and down the trade paths. The connection might even have been *The Five Scholars* being talked about, or put on, which led to the gossip and my name being mentioned; that play had definitely appeared first at Cloud Terrace. By whatever means, the duke's scouts had probably caught up here by last autumn. That gave the duke all winter to put together this scheme, and early spring to sail to Auspicious Prosperity Harbor himself to see it through.

If that was true, he'd know by now that the Hats and the *Pangolin* were only tangentially connected. If he wanted to present my shackled, miserable self to Xianti's grasping claws, it would be no use in going after the Hats. He'd have to get at me through the *Pangolin*. Due back on this day. With me.

I had to give Dinek enough time to get everyone to the ship. Then, I trusted that she would fall back to Benevolence Scrape, which at least so far neither Huyun Shandek nor the imperials knew about. No doubt, during the rain I could feel coming, she might employ those talismans she still had to shake off pursuit.

Keep him talking.

"I do appreciate the avoidance of bloodshed," I said as he sipped tea.

"My esteemed mother gained the distinct impression that the lives of your subordinates are important to you," he replied. "An attitude with which she is in sympathy."

Though I meant to hold onto the courtesies, I could not resist saying—in as even a tone as I could manage—"An attitude that seems to have stayed with her generation."

"You must not blame my mother for my shortcomings." He

saluted me with his cup. "On which she had plenty to say when she was, ah, resurrected."

I indicated his white sleeve. "You're still pretending mourning for her? That seems very risky."

"No, no. We arranged for her to waken miraculously at New Year's Two Moons—several weeks, as it happens, after my father's remaining aunt died peacefully in her sleep. She would have been gratified to discover that I ordered the island into formal mourning for the full three years."

A crackle from my lap reminded me that I was still holding Hat Tu's painstakingly written scroll. I laid it carefully by the untouched tea. It had uncurled slightly, the word *Virtue* written large.

Huyun Shandek glanced at that, then leaned forward slightly. "I believe we commenced our acquaintance badly. Let us begin again."

I said, "We began badly because you lied to me."

He responded equably, "You lied to me."

This was true, though for vastly different reasons.

He went on, "I comprehend that we both lied out of perceived necessity. You did not want your origins discovered. I did not want inquiry into my plans."

"To overthrow the emperor."

"You have to agree that he is a terrible emperor. And that his prospective heir is far worse."

"Yes," I said, glancing out the window. The island was slowly sinking behind us, but it was still relatively close. And, unfortunately, so were the heavy-laden clouds rolling in to obscure the mountains. Rain was definitely on the way, which would make sustained Essence pull more difficult.

"Whereas," he went on, "while you lived comfortably and undisturbed on my island, you must have perceived that I know how to govern well."

"Except for the matter of profiting off the human misery of those without homes, or wherewithal to make them," I said. "What would you do as emperor, establish a ministry of slave sales? I'm sure you'd rake in more profit than even silk or tea taxes."

"That," he said, "is a traditional solution." Yet as he spoke, his cheekbones edged with color, which suggested to me that either somewhere inside him there remained the vestiges of conscience—or perhaps I was seeing the remnants of anger resulting from his mother's discovery of his exploitation of this "tradition."

"Which is being mitigated," he said, and I thought, ha ha, his mother *is* using her considerable inherited holdings to pressure him!

Then he added, "As for the empire, you yourself could oversee the complexities of displaced persons. Don't tell me you haven't thought about it."

"Of course I have," I retorted—and then, too late, saw his context: he meant as empress. Not that empresses ruled in their own right. Though some had held more power than others. Always granted by either the emperor, or by the court when there was a regency.

I did not *at all* like his implication.

He eyed me in perplexity. "How old are you, anyway? I do not remember you, and I believe I was introduced to all the imperial children during my visit to the imperial capital."

I'd probably been in the sole charge of my nanny then, my world confined to the little frogs in Mother's nine-fold screen, but I did not say so.

He turned his fan over, then said smoothly, "Young, that much is obvious. And yet quite capable." He flicked Xianti's imperial order with a gesture of disdain. "As for today's events, though it was simplest to arrange matters through entirely legal conduits, it can always turn out that I was mistaken. This conversation, right now, uninterrupted at last, is my attempt to offer you alternatives. Once we understand one another."

"Mistaken?" I repeated, completely taken aback by this unexpected turn. I'd assumed that I was in that cabin to endure a lot of gloating and threats before I was chained up to be handed over to the imperials.

"I am quite willing to lie and say that Pangolin Ren—or at least the Pangolin Ren I arrested—was not Princess Lan Renti."

"What is the cost to me?"

"No cost." He laid the fan aside. "Marry me," he said. "I'm convinced that together, we could restore the empire to greatness. I would give you equal power, as long as we both agreed on matters of import. It is time for a new dynasty, is it not?"

There was so much wrong with these words that I was rendered witless with shock. But I hadn't the luxury of witlessness. I had to consider everything. This was a dangerous conversation, and for a heartbeat or two I wished so much that Granny Zim were here to listen—except that I was fairly certain he absolutely believed what he said. So far. And that was the problem: truth is not always the same thing to everybody.

I said very tentatively, "Is this why the three years of mourning? To postpone your marrying my imperial cousin Siarti?"

"I will avoid that if I can." His mouth tightened in distaste. "You ought to read the missive she honored me with shortly after your sudden, and may I add, mysterious departure the spring of the Dolphin Year." He gestured, indicating the spring previous. "A peculiar mixture of arrogance and platitudes copied straight out of the dullest lesson books, and presented as her own words. I surmise that the only truth in it was that she did not want to live among us while we were observing mourning for my mother." He opened the fan and turned it over, letting it express his dismay.

I had to suppress a laugh when I remembered Siarti planning that very letter while speaking to her brother.

"Even were it possible to avoid marrying her," I said, "my cousin Xianti would have objections. No doubt delivered with an invasion."

"He is probably already seeking an excuse for that, but the last I reliably heard, he has run into difficulties chasing one or another of his imperial relations," Huyun Shandek said blandly.

I was not about to let him know how much I knew about that matter.

He went on, "During the time the imperial crown prince has been pursuing other princes in the west, I've established communication with the emperor. I believe that he would agree to my substitution of one imperial princess for another, for he seeks my support."

"While you conspire against him."

"Everyone is conspiring. Even you," he added with a glimpse of humor. "True?"

Yes—it was true, but for the good of the empire. Except he seemed to believe that that was his goal as well.

Another subject! "You said there would be no cost to me. I trust you will forgive this ignorant one for her lack of wit, but I see a considerable cost in that I'm confined to a choice between marrying you or being handed off in chains to Cousin Xianti's tortures." I liked those words for their implication that these choices were equally dire. "You do know what he did to my brother, who had never committed even the smallest crime?" To bolster my fading confidence, I grasped the teacup like a boy and drank the cooling tea as a boy drinks, managing my sleeve with a boy's gesture.

"You," he said, eyes narrowed slightly, "would make a magnificent empress."

That so unsettled me that I dropped the cup on the table, just as the ship kicked up a sharp lurch.

Thunder rumbled in the distance, and the rain commenced.

I said firmly, "I had no such thoughts." My gaze shifted to that paper with *Virtue* at the top.

Virtue. A new idea: perhaps I could try to win Huyun Shandek's support for Guiza. But could we ever trust him? Not for a heartbeat.

To get away from the subject of marriage, I said, "How would you rule differently?"

He began to outline his plans for the empire. A lot of it sounded much like Guiza's same reasoning, the reestablishment of the laws of the previous dynasty, and encouraging trade with a hiatus of taxes for a year.

As he talked on, I was thinking hard. On the credit side of the ledger, Duke Huyun Shandek *was* a good governor to the inhabitants of Mountain Peony. He was well-respected, and even liked by all I'd met along Cloud Terrace's main throughfare. His guards liked him, and they were far better treated than those poor deserters had been, with their talk of forcing young boys into the front lines to serve as targets, and the grim evidence of surviving floggings consequent to a long list of stringent rules. Finally, though Huyun Shandek had set up this plan to trap me, he had indeed accomplished it without spilling a drop of blood. He could have gone the brutal route. Xianti certainly would have.

On the debt side, I still did not trust him. Also, though he'd contrived a plan to capture me without bloodshed, he still intended to overthrow the emperor. That meant every letter of friendship and alliance he wrote to Uncle Koza was a lie. *Isn't everyone conspiring?* he'd said so easily.

Ought I to try to convince him not to interfere with Cousin Guiza? This was another bridge of knives. Beginning with the daunting fact that I couldn't believe anything he said.

Ay! I needed Granny Zim after all. But I didn't want him knowing anything about Sagacious Blade.

"What are you contemplating so seriously?" he asked, startling me. "Might I hope you are considering my proposal?"

The arrow never returns to the bow, I wanted to say, so very badly. You lied so easily, I will never trust you. Especially with that smile looking so assured. But you know what they say about smiling tigers.

Time to exploit the tiger's might—even if I did not feel at all foxlike. Wishing On were with me to dance verbal rings around this tiger, I said, "I have to admit that I'm so hungry that my brain can only sadly contemplate the banquet that the Hats were probably preparing for us, until you came along. I thought I whiffed garlic-and-ginger seared whitetail, one of my favorites."

He smiled broadly, uttering a laugh. "An easy dilemma to resolve. I confess to a wish for the midday meal as well. We could scarcely demand the Hats to host our company to a meal while interrupting their ceremony so rudely. Ay! It no doubt will make an entertaining story for a time."

My fists curled in my delicate sleeves, but I loosed my fingers. He sounded so sure of his own cleverness. But I needed that complacency.

He raised his voice slightly, summoned a soft-footed steward and ordered a meal. Then turned to me. "I am accustomed to enjoy music while dining. Will that disturb your reflections?"

"Music is always welcome," I said, and in a very short time, a group of six young women more or less my age drifted in, dressed in floating silks of white (must not forget that mourning!) and I caught avid side-eyed glances that quickly averted when my gaze met theirs.

I remembered On telling me some time ago that young and hopeful entertainers competed vigorously to be chosen for these yacht expeditions. Such contradictions in this man. I was always off-balance. Xianti, I thought as servants brought in golden dishes from which wafted delicious fragrances, was in some ways easier to deal with: one expected, and would get, threats.

The food was as good as it smelled. The musicians were as excellent, and—as the conversation was at best desultory (occasional polite questions from him, short answers from me)—the performers ventured a couple of songs, and twice, decorous traditional fan dances, which take up very little space. As well as being appropriate for mixed company. Looking at those clinging silks, I felt quite certain that these dancers had probably been regaling him with sleeve or butterfly dances on the journey from Mountain Peony. Ah, he was welcome to their cajoleries, and I hoped that the girls profited well thereby.

All meals end, and once there was only tea left on the inlaid table—I had not touched the wine, fragrant and tempting—and the dancers had followed the servants out, I knew it was time for the second attack.

Was he going to attempt a more personal approach? Perhaps I ought to counter his advance with my own charge.

THIRTY

What is friendship to me, she is asked.
Here is my answer, she says.
This quick kingfisher sketch,
smudged by a dropped dumpling,
Is more precious than a thousand kingfishers
Carved artfully from gold.

"ON YOUR VISIT TO the imperial capital," I said, "did you have the fortune to meet my youngest uncle, Imperial Prince Guiza?"

Huyun Shandek's eyes narrowed. "He was a boy at that time, was he not? The emperor was inordinately fond of his talent with various musical instruments. Justly so," he added with a salute in the direction of the imperial island.

"We used to call him the Perfect Guiza among ourselves," I said. "Because he was. Never in trouble, never mussed his clothing, or spoke a word wrong. Advanced in scholarship. He, unlike the rest of the imperial princes, was taken to court often by the emperor, as his behavior was invariably impeccable. And it was said that he favored him over his other sons."

"Ah. And what brings this qilin to mind?"

"Only that word has passed among us that the previous emperor, in dying, wrote a will appointing him the designated imperial heir. Which lies behind Cousin Xianti's desire to see his demise."

"I see." The duke's voice was devoid of expression. "I take

it this is the one you favor among the warring princes?"

"He is," I said. "My fervent wish is that everyone would unite behind him, and compel the emperor to call an end to the fighting. Imperial Prince Guiza hates war. He knows that no matter who leads—whatever their motivations—it's invariably the empire's subjects who suffer. That is the worst betrayal of Kanda's Twenty-Five, which we all learn in our earliest lessons. It's the fundamental law of our government, that mercy and enlightenment are the best correctives, and not fear."

"All very well, but I don't think Lan Xianti will sit still for a lecture on the Twenty-Five," the duke said mildly. "Which is why the sages included patience as well as courage and determination among the necessary qualities for an emperor."

My mind shot right back to the library, and sitting with First Brother as he recited scroll after scroll of the sages—sometimes corrected by me. Altogether unwitting, I had been committing to memory a young master's education in preparation for taking the Imperial Examination. During the past five years I had thought myself becoming more ignorant as the days of my lessons with my mother sank into the past. It was only now that I was beginning to appreciate what I had learnt by rote. I had reached the age when the hopeful future magistrates and ministers made the pilgrimage to the imperial city to sit the examination, and my comprehension was fast catching up.

I said, "Mana Ta distinguishes between courage as exemplified in stereotypically daring behavior, by which I mean assaulting anyone who insults you, and a fearless, or firm, commitment to righteousness. That kind of courage is the highest form—an opposition to wrongdoing, but also honest submission when one finds oneself in the wrong."

"You have been studying the ancients diligently, have you? To what end?"

"Not to any end," I said, wary of the direction of his question. "Except filial piety. I was twelve when I helped my Second Brother to coach First Brother in preparation for the examination. It mostly fell to me, as Second Brother had his own tasks that took up more of the day than mine did. Acquit me of nothing beyond a knack for memory."

"It appears you did not waste that knack," the duke commented. "As you have not wasted your knack for putting to good use such tricks as charms on swords. Where did you come by that one? You agreed to dispense with lies. Why don't we begin with your Pangolin forebears?"

That was a bit of a sting. Only if I let it bite, I reminded myself. I did not care what his opinion of me was.

"I needed to break any trail of pursuit by Cousin Xianti."

"Understandable." He went on, "As for the sword. The fact that you've apparently given it away indicates that the charms did truly wear off. But you've still ambitions. It appears that you are exerting them on behalf of your imperial uncle the qilin."

I repeated, "He wants an end to war."

"An admirable goal. I respect it. I've also been counting back, and I believe that you are no more than sixteen, eighteen at the outside. Eighteen? There are many who consider sixteen the ideal age for marriage, but then most who do require no more than a winsome countenance in a wife, and an ability to ensure the continuation of his dynastic line. The winsome appearance will do for casual encounters, but I seek more in a wife. I seek a complement in wit and ambition. Not a spy." There was the slight distaste again, and I remembered Siarti, lurking like a snake in the grass.

He went on, "You'll be twenty-one when my mourning period ends. By then I intend to be prepared to act as I deem best. The world will no doubt look very different to you by then."

I clenched my teeth at the implication, but breathed out the ire. Was it possible…

I could not help saying, "The emperor, or more correctly, Imperial Cousin Siarti, might not wait that long." It was a fair guess that right now she was enjoying ruling over all the women of the imperial court, but if she tired of that—or if someone was promoted over her, forcing her back a step in rank—she might decide to put up with the much more relaxed requirements of second- or third-year mourning on an island where she would have precedence.

"I will have to take that risk," he said, and there was no hint of a smile. "Do you have any warnings in case this event does come to pass?"

What could I say? Honesty where the safety of the innocent was concerned.

"She will come with her own tasters," I predicted. "As her favorite method for getting rid of those who annoyed her was poison. But she also used to order maids to be strangled on whim. I do not know if she has grown out of that."

He gave a slight nod. "That can be planned for. Anything else?"

"Don't let her near any pets you might be fond of. Though that was mostly her sister and Xianti." I frowned at him. "Does this mean you're going to let me go?"

He held out his hand toward the window. "I did say that I could report I was mistaken. Have I not been straightforward during this, our much-postponed interview?"

"Yes, but you also said you are writing to the emperor, promising support when you are conspiring against him."

"I do not trust him," Huyun Shandek said equably. "I could trust you. I am endeavoring to begin now."

I was not going to say I trusted him. Nor would I lie. I was done with lies. I was doing my best to be done with lies. "When may I be set ashore?"

"We can put in at the next island."

I bowed, hands in my sleeves. "Thank you."

"Your sincerity," he said ruefully, "implying an eagerness to quit my company, is as sharp a reproach as any I've ever experienced."

It was that wry humor that got past my armor for a heartbeat. I recognized that in other circumstances—maybe if I had been betrothed to him from a young age, and sent off without any other experience—I might have considered myself lucky. I might even have closed my eyes to aspects of his governorship that were less appealing than others. Because after all, women did not interfere in government, I'd been taught. And he was so cultured, even attractive, in all other respects.

I did not like this insight into myself, and consequently I was very glad when that next day, after a brief rest in a comfortable cabin followed by a sumptuous breakfast during which Huyun Shandek exerted himself to be companionable, I found us coming into a small harbor, imperial banners flapping in a warm, earth-scented wind.

For the first time since that long-ago Journey to the Clouds, I was conveyed in comfort to the shore, and met with smiles and bows by assistants to the local magistrate. Huyun Shandek's stolid-faced steward did not give the assistants a name, instead calling me an honored guest of his grace the Duke and Governor of Mountain Peony Island, and a hefty purse passed from hand to hand.

In the flurry of greens seeing me to the shore and servants going off in search of fresh foods and smiling assistants outdoing each other in welcoming the "honored guest" I was not able to see if anyone else disembarked, specifically spies. I had no doubt at all that Huyun Shandek had ordered at least one spy to keep a close eye on whatever I did next—wherever I went. I reflected as I was tenderly led to the finest inn along the main street, and handed over to another set of smiling attendants, he could always have set them ashore elsewhere, out of sight entirely.

Very well then. I watched from the window of a spacious inn room that overlooked the bay as the yacht sailed away again, and at last I could breathe easy. I needed to make my way back to Hundred-Trees Island, but not before I identified the expected spy or spies and shook them off.

First thing? Establish myself as a perfectly innocent young woman having a splendid outing at the expense of a duke. As I expected, when I summoned a servant, I was told that I was to feel free to order anything I wished, and that included purchases made along the street—I was only to inform the proprietors that I was a guest of the Seven Sages Inn, Miss...?"

I did not want to lie anymore, but even stronger was the desire not to put up a beacon for any roaming spies of Xianti's. At the same time, I had no desire to associate Pangolin Ren with Huyun Shandek, which I was fairly certain he intended. I compromised on my first traveling name after escaping the imperial city: Ran, with a different tone, which meant a different character. "Ran Ti," I said.

"Miss Ran," repeated the servant.

I set out to explore the main street. I needed clothes and especially shoes. After two days of wear, my silk was looking limp, and though the beautiful shoes were holding up better than I'd expected, that would not last long. That much fine work deserved better treatment.

This is good, I told myself. I need time to think.

And think I did.

I was thinking when I found a clothing store. I ordered two practical summer travel robes, a night robe, and new linens. They took my measurements and promised to adapt the items that I had picked from what they had on display.

I was thinking when, farther down the street, I found a shoemaker. I had been reviewing every word the duke said, coming always back to the fact that I had three years—two, as the first had already passed—to do what?

Irritated with this oblique threat—for that is how I regarded it—I decided to take advantage of ducal generosity and get all new shoes and stockings. They also took my measurements.

I thought as I wandered back, until I spotted a bookseller, and to my delight, found among the new storybooks a version of *The Five Scholars*. I opened it right away, and found what I knew On would want to know: that the story was written after "the famous play by the mysterious hermit-scholar On Lu." He would not make so much as a tinnie from the storybook or its copies no doubt being written in the booksellers' back room right then, but the fame was what mattered to him.

I bought that and another, said loudly to put it to the account of Miss Ran Ti at the Seven Scholars, and then tripped back down the street to the inn, where I sat at the window watching the ships come and go, thinking about war, and armies, and Guiza, and eyeing all the idlers who passed by, in hopes of spotting the spies I expected.

My ability to catch spies was, as always, as successful as a basket hauling water. Equally unsuccessful was any conclusion to all my ruminations. Questions, always questions.

When darkness fell, I ate, read until my eyes tired, and slept soundly.

Early the next morning, I woke to the sound of rain, and the welcome news that the clothing I had ordered was here. All they'd had to do was hem modest sleeves and robe panels. I told the servant to bring them up with breakfast, and was going to retire to bathe when she said apologetically, "They insist that the clothes must be fitted."

"They?" I repeated, wondering why two people came to fit what I'd already approved. But I agreed, and a short time later there was a quick rap at the door, and two young women in servant robes walked in.

I looked at their faces—their familiar faces—and my mouth dropped open. "Cray? *On?*"

"Sisters Oriole and Pigeon," On said, preening coyly. "A quick bribe to the delivery girl, and here we are."

"But…"

"*Pangolin* followed that yacht out of Auspicious Prosperity Harbor," Cray said, pulling not only my new clothes from the satchel, but also my carryall. "Koi was planning attacks when On here said that as long as he had the sword, you were not in immediate danger. He watched it the entire time, as if expecting it to turn into a snake and dart into a hole."

"Dinek kept us at a distance, and we almost lost you during the night," On said. "I put my hand on the sword and I swear it pointed me toward you, though how I know that I can't really say."

"The sword didn't talk to you?" I asked.

"No mysterious voices," he said—with a disappointed sigh.

Cray went on, "Dinek hung the talismans about the *Pangolin*, and we followed the yacht in to this harbor. We saw you get rowed ashore, then sailed on to find an inlet and disguise ourselves, because we did not know how long the charms on the talismans might last."

"I found you last night, we bribed the delivery girl this morning, as I said, and here we are," On finished triumphantly.

"For which I thank you sincerely." I clasped my hands once again in the gallant wanderers bow. "I think there might be spies..."

"Two," On said, sober now, as he held up two fingers. "And two greens. Bodyguards?"

"Some kind of guards, since Huyun Shandek neglected to inform me about any of them," I said grimly. "I expected him to put *a* spy on my shadow."

"You can make your mysterious escape on the outward tide tonight," On suggested, his gaze then falling on the books. "*The Five Scholars!* Is this fame at last? Ha ha! You must bring it to the *Pangolin* so I can properly gloat over it."

"That's why I bought it."

"I will be your donkey for the next thousand lifetimes." He bowed, then pulled a folded paper from his sleeve. "I drew a little map of where to find our cove. The *Pangolin* is pretty well concealed. You might not spot it from the air, as there's an enormous oak and a lot of willow in summer leaf."

"We should go," Cray added. "Delivery, even fitters, won't stay around chatting. And we have to give this satchel back to the delivery girl. She's waiting at a tea place."

I thanked them again, then said, as I walked them to the door, "Thank Dinek. I was sure she'd go back to Benevolence. This is just the kind of political thing I know she does not want the *Pangolin* mired in."

"About that," On said. "Ay! You'll have to talk to her. We'll be waiting for you tonight. We will all exchange stories then."

They departed, and I bathed and put on my new clothes. Then, since I had an entire day on my hands, I used the plentiful water in the bath to wash everything in my carryall and hang them up to dry in the warm breeze.

My new shoes appeared in the afternoon, again quickly made because I'd asked for no embellishments. I packed up all my things, then took a walk in my new clothes so that the spies would see me, stopped at the bookstore again, and a tea shop, where I sat, sipped tea, and watched the street traffic. I returned to the inn, and ordered dinner as soon as the sun set.

I opened the window wide, and sat by it to eat and watch the sun set over the peninsula. Then I read — or at least tried to read, but my mind was full of questions — until third dragon, then blew out the lights.

I possessed myself in impatience until the stars had shifted to what I hoped was second Turtle, and the height of flood at last began to sink. I put on my carryall, shut my eyes, and called Sagacious Blade to me.

Smack! There she was, my faithful companion. I threw the obscuring charm over myself, climbed noiselessly to the window sill, stepped on the sword, and rose up above the inn.

At the back garden, I spotted a figure walking back and forth. At the bottom of the street, just in view of the inn's door, another.

I flew over their heads, and away to the *Pangolin*.

"Heaven does have eyes," Dinek exclaimed on my landing near the galley and clearing the charm away. "Sails! Anchor! Let's get back to Benevolence."

Anchor up, the ebbing tide was already beginning to carry the ship out of the cove. I ran to my cabin to throw my things in, then moved to the rail and began casting the obscuring charm over the ship as the wind caught the sail. Then I went to the dining area, where I saw Koi, his eyes marked with tiredness. On was back in his normal clothes, Cray as well.

I said, "Huyun Shandek said he wanted to begin again. Neither of us lying. He wants to overthrow the emperor. I explained that Cousin Guiza is the true heir, and that he has my support. He said he is in mourning for an aunt, and won't act for two years. Then said I could leave at the next harbor."

"He just … let you go?" Fan asked.

"If he's to be believed, his objection is to bad ruling. *If* he's to be believed," I emphasized, "his goals for good ruling sound roughly the same as Cousin Guiza's."

"Do you believe him?" Koi asked.

"They both seem to think that a good emperor returns to traditional roles. I'll believe him that far. As to how he plans to go about it, he did not share his plans and I did not ask. He didn't reject the idea of Cousin Guiza ruling outright. Perhaps the fact that Guiza is the true heir might weigh with him, if he truly respects tradition. Or, more likely, it occurred to him that my being in contact with my imperial relatives might achieve a lot of his work for him—assuming he can beguile me into joining him."

"That sounds more like him," On commented.

"But now we're getting into our old discussions of what if. To summarize, no, I can't predict whether or not he will invade the imperial island after his mourning ends if Guiza is on the throne or not."

"But he's definitely coming after you." Koi's expression didn't change.

"I think it's more he's confident about his powers of persuasion," I said, and turned to Dinek. "Thank you." I bowed. "I know you don't want *Pangolin* mired in imperial affairs, and here we are. Again."

She exchanged a fast glance with Fan, then said earnestly, "I'm beginning to see that we're mired anyway. No one is safe. Not even those at the top. I saw that wound on Prince Guiza. And hearing about that Prince Kandati and his princess in your ancestral island who can't even hold a private conversation in their bedroom is frightening. My objection was always to those of rank playing their games against each other, without a thought to the commoners like us. But it's different now. We'll support you as long as you think of the common people. We're all agreed."

"Thank you," I said, bowing again to show my gratitude, and those not on watch returned to their usual nighttime pursuits—everyone except Koi, who remained sitting, stolid as stone. And Cray, stroking a pigeon with one finger. The bird hopped from her shoulder to her head and back.

Koi said, "That wasn't all. What happened with that man?"

"That was the gist of it."

"And?"

"He wants to marry me and make me his empress," I said.

Koi's exclamation of *What?* Overlapped with On's voice outside the window, "I knew it. You seduced him."

It was my turn to exclaim, "What?"

"And what if she did?" Cray said, eyeing him narrowly.

On swung a leg over the window sill, laughing the while. "I can just picture it. You walked onto that yacht like the Empress of Heaven in silk and gold, and he tottered after, gloating and drooling—"

"There was no seducing! None! Not so much as a hairpin got

touched! On either of us!" I stated—a bit too loud, for there was sudden silence outside the open windows, except for the wash of the ocean against the hull, and the clatter of battens.

On shook with silent laughter—he never tired of teasing me in that way.

"Seduced by refusal," Koi said slowly, surprising everyone.

On grunted agreement, chin on his fist, elbow propped on his bent knee. "It's a tactic. He's intrigued. My guess is, no one has ever said no to him since the first time he showed an interest."

Koi said flatly, "I saw the way he looked at you, Ren."

Cray scowled at him. "Nothing wrong with that, either." And, sharply, "I had to listen to all those lessons Ren got about how girls must be modest and retiring and demure, and if anyone looks at them—though they are supposed to dress beautifully—then she is at fault for enticing them. The wandering way is freedom for both."

"I think he wants my imperial connections, oh, and Sagacious Blade, more than he wants me," I said to them all. "I let him think the sword is gone. And I did not tell him about our journey west. But he has to be hearing *something*."

Koi asked, "Does he truly want an equal working side by side with him, or does he assume you might be a weapon he can wield as he wants?"

"I'm assuming the latter, though he says the former. He might even believe it … as long as this partner of his agrees with him. There's also the matter of Siarti. He did offer to write to the emperor in order to swap me for her, but I pointed out that Xianti might insist on the marriage with his sister—along with an invasion. And that was it."

"Two years," On said, wiping his eyes on his sleeve. "I don't know if that is a proposal or a…"

"Threat," Koi said, even flatter.

"Doesn't matter, except that it determines me to talk to Guiza about the alliance as soon as possible." I plucked On's fan out of his hand. "I still don't know what to do next, but it makes me so happy that the Pangolins are not expecting me to go away and do it alone. I need the benefit of everyone's good counsel."

"I think you ought to chase after your ducal suitor, flutter your eyelashes winsomely, and get him to offer Prince Guiza that island's considerable wealth as well as its fleet, and have some fun while you're at it," On said jovially as he nipped his fan back. "Ay! If he gave me half as fiery a look as he gave you the night you cured the plague, I'd be with him right now."

"Stop." Koi raised a hand, his expression one of acute nausea. "Ren did ask for *good* counsel."

> *"Slim and slender, soft as jade-colored shavings from spring scallions,*
> *Flutter jade-green sleeves of fragrant gauze.*
> *Yesterday they lingered note for note upon the zither strings —*
> *And now the wood lies cast aside, forgotten..."*

"If you meant that," I said to On to stop his teasing, "you'd be off with Guiza right now."

On held the fan in guard mode, surrendering the point, and vanished from view.

Cray said seriously to me, "Do you want to communicate with Huyun Shandek? I can work him into our pigeon training. Jai says he remembers the Falcon scrape location word from the governor's island, and we could go from there."

"No communication." I shook my head. "I don't want him knowing where I am. It'll be communication enough once he hears of the emperor's conciliation, or whatever Guiza is able to achieve, once the alliance can act."

Cray gave me an inscrutable nod, and we all parted for the night.

I took my tea up to my cabin, looking around in pleasure. While the *Pangolin* was not home—I had ceased wondering what home even was—it was a relief to be back on it, and even better to know I was not expected to face the future on my own.

We sailed on, making certain that no ship followed us back to Benevolence. But as it's said, the swallow in the sky knows nothing of the turtle in the mud. While we'd been away, things had been happening elsewhere, unknown to us.

That became immediate the day we arrived back in Benevolence.

"You are here at last," Master Kuin said as we passed through the Guesthouse on our way to the Pangolins' building. "The Four Masters will return here at sunset, if you will join us."

"About?" Dinek asked, her voice sharp and anxious.

"A sizable company of newcomers seeking the Phoenix Pangolin Ren," Master Kuin said, and all eyes turned to me.

THIRTY-ONE

She learned: hope
The single lantern that forever shines
For thousand days away by land or sea
That illuminates many eyes

"THEY FOUND YOU BY the Snow Crane god, who turned human long enough to point them in the right direction," we were further told.

Master Durxu said, "Directed by a god or a demon, they still must be fed, housed, and given tasks. We are already crowded, and this stream of arrivals is not from any sect."

"More deserters," On said.

Quick looks toward the windows made it clear that everyone knew the danger of accepting known army deserters, who, if caught, were executed.

"The problem is, the imperials are not satisfied with just executing these poor unfortunates," one of the other masters said. "They're also punishing any village who harbors them. There are reports of smoke drifting across islands from the fires."

And, Master Kuin finished by fixing me with a steady gaze. "It is your name on these new ones' lips. I expect it will not be the first time we hear of these newcomers seeking Pangolin Ren."

They let us go, the implication being that we must think of

something. It was not the gallant wanderer way to issue threats or deadlines, but the moral pressure was there.

None of us spoke until we reached our building—left empty for us, in spite of the crowding everywhere else—and we put away our things.

Then we gathered along the kitchen side of our main room. I started a fire in the stove and gave the water a spurt of fire to boil it, then Hat Tu—eager to prove his worth—got rice going, and the rest of the Pangolins divided up the washing, chopping, and mixing of the second dish.

"Do you think it was Sun, sending these newcomers to us?" Fan presently asked Cray.

Cray looked puzzled. "Maybe. But I don't understand the reference to Pangolin Ren being a phoenix."

"Maybe they didn't say that. You know how rumors get muddled."

"Muddled indeed," On said. "But somewhere in there I detect a bit of actual circumstance, which is our first encounter with a pack of deserters on a small island before we sailed for Tortor."

"Ayoh," Cray exclaimed. "That was before we met up again."

"And that gossip might have got mixed up with the story about the lightning plague cure," suggested Hat Dove, who was the best at winnowing out truth from rumor.

Everyone turned to me.

I gathered my thoughts. While I got the fire burning properly, I said to Koi, "You've been reminding me that armies are not an evil in themselves, any more than swords are. I accept that. But I've been troubled by the inescapable fact that armies are put together to *do* something. Just as a sword is picked up to be used."

"Which is to fight," old Ayep stated in his rough voice.

"Or to patrol and look tough," On pointed out. "Didn't the Prince of Ran say something about that?"

I thought back. "Every two years he parades his fleets up north and back so that the westerners can see them. He said he believes that prevents a fight. That's exactly what I want. The emperor must learn that there is prospective power that can act, but isn't acting unless forced to defend."

Koi nodded. "Ready to act without having to act is the basis for the imperial guard. My second-cousin told me once, when he tried to talk me into joining with him, that mostly they spend their entire lives just standing guard, or marching in parades and entourages."

Heartened, I said, "If Guiza is known to have a considerable army, I'm hoping that that might convince the grand prince to support him, instead of the other way round." I turned to Cray. "Will the birds be ready to locate Oraiti if I want to get a message to Banti, and through him, the grand prince?"

The oil had begun to smoke. Cray tossed the chopped ingredients into the pan, adding garlic, ginger, pepper, and chili, as she said, "They should be. Lan Oraiti was very cooperative." She smiled a little, then began stirring. "He knew that Banti would be unhappy with him for not bringing you. The possibility of communication was what made him willing to work with me."

"Do you want army training for this army?" Koi asked me.

"No." I looked around at their faces. "I'm certain—unless you with more experience feel differently—that we ought to keep following the Falcon way: martial skills in the early part of the day, and the rest of the day would be devoted to work that has nothing to do with martial skills. Some—many—of those taken from skilled work could go back to that work, for example. There could also be a school."

On exclaimed, "I know there are some conscripted scholars among the deserters. I overheard one quoting Ar Laq's 'Ballad of the Three Tigers' as he chopped wood."

Everyone began talking at once, then Dinek raised her hand. "What happens when you get them trained? And how long is that going to take?"

"I don't know how long it'll take," I admitted. "I was thinking about that the other day, consequent to something Koi said to me before we left. As for what happens, summer is coming, and up north the days are bright and long. I can ask Guiza where to send them. They can always train there. All we need to do is start them on it, right?" I turned to Cray. "Do we have a bird ready to go to Guiza?"

"I'll know as soon as I go to the roof roost if the bird I sent to Ran is back."

"Will Prince Guiza acknowledge an army trained this way? He seems very traditional," On said.

"He is, but he's also been raised to two traditions, the imperial style, and the plains traditions of the northern islands. Order and peace are most important to him. I'm very sure of that."

There were some mutters and questions, then I said, "I won't disparage traditional thinking, though I know I talk of so many changes. It's daunting to be honest with myself and acknowledge that if I hadn't been forced out of the imperial palace, I probably would have been just the same. I have to find a way to convince Guiza that restoring the empire to the old ways is *a* first step. Not the only step."

"This is done." Cray turned the food onto a platter, and Hat Dove and Tu dished up the rice.

I faced them all. "I also acknowledge that everything I have learned since I left the palace has been because of my experiences with all of you, as well as others I've had the good fortune to meet. I've learned so much thanks to you."

We all clasped hands to one another, then the welcome declaration: "Eat up!"

As we helped ourselves, Fan said, "All this sounds good, but what if we get imperial spies among these newcomers? It's bound to happen."

"I know." I said. "I thought of that, too. But with Sagacious Blade I can determine when someone is lying right to my face. Since my name is being used anyway, I need to talk to each before they go on to the training. If they do. It seems a way to begin?"

Everyone agreed with that—and so did the Four Masters, when we presented our thoughts.

The following day, we put the ideas into practice.

Thereafter, for a stretch of days, were so many awkward questions and unnecessary talkings and "Try this!" and "Try that?" before we began to see order form out of chaos. It was frustrating at the time, but we carried on with determination, sure we were doing the right thing.

One observation I made was how, when newcomers came, there were mutual questions establishing kinship ties and shared locations. From the time I'd left the palace, I'd had to hide my identity, which meant avoiding such questions. Before then, we knew every detail about the people we met long before we met them. Until I heard the pattern of these exchanges—expected by both sides—I had not realized how my avoiding these questions had made me stand out.

The Prince of Ran sent back a terse acknowledgment, without mentioning Guiza's name, and added *carry on*. A few days later, the second pigeon returned with our first message from Guiza, written in an exquisite scholarly hand that I recognized at once from watching him inscribe all those sutras: *Your plan is excellent. My esteemed mother rec'd news Xianti summoned home. She desires to meet you.*

"I remember her," I said to Cray, handing the paper back. "But we never spoke. You remember! You were there with me. Are you sure you want to reuse this paper?"

"Paper is expensive," Cray said. "I don't mind soaking the ink out, drying the paper, and reusing it."

"You're the bird-master!"

She smiled a little. "Not yet a master. But I like working with the birds." No mention of Zi Tian—but that was her way.

I thanked her, and left her to it, aware that now that we were establishing communication with potential allies, my perception of my inner Circle board was broadening.

I spent a number of days flying over the many little islands lying to the north. Most were completely uninhabited. I made a map, and nights after full days of practice and work, we made plans—then in groups of five, began to shift the volunteers over to the islands. Most of the deserters seemed to prefer keeping together in groups, rather than venturing out into the solitary, wandering life. They could not go home—many knew they had no homes to go to—so they adapted to this new sort of life, half of which was martial training, and half other skills.

In retrospect, that was the mountain peak of summers, as the two islands I chose sprouted buildings and gardens. Spirits were high. Those with a thirst for fighting went away, or never showed up in the first place. Our newcomers were the people who trusted they would not be called upon to kill or be killed. That there would be an end to it, and maybe they might even see their families again. Around twilight campfires, cheery ballads were sung, or comedic skits acted out, the theme nearly always 'home.'

By the end of summer those islands were full, and still people kept coming. I sent away only three individuals, early on. "You are lying to me" acted on them like a jab with an invisible knife, and words spread fast that I could see into souls. No one ever noticed Sagacious Blade because everyone carried a weapon, even if it was only wooden.

We discussed the consequences. The three only saw Benevolence, so what they knew was that Pangolin Ren was currently at this Falcon scrape, but traveled often, no one ever knew where. "The solution is simple," Fan suggested. "We can say that Pangolin Ren rarely sleeps twice in the same place, but to be sure, Pangolin Ren has to be seen at other scrapes."

I protested, "I don't even want to fly to Ye. I don't think I'd survive flying from one end of the empire to the other. Not during winter, certainly."

On said, "You forget the power of rumor. All any spies need to hear is the possibility that you've been seen here, there, everywhere. I believe I can attend to that, through my player friends who travel."

He put his plan into action at once.

Meanwhile, Banti wrote to me. There was his dear scrawl, the same as it had been when he was a boy: *I nearly decapitated Oraiti for not bringing you when I found out he saw you! Then he told me you're Pangolin Ren, and the stories are true! But Grand-Uncle wants G backing him. X summoned home. Will you come to us here?*

I stared at the little strip of paper. So wonderful to hear from him, knowing it was only a few days old. And yet, so little! But pigeons could not carry pages.

After a day or two of frustrated thought, I wrote back: *Guiza true heir. Ran backs him too. Will you come to us? If no, talk to Gr.-Uncle about backing Guiza!* And soon watched the bird flutter skyward.

But though I'd avoided answering Banti about traveling to Whale Haven, I could not avoid conditions right before my eyes. The two islands I'd chosen were now crowded. The sun was beginning its southward arc. If we meant to send these men and boys to Ye, then it must be soon. But first, there were far too many questions to resolve for birds to carry back and forth.

It was time to go myself, and prepare the way.

I left before dawn one morning.

Exhilaration swelled within me as I rose so high above sea and land, looking down at the variety of greens in the tops of trees, and noting the patterns in roof tiles. It was so exhilarating that at first I paid scant heed to sun-Essence streaming off me as I flew ever faster.

This changed as the sun sank after a long day of flight. Hunger made me light-headed, as my skin itched and ached from the chafing of the wind. Mindful of the necessity of being seen, I zigzagged my way, stopping at Falcon scrapes that Dinek had marked for me on my old map. Though these scrapes were all quite different from one another, they were alike in wanting news.

The one Dinek had warned me was most nun-like in their withdrawal from the world turned out to be vitally interested.

The senior master, a woman white of hair and wrinkled of face, shook her head slowly, and in a quavering voice told of sons being seized off ships on their way to competitions.

"My own son, only twelve, though large for his age, vanished when he was sitting outside, eating haws while I negotiated an apprenticeship with a cabinet-maker," one woman protested. "My boy is tired of travel, and he's always making tiny chests and boxes, so I found a cabinet-maker who lost his apprentice to the last conscript. When I went out to bring him in to make his bow to his new master, he was gone! In his wake, people crying and lamenting in the street over the conscript gang grabbing them and tying them together with ropes."

After that a clamor of "Did you hear," and "My cousin's brother's second uncle said…"

Once I heard each of these personal grievances, I told them my plans, they listened and sympathized, and though I could see doubt in some faces, there was hope in others.

I flew on.

The last scrape, the most remote, was built into the stone of an escarpment, and here, for the first time, I met other flyers. Their method was their fighting staffs. They knew of the imperial conscript raids, but they were vitally interested in my talk of the alliance.

"We seldom involve ourselves in outside affairs," their elder said. "However, outside affairs have been intruding more insistently on us."

And a younger master said, "If you will trust us with a locator for messages, we will send hawks to you."

I gave them both Cray's and Zi Tian's names, and flew down from their mountains into the plains of Benevolent Winds.

The shapes of houses changed as I flew north. There were more of the round cottages, many tiled with thick thatch made of tough fronds. Finally Ye lay all across the horizon, marvelously flat from the sky. That flatness grew texture in streams and round hills as I approached the largest city crowned by a palace at the north end. The same sort of streets I'd grown up with — never straight, as everyone knows demons only move in straight lines — gave way to gardens with zig-zagging paths. This palace turned out to be empty, except for old servants, left to oversee the shrouded furnishings.

It took some searching and listening. Eventually I found Guiza having taken up residence in a long, low building above a rushing river. I noted, as Koi had bade me, the triple perimeter guard. No one was going to sneak up on Guiza—not even I, though I could have. But I did not want to startle anyone, so I landed outside the sight of the outer perimeter, and walked up the path.

To my surprise, as soon as I identified myself I was instantly conducted to a house as simple as a temple dwelling. I was left in a plain waiting room decorated by a beautiful screen depicting sporting herons and frogs on pads.

I turned at a step, and here was Fourteenth Consort Ye—no, the Princess of Ye, I corrected myself, and made my bow. I was glad I'd put on one of Arati's robes, though I had not been at all certain that mother and son lived in proximity.

"Renti," the princess said on a note of genuine welcome. "My son has spoken much of you. Thank you for troubling yourself over this foolish mother's wishes." When I just as politely demurred, she said, "Would you care to greet my son before we speak?"

On my assent, she led me to the far chamber. It had three windows, one overlooking the river, the second a pool, the third the path leading up to the house, lined with parasol trees, redbark, and chestnut. Chrysanthemums added a bright splash of color.

Guiza sat with a young man wearing healer's robes. His affinities were similar to Guiza's, which told me little. Normally I avoided sensing auras, as doing so invariably left me unsteady after jolting between perceptions. But this was important enough a moment to at least try.

His aura, a soft blue, almost silver, was a mirror to his affinities of water and metal. From that I determined that this new person in Guiza's life was exactly what he appeared to be.

Relieved, I took a moment to recover in that quiet room as I glanced about. A Circle board lay between them, but the game— at an impasse, I saw at a glance—had been abandoned: an open scroll lay across it, another next to it. Guiza had a third on his lap, and he held a fourth, which he was reading, his writing brush poised to make a note.

At my step, he looked up. The bandage was gone, his thick, glossy hair hiding most of the scar. There was a slash outside his left eye, no longer an angry purple, but fading in color. Even this scar could not mar his serene expression or his handsome features.

Cousin Guiza welcomed me with scrupulous politeness,

and introduced me to Healer Huan.

"I have come to report our progress," I said. And began to tell him about our companies of deserters and rescues, now designated the Lu Seekers, after Lu the Seeker in the ancient myth.

I did not expect effusion, but he listened to me with a face as expressive as a statue carved of stone. Without question or encouragement from him, I pushed on. "We could not call them army deserters, of course, though it would not take much questioning to determine what they are. But the gallant wanderers welcome their own kind. They avoid imperial politics, and this name gives everyone a modicum of protection," I finished. "We can send them north to you any time. They are trained to be self-sufficient, and many are back to practicing their old skills. There are two very promising silversmiths, a lute-maker, and a family of ropemakers who say the hemp up in these islands is the best in the world. And musicians," I found myself adding, as if I had to plead with him to take these volunteers.

Guiza gave me an absent smile, and observed, "That is very kind of you all. Huan, might I trouble you to light a lamp?"

I looked around for a candle, for I could light one for them at a touch, to discover there were none. The healer went out soundlessly and returned with a paper lamp, which he carefully set to Guiza's right, and a little back.

When Healer Huan sat down again, I hesitated, arranging my words in order to bring up the plans for approaching the emperor once we had the alliance united, and spread sufficiently across the board.

Guiza forestalled me by laying his hands flat on the table and saying, "Shall we have a little music before they summon us to dinner?"

Healer Huan bowed, and perforce I must consent, though I had not come all this way for a concert. Willow entered from the next room, carrying Guiza's guqin. Healer Huan produced a fine side-flute, and the two commenced playing.

To my admittedly inexperienced ear they were excellent, but as the music went on and on, I began to perceive that this was going to be the evening's activity. Eventually a gong rang softly, barely a swelling of sound, and the princess reappeared to lead me to wash my hands before dinner.

When I'd done that, on my way back to the dining area, I saw Willow at his place within calling distance of his prince's door.

I went up to him. The door was closed, the music unabating inside. Desperate, I said, "Willow, please tell me whatever you can that is not trespassing against his highness's trust: what can I do? Have I said what I should not?"

Willow bowed, then drew those long horse-teeth over his lower lip before saying. "Your imperial highness has committed no error known to this humble being of no worth. But if a suggestion might be offered, even by one less than an ant on a blade of grass—"

"Speak, Willow. I am listening."

"—if her imperial highness Princess Renti will heed her highness the Princess of Ye..."

"Of course I will," I said, on a note of question, for all this told me exactly nothing. Of course I would listen to the princess, a respected elder.

He bowed low, and began to retreat.

"Thank you, Willow." His worried expression sparked worry in me.

I went to the dining area to meet the others.

The meal was simple, yet excellent—freshwater fish, seasoned vegetables, and bean-paste cakes. A group of musicians played as we ate, a meal that lingered long without much conversation.

At the end, Guiza turned to us and said courteously, "Mother, Cousin, if you will pardon me, I will retire for the night. I trust you will sleep well." He bowed to us each and walked off.

The healer, who had eaten with us in a manner that appeared to have become habit, rose. "I'll take his pulse and bring his medicine to him," he said, and bowed himself out.

The princess turned to me. "If our esteemed young visitor would honor this foolish mother by accompanying her for a walk on the terrace?"

I assented. And as soon as we were in the warm, jasmine-scented summer air, presumable away from possible listeners, I said, "Has he suffered a relapse?"

"No—that is, not that he will admit to. He has always believed it to be unfilial to admit to pain of any kind. It is difficult to know how much his head has healed. If it has healed. Healer Huan says he thinks that recovery might be slower than my son will admit. He gets frequent headaches, and he cannot bear flickering lights, especially on that left side. No candles, only lamps that burn steadily, and nothing dangling that might reflect sunlight. He says nothing, but we can see him wince and turn his head."

"I hope he does recover soon," I said. "For his sake — and that of the empire."

She faced me, hands in her sleeves. I could tell by the line of her shoulders that her hands gripped tightly, hidden by that silk embroidered with peonies and rosebuds. "I hoped to speak to you about that." She hesitated, then pulled a much-crinkled scroll of heavy paper from her sleeve. Unrolling it, she said, "Here is the emperor's last will. Designating Guiza as imperial heir. You see the seal."

My nerves chilled at this, my first close sight of an emperor's imperial seal. I did not have to touch it to feel the Essence charm imbued in the complicated lines of red ink.

To the right of it, in a scribal hand, the words that appointed Lan Guiza to the dragon throne.

She rolled it up and tucked it away in her sleeve, saying, "Guiza has had much to say in your praise about your ideas for reparation of the empire as well as striving for a peaceable solution to our current troubles."

"This ignorant one hesitates to speak ignorant nonsense before her elders..."

"Please."

I gave her a swift outline of the present plan to funnel deserters up to the Ye islands. "Evidence so far suggests that Cousin Xianti is wary of invading these islands, unless he were to gather a far larger force. The emperor appears to be ambivalent about that. He has not turned over the imperial army to Xianti, who is leading his own generals."

"You are correct," she said. "My faithful contacts at the palace inform me that the emperor has been receiving a flood of memorials and testaments from the most powerful ministers of court, as well as from island governors, complaining of burned villages whose smoke stretches across the entire empire. His imperial highness Grand Prince Miluo, who as you might know is the emperor's birth father, though officially known as his uncle, and still commander of the Eastern Fleet, also receives these testaments."

I had not known that. Or if I'd been told, I'd forgotten it; then I recollected that scandal about the false monk who had prescribed a poison reputed to enhance the birth of sons, which had actually had the opposite effect. The emperor at that time had adopted the little Prince Miluo as his own, though later he had a very sickly son, and much later, Guiza.

Now I began to perceive the imperial Circle board a little. "And the emperor is filial?"

She said, "He dares not be. Though the grand prince does not interfere with governing, he is too powerful to be ignored. The Eastern Fleet is firmly loyal to him. And so, I believe at his advice, the emperor has summoned Xianti to return to the imperial city to lead the harvest ritual, as imperial heir, and to remain at the imperial palace for the winter. It is, of course, a way to curtail the excesses of Xianti's pursuits."

I exclaimed in relief, and she laid a hand on my wrist. "If he obeys, that perhaps gains us half a year, if he waits for spring before sailing off again in his pursuits. I cannot hope that Guiza is going to improve vastly in that time. He has never regarded the prospect of inheriting the throne as anything but a duty to be endured," she admitted, low-voiced. "This battle, and the wound he suffered, has not improved matters, though everyone attested to his bravery."

"He spoke a little of that," I ventured.

"This is my own heart's wish, Renti. Of the entire imperial family, he speaks well only of Eleventh Sister Taisa — she is the one who sent Huan to us, which means we could trust him — and your elder brother Yanti. Now, you. You most of all, because you are capable, and talented. Further, you share his hatred of the violence of battle, and prosecute vigorously ways around it. The best solution for all our problems would be if the two of you marry — "

"That's impossible," I exclaimed, then bowed. "Forgive this uncouth dolt for interrupting an elder."

"I understand your reaction. Such a solution is not traditional. That said, necessity sometimes requires amendment to traditions. There have been ways around the prohibitions. For example, if the Dowager Princess of Ran were to formally adopt you. She is willing — I could show you the letter, which I received only last week. You would keep your rank as princess. Even rise to princess of the second rank, behind her own daughter, who alas has been married these ten years to the Admiral of the Silver Circle. She is apparently irreplaceable as Chief Navigator of the Western Fleet."

I scarcely heard all this; I was waiting for a cease in the quick flow of words to once again say, "But this would not be possible. What would my parents say, to begin with?"

The princess said slowly, "That is testament to your commendable filial piety. I hold great respect for both your venerable parents, for I know they revere our traditions as well as our laws, but I have to point out that their status at present is … ambiguous. Though I believe your mother would understand the necessity of this arrangement." She touched my wrist. "Do *you* understand? You would be empress. You would actually rule. I am telling you what I would not admit to many others, but I don't believe Guiza would survive the poisonous air of that dangerous seat on his own."

Shock rendered me witless. Here was my second proposal! Huyun Shandek's empress would be limited to what powers he chose to share, the implication being she must be in accord with his ideas. Or, in plainer words, under his command. She would be in service to his summons for the purposes of progeny.

This proposal, by Guiza's own mother, ostensibly offered more power, and if I guessed right, it would be a marriage in name only. And yet, how much power did it really offer? I would still be confined, by tradition, in the harem, with the two them to convince to change tradition.

As if she read my thoughts, she said, "Your first act could be the restoration of your family to their rank and rights. And perhaps, eventually, you could adopt one of your brothers' children, who would be Lans. There are also other arrangements empresses have made…" She added delicately.

I understood. Old plays were full of wild references to women of high rank finding cooperative fathers in order to secure the all-important descendants, with or without the cooperation of husbands. They had also lost their heads over it; if anything went wrong, it was invariably the woman who was blamed. Such a possibility was not just repugnant, it seemed dangerous, a sure step along that thorn-flower path of the tyrant who began while meaning so well.

I turned to her, trying to find the politest words for rejection of the entire subject as impossible, but she raised her hand. "Think about it, good child. I beg you to return once we have concluded the alliance. I believe we all desire to be in firm accord before the imperial crown prince sails again next spring."

THIRTY-TWO

Since yesterday had to leave the Sage One and bolt,
Today had hurt her heart even more.
The autumn wild geese sent a mourning wind for escort
And bones of great writers served for her brushes
As she sent sutras along with the slain
Before the Court of Heaven.

I VISITED A SECOND set of Falcon scrapes on the return flight. At the first scrape, there was more grim news about burnings along the coast after the villagers had taken all their teenage boys into the mountains and turned them over to a martial arts sect. Once again, I promised aid when we could.

The second scrape turned out to have a case that was similar to Guiza's in appearance, that is, a child in a coma after a blow on the head from a falling beam. "We have heard that you are an Essence healer," I was told.

"I am only a beginner," I said yet again, though I knew that even very practiced healers without Essence training can be helpless to determine what might be wrong with skulls and brains.

I expected to be received with derision for my young age, and determined that I would refuse if confronted, but the healer was too distraught on his granddaughter's account to be resentful, if that was even in his nature.

He was truly humble, saying that at their remote height the

only healing he'd been called on was for stomach ailments, headaches, cuts and contusions — the usual troubles of mountain life. He told me that the child's village, down the mountain, had been burned around her, after their having been accused of hiding the local youths from conscription hunters. She and several others had been attacked while rescuing children who had been hiding in an attic.

I said I would try.

I had never spoken to anyone except Granny Zim from within that strange mental realm, but I remembered the Eel monk so long ago speaking to me, and presented as comforting an image to the child as I could contrive. For deep within that realm, she sensed me right away. Her spirit wailed in grief and guilt, that she'd been too late while fighting her fear. *Your brothers were taken away, but they live. And the small ones are all safe. They survived. You can waken now. The imperials are gone,* I repeated to her.

When she stirred, I broke out of that realm, dizzy and tired. They permitted me to sleep. When I woke again, I was told that the little girl had opened her eyes and taken a little healer's soup before falling back into a natural slumber.

I left soon after, regretting that once again I was gaining merit I did not truly deserve.

The other visits were notable only for their similarity in worry over the troubled state of the world. At least I was able to correct garbled reports about rampaging "princes." There was only one rampaging prince, though his declared excuse for his exertions was necessity forced on him by betrayal, thereby assuring that Princes Guiza and Yiuti joined my brother in having their names tarnished.

In two of my stops, the elders offered to host an army that was actually bent on helping get on with the work of farming, with harvest season coming on, and rebuilding: in both these situations, the Falcon scrapes were a lot like Benevolence, associated with local villages or towns for whom they'd provided a kind of protection.

At least here I could promise aid soon. And the higher I flew, the clearer my mental Circle board. I did know where to place our Lu Seekers! And in sending them where they could be of use, rather than finding a place to build a garrison where they would be isolated from normal life, and told to practice war day and night, I could see the pieces of a new Circle board, one whose points and pieces had been before my eyes all my life, but not counted consciously.

The weight of this new board both oppressed me and exhilarated me — much as did my flight, buoyed by the sun, but scoured by the wind. There was a cost to flying so far and as fast as I could. I couldn't help but wonder if it would have been easier if I'd been properly taught, rather than having to stumble through learning on my own. Then I remembered how On had taken to flying in moments, and had to admit to myself that yet again, I was taking a mite of talent and making a mountain against a dragon storm.

But the dragon storm is here.

As my long journey ended at last, I was very much looking forward to getting back to Benevolence, rest, and also a good helping of ginseng salve on all my skin wind-chafed to reddened roughness.

The late summer sun winked mercilessly off the sea as I began flying lower. I spotted the bay — saw no dreadful golden banner against crimson — then looked away, nauseated by the glitter and blur. It was tiredness, but I was now only steps from rest, I told myself. And Xianti was well on his way to the imperial island, if he hadn't landed already. I was safe.

I landed with a thump outside our Pangolin building, made an effort to wipe away the obscuring charm, and headed straight for the tea brazier, which always had hot water.

Hat Dove looked up from some sewing. "You're back! I think they have interviews waiting for you at the Guesthouse, Ren."

"Who wants me?" I asked, ready to avoid anyone until I'd eaten and slept.

"Koi. He's kept them there," she added.

"Koi? Kept some newcomers there? Why? Are interviews only with me insisted on now by the Four Masters?"

"I think… No, I am not certain, and do not wish to mislead."

While On might think it hilarious to summon me all that way to hear some gossip about *Five Scholars*, or some new and ridiculous rumor about Pangolin Ren, Koi was not frivolous of habit. I must put in the effort to walk the few steps to the Guesthouse myself.

Few steps. It seemed an impossible distance; after so much long flight, my body always felt heavy, as if I'd turned to stone.

The only cure was exercise, I told myself, sheathed Sagacious Blade, and forced myself to a vigorous pace. As I covered the gentle hills — barely more than mounds — between our building and the Guesthouse, I was distracted by the brightness of yellow mustard, echoed in some leaves already turning yellow in the chestnut trees, contrasting with the deep rose-purple myrtle. Nothing would ever be beautiful about the stark buildings of Benevolence, but nature was a glory in this season.

As I glanced over the surroundings, I became aware that there seemed to be more Falcons about than usual at this time of day. Maybe the masters had set the inhabitants some kind of game for training. My mind ranged back over what I'd seen and heard in recent weeks as I considered the conclusion I had come to while flying alone, above the world.

I reached the Guesthouse, to find unfamiliar gallant wanderers lounging about. With them—no, near them—our own people. Knots of two out by the kitchen gardens, the tool shed. Three here, by the practice weapon shed, and there. Five there, gathering wild onion, and five groping ineffectually for weeds in a desultory manner. Wherever I saw any familiar faces, there were new faces, hands gleaning chestnuts, eyes watching the clouds, mouths chatting. My focus shifted from my inner debate to tight hands, steady, unblinking gazes, light voices like the skip of water insects over very deep water...

In the interview room, Master Durxu himself, sitting with tea and snacks before a short, round-faced, mostly bald man who wore what hair he had in a long braid. He was dressed in road-stained robes, a staff leaning against the table, and a sword across his lap. Across from him, a tall, broad man stood, feet apart, a spear at hand. Fan was there, standing near a snake-thin young man with two axes through his belt.

Granny Zim said suddenly: "There is a demon here, an eater of souls."

Lightning ripped through my meridians as Master Durxu spoke. "And here is Pangolin Ren, as promised, Brother Turtle."

"Pangolin Ren!" Brother Turtle turned ordinary brown eyes toward me, their color not unlike my own. "Here, take this cushion beside me."

I took a step, then stopped. His gaze was so flat I knew instinctively that this man was the danger, half a heartbeat before he struck.

But Granny Zim—or the demon who was a part of Granny Zim—was faster. The blade leaped to my hand, lightning a blue and blinding flash through a sour-smelling wind, like a tomb full of rot. It took all my strength to hold the blade with both hands—as the big man and the snake man both charged me from either side.

The lightning had ignited every component of my body. In that moment I could not move as power surged through me. I was peripherally aware of a shadow before me as Koi whirled into action, sword and knife. The window smashed inward as four more of Brother Turtle's attackers burst through, two taken on by Fan, and the others meeting Master Durxu's blade.

The room was far too small for so violent a battle. Steel flashed around me as my eyes stung from the hot smell of burning metal, and my mind stuttered as the awe-filled glory of vast and shadowy wings beat over that strange realm, and swallowed the roiling entity within Brother Turtle.

The man's killing gaze emptied of life, and he fell like a punctured sack.

I staggered, the after-image of Koi's whirling assurance imprinted on my vision the way a false sun will blot out the world after you inadvertently look in the sky a heartbeat too long.

"Go!" Fan croaked.

Crash! Koi leaped through the broken window and the sound of clashing metal rang right outside, followed by Master Durxu joining Koi. Sounded like a horde out there. A premeditated attack. Then Fan folded quietly, one hand clasped to her left shoulder, where blood dripped frighteningly fast. The other hand hung lifeless.

I dropped Sagacious Blade—her scales still glowing with fire—and caught Fan before she could fall atop the dead snake man. What to do? "Staunch the bleeding," I whispered Grandfather Healer's first lesson. My shaking, tingling fingers scrabbled clumsily at the panels of Fan's robe, bunching it up as I shoved it against the wound.

She gasped in pain. Then roused enough to grunt, "Tell my brothers ... Apple Blossom Prefecture. Heaven's Serenity Garrison." Pink bubbles appeared at the corner of her mouth. She made a heroic effort. "Zelu family..."

"Hold on, Fan." I would swear that shoulder gouge from the axe was not a death wound. Still holding the robe against it, I felt over her—my fingers pausing when they encountered sticky wetness at her ribs, nearly overlooked. A stab wound from the snake man.

I glanced at the snake man's corpse, then to the thin-bladed knife in his loose fingers. The edge of the blade glowed greenish:

poison.

I flung my awareness into Fan as she whispered, "The king of the underworld comes … for me … I'll face him … straight on…"

"Granny Zim?" I cried. But she had been completely subsumed by that vast, shadowy presence, utterly strange to me. *I have fed*, this presence said, each word distinct, as if shaping words took concentration.

Heal her, I shouted across that measureless expanse; awareness swooped past my mind, and eddied, fast as a storm wind, then poured into Fan and coalesced around the lethal glow in that wound deep within Fan's body. A lick of flame ignited, an eerie green never seen in the material world. Fan grunted in pain as the fire burned the poison, fusing the knife wound, then withdrew.

Vertigo assailed me as reaching hands rocked me, then took Fan from me. Voices chattered but I could not catch the sense.

Then one I knew roused me. "Ren. Ren!" It was On. "Their ship."

I swayed, and he flung an around my shoulders. "Are you hurt?"

"No." My lips shaped the word, though no sound came out. Vaguely I became aware of Dinek crying somewhere nearby.

"There must be a ship," On said. "How do I look for a ship?"

Urgency forced me back to the present, and with awareness of the material world returning, the vertigo receded. I clung to On with one hand, the other grabbing for Sagacious Blade as I struggled to get my feet under me. He lifted me, his breath warm on my cheek. "Can you…"

"I can."

Together we made it out the door, as Fan was carried out by Dinek and Hat Dove behind us. "My sword … my sword," Fan muttered, rousing briefly.

Then On and I were outside, to find knots of hard fighting here and there, with still figures lying prone. I pulled free of On's grasp, running toward the bay. Where? Where? The problem with obscuring charms is, you have to concentrate right on the place the eye is told to sweep past. I squinted into the winking sunlight mixed with nauseating blur—and a warship flickered into view, slightly flattened behind the thick Essence. On its prow, a trebuchet was cranking back as someone lit a torch to a cask.

I brought Sagacious Blade around, and flung a firebolt

straight at that cask—which exploded, sending the trebuchet crew flying about the deck. The machine came apart in splinters.

But that did not stop two long boatloads of enemies now rowing hard for shore, bare weapons glinting in the sun.

Farther along the road to the town, a line of Lu Seekers advanced toward the reed-clustered beach. Every line of their bodies expressed uncertainty and determination. Already a boatload of attackers had run ashore, and they leaped out to charge. It was clear who expected to win this encounter...

On began to run, swinging his double sticks. Only then did I notice a great sword rent in the side of his robe, and dark dots along his leg, probably from a cut.

I braced myself, brought Sagacious Blade up, and said to whoever that vast voice was, "Give me fire."

It gave me fire. I shot a firebolt at the chargers on the shore. They faltered, faces turned toward me. The four at the front dropped to their knees, slapped arrows to crossbows, and shot at me.

I ran behind a myrtle tree. Thwack! Thwack! Bolts sent splinters flying.

I threw the obscuring charm over myself, tossed down the sword, and bent my knees as Sagacious Blade and I rose steeply into the air. I scattered a rain of sparks down on the chargers, who were still shooting at that myrtle tree below me.

Then I swooped over the boats rowing toward shore, and gave them a rain of fire sparks. The oars clattered to the bottom of the boat as the enemies hastily began dousing the flames with handfuls of water.

Relying on my invisibility, I dove down and snatched up oars to toss overboard. Mistake!

"Where?" an enemy bawled.

Several looked around—then two looked up. One squinted, and pointed. "There! On the flying sword!"

Up jerked the crossbows, as one by one they began peering past the now-useless charm: these enemies, having been secreted on an obscured ship, knew all about obscuring charms and talismans.

I rose as fast and as high as I could, zigzagging desperately as lethal bolts hissed and skimmed around me. I swung around behind the ship's stern mast, as most of the crew left aboard was fighting the fire from the ruined trebuchet.

Gathering all the sun I could pull in, I dropped a massive firebolt into the middle of the tower ship's deck, then raced away, out of range of the bolts arcing into the sky, my heartbeat so frantic it crowded my throat. I retreated behind the shelter of the myrtle trees, where the enemy couldn't see me, and then landed to assess from behind a trunk.

In the short time I'd been aloft, everything had changed. Koi raced down the road, leading a wedge of martial artists. They slammed into the enemy driving back the Lu Seeker line. A violent melee ensued, some enemies trying to retreat until they saw their tower ship on fire, smoke gouting toward the sky.

They massed together, shields held edge to edge as they ran for the two longboats on the sand. The gallant wanderers leaped rocks and reeds, bearing down on them before they could get the boats into the water, and another melee broke out.

I caught up with On, who held one arm against his side, blood dripping off his hand. "Who are they?" I asked.

"Imperial elites," Koi said, pelting up. "In disguise."

The battle at the longboats ended, the enemy either dead or swimming out to sea. No one chased them.

Koi's eyes moved constantly, assessing. When some faces turned toward him, he called, "Master Durxu has the scrape in hand. I think we're done here."

"Let's get the wounded," called Master Kuin's sister.

We turned to help those few who needed it, and started toward the road. I had no one to help; the martial artists got to their brethren first. I saw with sorrow corroding my heart that all those lying prone were dead.

Koi's head lifted, and he saw us. His face eased slightly. "I was afraid they'd shot you," he said huskily. "You looked like you were going to crash beyond the trees."

"It was a retreat," I said. "They saw me."

On said, "As soon as they get back, they'll report. And start watching the skies." He pointed at me. "That means watching for you."

More Benevolence martial artists arrived at a run, and began to help with the wounded, and lay out the dead. Koi said, wincing, "I recognized one of them, in that second longboat. One of Xianti's old bodyguards, from the elite arm of the Imperial Vanguard First Camp."

There was nothing to say to that: everyone had known the possibility that Xianti would catch up with us. Either he or his followers. I was the target, not the cause. Martial artists understood that. There were no wry looks, no mutters, as I joined the rest in the heartbreaking task of gathering the wounded and the dead, then cleaning up the worst of the detritus.

When we reached the Guesthouse, we found people roaming around, some purposefully, others purposelessly looking, talking, clutching minor cuts, rubbing heads, in the way that I'd seen before after events of great exertion. It's as if they must shed the Essence of endeavor racing along meridians.

"But we don't have a Hall of Ancestors," one of the Lu Seekers was saying, distraught, holding a length of wood as beyond the kitchen garden, some began building a platform atop the flat rocks used for those known to prefer the cleansing fire, to ensure the soul's rise to Heaven. Others carried the dead on stretchers toward the forest, where tomb mounds lay undisturbed.

"Memorial plaques are proper wherever you set them up," Master Durxu answered the young man.

"What does Kanda say?" someone else interjected.

Faces turned toward On—the known scholar—in appeal.

But On turned to me, unable or unwilling to say that most of his education had been military—and then entertainment.

I said, "That's correct."

Father had told us that when Second Brother had asked how Father could go to the Hall of Ancestors with the imperial family to pray for his own father, but our grandfather also had a tablet in our palace Hall of Ancestors.

"If you make a memorial tablet here, and take it to their family, and they burn incense and say the sutras, I think the ghosts still are guided the right way." As I spoke, I listened for the eerie voice-without-words again, that sense of something as broad and as dangerous as a thunderstorm somehow encompassed in Sagacious Blade. That voice had nothing to say to memorials. "Granny Zim?" I asked within me, very tentatively.

"I am here," came her reassuring voice. "That which is left of me. Fear not, my Bu. You will learn there are as many types of demons as there are flowers or birds or animals or denizens of the sea."

Some listeners accepted my words as reassurance, and I left them to discuss their different customs according to their islands of origin. On volunteered to help with the burial detail, and Koi was detained by Master Durxu.

They both sent me looks, as if to invite me to listen, but my head was too light again. I left them and made my way back to the Pangolin house, poured and drank three cups of scalding tea, then devoured a stale pancake left from morning. My body still felt as if weighed down by boulders, and the wind chafing hurt every time my clothes shifted. I was too tired even to go upstairs, but I reminded myself that at least I was not wounded. There was work to be done. At least I could do kitchen tasks while sitting down.

Cray appeared, carrying two buckets of fresh water. Others began to drift in, and I learned what had happened while I was gone. It had been largely peaceful, with newcomers turning up now and then, as usual. A few days ago, these newcomers began arriving in groups never larger than five or six, but too close together. They all claimed to be gallant wanderers, and were outfitted like gallant wanderers. But the Masters could see in stances, and in assessing gazes, that these were men of a different quality.

"They said they were seeking Pangolin Ren," Cray told me as we washed vegetables together. "The Four told them they had to wait. They camped along the road, effectively cutting us off from town. Others settled in points outside the scrape. Koi, On, and a a couple of the older army deserters said they were too much like a perimeter, which could turn into a surrounding attack."

"Where is Master Kuin?" Hat Dove asked, setting down a basket of rhubarb, carrots, scallions, and turnips.

"Not back yet, far as I saw." Cray turned to me. "She took some tough volunteers to the town during the night, to see what they found there." She wiped her grimy cheek on her shoulder, her profile troubled.

Dinek appeared. "How is Fan?" I asked.

"Asleep," Dinek reported. "The healer can't account for the burn at the stab wound, but says it stopped the bleeding inside. Her shoulder wound is messy but not threatening."

"Good," I said, and to the others, "It's time for me to take the Lu Seekers still willing to join the alliance, and depart from Benevolence."

Some looked relieved, others unsure.

I said, "Everyone is tired. Nothing is going to change right now. My suggestion is, let's discuss details tomorrow, after we rest."

This was agreed on, and talk turned to meal preparation, after which we ate. Then Dinek left with a bowl to coax into Fan. Other Pangolins trudged tiredly out.

Koi, Cray, and On remained.

Koi turned to me, but On spoke first. "Xianti's spies are getting better. He must have launched these at us on his way back to the imperial island."

"Next time," I said, "it'll be what I always dreaded, an army."

Koi had been waiting. He looked at me soberly. "You said 'join the alliance'. Not 'Guiza's army.'"

On's head turned quickly, and his expressive brows rose.

I said, "This is what I never got a chance to tell you. Guiza is an ally. But I saw it on this visit, he's not a leader. His mother proposed marriage to me on his behalf. I don't know if he even knows. Doesn't matter, because he will surely do what she wants. What does matter is that I've talked and talked about women having a chance to do what men do. And yet I kept looking to the various princes for the right leader, because most people are used to tradition, and they'll follow a prince before they'll follow a common man. But never a woman."

Cray's head came up sharply, and her lips parted.

"I didn't consider the fact that I've the same blood, the same name, as most of the princes. It's not Guiza's alliance. It's mine."

"*You* should be emperor," Cray said, her voice low. Yet she spoke with utter conviction.

Koi smacked his hands on his knees. "Yes," he said. "But Ren, you had to see it."

"I couldn't," I said. "Partly tradition. Habit. But also, I think of the prestige, the power, and of course I am not worthy, not ready, too ignorant, too young, too … impossible. But here's what I realized while I was in the sky, looking at the world below: the dragon throne itself is impossible. How can an ordinary person, born naked, as my mother once said to me, presume to rule the world? And yet it's equally in our nature to look for leaders. Especially in danger."

"You're better than any of those other princes," On declared. He grinned, and said, "That includes…" His gaze shifted. "The upstart prince."

Cray waved dismissively. "He's been dead for years." She said to me, "You will be a good leader because you *listen*. Not just to those of rank."

"True," Koi said, so softly I almost didn't hear it. He gazed steadily at me, but his gaze seemed confused, and he blinked, as though trying to force his eyes to focus.

I gazed back at him, and it was only then that I began to see that the dark blotches on his dark gray robe had grown bigger in the time it took to eat our meal. A meal that he'd scarcely touched. "Koi?" My voice came out sharp.

Cray looked from me to him, then her eyes widened. "I'll fetch the bandages."

On rose slowly, rolled his shoulders, listened to his neck crack, and flashed a rueful smile my way. "I'd offer to help, but you're the healer. As for me? I need a bath before I bandage up this arm. No, no, don't protest, it really is nothing. I can wrap it up." He sauntered out, leaving me alone with Koi.

Cray reappeared from the back room—the clothes-drying room in winter, and a kind of sick room, where Fan had been put—and set our shared healer basket down. "Want help?"

Koi turned to me, question in his face. No, appeal.

"I can take care of it," I said to Cray, and watched relief relax Koi's expression slightly.

I didn't know how many cuts Koi had taken until I helped him to ease his robe off. Every piece of the dark gray fabric bore a cut or a rent, nearly indistinguishable in the light of the single candle. The many blood splashes on his once-white under-linen shocked me.

Cray reentered, soft of step, and murmured, not quite at either of us, "Hat Dove is up at the Guesthouse, helping with the nursing there. Dinek put her bedroll beside Fan in the back room. Says she needs quiet. I'll stay with Zi Tian." She walked out.

Koi winced, and winced again as I gently sponged off the wounds. In the cool air his flesh roughened, but he didn't move as I daubed salve on the clean cuts, then wound each with bandages. I tried not to stare past each delineation to the whole.

How laughable are we! I knew the human body. Grandfather Healer had made us memorize all the parts, and their attendant meridians, when I was at my first scrape. The differences between man and woman had not interested me at all beyond the acupoints I needed to know. But now, suddenly, I was alone with Koi sitting there naked from the waist up, and my face ignited to a sun glow as I tried not to stare at the compelling contours of shoulder, arm, the inviting dip between his collarbones, the entrancing musculature of his chest, drawing the eye downward.

I tried … and failed.

Koi stared straight at the wall, his fingers gripping his knees. "Brother Turtle. Master Durxu pointed out that martial sects haven't adopted animal names for a couple of centuries. But that was hindsight." His voice was husky.

"Am I hurting you?"

He turned that honest, sober gaze to me. "Ren, I don't even know how many I killed."

Oh, how tangled is human nature! How vivid my memory of him whirling and striking, every move sure with economical grace. Now I understood how poetry could admire the graceful yet lethal strength of the tiger on the attack. But that was a tiger's nature. It did what it did, and then it basked in the sun, untroubled by the death it left behind.

I said, "You saved my life."

"No... Yes. Perhaps. But you took out that white-eyed wolf. He smelled of blood, that one. Not here." Koi tapped his nose. "Here." A finger to his forehead, then a wince.

"He was possessed by a demon," I said.

Koi's startled gaze met mine.

"I don't know more than that. Yet. He was so possessed that it looked out of his eyes, not the man. This was a new thing for me, too. The sword ... has more than one..." Person? Living entity? I remembered the eel monk so long ago. Koi had been there, but I already knew he'd only seen a monk, never the eel. "I need to learn more," I finished.

"There will be a lot for you to learn," Koi ventured, and here again was the shadow of the dragon throne. A jolt deep inside: it would never again be far away.

"But all of you will help me learn it," I said, pushing it aside for now. "Come. Let's get you upstairs."

He half-rose, then hissed, staggering.

"You lost a lot of blood," I observed.

"There's plenty left," he murmured. "Enough to feel every one of these cursed cuts that wants to start bleeding all over again."

By the time he was half-way up the steps, he was leaning heavily on me.

The women's side of the sleeping area had its door directly at the top of the stairs. We stumbled inside, and I hip-shoved the door to close behind me, cutting off the noise of the men and boys already snoring in their area on the other side.

Cray had dragged in Koi's bedding, thoughtfully piling it on top of a stack of our winter quilts. I eased him down, and then thought, what now? Do I drag my own bedding over, or go sleep on the roof with the pigeons?

"Stay?" he asked as I began to rise.

I sank back down, and he relaxed against me, heart thrumming. I could feel it all through my own body. The wind-chafing could not be said to be gone, but it no longer mattered to me. Koi was in enough pain that I gave in to impulse at last and raised my hand to smooth his hair, damp from my sponging, off his brow. He sighed with pleasure, and emboldened, I combed my nails lightly through its silken ribbons.

He gave a kind of half-wince, half groan, and he whispered, in another key altogether, "Stay."

It was my heart's turn to thunder. "But your wounds..."

He gave a peculiar, gulping not-quite-laugh, a sound I'd never heard from him before. "Here's a truth about me. Maybe all men. We can be half-dead, but we'll still—"

I smothered that laugh with my lips.

THIRTY-THREE

…Conquerors and their valor perish
But masters of art live forever…

HOW MUCH TO SAY when writing for the eyes of one's progeny? And yet every one of us comes from such acts. But just as we hide the fact that we are all born naked, so we choose what is to be shared with the world, and what is kept behind the nine-fold screen of reticence.

'Reticence' can encompass all the range of human emotion, many of which we must struggle to suppress. Others? I believe that giving and receiving tenderness is one of the highest of human emotions. It has an infinitude of forms. It is there for everyone, from the youngest and poorest to the most illustrious of ranks, and it—like anger—is contagious. But it heals where anger cannot.

I had experienced tenderness in fleeting moments during my young years, but it had been there in my mother's soft hand on my brow when I was feverish, in the purr of a cat when I went to the back garden to pet them. I discovered a new form of tenderness in the very early hours, well before the sun was to rise. For a blissful time, the entire world under the heavens narrowed to the exquisite pleasure of tracing the silk of Koi's eyebrows with my forefinger, as he slept.

But pain, and leaky bandages, interrupted that sleep, and the world once again crashed insistently around us. I lit a lamp and put him through the agony of having bandages changed. After which I stole downstairs to bathe, dress, then bring up tea.

When I returned, I was in time to see Jai flinging open the door and bawling, "*There* you are! Why did you sleep over..." The obvious then occurred to him, and I smothered a laugh as his astonished gaze shifted from Koi to me and back about three times, before he let out a squawk of a laugh.

Then Koi shot him a look that stopped the laugh abruptly. "Ay, big brother!" Jai said hastily. "I'll help you to the bath. The Hats are making congee."

Once we had breakfast we all had to face the new day. My thoughts slammed between the rush of necessary tasks and the utterly daunting idea that I was going to head the alliance myself. As I helped tend the wounded, I veered between conviction that of course I'd fail humiliatingly, and determination. The only way not to balk at the impossibility was to once again heed my mother's lessons, and break an impossible task into portions that I could accomplish.

And so, when I faced the Pangolins over the midday meal, I said, "Here's my idea. We help get the harvest in here, and then leave Benevolence—the Lu Seekers as well as ourselves. Xianti's spies will be back. They need to find us gone. We need to use the time before winter sets in to deliver the Lu Seekers to all the places I promised aid. Then I must go to the Grand Prince, and convince him to join us, so that before spring, the alliance can demand peace."

Dinek looked uneasy. "It's still not safe for you to go to Whale Haven."

"What is safe anymore?" I asked, pointing out the window at the fresh burial mounds in the forest. "I refused to go before because I was one individual. But I'm going now as the head of our alliance, and I plan to have letters from the Prince of Ran, and Imperial Prince Guiza, to prove it. The grand prince is ambitious, but I don't think he's unreasonable, or my brother would not have stayed with him all this time."

I said it, but I had doubts. *Plan for anything*, I told myself as people dispersed to the afternoon task of repair and restoration. I did not have an immediate task, as the wounded were all resting. I could check on them after some healing sleep; others were also there to watch over them.

I turned to Koi, who—wincing, moving slowly—stacked the dishes to be washed and set to dry.

"I'll do that," I said. "Just looking at you, how you move,

hurts me, too."

He gave me a questioning glance, then sat down, mute evidence of how much pain he was in.

"Is it your doubts or mine?" I asked, taking his face between my hands. He leaned his forehead into my palm, then a shout outside recalled the world.

I took up a dish to scrape into the slop bucket, then a sudden thought chilled me. "Are you regretting my decision? Thinking I have overreached myself?"

"Not at all," Koi said. "Hand me those. At least I can rinse and stack them while sitting. You'll be a far better heir to that throne than any of these others. I think Cray has been hoping for just that, ever since we left Lan. But Ren, you cannot do away with all the laws and traditions."

"I know that. I'll have to begin slowly. Important things first: peace. And once we have that, an end to slavery. Then wait for adjustment before going on. So very much to go on with. But it's like the thirsty crow in the tale, confronted with a half-empty cup of water. A pebble at a time spills not a drop as it brings the water level up where the bird can reach it; a boulder splashes everything out."

"Yes, but there will be matters of rank."

And he waited for me to shift from the empire to the two of us.

"You will never be my servant," I said. "We'll find our proper roles if we get that far. But behind closed doors, we are as we were last night. Just you and me. No roles."

He said, "And On?"

I sighed, knowing that On—with the delicacy that the experienced Xuan cousins had taught him—had been waiting for me. "We're alike. A lot," I said. "We'll ... find the right roles. It helps that he's a butterfly."

"This alliance. They're going to expect you to marry Lan Guiza. Or some other prince," he said, and I knew from that he was thinking ahead as much as I was.

"I know. I thought about that all the way back to Benevolence. But—if this is at all successful—I mean to sit on the dragon throne. There is precedent for that, too, in the unwritten history."

"The Sage Empress," Koi said. "I remember Banti's lessons. Chosen by Suanek herself."

"Ay," I said, sighing. "I realize that to speculate that far ahead, right now, is like expecting rain at the first breath of wind, but…"

"You ought to speculate. Plan. I don't think you have the luxury not to," Koi said.

"It still supposes that I've succeeded. That I put myself at the center of the alliance, and not Guiza. I'm easier about it if I think of myself as the *target*. Instead of my brother, or Cousin Kandati down in Lan, or especially Guiza. Because I think of myself as easier to replace than any of them."

"Not to me," Koi said.

"But to all those who depend on them? Banti is important because he is the calm where Yiuti is wind. Kandati, ay! You saw the tragedy of Lan. But if one of those bolts took me out yesterday? The stream of life would close right over my head and flow on with scarcely a ripple. Oh! To be truly *chosen* — that is, to know that you are *right*, in the eyes of Heaven. What a gift that would be!"

Koi seemed unconvinced, but he said nothing further, and he looked so tired that I decided that my words were merely a weight on his spirit, adding up to a problem he couldn't solve. "I'm done," I said as brightly as I could.

We finished the dishes soon after, and I lugged the water out to dump on the vegetables. By the time I got back with fresh water to refill the pot on the simmer, he was asleep.

I looked in on the wounded, found two Falcons there with the slumbering patients, and tiptoed out to walk around the scrape to see if there was something that needed another pair of hands. My mind engaged with all that must be done before we left. And questions, always questions.

All that faded when I saw a flash of yellow among the purple myrtle blossoms, and discovered On sitting against a venerable tree, a writing desk on his lap, brush in hand, moving rapidly. He had nothing but a tea jug with him.

I realized then that I had not seen him at midday, so I went back to the Pangolin house. There was no food left, but there was still half a basket of fruit that one of the Hat boys had picked that morning.

I picked out three of the nicest pieces and crossed the field toward that clump of trees. On had not moved. He looked up at my approach, then blinked as if struggling to replace his mental stage with the real world.

I held out the fruit. His lips parted and he began to reach, then he stilled, his gaze wary. I looked at the fruit. Had a giant insect burrowed through? Peach … pear … apricot… Oh.

"No," I said with some exasperation. "My very practical parents kept the more romantic stories from me when I was young, so the tragedies that commence with the giving of peaches or pears don't occur to me. If I'm to say a permanent farewell to someone, I wouldn't do it through fruit."

His cheeks glowed, but he grinned and said carelessly, "Did not think so. However, last night..." He lifted a shoulder. "You might have decided you're a tree after all."

"If I had, I would honor us both by speaking, and hope that words would be said to me in return. This is a silly subject. Eat these. You skipped the meal. Need someone to grind ink for you?"

"I have a method." He laid aside the brush, and devoured a peach as if he'd just discovered hunger.

"More *Donkey Duke*?" I asked.

"No." His brow met over his nose. "After yesterday, I wonder if it's too simple. Too stupid. I'm back to Gan, my hero. I finally have the right story for him."

"Not a battle like that yesterday?" I asked in dismay, and quickly corrected myself. "Though I can see that such a thing would be popular. And at least the players pick themselves up at the end, and the blood is only pieces of crimson silk fluttering."

"It's not the battle," On said, tossing the peach pit. He took the apricot, leaving the pear to me, and when he was done, he flung a few drops from his tea jug onto the inkstone before picking up the ink to begin grinding. "My mistake was thinking *I* had to become Gan in order to write him. To try to think like a hero, to act. But I'll never be a hero. Even when I was defending myself, I was thinking about myself defending myself. If that makes sense."

"You are conscious of self?"

"Yes. Always. I had to be. Whereas Koi never seems to consider himself at all. Modesty is in his nature. Did you know the defense plan was his?"

"I did not."

"It was. He said he was trained by a Master Sima, who incidentally fought in the battle that defeated my uncle."

"I remember Master Sima," I said. "He was at my first scrape."

"This Master Sima trained Koi in strategy while he was up there in the mountains beyond Cloud Terrace Harbor. Master Durxu was in the army for ten years, and saw a lot of action when the easterners attacked us. Once he was released, he took to the wandering life, but he remembers what he learned. He was suspicious about Brother Turtle and his sect brethren, but it was Koi who convinced the Four Masters not to say anything until you got here. Instead they took defensive positions."

"He'll always give someone a chance," I said, remembering Brother Turtle's flat eyes. I did not know his true name. But then his soul had probably been consumed long ago. Perhaps it was fitting that he died with no one of his kin to know, to mourn.

On wiped his hands on the grass, then picked up his brush. "The sure way he set it up, and then ... did you see him yesterday? He was like ten men. You know I hate war. But there's something so exhilarating in watching him."

"I know. I saw."

On grinned. "I thought you did."

I could see teasing coming, and forestalled him. "He doesn't talk about war. Doesn't want it. But he knows what to do if it comes. There's a comfort in that. As for you ... you know the saying."

"Which saying? If the world had to rely on me, they'd do better to drink the wind?"

"No—"

"That me trying to be a warrior is like the dog trying for the cat's job?"

"No—"

"If your saying has anything to do with donkeys, I'll—"

It was my turn to interrupt. "Musicians! But it will do for 'player', or 'play-maker'."

On smothered a laugh. "Ayoh! I'll accept that." And, striking a pose from where he sat, "To a battle you don't send a musician, and to a festival you don't send a general."

"Isn't it true?" I asked.

"True enough. And it gives me another idea for how to shape Shi Gan the Hero's adventures... Ay, this is going to be my best one yet..." He dipped the brush, and began scrawling madly.

I left him to it, knowing that there would soon enough be little time for such endeavors.

So it proved to be true.

By the beginning of the Year of the Pig—pig years being regarded as hopefully auspicious—the last of our Lu Seekers was in place. They were not quite an army, not in the customary sense, but they already were welcome as defenders, we'd quickly discovered. I'd insisted we make sure that no island got all the skilled artisans, spreading them among all the companies. We also tried to send people as near to their home islands as possible.

Cray, with Zi Tian's aid, had expanded our communications, so that each Lu Seeker group was able to communicate.

As for us, we celebrated New Year's Two Moons unable to see the moons at all, mired by a snowstorm in a cove off the northwest corner of Benevolent Winds. An imperial stronghold. But we were only there for the three days the snowstorm lasted, and then we pushed on, heading for the territory of the Grand Prince—knowing that the closer we got, the stronger the inevitability that we'd be spotted by imperial spies. Even so, I refreshed the obscuring charms over the *Pangolin* every morning, no matter how bitterly cold. Though we knew that Xianti now had at least one Essence expert working for him, and his spies were surely taught to scrutinize every blur or blot, that did not mean we would not try to stay invisible.

Once I'd been content to spend my days cut off from everyone, praying for the safety of my family and hoping that one day I'd find a way to free them. Now I often scanned the skies for the little shapes of pigeons, and fretted if a day passed without a message.

Through the Princess of Ye, we learned that Xianti had summoned the fierce General Zoa away from Lan, which meant that Kandati could reestablish contact with Arati, our mutual cousin.

We believe you can do anything, (Kandati wrote to me, through Arati) *but I hope you will forgive this incompetent one's earnest entreaty that it be done before next harvest, or you will have to lead the ritual to bless an island of ghosts.*

THIRTY-FOUR

The formidable path ahead grew dark, and darker still
With nothing heard but the call of the wind
Hemmed in by ice…

THE NORTHERN WORLD WAS a vast expanse of icy gray and blue under an early morning sky the color of milk. We had expected Whale Haven's bay to be frozen, and it was. I'd spent considerable time making talismans to aid me in applying steady fire. This way I melted enough ice permitting *Pangolin* to forge a narrow path toward the shore. We flew a white envoy's banner over the *Pangolin* banner, the Ye banner, and Ran's blue.

Icy slush churned greenish-white to either side of the bow as we passed a very old pagoda built at the extreme end of a long, thin peninsula. The watchtowers remained still—no drums of alarm, no rains of arrows or crack of cannon. The crew was all on deck in spite of searching gusts, weapons to hand. But there was silence, except for the moan of the wind as we wondered what sort of a welcome we'd encounter. They'd certainly had enough time to prepare.

I had prepared, too. Beginning with myself. After much consideration, and discussion with Cray and On, I'd decided that for our arrival I'd wear the lavender dragonfly robe, even though I was not going disguised as a boy. My hair was pulled up in its tail, fixed with golden pins. I added a jade ornament to my sash, a reminder of my Lan rank. But I was going to use my boy movements. No demure princess of tiny gliding steps, with demeanor small and meek.

There was a pier with no ship frozen next to it. I melted ice all the way there, water surging and splashing until we eased to a halt.

A tall figure stamped his way down the wharf. In spite of the bulky coat and the hat pulled down nearly to his nose, I instantly knew my brother by his gait.

I waited impatiently for the ramp to be slid over the rail, then ran down. "Banti!"

I threw myself in his arms. He gave me a rib-cracking hug, then let me go and pointed back at the green-blue trail carved through the ice. It had seemed so straight when we sailed, but I could see an arc. "I can't believe it," he said, his breath clouding. "But there's the evidence." He gave me a comical look, his nose ruddy from the cold. "Can you get your ship out again?"

"With the right wind, I'm told," I said. "I just make fire. I'm no navigator."

"'Just make fire.' How many can claim that?"

I was ready to disclaim—*ay, it's nothing*, the words were there—but I must no longer regard whatever I did as nothing, just because it was not all I wished I could do.

"I can't really believe you're here," he exclaimed. "Tell me everything!"

"I was going to say the same to you. Is there news about our family?"

His entire face brightened, but he caught himself, his gaze shifted, and he said, "Yiuti and his imperial highness get the news first."

"First tell me what kind of welcome to expect?"

"Ayoh! Grand-Uncle has a banquet in preparation, musicians, probably speeches. Yiuti should be along. He started beautifying as soon as word came you were sighted," Banti said cheerfully.

"Is that what I'm to expect, then? Another proposal of marriage?"

"Another?"

"Not from Cousin Kandati. Who is already married. I really liked his wife. She goes shares with him in everything, and it hasn't been easy. Nor from the Prince of Ran, who married Arati. You remember."

"Do I," Banti exclaimed with a wince. "Poor old First, he was gutted by that."

"I hope he's gotten over it. She has, I'm glad to say. The Prince of Ran listens to her, and no, Banti, hear me. I can see you're impatient to get to your questions, but this is important."

I stopped, right there on the wharf, though the Pangolins were waiting for a sign from me, and farther up on the shore a cluster of muffled figures waited with a carriage. "Banti, look at me. Hear me."

He stilled, and brought his gaze, which had been darting all over the *Pangolin* and beyond, back to my face in question.

I said, "I hope that someone here will support me. I'd like that to be you, my own brother —"

He cut in earnestly, "I'll *always* protect you. If I can — if I can even see you —"

I waited, and he stuttered to a stop.

"Banti," I said, shoving my cold fingers farther up my sleeves. "I need you to understand. This is *my* alliance. *I* put it together. With help, of course. And advice from people I've come to trust. Yet so far, all I'm hearing are marriage proposals."

"Marriage treaties," Banti said in a tone that made me suspect that yes, I'd shortly be hearing another. "It's traditional," he added uncertainly. "An honor."

"I know. But look past the immediate circumstances, will you please? If I were a man, then all talk would be of following me, or dividing up territories between me and some other leader, or killing me. But I'm not a man, so the talk is of taking everything I've done and handing it off to a man. Easiest way is through marriage. It's not just men who assume I need to be directed by a man. Remember Fourteenth Consort Ye? She promises I'd have more than my share of power, but that would still be granted by a man, bound by custom. There are other women who cling far more tightly to the old ways. The rest of us? Never are permitted to choose for ourselves. If I succeed, I'm not going to marry any of these men and make him my emperor."

"But..."

"If I marry, any man I marry will be my *consort*. I might even marry two, or three. Or nine."

Shock widened Banti's eyes, then mirth crinkled them. "Ay, Renti, I would love to see you managing nine men. Everyone knows there can't be even two roosters in a pen."

"Believe me, harems aren't any more peaceful, as a rule. Women are just sneakier about their warfare. And more desperate to hold onto the tiny bit of power left to them — but that can wait. There's so much to happen first. So much. And I might be dead by tomorrow—I learned that lesson at my last Falcon scrape, when I came face to face with an assassin Xianti sent specifically to kill me. I remind myself of that every single day."

The mirth died out of his face, and he made an abortive gesture, meant to be protective. Then he dropped his arm.

"I will probably keep on using the word *empress*. It's buried too deeply in the language, and I think my model must be the first Sage Empress. But I am determined to become emperor. Not because I want to. Certainly not because I deserve to. But because I believe there needs to be change, real change, or we'll just have more warring princes in the next generation."

He nodded slowly. "All right. I think I understand. Then ... take it I tried to speak in favor of Yiuti, as I promised to do as the condition for getting to greet you first. I won't go against you. But I need to warn you. It's going to be difficult. Grand-Uncle Yiulo has everything all planned out."

"That was exactly what I wanted to hear, so that I'd know what to expect." I gulped in a shaky breath, aware that I was sweating inside my coat, though my extremities ached from the chill. "Thank you! Secondly, I don't want my companions pushed over to the servants' wings. Think of them as my entourage—fellow envoys, not servants."

Banti looked uncertain at this complete upset of all expected rules. "They can go with you in the guest suite. I'll tell the steward. Ho, is that Koi up there, with the sword?"

"Yes. He's my ... my captain of defense."

"Ay! Come, come, come! Inside, and to warmth. Expect Yiuti to turn up at the door. Oraiti will be along, too. He had some amazing things to say about you. No one believed him—thought he was enamored." Banti chuckled. "You'll get all the news we have, and then you can tell us yours."

I gave Dinek the hand signal that it was safe to disembark, and we were taken up to where Oraiti waited with servants to handle trunks (which none of us had—we bore our own travel gear, as usual) and a covered carriage.

The grand prince had turned a garrison into a fortified capital. Those watchtowers had been placed with reach over all the bay, and there were more along the top of the lower wall. Trebuchets lay behind that first wall, big enough to launch ship-killing loads. Higher walls lay behind, earth and stone both, and I noted Koi examining all these defenses as well as we proceeded to the south hall. My thought as I looked about was of the cost in labor and gold; all of that could have gone to relieve Lan, for example.

First there must be peace, I told myself, squashing the urge to dwell mentally on the Circle board of trade that I had been building during all my journeying.

Yiuti came to the palace's outer door to greet me, a deliberate honor considering our respective ranks. "Cousin Renti," he cried. He wore a military-looking outfit richly decorated to mark him as a prince. His big, broad chest looked splendid with a crimson firedragon embroidered across it, and gold accented the edges of his robe. He was barely my height, but his golden hair clasp and topknot and his fine boots worked with gold added stature to his appearance.

He was full of compliments as we proceeded through a splendid hall and out to a winter garden, and then to the guest building. First on my looks, which I accepted politely. I have to admit that I was tempted to turn them back on him, just to disconcert him, except I suspected that the effect would work against me in that he would assume that I was smitten by him at first sight.

Then came the compliments on what I'd done, interspersed with questions, which I answered easily:

"Did you really cure a plague before it could spread by calling down a lightning storm?"

"No, I don't call storms. I'm told by true Essence experts that meddling with weather can cause famine for months, at the least. The lightning was there, it's just that I can use the Essence from fire within it."

Truth, always truth, just not all of it: for example, I did not want that plague ruse getting back to Xianti, to protect the innocent citizens of Mountain Peony.

Yiuti took me to the readied suite. I barely had enough time to unsling my carryall before he shouted for tea to be brought, and he headed for the seat of honor, gesturing to me to take the seat to his right, where a wife would sit. I took three broad strides and got to the principal man's seat first, and lounged back, Sagacious Blade across my knees.

Yiuti stopped short, blinking at me.

"Leader of the alliance," Banti murmured to Yiuti.

"Ayoh!" Yiuti exclaimed, visibly smothering an outburst of temper, which left his face almost as red as his firedragon. "Of course!" He bowed, and gingerly sat in the other seat, as if his contact with the chair in the wife's usual place might unman him.

I bit my lip against a laugh, and said as graciously as I could, "This cousin has grown sadly uncouth while learning to master many arts. I beg my good cousin to overlook my manners, and please! Tell me the news?"

Yiuti grinned. Now he was sure of himself. First a glance at Banti, who gave his head a tiny shake, and Yiuti said triumphantly, "There *is* good news. There was a general amnesty declared at New Year's Two Moons this year." He paused, and added, "That includes your family!"

I looked from him to Banti. "They're free? They're safe?"

Banti opened his mouth, then deferred to Yiuti, and I understood at once his hesitation when first we met: it was Yiuti's design (or, more correctly, his grandfather's) to have the excellent news delivered through Yiuti as a way of advancing his prospects. It was that thought that kept me from weeping, but I could not prevent my eyes from stinging.

"Safe, that I cannot say," Yiuti stated, looking unwontedly sober. "No one is truly safe in the imperial city. But they were released. Xianti himself went to let them out—he was trying to impress Princess Meiti." *Meiti* being the adoptive name given to Namath Vaha, the Cinnabar Princess. But no one seemed to use it outside of formal court affairs.

"He's still courting her?" I asked. "Xianti? After all these years? I did not think he could be faithful in that way."

"Faithful?" Yiuti uttered a crude laugh.

Banti said, "No one knows what's in his mind. And there is a steady stream of dancers and comfort women in the palace—"

"Banti, you ought not to mention such things before your unmarried sister," Yiuti said with a proprietary glance in my direction.

Annoyed, I said, "I hope he pays them well. I can't imagine that he's anything but the most self-involved lover."

Yiuti looked as if did not know what to make of this, and Banti said hastily, "Xianti still wants to marry Vaha, whatever his reason. He has not changed in that. Or in his care for Kianti, now governor of Benevolent Winds."

"I remember that." Benevolent Winds had been under the governorship of Oraiti's branch of the Lans for several generations.

Xianti would leave Benevolent Winds untouched for his

brother's sake, but Princess Vaha… "Why hasn't he forced her to marry him?"

"Vaha was promised that she could choose. And the emperor does not dare to contradict an edict made by the former emperor, not with his birth father right there before the throne every time he calls court." Recollecting that Uncle Koza had been thus raised to call the imperial couple Mother and Father, and his cousins, brothers and sisters. But with their deaths, that fiction need no longer be heeded.

"The Eastern Fleet is still very loyal to Uncle Miluo," Banti finished.

Though military organization had never interested me, I knew that the Eastern and Western Fleets included marine warriors as well as the navy. So, in effect a good portion of the imperial armed forces.

"Which is why Xianti's been building his own army," I said. "So that situation has not changed."

Yiuti said, "According to Yuen and Janek, whose fathers are both ministers, on the first day of the new year, when the divinations for auspicious predictions were read out, Xianti promised before the throne that he would defeat the rebel princes by summer, cleansing the empire and establishing peace. He said that if the emperor would give him the tally for all imperial forces, he would lead a two-pronged attack, one against Ye, and the other against us here. But the emperor said that trade must be protected, and all treaties observed, so Xianti can't strip the big garrisons like those at the Jade Islands or Flowering Plum or Te Gar, and of course at Ran."

I was mentally surveying the map that Koi and I had made, tracking imperial forces—as much as we could gather. The Prince of Ran had been principal in gathering that information for us. "Xianti always wants to outnumber his foes. He'd have three fronts in the west. No, two."

"Exactly," Banti said. "He'll discount Cousin Kandati down south in Lan. From what we hear, they haven't the strength to do anything."

"It's true. I was there. Our ancestral island is in terrible shape," I said. "Or Xianti never would have pulled Zoa out. My guess is, he will be sending Zoa north to keep the Prince of Ran from reinforcing Ye."

"That's what my grandfather says, and his general agrees," Yiuti stated.

"But…" My mind soared over that mental map, covered

with Koi's meticulous handwriting. All those imperial garrisons with harbors we had made sure to avoid. "He won't want to attack here without a far larger force than he's got..." I drew a breath.

"What?" Banti asked, and Yiuti looked uncertain.

"Mountain Peony," I said. "I'll wager anything that Xianti will be forcing that marriage on Huyun Shandek, so that he can then commandeer the greens to send up here against Whale Haven, with his own favorites as backup, once the greens take the brunt of the defense."

Banti raised a hand. "The latest we heard was, Siarti herself is insisting on the marriage. They exchanged some letters, and she got hold of a drawing of him. According to what she's been saying all over the women's side of the palace, she'll have the handsomest husband in the empire at her feet."

I uttered a foreboding laugh.

Yiuti gazed at me fixedly. "Do you have spies *everywhere?*"

"I don't have spies anywhere. We're only beginning to get communication going. But I know something of Huyun Shandek. Who has been corresponding with the emperor. Whether or not he finally has to marry Siarti, I'll wager anything he's made some arrangement with the emperor so that he can save his greens. But we can't count on it," I added. "That's why we need to present our case to the emperor well before spring."

Yiuti's gaze shifted. The talk dwindled to promises of various treats, and the boys left soon after — Yiuti reminding me that the banquet would be held at midday.

Koi and Cray appeared from the side rooms.

"How much of that did you hear?"

"Everything," Cray said.

"Good! Where's On?" I asked, and sighed. "Never mind. He always vanishes." The grand prince would surely remember his family — his father had probably been about the grand prince's age. But as yet, I was the only one among us who knew On's true identity. "He's off to spy around here, I hope," I finished.

Cray and Koi both expressed pleasure at the news about my family, but that didn't last long. I gave voice to my own worries: "I'm afraid that if he gets any kind of setback, Xianti will be after them again."

"Yes," Koi said reluctantly.

Cray said, "I sent a pigeon from the ship to our Falcon safehouse in the imperial city. Though she's a young bird, still training, she ought to be able to find us again. They'll know through Bao where Chief Censor Lan and Madam and First Young Master are."

Bao had been a general purpose yard man, one of Mother's people. He had been the one to save Koi after the arrest.

The gnawing worry about my family was back again after that brief respite. They would never be safe from Xianti unless they could be hidden from him.

"I had better get ready for this banquet," I said, my mood souring. "Get out *all* the gold. I think I'm going to need it. The silk slippers, too."

I laid Sagacious Blade in the bedroom, and went to take a bath.

THIRTY-FIVE

Lu the Poet, Lu the Madman, Lu the Drunkard
Chased the sun till he spied the place where the sun sets.
He leaped over the Great Sea and climbed the Heaven-Piercing
Mountains
He broke through the clouds to dart toward the sky
Bowing toward the stars to the left and to the right.

I ASSUMED THAT YIUTI would have given his grandfather a full report on our earlier conversation. They'd plenty of time to make their plans, whatever those might be. Cray and Koi and I talked out possibilities, with me wishing now and then that On would turn up. Koi was excellent for strategic speculation, and Cray knew what was possible with regard to communication, but On was our acknowledged expert on theater. And I was beginning to play my role. I had to be ready for anything.

A distant gong boomed.

It was nearly time to step onto the stage.

As always in these moments, I was aware of my heart beating in my throat as I shook out my gauzy silk sleeves that rippled to the floor. The golden chimes in my headdress rang sweetly as I crossed the long corridors, and a waiting steward bowed me into the banquet room. I used a good, broad stride, causing the layers of my gauzy robes to swing about my feet.

The mirror in the guest room had reflected a tall person with a strong resemblance to Banti, but without his humor. My mouth was shaped like my mother's, otherwise I was very much a Lan, dressed in gold and celestial blue, embroidered all over with crimson amaryllis.

The grand prince had arranged a table for two on a dais. He conducted me himself to one of the two cushions.

My great-uncle had the Lan eyes and brows, the rest of his face even browner than our shared skin shade, seamed by the sun. Gray streaks in his hair added a tigerish aspect to his challenging smile, but I detected no malice in it. I did wish I could have brought Sagacious Blade—but I reflected that we would surely meet again, and I could find an excuse to have my sword with me, if I came to distrust his words.

I did not want to distrust his words. But I could see that he was watching me as closely as I watched him as we complimented the day, the new year, the food, and each other. I also returned toasts from Yiuti, Banti, Oraiti, and the more prominent of the ministers' sons. It was soon clear that they were all in the habit of drinking hard, at least in winter.

And there was a challenge to me in these many, many compliments, each over a full cup of fragrant hot rice wine.

I will not describe the elaborate politenesses and the many, many toasts as dish after dish was brought out. I had to prove myself, which meant drinking cup for cup. That meant concentrating after each swallow on using fire within me to burn off the part of the wine that otherwise would separate my mind off from my physical awareness, setting me afloat in that Essence realm when I needed to keep my senses sharp.

All the boys were there, of course, plus a few wives seated across from them, or consorts behind them. None of these spoke. When I could, I glanced across from Banti to see if the lover Koi had reported him having had been elevated to consort, at least, and discovered that either she wasn't, or she had not come, for there was no table either across from him or behind him.

My heart knotted as I wondered if I was going to get a chance to speak to Banti without anyone else around, or expectations from his host. At least our family had been freed, I reminded myself as I forced down a few bites of excellent whitetail cooked in sesame oil with ginger—a dish that ordinarily I loved. Banti had probably told them that. We had been close once. I wondered if that sibling alliance, so natural and unthought, could be retrieved.

I forced my gaze to shift away, for I had to concentrate.

The grand prince had been watching me. Alarm shot

through me, igniting the singing meridians of anticipation.

He lifted his cup to me again, saying, "Yiuti reports that your strategic awareness is as the gods looking below. He is not used to such brilliance as well as beauty." Another bow.

I bowed as well, suspecting that this was the first step toward the labyrinth of the marriage proposal. He probably had a respectable and high-ranking dowager ready to offer to adopt me so that in the eyes of the world—and especially in the eyes of future generations—our marriage would be correct with respect to the degrees of family relation. Hat Dove had done some checking for me, and as I'd suspected, it had happened more often than not with marriage treaties between imperial or important noble families with great landholdings or wealth to preserve.

Resisting a proposal would set me back onto my hind legs, requiring yet more compliments and maybe even compromise to preserve face as I persisted in refusing. It was time to charge ahead.

"Talking of strategy is necessary," I said. "Though my goal is peace."

"Ah, peace! We are of like minds in our desire for peace."

Here, yet another toast.

"If I may invite my illustrious young guest to deign to listen to the plans of us old graybeards, whose young years were spent in military experience to the glory of the empire, I believe we will attain that peace the soonest."

Toast. Bow. "I would be delighted to be instructed by my venerable elder," said I. "And in turn, might this young relation of no talent presume to offer her own plan under correction?" Then—my heart drumming hard—I raised my hand. "Stay! An idea occurs to me, perhaps entertaining on this long, cold wintry day."

Grand-Uncle Yiulo's brows shot upward. I was distracted by two white hairs in one eyebrow. Below those, his gaze was a little surprised, and very amused. "Please! We've only ourselves for entertainment, and the days are short, the evenings long."

I was very sure that a horde of dancing girls were waiting elsewhere for when they'd rid themselves of the women of rank, but that was irrelevant. I said, "Why don't we discuss strategy while at the same time playing a game of Circle."

"Circle?" the grand prince repeated.

"My father never wrote down his teachings. He was too humble to assume anyone would desire them, and also far too busy working for the good of the court; except for us, his children, he did not consider his words of interest. But I remember so much of what he taught us. For example, he taught us that Circle is a metaphor for history."

"Oh? And what did my very esteemed nephew say about history?" the grand prince asked.

"He said that the board, the pieces, the rules, are constants, just as are islands, the people on them, the creatures of sea, land, and air. Our empire is the board, and the games represent the flow of history, which is like a river. Though it has its boundaries—its rules—it is never still. We strive for balance in the game, and we strive for balance in the world."

"This is true enough," the grand prince said, with smiling tolerance. "I can send for a board, if it would please my young grand-niece."

"I would like to suggest that we forgo the board altogether. We can conduct the game on a mental board, as we discourse on the present situation, and possible solutions."

Banti sent me a startled glance, and I wondered if he had not indulged in this type of game since youth. The other boys murmured a little, and Yiuti, I noticed—already red-faced from too much wine—looked a bit like a stuffed fish, his eyes shiny.

All gazes turned toward the grand prince, who uttered a laugh, and this time when he toasted me, it was with the air of one acknowledging a very fine move on the board. "Interesting! And is there a stake? What does the winner gain? Treasure? Ships? Men?"

"The support of the other in their quest for the dragon throne," I said.

All eyes arrowed to the grand prince, who laughed heartily. "You play for lofty stakes, child? Ah, that you were born a man!"

I don't *play* for anything, I wanted to say, except right now I was doing exactly that. But only to prove my brains within a familiar metaphor. My challenge had circumvented—for the moment—all the tedious reasons why marrying Yiuti and submitting to Grand-Uncle Yiulo's experience and traditional thought ought to be done. Now I had to win the game that was no game.

I no longer remember the sequence of moves, or which of the various contingencies we countered back and forth. His strategy was war. To his credit, he truly believed that with the alliance holding off the rest of the empire, he could sail straight south, gather in my Grandfather Gu's forces at the north end of the imperial island (after I convinced my grandfather that it would be good to do so) surround the imperial capital, batter the straitened imperial guard to surrender, and dictate terms. It was a much less bloody plan than Xianti's thirst for rampaging across the entire empire.

While we went through the steps of these outcomes, we conducted a game without board or markers. It was not a particularly elegant or complex game. I was working so hard to maintain the two separate threads of discourse that my toes bunched tightly in my slippers, and my body was taut as a guqin string. My grand-uncle, again to give him credit, worked gamely, though he knew as well as I did that this was mostly a trick. Mostly.

I knew I was going to win about three-quarters through. He was losing sight of the board, just as I had game after game after game all that winter at Tortor. But I played on until at last he clasped his hands to me and said, "I surrender the board."

Yiuti had begun writing the moves on his table, or trying to, using his eating sticks and peas and currants. He also had been gulping more wine. He looked up, aghast, then said, "Grandfather! This is not just."

"It is just, my boy," the grand prince said. "In that it was a refreshing mental exercise. And I agreed to it. I thank you, my esteemed young grand-niece. But it is merely a game, no replacement for experience. And experience is all you need to add to your excellence. I venture to suggest that as my grandson's wife, that experience would be the making of the both of you."

And there was his counter-charge. My trick had failed. Time for reason.

"May this grand-niece observe to her esteemed grand-uncle that experience is destined to be the outcome whatever we do, unless we cease to exist in this life and forget everything before the next?"

"A true observation, grand-niece."

"I further desire to observe, if my esteemed grand-uncle will permit me, that of all the empire's long and venerable line of emperors, not a one could have experience of being an emperor before ascent to the dragon throne."

Grand-Prince Yiulo chuckled. "It is true. One of the reasons why we say that the emperor is Heaven's Chosen — in other words, the Jade Emperor himself designated the choice with imperial birth."

"This grand-niece entreats permission to thank her generation's grand-uncle for another wise observation, but begs leave to observe that—as happened with the recent change of emperor—designated heirs are not necessarily given their designated place."

"Is all this," he said, "a hint that you prefer to marry young Guiza in preference to my grandson?"

"It is, if I may be allowed to clarify," I said as quietly, but as firmly, as I could, "a statement that I do not intend to marry, now. My Uncle Guiza furthermore supports my bid for the dragon throne."

"You cannot be serious. A girl?" he exclaimed.

"A Lan," I corrected. "I'm young, but I am not the youngest by any means to step forward to claim the dragon throne. I can name ten younger without looking at the records, and out of those, only two were designated heirs. Every one of those ten emerged out of the wreckage from revolts, counter-attacks, defenses. Not all that strife was the result of mere greed. Many were desperate actions caused by very bad government."

"True. Though I do not see young Koza as any improvement over his father. But you wish to favor us with a point?"

"Thank you, esteemed Grand-Uncle Yiulo, for your forbearance. My point is that Mana Ta instructed us centuries ago by reminding us that Kanda's laws of civilization regard rulers highly, in their proper place, but warns that it is acceptable for the subjects to overthrow or even kill a ruler who ignores the people's needs and rules harshly. This is because a ruler who does not rule justly is no longer a true ruler—one could then say, not the true Heaven's Chosen."

"I have to admit I have never read of a rebellion being led by a girl who justified herself by quoting the ancients," the grand prince began, and once again his indulgent tone, if not his words, seemed to pull the discourse back in the direction of it all being a game, a jest. Not to be taken seriously.

"Under correction, permit me to observe that my quoting Mana Ta should not be taken as an instigation to violence against law but as an application of Kanda's philosophy to society. Kanda states in the Twenty-Five that all relationships should be beneficial, but each has its own principle or inner logic. Rulers must justify their position by acting benevolently before they can expect reciprocation from the people. Is this not true?"

"It is true, but…"

I bowed. "This grand-niece begs leave to finish discussing her possibly deficient understanding of Mana Ta's meaning: In his view, a ruler is like a steward. Although a ruler has higher status than a commoner, that ruler is actually subordinate to the masses of people and the resources of society. Otherwise, there would be an implied disregard of the potential of human society heading into the future."

"One cannot quarrel with the ancients," he said, still smiling.

"To finish," I said, aware that I was close to repeating myself—which would weaken the whole. "Is there any reason why I ought not to lead the alliance, outside of my form happening to be a woman's? I have proved that my brain is as nimble as anyone's here. I have presented my plan. I am fast gaining experience that, may I point out, none here can match, unless any of my esteemed cousins and colleagues have studied Essence skills, healing, and have traveled to the west and back, observing the broken links in the major trade routes?"

"Have you learned to lead a battle, or defend your life?" the grand prince asked.

"Actually, I have defended my own life. And I believe I understand general strategy, again as well as anyone of my generation, but my entire point is that we do not have to rely on violence to solve this dilemma. It might be forced on us. But I intend to exert every wit to avoid it. This alliance so far has been put together without violence. That is, not on my part."

The grand prince slowly shook his head. "I grant you most of those things, my good child, and I am impressed by your determination. But so great a change—the world won't stand for it, I fear. To try to wrest the flow of tradition is to force a river to run backwards. If we had some sort of…"

"Sign?" came a familiar voice from the back of the hall.

And so we come to that famous moment that so much has been written about by those who were not there.

The voice belonged to On, with his usual impeccable timing. He sauntered in, drawing every eye. Who was he now? On Lu wore scholarly robes with ragged hems, as expected of a poor hermit-scholar; was this Shi Gan the Hero? But On was dressed in layers of deep cobalt blue over crimson and white, with accents of gold in dragonflies and lilies, his hair drawn up into a hair clasp of pure gold edged with pearls, very much like a young prince.

Lilies? Then I noticed the jade ornament suspended on a

silken cord, tied in an Eternal Amity knot, with a long tassel dancing below it. I knew that jade ornament. It had a lily etched on it—it had been handed to On by his elder brother, before that brother was killed on the emperor's orders.

"His imperial highness, Prince Kwai Sheion," announced the steward.

On stopped ten steps from the dais, and snapped his fan open. Across it, above a spray of painted hibiscus, was written *Lift the window—see Mt. Lir.*

The grand prince learned forward, squinting. "Yes, you've a look of Kwai Xukanda! Where did you come from? Are you with anyone?"

"No prince comes without an entourage," On said, laughing over his fan. "This individual of no talent is here as one of Princess Lan Renti's allies. As for my entourage: listen," he invited, with a graceful arc of his fan toward the windows.

So intent we all had been that the gradually increasing rumble from outside had scarcely registered. It was louder now, a sustained clatter unlike any sound I had ever heard.

The windows had been pulled shut against the wintry wind, but low as the sun was, it ought not to be setting now. Yet a gloom darkened the room, only lit by the branches of candles behind every table.

The grand prince gestured, and servants sprang to open the windows. We ran to them and gazed up at a wind-scoured sky of silver and tarnished brass, the glow of both moons beginning their parting dance diffusing a still and muted luminosity as they crested the horizon.

The sky had blackened with thousands upon thousands of shapes nearly obscuring those moons: birds. A vanguard on the wing soared, calling and calling, from seabirds and sand hoppers to the long shapes of storks, snow-plumed except for dark flight-feathers striping their inner wings, ragged and gray save for flashes of pink reflecting the setting sun. Above them the cranes, riding the high currents. Below them, crested starlings swarmed, sinking then re-cohering as though their gathering numbers turned on a thin ribbon, the line stretching from horizon to horizon.

We watched, astounded; the sun, sinking as the moons rose on the opposite horizon, took much of the light with it, the vast army of birds darkening to silhouettes before the unifying shadows dissolved them.

Then high, fluting trills unfurled, honks and caws

trumpeted, as from the north a golden glow rose to drift magnificently over the palace.

It was a phoenix.

It was that same phoenix I remembered from that faraway sacred isle of Ys, her feathers a thousand shades of color shimmering with a golden overlay.

She gave one beat of her wings, sending tiny glows, not unlike fire, to shower down over the palace roofs, walls, and courts. Most of these burned out and vanished before they reached the ground, but one spark fell toward us, eddying on an unseen current, until it drifted inside the window, evading the snatching hands of Yiuti and a couple of the boys, to land on me.

Essence burned through me, and I almost didn't hear Grand-Uncle Yiulo say on an exhaled breath, "It seems we have received a Sign."

THIRTY-SIX

…She descended in winter's bitterest hour,
Riding a phoenix and leading a phalanx of white cranes,
With banners of hibiscus and all the horns of Heaven….

"DIDN'T YOU SEE THE birds when we first arrived?" On said much later that night, when we were all alone in the suite. Truly alone—even the listening ears of servants had been prudently withdrawn, or perhaps they had withdrawn themselves. "Black specks all over the ridge along both sides of the bay? How could you miss them?"

"Because I was watching the towers," I said. "And complaining to myself about the cost in labor and material building this fortress, and calculating what we could have done with that gold."

"You could have told *us* who you were," Cray said, giving On a flat look.

I sensed that she did not like his revelation of imperial birth (which would explain a lot of his reluctance!), though even Cray had to admit that his revelation had enhanced our prestige more than I would have expected.

After the phoenix vanished, the banquet hall had become a cacophony of sound as everyone gave voice, not unlike that noise from above. Over it had risen the grand prince's shout, insisting on order, as I held onto a veneer of calm and met On's eyes.

He mouthed the word, "Sun."

Then On became the center of attention—an act of risk on his part, for he and I both knew that the grand prince had led the forces that had annihilated Ing Moa, On's maternal uncle, who had gone to war in On's name. Thus earning On the unwanted label of "Upstart Prince."

But it became instantly clear that On's fears all this time were unnecessary. "Kuai Sheion," the grand prince bellowed in surprise and delight. "We were unsure if you had truly survived! I strove in every way to get Ing Moa to give you to me, if you still lived—I would have protected you. Your grandfather Kwai Xukanda and I were the closest of friends all through princes' school..."

He continued in an injured voice, explaining that the very vigor of his defense against Ing Moa's attack was because of Ing Moa's presumption in using the Kwai name to excuse his bare-faced ambition. "We thought you were truly dead, and he was pretending you were alive. Why, except for his unconscionable greed you could have grown up with Yiuti, here, side by side!"

The grand prince had gone on about the excellence of Kwai Xukanda, On's grandfather. He had been considered a qilin, as well as On's father—which might have been why the emperor destroyed the entire family.

We'd then been swept off to an entertainment that I strongly suspected had been arranged initially to celebrate the betrothal of me to Yiuti—but though the musicians and players gave us an excellent rendition of *The Swordsman and the Fairy*, all attention was pretty much divided between On and myself, until at last we all parted for the night. The grand prince, I felt certain, to reform all his plans.

In our suite, Cray continued by saying, still a little affronted, "Why didn't Sun come to me?"

"Because you were not outside," On said. "She flew with the cranes. She told me that they've been following us ever since they sensed that demon inside Brother Turtle. They also want humans to stop burning nests and habitats, and it seems they think Ren's going to do that."

"How do they even know my plans?" I asked.

"Sun only changed to her human self for long enough to tell me that much, and to ask what they could do to aid me. You have to understand that we were right above one of the windows of the hall, where I'd been listening. I could hear the grand prince trying to muscle you, Ren, into his grandson's arms, and I'd just about decided it was time to intervene when she turned up. I told her that the one thing I needed and didn't have was an entourage. She said, *You don't need people when you've got us!* I told her to stand ready and ran back to change. That was all we said. Birds don't wear clothes, so she had none with her, and she didn't want to stay human long. As I said, we were outside on one of the rooftops, and she was freezing in mere skin. She said she would come to the *Pangolin* to talk more when we set sail again."

Cray's brow cleared.

Koi had accepted On without any change in word or tone. I think he had always suspected something of the sort, for the same reasons I'd suspected early in our acquaintance. "Did *she* bring the phoenix?"

"I don't know. I spoke with her before the birds swarmed," On said. "I think the cranes were surprised, too. We can ask later who the phoenix is. If she's the same one we saw at that island when we had to let Sun go." He grinned at me. "You might get an explanation, you might not. But sometimes you have to let a miracle be a miracle."

We were interrupted by a knock, and Banti was let in, late as it was. "I saw light," he said. "Is it too late? I hoped to have a chance to talk to you…" He was speaking to me, Koi, and Cray, but he halted when he perceived On.

"He knows everything," I said.

Banti blinked, then said, "The grand prince thinks we'll be ready in a week to depart for the south. If, that is, you can melt the bay again. It's already freezing over, I just heard." And in a lower voice, "I think Grand-Uncle Yiulo considers your ability to set fire to the bay even more impressive than that phoenix and the army of birds. Which I still don't believe happened. Except that the guards and the servants and everyone else are all out there in the icy wind collecting feathers wherever they can find them, as good luck talismans."

"A week?" I repeated. "What if news gets to the imperial capital before we do?"

Banti said confidently, "All birds are under the control of the bird-master, who is very loyal to our grand-uncle. No birds are permitted to fly out—they'll be shot from the towers."

"I need to be able to send messages," I said. "Though I can get around it if I must."

"No need. Cray, first thing in the morning bring your birds to the bird-master. I'm sure they'll be excepted—now."

Cray nodded, and I turned to my brother. "About communications. Xianti knew the grand prince's plan to winter over here. Did you ever get the letter I sent to Koi about that?"

"Ah! Yes. Grand-Uncle Yiulo had everyone in the birdmaster's area put to the question."

I winced. "What happened?"

"I don't know exactly. He did not talk about it before me or the boys. A couple of people were executed, that much I do remember. No one ever said if they were identified as spies or not. You know the military tradition, that it's better to kill a few innocent than to let a spy or rebel go free. But he's certain that he now has complete control."

Nothing was certain. I winced again, and decided not to bring up the subject of a possible spy to either Yiuti or the grand prince; I would find excuses to wear Sagacious Blade, and only if I heard a liar would I speak up.

I did share my concerns with my own people, who said they'd keep their ears open, and so a few days wound their way slowly by. At least I got some chances to talk to Banti, to discover that the lover that Koi had mentioned had left him when she found out that our family had been freed, but not restored to their title.

"That hurt," he admitted candidly to me. "Can't blame her for wanting to marry a prince. I'd thought she wanted me instead of a title. I'm not the first to get my toes trimmed." He glanced ruefully down to his handsome court shoes with the turned-up toes, embroidered with lotus leaves in the *walks on lotus* mode. "Haven't been with anyone twice since Song left me."

It was interesting to see him striving to accommodate himself to Koi's not being his servant. It helped a great deal, I noticed, after Koi consented to practice martial arts with Banti, Yiuti, and the ministers' boys.

As expected, after being shut up together for so long, they played as hard as they drank, shot, and probably rode, during the seasons of good weather. Martial arts was the favorite activity they sought together, but there was a difference between wealthy nobles' sons competing against each other and the training that Koi and the Falcons got, which recognized that there were dangers in the world. Koi so easily beat them all — including Yiuti — that he didn't have to say a word. Their respect for him shot from nothing to very high regard.

There it was again, that awareness of how men gauge other

men by their capability to destroy one another.

I agreed to practice with them, though I knew I would be avidly and disparagingly watched, especially at first. But I also knew that they would gauge me as a man since I was insisting on a man's place in the world—that is, some were, consciously or unconsciously, seeking proof that I could not meet a "man's" standard.

I needed to beat a few of them and I did, using my knowledge of acupoints. Both sword—as an excuse to keep Sagacious Blade with me—and fighting fans. Surprise and strike, two moves or three. At that, they deferred, many with thoughtful airs, and more than one, alas, demonstrated a tendency to offer to marry me when the wine fumes were thick in the air. That's usually when I retired.

On handled them in his typical manner, fast and potentially lethal, keeping up a running commentary interspersed with quotations, as often as not crude enough to cause would-be opponents to erupt into laughter. His being a prince of an even higher rank than Yiuti, the only descendant of a former dynasty, probably ensured that.

And so a few days passed very slowly, as the grand prince continued to try to convince me to favor his grandson. At least the Sign from Heaven, as they had begun to refer to it, kept him somewhat more reticent about it than I suspect he was used to being.

The most common topic among the boys when the grand prince was not with us was cursing Xianti. They'd bring up every brutish incident they remembered from their boyhoods, rehashing them over and over again. I admit that at first, my angry heart relished these stories, but they palled by the second repetition. By the third reiteration (usually over the third jug of wine), I only heard *quack quack quack*—except for the very rare incidents in which Xianti did act like a human being. These became the more interesting as I wondered at his motives. I don't mean his courtship of Princess Vaha from the East, which might be mere lust both for what he couldn't have and for her elusive power.

It was his kindness for his twin that interested me most. Kianti, I remembered well, had been sickly and clumsy and forever in the way, but unswerving in his admiration for his twin brother. Xianti could so easily have kicked Kianti around. Who would have interfered when the boys were alone? They mentioned that Xianti had slapped Kianti once or twice, but never hard. And if anyone else touched Kianti, Xianti would turn on them like a tiger.

I knew that it was inevitable I would have to face Xianti. How to find leverage to convince him, without bloodshed? I had been afraid of him as a child. He wanted to kill me. How to comprehend his mind? Could he be convinced to become a human instead of a monster?

I did not see nearly enough of Banti, but he readily — enthusiastically — agreed to sail with *Pangolin* when we left, so I contented myself with those few visits, mostly in company with the others.

Right before we departed I inadvertently discovered who the spy was. If he could even be called that. We'd mentally ruled out all the boys, whose fathers were all friends of the grand prince's. They got along well, and had for all this time. All of us had been sure that Xianti, or one of his followers, had somehow insinuated some low-ranking individual among the warriors or servants, one who either had their own birds, or could get access to the grand prince's.

But the night before we were to leave, on our way out of the practice hall to get ready for the farewell banquet, the grand prince — who had come to watch the sparring — rubbed his hands and declared, "Ay I can hardly wait to see Koza's surprise when he hears about the phoenix."

All the boys sycophantically offered agreement. He liked enthusiastic agreement to his declarations, and they had been trained to offer it. But this time, as I listened with part of my attention in that other realm, I caught a flash of resignation and regret underscored by alarm.

"The young one," Granny Zim said.

Yes. It was Norek Bin, the son of the Director of Pasturage, under the Minister of War. I looked over at Bin, who stared down at his feet. He was one of the smallest of the boys, definitely the youngest, soft-spoken and friendly. His friendliness had been genuine.

Was he really the spy? Or rather, had he been, before my message to Koi arrived, delivered by the Hats? Bin could not possibly have got a bird past the present communication arrangement, not as it was demonstrated to me so proudly by the grand prince. I considered what to say, hesitated through dinner, hesitated afterward, and the next day we were to leave, so I thought it more merciful not to speak at all.

Spirits rose high when we left Whale Haven, though I noted

that On, Cray, and Koi made a decent effort to hide it. On had been strongly invited to join the flagship guests with the other boys, but he insisted on staying with us. The grand prince had to accept that, but he insisted with jovial firmness that we sail in consort with his fleet to enjoy its protection—and we knew that he would be insisting that we row over for banquets and entertainment, not only in order to continue to push Yiuti and I together, but to draw On in as a follower in case it was On I would choose to marry.

I had used those few days to make fire talismans for all the ships, layered with enough Essence to burn through ice until we reached the open sea. It was very slow going at first, but the ice cracked, snapped, threw out a thousand lines, then diffused and crumbled. I could feel the wondering stares sent our way, and was glad to be aboard the *Pangolin* again.

"If we succeed, Essence studies are going to be on the rise again," On remarked to me as he perched in a window, apparently impervious to the cold. "War-related first, I fear."

"I know. If I survive, I will consult the wise ones for ways to counter that."

The ships reached open water, and set sail. Banti shivered at the bow, grinning into the wind. He had uttered no complaint about his years sequestered with the grand prince's branch of our family, but I could see in every line of his uplifted face that now he felt set free. It was also clear that he loved sailing as much as he had hoped he would when we were small.

On came to me to request Sagacious Blade. I turned it over to him, and he soared up into the sky, startling Banti, who fell against the rail, laughing. I believe if his inclinations had been toward his fellow man, he would have fallen in love right then, but it was surely the next thing. He watched in delight and admiration and yearning as On spiraled up into the sky, and I wondered how much they could see from the flagship. Probably not much, as On's coat was a silvery gray, and he was soon surrounded by circling birds.

He came down a short time later with a gray and white crane whose Essence demeanor was familiar. Her shape blurred, and Sun stood naked on the deck, her long dark hair blowing about her clay-brown, fast-puckering skin. Banti stared, mouth open—and there was the ardent gaze!

Cray appeared from her cabin. She crossed the deck in three strides and threw a robe around Sun, who, utterly unbothered by her nakedness, was more intent on working her lips. My awareness widened to the captivated gazes of the Hat and Ayep boys—and Fan, until Dinek reached up, placing a hand over Fan's eyes, calling, "Crew! On station!"

Those on watch startled, then scurried off, with some backward glances. Fan chuckled and ran off to the helm to reinforce it, as the waves were rolling significantly higher.

Sun's slim form was now robed, only her face, hands, and feet bare as she said, "It's odd to have a tongue that moves sideways. And teeth. Myam, myam, mum mum mum!"

"Would you like to eat something?" On asked.

"Oh, yes! When I'm a human, all my love for human food rushes back."

"Let's get you fed," Cray said, and we entered the dining area, warm with the steam from the hot water stand, and smelling of baking pancakes with plenty of onion.

Banti followed, that open, wide-eyed expression of wonder still on his face. I had to laugh: he might not have fallen for On, but he certainly had for Sun. Who was in many ways so like On, when she was human.

"Did you bring that phoenix?" Cray asked.

"I wouldn't dare," Sun said, cradling her tea between her palms as she sent a long, appreciative sideways glance at Banti. "Grandmother goes where she wills."

"Your actual grandmother?" I asked.

Sun flashed a smile my way. "My grandmother, Father's mother, is a crane. Mother's side are all humans. She promised Father I would come to the cranes once I reached adulthood. I didn't want to leave *Pangolin*, but now I'm glad I did. Being a crane is so ... so different. So wonderful! I'm still learning how to understand and to be understood by those with ... ayah, there are no words. I guess you could say demon blood."

"Do you know why Grandmother Phoenix came?" I asked.

Sun shook back her hair, drank tea, frowned, then said, "I don't have the words—or the understanding. But there are so many birds, and animals, who have lost their homes to the fires Xianti set and let burn, especially during the dry times. You are the human who listens to the powerless, that much I could share. My being a human meant something, I discovered. I could in some wise explain the senselessness of human actions." She lifted her shoulders. "Think of me as a child of four or five, trying to comprehend what adults are saying."

I brought up a hand. "It's enough. Thank you, Sun. What they want is no more than what I want."

Hat Tu appeared at the door. "I see flags going up at the flagship."

"Probably a summons," Hat Dove said to On and me, with a slight nod to Banti.

Sun went off to chat with Cray as the rest of us got the rowboat let down. Banti helped. He was eager to help, and to learn all the workings of the ship.

We rowed to dine with the grand prince, who promised that we should soon have the latest news from the imperial island, which he would share with us first.

This began the pattern for the next few days. Sun stayed often with us, her attention mostly divided between On and Banti. The older of the boys in the crew sighed over this, but they'd had complete liberty during our stay in Whale Haven, which meant access to all the entertainments arranged when a lot of men are cooped up in one place. The younger boys still had a tendency to snicker when Sun transformed, walking about blithely with only her loose hair as covering.

We'd sailed in reasonably high spirits, glad to be on our own ship, when—as is inevitable—everything abruptly changed.

THIRTY-SEVEN

Watch the cranes drifting high among colored clouds
Toward Heaven's Jade City,
With hibiscus in their beaks. They only desire peace.
Can humans do less? the Phoenix Empress asked.

THE GREAT MIGRATION OF birds had dispersed, but a few cranes remained, circling high above us. I noticed the grand prince looking upward from time to time, when Banti, On, and I rowed over.

We'd sailed through two snow storms when at the first pigeon from the imperial island reached the flagship. One of Cray's birds fluttered down to *Pangolin* a short time later, landing on Cray's arm. She took the bird off at once to get rewarded and warmed up, then called to me, "I think you'd better come."

Her face was stony as she handed me a thin strip of rice paper:

Cray: Pangolin Ren is truly Lan Renti? News all over imperial palace – phoenix – Sign from Heaven – Cedar insiders report sounds of arguing within imperial palace: emperor grounded Xianti.

Cedar, I remembered, was the graywing that Xianti had burned badly when we were all young. Koi had told me that Cedar was one of the leaders of a covert group among the servants. They saved as many as possible from the whims and cruelties of the imperial family.

"The emperor—and Xianti—knows about the Phoenix already," Cray said.

"Yes. It seems that Bin somehow got a message through." I stated the obvious because now we had to consider the consequences, beginning with how the grand prince would react.

Banti pelted up, breathing hard. "Bin? Did I hear you mention Bin? What about him?"

"He's the spy. I found out the day we sailed. The grand prince will probably be incensed."

"Incensed? The grand prince will kill him," Banti whispered, eyes horrified. "You've only seen him at his best. He has a very hot temper."

The grand prince was already as volatile as fire! "Let's bring Bin over here. Find out what he's said. What he knows. Then decide what to do."

Banti shook his head. "It's already too late, if you're trying to stop Grand-Uncle Yiulo from executions. If he got a message back that they know about the Sign from Heaven in the imperial city? He'll kill *all* the bird people. In fact, he must be in a rage right now—"

"Let's go over before they invite us for..." I began. I'd stupidly been relying on the grand prince's promise to share news as it arrived. "I think it might be time for me to remind him."

Banti and Koi ran to let down the boat, Banti having refused to fly after On tried to teach him—not only had vertigo seized him, he'd been convinced that he would drop dizzily into the icy water and drown.

I left them to it. I was better off facing the grand prince on my own.

I changed to my second 'boy' robe, brought out the sword, and flew. This time I made sure the lookouts on the flagship all saw me as I sailed slowly overhead, and then brought myself down to the deck. It would not do to stumble, though the ships were rocking on the choppy waves.

Yells cracked in the air, and many ran out to see me just as I landed. I sheathed Sagacious Blade with a fast stroke, and walked into the command room.

Sickened, I saw I was just in time—or barely.

Three men knelt before the enraged imperial prince, their

backs bloody. A burly warrior stood over them, stick in hand. I recognized all from the communications roost at Whale-Haven.

I bowed to my grand-uncle. "This bereaved grand-niece entreats her elder to forgive her for a reminder that he promised to share all news as soon as it arrived."

"I would spare you the sight of these traitors," Grand-Uncle Yiulo began in a voice thin with anger. But beneath he was still uncertain, which frustration only made him angrier.

"These are not traitors," I stated. "I know who sent the messages. The sender is not among your servants. I entreat you to let these innocents free. And send a physician to them," I added.

He stared at me. "Is there someone you planted among —"

"Impossible, your imperial highness," I interrupted. "You must know it is impossible. I know when people lie, or are hiding something. I found out the day we left Whale Haven. I will tell you why I did not speak, but not until these get their wounds addressed."

The grand prince stared at me, his breathing audible. I did not need Granny Zim to warn me that Grand Prince Yiulo balanced poised on the knife edge between anger and desperation. But I waited, hands together in the clasp of a bow, and he jerked a hand toward the waiting guards, who took the stumbling men away. Two servants scurried forward to wipe up the blood, and the grand prince sat down heavily. "I don't understand," he admitted, as we were pretty much alone, except for the silent servants, and Yiuti over in the corner, his eyes like darting fireflies between us all.

"I did not speak because I wanted to prevent what just happened. We can question the correct person together," I offered. "Not interrogate. I don't think it's a situation where it is easy to say that this is an enemy, bent on our destruction."

"Very well, very well," the grand prince said, bowing. But I saw his gnarled fingers tremble. "Do what you want. You are going to do that anyway, are you not?"

"I will do what I deem right, but always under advisement," I said, with a deferential bow, for it was important to save his face before his command if I wanted to keep his cooperation, which was indifferently willing. I was already robbing his cherished grandson of the throne the grand prince believed Yiuti deserved. "Including from my elders. It so happens that in my Essence training, the ability to detect lies became one of my skills."

I went out. By then Koi and Banti had reached the flagship, and had just climbed aboard, wind-tousled, their cheeks reddened.

"Banti," I said, "go and get him."

Banti did. When he and Bin reached the grand prince's command cabin, Grand-Uncle Yiulo roared, *"Norek Bin is the traitor?"*

Bin had looked concerned, but on the word 'traitor' terror slackened his jaw, and he gazed from one of us to the other, his knees giving way. Thump! He knelt on the still-damp deck, his head bowed.

"Just tell us the truth," I said.

"I don't know what you're talking about," Bin replied, his voice high.

"Yes, you do. You regret sending the message, but send it you did. Did you not? We need to know how you sent it, and why. Also, what it said."

Twice more he tried to lie, but each time I called him on it, which seemed to frighten him even more than the prospect of retribution from my grand uncle, for he was by then speaking solely to me.

It was dispiritingly predictable. Coming from a ministerial family losing its once-prominent place in court, Bin had admired Xianti for his strength and his leadership among the imperial princes and the nobles of court. To him, Xianti appeared to be the perfect candidate for crown prince. His attitude that if anyone was not following him was necessarily an enemy made sense to fourteen-year-old Bin, and he was proud of being considered part of Xianti's elite circle. That was what Xianti called it, an "elite circle."

When Xianti asked Bin to spy on Yiuti, Xianti's main rival second only to the Perfect Guiza, Bin was delighted to be trusted. He began following Yiuti to report what he said and did, and after Bin brought gossip that Yiuti thought secret from the world, Xianti rewarded him with gold—knowing that the Narek family was in desperate straits.

When the grand prince left that spring after Koza seized the throne, and the boys were sent to safety with the grand prince by their frightened fathers, Bin was also sent by his own father— after strict instructions in how to write in juice, which would be invisible, on an otherwise unexceptional note to his family. It's an obvious code, he was cautioned. His behavior must never give anyone cause to hold his letters over a candle.

Bin soon began to want out. He said so by code, to receive instructions that if he did not cooperate, the Narek family would follow the fates of other traitors. Everyone in the family. Including Bin's mother, who knew nothing of what was going on. His little brother of three. His nanny. The grand prince let the boys write home from time to time via pigeon; the steward read their notes, but never suspected a code.

Bin had no choice but to comply, he admitted as he knelt before us, tears freezing on his face. "The last note I sent was the other night, before the order came that we ought not to write anymore because we were going to surprise the imperial capital with our appearance. And our news of the Sign from Heaven. I tried to stop my note. But it had gone out along with the military report. I hoped that it wouldn't reach Father."

But it obviously had. The hard silence after he finished implied that much, and poor Bin broke down then, as the grand prince began to rave. He wanted Bin tossed overboard—into the brig—flogged to death right there on the deck before all.

I said as soon as he paused to draw breath, "We will take him."

Banti and On hustled Bin to the side, and they rowed him back to the *Pangolin*, where he was sick over and over again until Dinek dosed him with ginger brewed in tea, with a tincture of poppy in it. That put him to sleep at last, leaving us to try to figure out what to do with him.

When they all turned to me, I said, "Let's leave him at my Grandfather Gu's until peace is resolved. Then the matter will take care of itself."

We agreed. When he woke, we told him what would happen. He ate a little, but remorse and guilt were I think far worse lashes to his spirit than an actual flogging might have been to his back.

Sun returned that night, concerned. From her appearance I guessed that her particular flock of cranes was staying with us for their own purposes. She and On went up to On's aerie, leaving Banti sitting ruefully with the rest of us in the galley.

"Cheer up," I said to him. "You'll still get your turn. Sun likes variety as much as you do."

"Variety," Banti repeated, his eyes full of humor as well as wonder. "I want to *marry* her."

Cray scowled. "Ay, mighty Prince Lan Banti, crying rain at the first breath of wind. You assume to ask is to have?"

"*And* you're betrothed," I reminded him.

Banti tipped his head. "If both the Mu and the Diseg families didn't send letters cancelling the betrothals within a week of Father's arrest, I'll be a donkey for the next ten lifetimes. I'll wager those would be the only letters Father ever received in that prison." He glanced out the window, then upward, and murmured, "Supposing she'll have me. If we have children, will they be cranes?"

"Don't be silly. Women don't lay eggs." Cray glared at him. "When she's with us she's human. When she's in crane form, she's a crane. She told me once that if she mates with a crane, her children will be cranes. And they probably won't be able to become human. Likewise, if she mates with a human, her children will be human, but might not be able to be cranes. No one knows how demon blood works."

"Demon," Banti repeated, then shook his head. "Everything has become so strange."

"These things have always been there," I said. "We just don't see them. As for 'demon,' I'm discovering that it's about as vague a term as water, which can stand for the Great Sea, or a river, or the drip from an icicle, or a pond full of floating lotus," I said.

"And tea," Banti replied. "And wine—" Here, raising his cup of hot rice wine, brought over from the flagship. "Speaking of wine. I think I need a jug. Poor Bin!"

Poor Bin indeed. He dared not step on deck. He was afraid that the grand prince had issued orders for him to be shot on sight if he did. There were certainly crossbow-carrying sentries on duty on the flagship, though we were in the middle of the sea, the current carrying us strongly west as we fought for southing.

The northwest wind finally came, bringing with it a howling storm.

The storm could not have been more vigorous than the emotions dancing wildly through the ship like kites on strings. Sun laughed at Banti's adamant proposal, saying, "Even if you'll feel the same in a month, a year, I will *not* be stuck in a box!" And On leaned down long enough to hoot at Banti, who hooted back, and challenged him to a duel. Any weapon.

I have to admit that I was bewildered and anxious, so quick and so intense were these emotional changes, until I was able at last to catch the undercurrents of laughter, and of not-quite-resolved attraction between Banti and On. That is, On knew exactly what it was. Banti was the leaf in the breeze.

"Any weapon?" On shouted against the wind-flung snow.

"Any!"

"Poems!"

"Snake!"

"Boar!"

Cray stuck her head out of her cabin window, glowered at Banti, and muttered about playing flute to a pig.

The storm blew out in three days, and to our dismay, we discovered that we had been blown in sight of Benevolent Winds. Dinek put us all to work hauling sails over, and we turned east again.

Against a white sky late that day a bird appeared, drifted down—and everything changed again.

Here is the report from Bao, every stroke in his characters resonant with horror:

> *Xianti killed the emperor. The city is under military law. He loosed Tiger Li to hunt down Censor Lan and family.*

Banti was with me when Cray read that out loud, her voice breaking. "What can we do?" Banti asked, his gaze wild as he peered up at a sky streaked with iron-gray cloud. So cold, so bleak. A few flakes of snow drifted down. "I'd better go over to the flagship. Beg on my knees that we sail as fast as we can to the imperial island—"

"And then what?" I asked.

Banti flushed. "And take the war to Xianti before he burns down the entire empire. Renti, it's all very well to say you will not fight, that you want to negotiate for peace, but are you going to let our parents and First Brother be the first sacrifices to your determination not to shed a drop of blood? You *know* they will be. Xianti will hang their mangled bodies over the wall for all to see!"

My heart thundered as my mind raced and raced. Time. Distance. Place. Influence. The right lever, and you can move the world...

"No," I said, and ran in search of Dinek.

She blanched when she heard the news. "You have that fierce eagle look in your face. That means you've a plan. Yes?"

"Yes. Can you take me west to Benevolent Winds? I will construct talismans to hide the ship, though now there is the risk that the imperials will be on the watch for the blur of the obscuring spell. But that is no reason to make it easy for them to spot us."

"It's still very hard to see the blur," she said. "Especially in conditions of rain and wind and snow."

"Good," I said. "Here's my idea. If Xianti's first order is to hunt down my family, I believe his second order is to protect his brother. He'll be expecting a retaliation of the sort that he would instigate: an attack on Kianti."

"But we would never … would we?" Dinek asked in a weak voice.

"Ay!" I said, and laughed. "I am going to take Kianti right from under Xianti's nose. Let *him* get a dose of the agony he causes in everyone who has beloved family members as hostages."

"You're not going to kill Kianti?" Banti asked, staring at me in doubt.

"Of course not. We'll just take him. And sail for home, and once we get there, let him go. I'm hoping it will halt Xianti long enough for us to reach the imperial island." My stomach boiled. "It's time to face him."

Dinek said, "Do we signal the flagship?"

"No, sail for Benevolent Winds *now*."

Koi gave a short nod of agreement. "Xianti's order to establish a protective ring around the bay where Kianti lives has probably already gone out. Xianti's birds will be arriving any time. If they aren't already there. Cray, what can we expect for time measure between dispatching and receiving messages?"

"A matter of a few days. Each day we sail, subtract two days of flight by pigeon."

"Then I'm going ahead on Sagacious Blade," I said. "They will be preparing for assassins and the like. They won't be prepared for me. But I'll need backup…"

"Ayoh! Let me, let me!" The cry came from above, at the third floor rail, as On and Sun peered over, very much tousled.

"Sun, if you could be our communication, this might even work," I cried.

She clapped her hands.

On called, "Shi Gan needs some more adventure experience…"

"Shi Gan?" Banti repeated. "Who's he?"

Koi was already putting weapons into the longboat.

"On is a man of many faces," I said to my brother.

"*He's* a bird, too?" And at the sight of everyone running

around, he said plaintively, "Did anyone ever tell you people you're all mad?"

Hat Dove, usually quiet and mild, gave him a stare like a poke from a dagger, and uttered a very old country comment about the long-tailed squeaker who complains of rats, as old Ayep chuckled in the background, muttering that it was better than a play, better than a play.

I was already rising on Sagacious Blade. I let the wind carry me to the flagship, where I landed running, and sheathed my sword as the grand prince himself banged out the door of his command center.

"Just let me see that boy and I'll throttle him myself," he snarled.

I bowed, and, as if he hadn't spoken, "This grand-niece is here, as promised, to explain a new plan." I sketched it out fast, watching the twitches of brow, eye, and lips as a parade of reactions changed his face.

At the end, he grinned, looking very much like Yiuti as he said, "And you will hold Kianti until we reach the capital, eh?"

"That's my plan. But if I'm to get him safely off the island, I must leave now."

"Can I come? I want to come," Yiuti said. "If we're going to torture Kianti right in front of that white-eyed wolf Xianti, I want to..."

His voice vanished in the wind behind me.

THIRTY-EIGHT

YOU HAVE NO DOUBT observed how *large* Benevolent Winds Island is. I was astonished to discover that the west-most reaches are not far (on the map) from the east-most peninsula of Ran, lying south of it. Thus, because of winds and currents, Benevolent Winds is often said by sailors to be "above" Ran. These two enormous islands form the bulwarks of the west end of the empire, the western trade route running between. The storm had deposited us at the edge of the eastern trade route.

Flame-In-Ice, the capital, is like most imperial harbor-capitals, at the southeast. More east than south.

Jai captained the longboat carrying Koi, Cray, Fan, and a few of the others from the *Pangolin*. They slipped past the forming perimeter of warships in the middle of the night, and sailed quietly into harbor, looking like one of a hundred fishing boats.

I flew in on Sagacious Blade, having to use a fierce amount of Essence to keep myself in the air, and from freezing. It did not help that the air, even in winter, reeked the farther north one went in the city, as the mountain blocked the cleansing west winds from reaching that end of the bay. Nevertheless I took the time to inspect that northern part from the air, for I wanted to see what kind of governer Kianti was. I believed that going where the poorest lived was the surest beginning of evaluation.

Cousin Oraiti had told me when I questioned him one night during a rainstorm that there was nothing to be done about the reeking wind, but his father had only the year before made him liaison to the temples for street maintenance.

"The streets?" I'd asked. "It's not a matter under the governor?"

"My father says that the archive is full of secretaries caught embezzling, generation after generation. It's so large a charge. The temples do a better job as they aren't permitted to own anything," he'd explained. "The monks and nuns do their good deeds, for they don't seem to mind that the grit carried on the wind is always there. The constant sweeping is part of their ritual. That brimstone dust grinds down everything. Especially on the north side, which is where the hard labor comes from. Boat loaders and builders, miners and servants who eventually go up on the hill. They stay northside because rent is a few tinnies, so they can spend their earnings gambling, or however they want. It's also full of drifters and the like. It's been that way for ages. Mother says it ought not to have been built up at all. Father said, kings must have gunpowder."

From the sight of the brimstone eddying along the streets, sweeping and repairing was no longer a priority. It was a grim place, even in the moonslight. Dilapidations evident not just in the streets. Was all the labor swept off to the mines?

Of course it was. Xianti would want ever more gunpowder.

The southern end was where the fine palaces lay. At the highest point the three-tiered roofs marked the governor's palace. I circled around that, marking guard patterns, before I descended to the ruler's wing. Flaws in the wind brought the odor of brimstone occasionally, making me wonder how Kianti, who (the boys had attested) had suffered from one cold after another all his life, endured it. "Maybe he can't smell it," Banti had said.

How to get him out?

A rustle and the soft thump of bird feet beside me announced Sun's arrival. I knew she could understand me, and if I concentrated in the Essence realm, I could even hear her.

"I'm afraid it's going to have to be a fire," I said. "Xianti will have the entire garrison executed unless there's overwhelming reason for Kianti to vanish. A fire is sufficiently overwhelming."

She shifted from foot to foot, ruffling her wings, then dipped her beak.

"I'll start fires at the top and to either side of Kianti, to drive them all safely down. But I'll need a route to get him away from the bucket brigade as well as sentries."

We surveyed the complication of rooftops and balconies and stairs, then she lifted her wings, flew off, and drifted along these, showing me a route down, between sentry lines-of-sight.

I waved in acknowledgment. She flew off to apprise Koi and Fan, busy dodging those sentries, as Jai remained behind to defend the boat. I renewed the obscuring spell over me, and flew up to find a window I could pry open.

It was all soon done. The wind brought flurries of snow. Scented candles glowed everywhere, not just to beat back the darkness but also to cover the occasional whiff of brimstone.

A window whose oiled paper was torn by a branch borne on the wind—a curtain that caught a candle—the candle branch knocked over so that fire spread to carpet, table, screen—I constructed the scene so that no one but the wind could be blamed. I spread this fire with care, and the royal wing of the palace was soon in an absolute panic.

Kianti was easy to pick out. Thin as bamboo shoots in his night clothes, half-bent and coughing hoarsely, he stumbled along between a couple of graywings and two guards. I whipped up a shower of sparks to scatter over them—brought up smoke to blind them—and while the graywings and the guards batted desperately at the sparks in cloaks and hats, I dropped down, jabbed Kianti's acupoints to freeze him, caught him round his thin waist, pulled him onto the sword, and burning a furious effort, launched us into the air as I obscured us both. Ayoh! Kianti stank of sour sweat, even in that cold air.

I flew as far as I could sustain the Essence, and caught up with Koi and Fan, who took Kianti's inert form as his eyes gazed startled and fearful into the sky. Sun and I both flew ahead, marking the way between the sentries rushing with clattering buckets upward toward the fire. Koi and Fan lumbered with their burden down, down, down to the boat along the river's wharf.

I flew back to give the sentries some more fire to fight, enough so that there would be plenty of excuse for missing the imperial prince, hopefully until morning, and we set sail in the longboat, out of the bay. All before the sun came up.

After a bitterly cold trip over choppy water, Sun swooped

down and around us, leading the way to the *Pangolin*, which was very hard to make out beyond the snow flurries. The boys muscled Kianti aboard, where he collapsed, wheezing and coughing thickly. "Did he choke on smoke?" I asked. "I thought I got him out before the smoke thickened."

Fan and Koi turned to one another—neither of them choking, or even smelling of smoke.

"He sounds a lot worse than he did seven years ago," Koi said slowly.

"Let's put him in the cabin next to the galley, and open the window so he gets pure air," Dinek suggested.

In the light of a lamp, Kianti looked even worse. The hollows in his cheeks, the marks under his sunken eyes, could be partly attributed to the bone structure peculiar to that branch of the Lans. It was like someone had sculpted their bones to exaggerate those features. Xianti had managed to carry it off, with his head flung back to make most of that dramatic jawline and those jutting cheekbones and that hawk's beak of a nose. I remembered that as a child I'd thought Xianti ugly, though in certain poses, he could be quite striking. But that bony head on a skinny neck, and Kianti's grayish complexion, made him look decades older than he really was.

Koi and Fan hefted him once again and laid him on the bed. His short-sighted eyes strained toward us in impotent fury, but as yet he couldn't move. We made him as comfortable as possible, piled blankets on, and before we left, I said to his stark, staring eyes, "You are on a ship. We are far out to sea. No one will harm you. When it's safe for you to swallow, as I froze your acupoints, I'll be back with tea and food."

We retreated to the galley, where I sustained a variety of dubious looks. "It's the only way to keep Xianti from launching war right now," I said. "We already know he uses family members of those he deems enemies as hostages. Let him think I'm doing the same. I predict he'll now order all loose fleets to Benevolent Winds to surround the island and chase a phantom, while we sail straight for the imperial island."

Kianti staggered out sooner than I'd expected, while we were all in the middle of a breakfast preparatory to getting some sleep. He leaned in the doorway. "*There* you are," he wheezed, glaring at me through bloodshot eyes. "My brother … will kill you … when he catches …"

"He's been trying to kill me anyway," I said. "Though I've done nothing to him. Nothing will happen to you, either. Want some tea?"

He spat on the deck, whispered vituperations, and pushed away from the doorway, swaying before he fell against the wall.

Koi dropped his eating sticks and sprang to catch him before he could collapse to the deck. He was so feeble I was afraid he'd shatter his bones just falling.

"I know you," he gasped, squinting at Koi. "Servant..."

"You remember me, I hope," Banti said, appearing at Koi's shoulder. "Koi is no longer a servant. You ought to be used to that," he added cheerfully. "Your brother has been promoting all his servants into village-killing captains right and left, ay?"

Kianti cursed him hoarsely, gasping for breath between words. *Traitor ... rebel ... treachery ... death by a thousand cuts ...* He spewed it all out, though the effort nearly bent him double. Koi walked him back to the cabin, where Kianti dropped onto the bed, his forehead dotted with sweat in spite of the icy wind.

There we left him. He eventually burrowed under the blankets and composed himself, breathing in short, snorting gasps. After peeking in at him as he stared up at the ceiling, I went to Koi and Banti, who had the Circle board between them. "He's still gasping. It's like he can't get a breath."

Both shook their heads. "I remember he always had colds," Banti said. "Xianti used to yell at him. Slap him. Say he was a coward, and if he just made an effort he'd get stronger. But he stopped doing that a year or so before we ran. Seemed clear that Kianti was never going to get over that cold. Or get some heft to him."

Kianti refused to speak to any of us for two days, his eyes wide with fear when the grand prince's flagship caught up with us. I saw him squinting at the round mouths of the cannon, and at the archers with their crossbows pacing along the rail. But he said nothing as the ships plunged in parallel without coming together. Despite the pure air, he still wheezed in short spurts, and walking apparently took all his strength. But walk he did, skulking from one rail to the other, with anxious profile. Probably in hopes of sighting imperial ships.

I was anxious as well, for each day that passed without a bird was a day in which fresh worries about my family gnawed at me. Banti was more resigned, or else he, too, kept his worries inward. I saw him playing game after game of Circle with Koi or Bin—when he wasn't on deck doing seeds, forms, and sparring, or sitting over rice wine and pressing the Pangolins for more stories about our adventures.

Kianti lurked about, listening, too. When he finally spoke that third day, it was to Banti first. It was a clear morning, after the usual exercise on deck, under Fan's direction. After seeds and forms I ran to get tea, but when I came out, I saw Kianti go up to Banti. His jaw moved. His thin hands gesticulated. Over the sound of the waves slapping the hull and clattering battens his voice could just be made out, a raggedly angry whine that was difficult to listen to. It reminded me of the sound of an angry baby wailing—a sound that as sound goes is not loud, but it claws at the nerves in a way that other sounds of the same intensity don't. The urge to fix it is so visceral.

Then he holed up again, cursing Hat Dove when she offered to fetch him a meal.

Banti joined me when sparring began, saying, "In between all the curses and threats, he wants to know if it's true you kill with Essence skills?"

"*Kill?*"

"That's what he said, and, how did you get so powerful."

"And you said…"

"To speak to you!" Banti pushed the matter away with his hands. "I'm not dealing with him."

The following morning, as snow scudded across the deck, Kianti truculently demanded as I brought his breakfast, "When is the execution? Or are you going to do it with your demon charms? You want my brother to see me die, is that your plan?"

He stared down at the food. Since the beginning, he had eaten furtively. Sun, peering through the window as a crane, said she saw him take the tiniest bite, then sit, arms pressed across his stomach as if waiting for the effects of poison, before he'd venture to eat more. Every. Single. Meal. As if he fully expected us to be toying with him before we struck. It was not difficult for any of us to see in these behaviors shadows of actions he was used to seeing, if he had not ordered any himself.

I looked into his haggard, furtively darting eyes, and wondered if it wasn't just the shape of his wary gaze but his entire countenance that had been molded by fear for an entire lifetime. That grating whine in his voice clawed at my nerves. "First, I don't kill with my Essence skills. I know a little about healing. And I can obscure things." Instinctively I avoided mentioning fire. It seemed a dangerous subject for so angry a person. He did not need to know.

"Healer," he repeated.

"A little."

"How did you learn to fly a sword?"

"Essence studies."

"It's forbidden. The sword, I mean."

"I know. That's probably the only actual law I have broken. The rest of the accusations against me are lies," I added.

"You nearly got Xianti killed off the Tiger Islands."

"No, that's a lie. I believe I saved his life. But I did it in such a way that he lost face before the locals. I probably should have done it a different way, but I was still so angry about how much he hurt my family."

His squinty gaze shifted between my eyes, then he said, "What did you do?"

Ay! An interrogation was happening after all, only he was the interrogator, not I.

Mentioning no names, I said, "I overheard something that made me believe there was a plot against Xianti and the grand prince's envoy. And I warned your brother."

Kianti seemed to put it together for himself, for he said, almost musing, the whine lessened, "That had to be Huyun Shandek. Xianti believes he was plotting against him. And now Siarti is married to him."

"Oh, the wedding took place?"

Kianti uttered a short, sardonic laugh. "She insisted. Got what she deserved."

"How?"

"He keeps her locked up in a treasure box. All the gold she wants. Food. Music. Books. Clothes. But no court. No court ladies to order around. No entertainment. Mourning. Everything outside her wing in mourning white." Another wheezy, gasping laugh. "After the wedding, he doesn't go near her. No wedding night." He breathed with his mouth open, as if the effort of speech had been akin to climbing to the top of a nine-story pagoda.

Then he began to toy with his fish in black bean sauce, which the cook had said would strengthen so flimsy a frame.

I said, "I could at least prove that I know a little Essence healing. Want me to try?"

He gave me a contemptuous glance. "What could you do … that the physicians can't?"

"I don't know until I try." I got up and went out. At least I'd made the effort, I thought. Though half-hearted. I didn't want to be anywhere near him.

But the subject did not end there. After morning exercises, I went to get more tea, and overheard the last of a conversation between Kianti, who leaned against a wall, and Banti.

"…let her try," Banti was saying.

"She's younger than us!" Kianti retorted.

"Yes, but she healed Guiza. One of your brother's jackals nearly brained him during his attack on Ye, is what Oraiti told me. My sister did something inside his skull. Oraiti was right there as witness."

I turned to leave, sorry I'd ever brought up the subject. I should have let Kianti believe me a liar. What did it matter what he thought? We'd be rid of him as soon as possible.

He seemed ambivalent, until that night. The air was humid with the breaking of winter. Gasping and coughing, he glared at me when I brought him a tray — the others had refused — and said, "Do your worst."

I could have pretended not to know the context, but what would be the use of that?

He went on, taunting, "I don't have long anyway. So if you kill me. What do I lose? Xianti is going to hunt you down…" He lost the rest of his threats in a morass of nasty, gasping coughing.

"What do you mean, you don't have long anyway?"

"Physicians. When I turned fifteen. Said I wouldn't live past thirty. That's five years off. Less."

Chilled, I said in doubt, "All right. Let me try. Do remember I'm a beginner."

"What do I do?" He eyed me apprehensively — he seemed surprised that I'd agreed. And not at all pleased.

"Just eat your meal before it gets cold. I'll be behind you. I have to touch your back."

I did not want to, for he smelled worse than ever, but no one was going to insist he try to bathe on that windy ship. Not with that gasping, terrible cough. The rest of us shivered and gasped enough even with a basin of hot water.

He bent over the meal, and I moved behind him, touching a forefinger to his bony back as I searched within me for Auntie Breeze's views on breathing matters. She'd not been primarily a healer, but she was wide in her knowledge.

Not wide enough. All I got were some differentiations between obstructions of the lungs and various illnesses.

Obstructions of the lungs?

I reached within him via the Essence realm. It took some time to navigate, and what I found shocked me so much I propelled myself out of there. Then closed my eyes and formed mental words: "Granny Zim. Have you ever heard in all your years of someone with big ... bags, almost, in their lungs? I don't think he can breathe past these. They are slimy and ... diseased," I finished inadequately.

She did not answer, which meant this was new to her, too. Not surprising, as she had been a musician, and most of those who bore the blade after she entered it had been martial wanderers, including Auntie Breeze.

I gritted my teeth, and cautiously felt my way in again. There was that huge, vibrating ... *thing*, right at the top of one lung, large enough that air had to squeak past. That was the wheeze. The shininess reminded me of the slime that blocks one's nose during illness. I ignited the tiniest pinpoint of fire, and touched it to the slime. Which promptly dried and shriveled. The vibrating, wobbling bag, probably years old it was so scarred over, also shriveled a little.

Kianti straightened up. "What did you do?"

"Did it hurt?" I asked, concentration broken.

"No..." He sucked in a breath. A slightly deeper breath. Once again, more quickly, I made my way back inside, and again touched a pinpoint of fire to that horrible thing. It shriveled like burned paper, and air *whooshed* by, deep into his lung. That had to be a good thing, yes?

Very well, then. This had to be a right thing. I reached deeper, cleaning out the rest of those bubbles and bags. His breathing eased more with each, until he was drawing in air as if he'd never breathe again. Deep lungfuls. Then he coughed out the residue of that stuff inside him, almost like ash, except white. It looked merely like the vapor we all breathed out, and he didn't notice it settling on the deck as he staggered to the bed and flopped on it, red in the face.

"What did you do... what did you do... I'm so dizzy," he said—unfortunately, the whine in his voice stronger. But his scrawny chest rose and fell with those deep breaths.

I walked out, a little dizzy myself, and went to my room to compose myself. Using Essence that intensely always consumed strength.

Presently Dinek and Cray came into my cabin. "What did you do to him?" Cray asked.

"He said to try to heal him. So I did."

"He's yelling," Dinek said. "Banti says he didn't think Kianti could yell, but there he is, louder than a donkey braying. I think

he surprised himself at how loud he is. He wants to be taken
back to Benevolent Winds."

I said, "It was lucky that my Essence fire was able to do
something. But I need to speak to an Essence healer to find out
if what I did was right, or if those things will grow back and
choke him again."

"His coloring is almost like a human," Cray observed.
"Rather than like a corpse. I didn't think that was even possible
with him."

They walked out, and I made to sit up, and discovered that
I had neglected to take off my harness, when Sagacious Blade
scraped my shoulder. As I unfastened the harness, Granny Zim
remarked, "You must remember that that request was a rice
grain of trust. I think it was a new experience for that lost soul."

Lost soul was one way of describing so unpleasant a person.

When I went to the galley for tea, he was there. He followed
me out. I changed direction to his cabin, for I did not trust him
climbing stairs—and I didn't want that sour sweat smell in my
cabin, though Koi's smell was welcome any time.

"Why did you do that?"

"You asked," I said, leaning against the wall just inside the
door.

"I know nothing. Just so you know that. My brother tells me
nothing."

"Not even news?" I asked.

His lip curled. "I know he'll kill your arrogant, self-
righteous brother Yanti with his own hands once he finds what
hole he crawled into. Wherever it is it's not far enough."

"He still doesn't know my First Brother at all if he thinks he's
arrogant. First Brother is always the first to blame himself when
he makes mistakes. If he thinks he might have caused someone
else to err. The truth is a living thing for him. As Ar Laq says in
the poem about phantom butterflies, my First Brother spends
his days, and his dreams, trying to grasp and hold the butterfly
of truth."

Kianti's eyes shifted when I mentioned 'The Butterfly
Ghosts' and I remembered once seeing him reading. He was by
himself, his head bent over the pages. That had been on the
Journey to the Clouds not long before my family was arrested;
Xianti had not come along that time, which I guess left Kianti to
his own pursuits.

Kianti sneered, "Not arrogant! Everything he said always
began with *You're wrong*, and then he'd blather from the

ancients. As if he was the emperor! Not arrogant…" He went on cursing First Brother, who had dared to speak up to Xianti, and I walked out before he finished.

"It is so very hard not to let his anger infect me," I said to Granny Zim as I went to the rail to let the snow pat against my hot face. It was so wearying to be in his proximity.

"Breathe, my Bu," Granny Zim said. "Breathe. It is difficult to listen to that young one's voice. It's like a guqin made from a five-hundred-year-old parasol tree fitted with broken strings always out of tune. Think how much fear must wrench such gifts into utter futility."

"Gifts?" I thought. I had not even tried to sense for Essence capability. I was used to there being nothing of the sort in my family, and Kianti was so unpleasant to be around.

But the next time I brought him a meal, I made sure I had Sagacious Blade with me as I reached toward him in the Essence realm. At first I found nothing beyond the usual roiling colors, though with far less putrid orange and yellow than when I'd first snatched him.

I would not have reached deeper had not Granny Zim spoken. And when I did, I was appalled, and chilled, to discover that Kianti had the same affinities as his brother. And me. No, there was tremendous potential in him that Xianti did not have. Perhaps fear, and helplessness, and the effort it had taken to draw a full breath while growing far past dwindling strength, had choked that potential off just as thoroughly as his diseased lungs had choked his air to a trickle.

It was almost overwhelming, this discovery, and the awareness of so much potential wasted on a life of fear and futility filled me with sorrow. My eyes actually began to sting, and I had to get away before he saw it, for I could not explain to him now about these talents that had been rendered barren. I sensed that my explanation would worsen things for so angry a person; he would despise pity, and he was angry enough to torch the world. Could Granny Zim even fix him?

I walked out, and Granny Zim said, "He cannot hear me. There is too much shrieking in his mind. His memories are a torment, I found that when you burned the disease from his breathing."

"Could you heal him through the memories, if I were to touch him again while he slept? No, not through memories. Those ought not to be tampered with. Through dreams?" Even as I asked, I knew that that, too, would be a trespass akin to lying. Only worse, because he would have no defense. That kind of healing he must seek himself.

The next day he was exactly the same as ever, and the next, but the following day, when word came that we might come within sight of the imperial island within a few days, and I must keep my promise to make obscuring talismans, Granny Zim said one morning, "His sleep is better."

"Is it from better breathing, or ..."

"I tell you what I sense," Granny Zim said.

She had been a lot more present of late than she had for quite a while, I realized. I'd been used to longer and longer silences, broken by brief comments. Perhaps it was Kianti's demon blood, or the demon in our blood, for didn't Banti have the same blood? And yet Granny Zim seemed largely unaware of him.

The next day, as I began to go up to my cabin to work on making talismans to obscure our ships, Kianti stopped me. "Are we nearing the imperial island?"

"Yes."

"Then what?"

"To the capital."

He turned away.

That night Cray came to me as I was finishing up a talisman. "My bird is back," she whispered. "I just told Banti. Bao says your family, and the staff still alive got over the mountain to Governor Gu."

THIRTY-NINE

This is the road by which I fled.
Who is this now returning?

BANTI AND I STOOD at the bow during a late-winter storm, both watching anxiously as we rode the high waves between the imperial ships on blockade far outside my Grandfather Gu's formidable guardian fleet. I was there with Sagacious Blade to hand in case I was needed for further Essence obscuring, but Dinek had chosen an excellent storm to aid us in passing through the imperial blockade, each of the Firedragon ships equipped with obscuring talismans. I had gone around *Pangolin* myself.

Now we scanned past the sleet for the outline of the mountains above Peaceable Breezes Harbor. I had to ignite Essence within me to keep from shivering violently. I don't know how Banti endured it, but he did, until at last On cried from above, "I see the imperial island!"

Banti's eyes closed briefly, and he huddled into his coat as he retreated to the galley to warm up.

On leaped down to the deck and came to my side, his long hair wind-tousled. "Life," he said with a smile, "can be so very strange."

"You never thought to come to the imperial island?"

"I did, but never as myself. It's On Lu I wanted to be, a great talent renowned in the capital. As does every writer of plays."

"Are you regretting revealing your true name?"

"Not the least," he said. "I'm sure it's merely my excellent imagination, but I feel all my ancestors resting easier now that I've done that." He frowned. "It has to be my imagination. They wouldn't all be waiting in the grave for generations against the chance that... No! They certainly did not expect their progeny to be annihilated. This feeling of mine must be something else entirely. *Do* souls forget? We're told that the king of the underworld sees to that, and yet there are so many who insist they see ghosts... Ay, you don't know any more than I do, even with that talking sword, is that so?"

"Granny Zim isn't dead. Strictly speaking," I said. "Though her body was gone long ago. So no, she can't tell me what exactly lies on the other side of death. If life is not strange because you arrived here and under your true name, then...?"

He lifted a shoulder. "It is so very strange that the first person to read my entire Shi Gan play is Lan Kianti, of all people. Sun has heard bits. Banti, too. And a couple of the Hat boys. But Kianti sat up there all yesterday, with his nose almost scraping the ink as I wrote so small, reading the entire thing. About the only thing weirder would be if Lan Xianti had turned up to say, *Wait, I'll stop the war if you'll just let me read your next play.* O! To be so popular! To be remembered! That's true immortality. But then I'd have to write something serious. Even ... instructional." He affected a shudder.

"You," I said, "are a madman."

"You've only just noticed?" he retorted with that foxy flash of smile. "Shall I fly up and remove the talismans, now that we've safely passed the imperial blockade? Soon we will be on land and I shall have to give it up."

I laughed, handed him Sagacious Blade, and then went to find Cray. Birds had been flying back and forth more frequently, especially once we'd safely passed the imperial blockade.

"No change," she said.

On soon returned, grinning as he always did after a flight, complexion glowing, clothes and hair damp from the spitting sleet, which he ignored. He handed the sword back to me. I put it in the harness, for I'd decided to wear my gallant wanderer clothes, though I was coming back into the realm of imperial manners. But these clothes, and my headband, had been so much a part of who I now was that I had no desire to hide that aspect of my life.

Our fleet approached the Gu fleet, the proud Gu oak banner

flying from their every mast. Cray had told us that the Gu defenders had been told to watch for the pangolin banner as well as the grand prince's firedragon against gold. There was no cannon shot, no warning flag put up. Many sailors lined the rail—and as we passed, bowed three times.

"Who were they bowing to?" I muttered to Dinek.

"Sun," stated one of the Ayep boys.

"It was Sun," agreed Hat Tu.

"It was me," Fan retorted, fist striking her other shoulder. "I'm the tallest and might I say, *most* imposing."

"Koi and Jai are taller," Hat Dove pointed out.

"But those two won't be mistaken for Pangolin Ren," Fan said with a shrug. She grinned at me. "The fame is yours, whoever they bowed to."

"Get used to it," Dinek said earnestly.

Perhaps. But between matters of popularity and protocol lay the glowering threat of Xianti, who now sat upon the dragon throne. No doubt after the most elaborate ritual in the entire Book of Rites. Bao had not been able to report on that, only the very elaborate parade beforehand.

I looked back at the grand prince's flagship, directly behind us. It was a relief to know that we soon would be able to leave him to my grandfather.

There was the bay, visible now. I had to grip myself against rising impatience. For years I had yearned to see my family again, but now that it was about to happen I was filled with trepidation, as I strongly suspected that my very traditional parents would disapprove of Pangolin Ren. And yet it would be false to hide.

Kianti appeared from his cabin. "What now?" he demanded truculently, his fear sharp beneath. "Chains, a wooden yoke about my neck, until I reach the dungeon?"

"No," I said. "Here's a summary of all recent communication. Your brother knows that I have you. Between him, my grandfather and our grand-uncle Prince Miluo—who still commands the Eastern Fleet, as the Prince of Ran controls the west—there appears to be a standoff." *Not quite a truce*, Bao had reported tersely. "As I told you from the beginning, I'm going to the imperial city to talk your brother into a peaceful compromise if I can."

He muttered, "Xianti won't believe a word you say."

"Perhaps. But I am going to try anyway. Right now he is aware that, without attacking anyone, I've brought about a balance of forces. I hope I can negotiate a peace with him."

Kianti looked down, his head wagging slowly. "He'll kill you for forcing his hand."

"He'll kill me for forcing his hand not to kill?" I said. "How can you not see how very wrong that is? Ay, never mind, never mind. As for what is to happen immediately, my Grandfather Gu has arranged a suitable parade welcome for the grand prince and the ministers' sons. Everyone will thus see the alliance's leader."

Kianti shot me a quick, squinty glance. "I thought you were the leader."

"A month ago, it was our uncle Guiza. Doesn't really matter to me who is the face of the alliance. All I desire is no killing. The people like a parade. A parade is reassuring, and inspiring to look at, because when there is a parade, no one is attacking anybody. That ought to distract all eyes from our very quiet entry. Here we are."

The ship came to a stop, rocking against a pier as ropes snaked back and forth, making all fast. A vast crowd pressed front to back all along the entire quay. Gu guards in armor over rich brown kept the multitudes back using only their halberds.

As the crew lowered a ramp to the wharf, Jai and the Hats got our smallest boat over the other side, and Banti, Koi, then Kianti dropped down, with Cray and me going last. A last glimpse of On's rueful face, as he was going to ride behind the grand prince—and keep an eye on him, Yiuti, and the ministers' boys (minus Bin, who was staying with the crew), to be reported later.

A space had been cleared, leading to the road up to the palace. At the edge of the wharf, a steward waited, his "loaf" or steward's hat the first familiar sign of a life I'd thought never to return to.

As the Hats rowed us to the commoners' side of the quay, I looked back. I glimpsed that steward bow in welcome to Grand Prince Yiulo, who glittered in crimson and gold. Caparisoned horses were brought forward, then I lost sight of them as a fisher interposed.

I turned back, impatiently counting every lift of the oars, anxious to see my family. After all these years, the thought of waiting another heartbeat was too exasperating to countenance!

We beached the rowboat, amid a gaggle of children gathering broken shells to be made into soap, fishers and traders and laborers. The crowd was thick here, too, everyone busy. On a rise behind, I saw a village of round tents.

Banti and I searched the faces of the crowd.

"There's An Gui!"

I spotted one of my parents' most trusted servants, save only Father's Fumek, who had lived beside Father since they were boys. Gui lifted his hand to Koi, his austere face easing, and we saw his lips move as he addressed some plainly dressed people with him: *There they are.*

We could hear the brassy sound of the gongs and the screel of the gourd pipes in the distance as we climbed up then stepped into a very plain covered cart. Kianti's gaze darted around wildly, but Jai and Koi were on either side of him—actually for his protection. Nobody thought he'd make it far if he bolted. Not on his own; until so very recently it was all he could do to breathe. He would not know how to survive, especially if anyone recognized those distinctive features.

He appeared to think so, too, for as no black-clad assassins leaped out to slaughter right and left and waft him away, he seemed resigned to whatever was to come next.

We had a quiet ride up the zigzag path to the palace above the garrison, seeing yet more crowds, more jumbles of tents. Refugees, I realized. So very many.

We finally reached the palace's grand entrance, guarded by two great stone qilin. The doors were thrown wide by servants, and I saw movement just inside.

"First!" Banti shouted, his voice cracking.

"Banti?" That was First Brother's voice.

The two of us sprinted past everyone else, deportment utterly forgotten. There they were! As soon as I saw my dear mother's face—so much thinner and more lined than I remembered—the urge to halt, to fold my hands and return to tiny floating steps seized my muscles, and I had to shake off that instinct. But I compromised by advancing with measured step as her gaze searched my face.

I stepped over the threshold and there she was. How had she gotten so *small?* I was half a head taller than she was! I threw my arms around her. She trembled against me, rubbing her hands up and down my back, and whispered, "It is really you, Renti. You are so grown!"

Then she stepped back, composure so habitual, though those lines of sorrow at her eyes and around her mouth would never go away. "Renti..." she began, her brow puckering as she looked at my clothes.

"Daughter?" Father said, one hand on Banti's shoulder, and the other on First Brother's.

First Brother's head turned. He wore a band around his eyes. As tall and gaunt as Father, he groped with his free hand. "Sister Renti?" His head turned from side to side. "Who is that next to you? I can hear his breathing. It sounds almost like … no," he said to himself. "It cannot be."

I took First Brother's hand in mine. His hand was thin, but stronger than I'd expected it to be. "It is Kianti."

"I thought he would be in a prisoner cart." First Brother spoke in the direction of Kianti.

Kianti flushed, and I said, "I think there has been too much of that. Where will it ever end?"

"Only when we are all dead, if Xianti gets his way," my brother answered flatly. "But we will speak more when *he* is not by." And he would say nothing more.

My grandfather, whom I had never met, was still with the grand prince and On. My grandmother, who held tightly to Mother's hand, said, "Come within, come within. From the look of the sky, we're to have more of this wretched icy rain. There is warmth and good things waiting!"

First Brother turned his head. "What about *him?*"

"I promised Lan Kianti my protection," I said firmly, looking from First Brother to Father and Mother to my grandmother. "As Lan Kianti is my responsibility, so ought guarding him fall to my people. Koi here is my honor guard captain. Cray there is my chief of communications, so I entreat you to provide her with a tally so that she can tend to her birds, still aboard the *Pangolin.*"

We were first shown splendid rooms. Grandmother Ou appeared far less nonplussed than the steward at the fact that neither Banti nor I had servants to take charge of our things, but then she came from a long line of traders, half of whom were Falcons.

She patted me on the shoulder, saying, "Just as well, just as well. Your two maids are waiting to see if they are wanted. They can see to that." She nodded at my battered, dusty carryall. Cray looked pleased at the prospect of seeing my childhood maids, Perch and Minnow, again.

We moved on, and I heard Koi in the background taking charge of Kianti by ordering a bath and new clothes.

Grandmother Ou gracefully excused herself as we entered the fine room made over to my parents. Now, for the first time since we traveled on the Journey to the Clouds that fateful spring, we were all together.

Mother and Father exchanged glances—how painfully familiar, those looks. Only no longer inscrutable. Mother seemed bewildered and anxious as she leaned over to take my hand and squeeze it. I sensed a tremble in her fingers as her emotions roiled.

Father said, "I am more happy than I can express that my two youngest are alive, and well. But Second Son, I venture to observe that you neglected to care for your sister."

Banti bowed his head. "The day of my arrest I could think of nothing except escaping the imperials, who were accusing me of Yiuti's crime. I went to Grand-Uncle Yiulo as the only one who could straighten everything out, and who I know the former emperor would not dare to blame, and he took us away, and then would not let me go. I would have tried to escape, but he had communication, and once he told me of your arrest, he promised that he would get first notice of your welfare. He also promised that if I stayed at Yiuti's side, freeing you would be his first order once he established himself as emperor. As I did not know what else to do to free you, I had to stay with him."

Father said, "You were to be the voice of reason for Prince Yiuti?"

"Yes!"

Father bent to cough into a handkerchief. It was a dry, scraping cough that harrowed my nerves.

"Father, this daughter begs forgiveness for interruption, but has a physician seen you?"

"As soon as we arrived," Father said tiredly, then he sat up straight and strengthened his voice. "I am well enough. The Princess Meiti—Princess Namath Vaha—preserved my life through her eastern healer skills, or I would not be alive now. The rest can wait. Daughter, we come to you now. I scarcely know where to begin."

Ever since I first heard that my family lived, I had dreamed of this day, and imagined conversations. And they always began with this question. I had judged myself according to Father's imagined strictures, knowing that one day I must stand before him and Mother and justify myself.

And so it had come time to explain, which I did. Having thought so long of this day, I had arranged what to say countless times, and it came out smoothly, and in the manner we'd been taught: begin at the beginning, with the finding of Sagacious

Blade. Then the chain of choices, consequences, reasons for choices, offer of witness should that be demanded.

Father only asked two questions: the first, to clarify the chain of evidence that led me to believe that Huyun Shandek was plotting to kill the envoys at Tiger Island Bay, and second, exactly what the Prince of Ran and I discussed over the map. Then he fell silent until I reached the present.

At the end, he turned to Mother. "This is the same sword your esteemed mother wished to introduce to the boys?"

Mother bowed her head. "It is. I did not know that Renti had found it—I was striving to get it sent back to Grandmother Ou when she discovered it at the bottom of a trunk full of my childhood things."

Father turned to me. "Is that this sword?" He indicated Sagacious Blade, lying beside my leg as I sat on my cushion.

"It is."

"Let me see it, Daughter."

I drew the sword, whose scales flashed in the candle light as he turned it over in his hands, then he laid it carefully across First Brother's lap, and guided my brother's fingers to the gleaming white stone in the hilt. "First Son Yanti. Do you sense anything?"

My First Brother took his time running his fingers along the hilt, the stone, the blade, then shook his head.

Father said, "Banti, take it."

Banti did, holding it up to admire the blade anew. Of course he was long familiar with it by now, after sailing with us, then trying unsuccessfully to fly on it with On. He handed it back to me. "Not so much as a peep, much less ghost voices, or whatever it is you say you hear, Sister."

Father said to me, "It seems you inherited a talent. And you deserve praise for continuing to seek education. That is exactly what I would expect of my children, boy or girl. If you choose to pursue Essence training in healing, I will support that decision as far as I am able. Which, alas, is not far, these days. But the future is uncertain, as you know."

"Perhaps someday," I said. "Once my true goal is met."

"Your goal being?"

"Peace. Which includes everyone. That means an end to slavery."

Father shook his head slowly. "It is a fine sentiment, but that is what it is. There are ranks for a reason, each with their work to do. If they do well, they are reborn in a better for the next life."

"With respect, this still-learning daughter ventures to suggest that that does not preclude bettering life now," I said.

"And so you intend to thrust yourself into a sphere into which you will only be regarded as an interloper, a figure of derision? Why not seek the respectable calling of healer, as you've been given the talent for it? Do you despise it? Or do you assume that you deserve better things?"

"No," I said, fighting the constraint of tears threatening my throat. "I am proud of the few healings I've done. But that is one person at a time. Though it means everything to that person. It seems I also have a talent for finding that point of balance that avoids violence, and it's that which motivates me now. Again, I am still only a beginner. So much to learn. But it has *worked*."

"Balance. Ay! What is the difference between Kanda's words on the Golden Point of Balance and those of Mana Ta?"

This was interrogation from another direction, but even so, I recognized immediately that this one of the questions from the Imperial Examination that First Brother had studied for so long ago. Father was taking me seriously, at least in this moment.

"Kanda states that the wise ruler seeks to maintain balance and harmony by striving to direct the mind to a state of constant equilibrium. The ruler thus treads, decision by decision, the path of duty, and must never leave it."

"Good … go on."

"Kanda then says, and this I have seen proved from day to day, that the true follower of the path of balance is cautious, gentle, and shows no contempt for one's inferiors, for common men *and women* can carry balance into their practices. The Golden Point of Balance is thus measured by moderation, rectitude, objectivity, sincerity, honesty, and propriety — and its guiding principle is that one should never act in excess."

"And Mana Ta's emendation?"

"That the doctrine of balance has three parts: the Knot, or the rites, traditions, and customs, including divinations, that show the path; the Process, or how men — that is, he wrote men, but —"

Father held up a hand. "You may, for now, say 'human.'"

"Thank you, Father. How humans agree on laws and treaties. And third, the written wisdom that is taught to those expected to govern, or the Word. We can also say Education."

And though none of us had drunk or supped — and Father waved off servants bringing trays and teapots — he proceeded to grill me on the Six Measures and the Three Parts.

To these, I could quote a great many of the supporting passages (or at least summarize, where exact memory faltered) that I'd coached First Brother through over and over. I did quote many, but I found myself offering examples of my decisions over the past year or two as related to these. How they had guided my thinking.

It was very late, and I was heady from hunger and thirst, when at last Father beckoned to the latest steward's attempt to offer refreshments. "I begin to comprehend," he said finally. "My first thought, I must admit, on hearing that this wild Pangolin Ren was none other than my own daughter was to request your grandfather to lock you up until we could restore you to good order."

I could only bow, though by now tears dripped onto my folded hands.

"However. I thought such things were metaphor, but there are enough witnesses of that phoenix marking you, and only you, that it appears Heaven truly has bestirred itself to indicate its choice. First by seeing to it that yon sword reached your hand. You were always an apt student, and there in this sword's memory were the teachers. Seen in this light, this matter of Heaven's choosing becomes a duty."

"We have always taught you children not to shirk duty," Mother said quietly.

Father bowed her way, and said on a sigh, "It is a very strange business, but the world is so chaotic that traditional customs have been overturned. We are all testament to that."

Mother had been pouring out tea for Father, First Brother, Banti, and then herself and me. Father finally turned to First Brother, who had not spoken a word to me, or to anyone else, since I said that Kianti was to stay with me. "Yanti. Have you thoughts after hearing your sister's testimony?"

First Brother took a few moments to drink tea, then said, "I apprehend, Father, that your question is in some measure a criticism aimed at me. And I bow to its rightness, and to your perspicacity in observing that I have been straying off the path in my wanting to see Kianti suffer for his brother's evil decisions, though he never instigated anything on his own. He was always enjoined by his brother in that. I will rectify myself."

"And I shall make time to speak with my young nephew Kianti. Who hitherto I never saw except in the shadow of his brother."

Father then gave me a look more like a weary parent than like the censor presiding over a state interrogation—which is what he had just done—and said, with the rueful mildness that was about as close to humor as he ever came, "I suspect that you would go and do what you considered right in any case, but for what it is worth to you, you have my blessing."

FORTY

"ILL-GOVERNED? YOU TOLD your father that Benevolent Winds was ill-governed by me. Why did you say that, unless to make yourself look like some sort of sage?" Kianti burst out the next day, when I returned from waiting upon my grandmother. He, like the rest of us, was clean, dressed in new robes. "I governed Benevolent Winds well. I listened to every case. I judged it on its merits." The hectoring whine was back in his voice, a defensive shield, I began to see.

"I bow to you in respect for that intention," I said past a crashing headache. In spite of a hot bath and soothing incense, I had not been able to sleep. My mind insisted on reexamining my father's questions and my answers. What I ought to have said.

Before dawn my mother send her maid to see if I had woken, which I took as a call to filial duty. My grandmother presided over a crowded court of refugee noble women, each with anxious questions I could not yet answer, especially the one heard most often: *When can we go home?*

If I am successful, it's always going to be like this, I warned myself. I had seen that as a child, when Father came home from the Censor's Wing of court when most families were preparing to retire, carrying a stack of testaments that must be read and written up before he himself could rest.

I bent my attention to Kianti, who was just as anxious as I was, if for utterly different reasons. I said, "I did not utter those words randomly. I inspected the north side of the city before I came to get you."

"Ayoh! You cannot judge me by *that!* The north side is where the loafers, the gamblers and trouble-makers hide out. One step above beggars, though we had enough of them, too. You can't get rid of them. Like flies."

"The benevolent governor finds ways so they don't have to beg. Or tries to. A good beginning would have been to continue giving that tax on the south side to the temples."

"You know about that?" Kianti shrugged sharply. "I saw Lan Oraiti over on the other ship. Whatever complaint Cousin Oraiti made about me was a lie. Eh, perhaps not a lie, but *they* had it easy during their tenure. His father left a long rant for me, under the seal. There was a long list of things I *ought* to do. I found it when I first entered the governor's palace. *I* was sent to new governorship with an edict to double the brimstone quotas instantly. I saw no recourse but to send conscription parties to sweep up all the idlers and put them to work in the mines. They were fed and housed!"

"Acquit me of malicious intent, is what I ask. Let us have peace between us. We must be on the road tomorrow, for I don't know how long this truce can last. Get what rest you can."

"There's nothing wrong with me," he muttered truculently.

"What?"

He reddened. "Before your father sent to interrogate me. The governor directed a physician to examine me. If he did not lie, he said there is no reason I ought not to live a normal life." His fingers brushed his ribs. "I don't even have to sit up to sleep anymore."

Then, as if he felt he had said something complimentary where he had not meant to, he left abruptly — to return to his room and a pile of books, according to Jai, serving as bodyguard, watcher, and servant.

With Kianti gone, Perch and Minnow entered, soft of step and full of bows. Perch gave me an assessing glance and offered to fetch tea with willow bark, as Minnow offered to brush out my hair and rub my temples.

I very nearly wept at this, a reaction followed by a pulse of guilt at what a sheer relief it was to have servants once again. All my belongings had been exquisitely cleaned and repaired, and Perch had marveled over the lovely robes that Arati had given me.

Just this once I would let myself be the focus of their lives. But not tomorrow, I sternly promised myself. At my encouragement, Minnow talked about their prison survival. It had been harrowing indeed, beginning with First Brother's personal servant being killed by Xianti when he tried to put himself between Xianti and the guards holding First Brother when Xianti blinded him. The grand princesses had apparently enjoyed coming in to threaten the same to the maids, while the wretched pair did their best to humiliate Mother, but Princess Vaha had put an end to that through Grand Prince Miluo, and Siarti and Liarti had been forbidden to enter the prison after that.

The days of terror over, it had been dreary endurance until they were abruptly freed, turned loose right on the street along with murderers, thieves, and political prisoners. Bao and An Gui had been able to whisk them away to the underground safehouse that I had first stayed at when I was a refugee of twelve, and from there they were spirited over the mountains, much of it spent lying under trade goods in carts.

"And we're to go back now?" Minnow asked.

"Only if you wish to," I said. "If you would rather stay here in Peaceable Breezes, I will speak to my grandmother. You are free to choose."

That night, my grandfather gave a banquet. The seating was a quiet, deftly done statement of what was real to my grandfather: in honor, he accorded Grand Prince Yiulo and Kianti seats at the head table, but Yiuti was no higher than On or my brothers. Father was in his rightful place above the boys, Mother across from him, next to my grandmother: their demotion to commoner was as nothing to Grandfather Gu.

My place was across from my brothers, next table down from my mother. I learned much from this exercise in unspoken diplomacy, and tried to inure myself to all the staring from the noble refugee-guests at the lower end of the room as we ate from many beautiful dishes. There were not the usual wasteful heaps of food on them, but what might be lacking in quantity was

more than made up for with plenty of rice wine and entertainment.

During the many toasts and complimentary speeches, I
learned that Grand-Uncle Miluo—who still resided in the
imperial palace—had jointly with Xianti sent an envoy to
Grandfather Gu with a formal request for a truce. The wording
invited the Lan family members of rank to meet in the capital,
to negotiate a compromise among themselves, for the good of
the empire.

"Father is not going to agree," I asked Mother under cover
of the musicians playing. "He'll stay here in safety, will he not?"

Mother gave her head a tiny shake. "He insists on being
there. It's a gesture of trust toward the Grand Prince Miluo, who
has faithfully held to a firm but merciful standard all this time."

"Too powerful to unseat without disastrous consequences,"
I said, appreciating this lever of influence: the mighty Eastern
Fleet was still very loyal to Grand Uncle Miluo. Not only that,
I'd discovered during the course of the day, but a great many of
the naval deserters had fled to them, where law required them
to be put to death, but apparently they were regarded as …
volunteers.

"Your father wants the imperial city to understand that he
supports you." She saw my worry, and said gently, "We cannot
hide forever. And as your father said to me, we endured the
journey here while buried in hay and under sacks of grain, we
can certainly endure a more civilized journey back."

I bowed my acquiescence. Father's health had suffered
severely. We had all seen that. But I could also see that the
decision had been made.

I longed to discuss it with Koi. I surely was not the only one
who did not believe past a breath that Xianti would honor this
truce. It was not until late that I finally met with Koi and Cray,
who agreed with me.

"I think even Kianti is expecting some sort of stealth attack,"
Koi said. "Or rescue, as he probably sees it. But we're to have a
full company of your grandfather's best, along with all the
warriors Grand Prince Yiulo brought."

With this I had to be content, I decided as I dragged myself
wearily to my rooms.

Here, Minnow and Perch were waiting.

Minnow said, "We talked about it. I shall go with you. I
don't know what I would do else."

"And I. You were chosen by the phoenix god," Perch said, with awe, then dropped forehead to the floor—mimicked by Minnow. "Please do not make us go away."

"Up, up, up," I cried, resigned to beginning over again to break that wretched habit. "Get your rest. We've only a few hours until our departure!"

I slept hard, and woke to rustlings and whisperings. It seemed I had just shut my eyes, but the household had roused. Everyone was fearful, fretful, apprehensive. My grandparents had admitted that the city's resources were strained to the limits by holding a populace three, four, then since Xianti's taking the throne, six times its size. The granaries were nearly empty. Yet the mountain paths, even in mud and slush, had been alive with people escaping the south.

We rode out in column under low skies, surrounded by warriors bearing banners, spears, and halberds. Along the road, even up in the rocky palisades, uncounted people watched. Some waved, many bowed, and called, "Pangolin Ren! Pangolin Ren!"

Riding at the front in an open carriage (for I did not know how to ride a horse), I was thus able to see Grand-Uncle Yiulo forcing a smile as he waved his fine sword. When we reached a summit, and a booming voice called, "Bow!" before a great crowd bent low, I caught the grand prince urging his grandson to ride beside me, and to wave.

On trotted up on my other side, so the three of us were abreast, and he waved to the people. As I waved, Banti joined us, also mounted, and the appearance of Yiuti and me as a pair had turned into a cluster.

We rode on, Banti riding beside Yiuti and entertaining him with a steady stream of jokes and anecdotes. Hearing Yiuti's occasional guffaws, I promised myself to thank him sincerely later. He had to be engaging Yiuti on purpose.

Sure enough, when we halted for a refreshment stop, On handed the reins of his horse off to one of the servants pacing beside us (for we proceeded at a sedate walk) and hopped up beside me. "Told Banti to deflect Yiuti."

"Thank you," I said. "I'd better find my family."

"Your father is asleep in their cart. Your brother is being read to by someone. Your mother—"

"Renti?" Here was mother, having walked up on her own. She looked from On to me, and he hopped down with a bow and a smile. I looked after him, feeling a pang. I would have liked his company, for he could always find a way to ease the clamor of voices in my head.

Mother climbed up beside me, as grooms brought water and fodder to the horses. "He is the surviving Kwai prince, is he not?" Mother asked.

I was ready to exclaim *Not marriage talk again*, for there was no mistaking the reflective interest with which she looked after On, but I suppressed it. That would not be filial behavior, and already I was amiss, having not been the one to instantly go back to see if there was anything my parents needed.

"He is," I said.

Mother turned her searching gaze to me, and observed, "You have experienced so much that I do not comprehend a part of, Daughter. Except to compare you with my cousin, and Grandmother Ou, though neither has Essence skills. I also had to become reacquainted with my own mother, unseen for so many years. All we've had were letters, and after we were imprisoned, not even that."

"I'm sorry you suffered so," I said, taking her hand. "And that I could do nothing."

"We are alive. And together. That is what matters," Mother replied, and I sensed her conviction.

I said, "Tell me about First Brother. We have had no words. But that was true even when we were small, save when I studied with him before he took the examination."

"Your brother ... suffered the most," Mother said. "We were helpless to prevent any of it. It became apparent that the imperial crown pr—no, he has now made himself emperor."

Even now Mother was being scrupulous about honorifics. "Just call him Xianti, Mother. I know who he is."

She gave a tiny nod. "There was always an antipathy between him and Yanti. Your brother saw it as his duty to correct one who might very well command the world one day. He never spoke against that inheritance. His entire purpose was to do what he could to help shape a good ruler. But those imperial grandchildren had been raised to consider themselves at the center of everything. And so, all matters had to be personal. That young man took every word Yanti spoke as an affront, if not an attack."

"I know. I saw some of it, even when I was small."

Mother lowered her voice. "Your brother would be dead if

it were not for the Princess Meiti. Princess Vaha," Mother corrected herself. "She requested us, among ourselves, to use her birth name. She came every day. *Every* day, without fail, even if she could only stay a short time. After she did her best with eastern medicine, for Xianti would permit none of our physicians to attend Yanti, she sat with him to talk. And always to us as well."

Mother glanced around, as if for listening ears. "In ordinary days, we could not have permitted two young nobles so much time in one another's company. But there we were in prison, our rank rescinded, and there was no custom to dictate what is right under these circumstances. I will confine myself to two observations. First, that Yanti's heart is very deeply engaged. Very deeply. With his sight, he believed that his use in the world was taken away—everything he had trained for. But for her company, and the fact that he believed it would be unfilial, I think he would gladly have refused bite or drink until he died."

That sounded so very like my brother that I had no trouble believing it.

"Second, we had to be so very, very careful not to let any sign of that friendship appear as anything but mercy visits to your father and me."

Xianti's jealousy, in other words.

"Understood," I said.

"I do not know what is to become of any of us," Mother said with a tired smile. "I do not even feel I can rightly caution you in behavior or intent. So much has changed. Except I know it is my duty to encourage you to reflect before acting."

"I've had your voice directing me all along," I said, pressing her hand. "Though you might not agree with my actions, I tried to heed your teachings."

"That's all I can—" She broke off as the call to mount up echoed along the long column, and we were in motion once again.

Bao reported through Cray that the Falcon Watchers had not detected any armies moving to intercept us. Sun and the cranes flew above us. Sun reported many refugees, but no armed parties. However, none of these could guarantee no stealth attacks.

Koi formed a safety perimeter around our tents, drawing on certain among the grand prince's warriors known to Koi from his early stay at Whale Haven, plus some Falcons among

Grandfather Gu's defenders. This was in addition to the posted sentries that the Gu company commander and the grand prince agreed to; theirs was the face of the military might. Koi and his group watched for those trained to infiltrate regular military defenses.

I spent my time with my family, doing my best to fit myself among them again. It helped that Father had decided the best way to aid me in my new duty was to revert to our childhood habits: over the simple camp food, we had lessons.

Father decided to begin with the ritual of court, about which I was completely ignorant. He turned to my First Brother. "Yanti? Enlighten us about the imperial robes."

My elder brother said, "There are different robes for different seasons and circumstances, but each robe must include the Twelve Symbols of Imperial Authority: the sun, moon, seven-star constellation, mountain, divination talismans for prosperity, the axe head of order and security, and of course the five-clawed dragon. The hems are worked with lotus, osmanthus, and seaweed, the back below the dragon depicted the sacrificial cup surrounded by flames and the grain."

"Excellent, thank you. Renti? Can you repeat all twelve?"

And so it went. Father and First Brother traded off instructing me on each move in the elaborate rites, and the historical significance of each, as Banti sat as silently as Mother, he by First Brother, and she by Father.

From court etiquette and protocol we branched into general discussion of changes in the organization of government, from the time of the Three Departments to the evolution of Left and Right sides of court, which ministers stood where, and why, until we got to the present court organization based on the Six Ministries.

I began to look forward to these discussions each night. Once again, the metaphor of a Circle game applied, only now the board was law, tradition, and custom. Whenever I faltered, First Brother would be there with remembered texts. He was patient in repeating these as many times as I needed until I got the gist, if not the precise words. We had no books. I asked for no books, mindful of his blindness. But I soon saw that we did not need books, for his memory was exceedingly good. I'd always known that—but he'd only gotten better.

When First Brother spoke without faltering, I saw Father's face relax, and he'd shut his eyes, smiling a little, as if enjoying each word. The way other people listen to music.

At first we sat alone in the tent set up for my parents, but when we discovered that some listened outside—including Kianti—Father said that they could come inside, and put questions or offer quotations. The grand prince did not like Kianti being there, much less speaking, but Kianti had been well tutored, whatever else had happened in his life, and surprisingly, Father was firm in permitting it. "We discuss nothing that cannot be heard by every imperial subject of whatever rank." Education, for him, was second only to law. The more serious among the ministers' sons also crowded in, sitting with Banti at the back.

Yiuti was left with his grandfather and the wilder among the boys.

The grand prince relented, shaking his head as he withdrew. "Have it your own way, Nephew. You always were stubborn, even as a pipe-voiced boy." And he went off to talk military preparedness with the Gu Defender Commander.

The days began to be broken by refugees appearing along the road. At first furtively. Then in clusters, and in greater and greater numbers.

They were there to speak to me.

"Pangolin Ren, can you find my son?"

"Pangolin Ren, I beg you to send the phoenix to our village. There are only eight of us left, and…"

"Pangolin Ren, can the phoenix see everyone? Is my husband still alive?…"

"…taxes are worse every season…"

"…no one left to repair the roof…"

At first Koi and the others questioned and searched them, then accompanied them to wherever I was, but after a time there were too many, and we were always moving, so they knelt by the roadside and called out. On had managed to acquire more paper from my grandfather's scribes, and he brought me brush and ink so that I could write down names, villages, problems.

But as their numbers increased, I could not keep up. On was a far faster writer; he and then a couple of the servants offered to help record these petitions; I repeated hundreds, thousands of times that I would do my best, that their problems mattered. On and his scribe friends crouched in the carts, writing, as volunteers ground the ink for them.

Grandfather Gu's escort hated these interruptions. They had gone on high alert, especially as more and more appeared, in crowds now, following us toward the imperial city.

"Every day I expect a stealth attack," Koi said when he stood with me under the cart roof very early one rainy morning. "Xianti won't honor a truce if he thinks he can get away with it. He will think himself clever, capturing real arrows with boats of straw—"

A dark cloak passed before the dripping opening. It was Kianti, a scrawny, slouching figure. Koi fell silent; unlike Yiuti, he did not like baiting Kianti. Maybe because Yiuti did it, usually before an audience of the ministers' sons, who gave him the laughter and applause he craved.

Kianti moved away, and I said, "I know Xianti is likely plotting. But turning those refugees away because Xianti is likely to strike against us would be my own kind of betrayal."

"You're right. I'll tell Sun to keep searching from above," Koi said wearily. I pressed my hand over his cold one. He turned to give me that private, sweet smile that only I saw, and then he was gone.

I went back to looking at auras, though if I did it too long while moving it gave me stomach-clawing vertigo. I still didn't really understand the roil of colors well, except in a general sense—and it was easy enough to see those expressions in eyes, mouths, hands, stances, without resorting to the Essence realm.

As it turned out, I did not need subtlety. It was I who discovered the stealth attackers. Their auras were an intense, blue-white, not unlike lightning. When I spotted them at the back of a mass of refugees, I said, "There's five assassins—"

Hiss! Thwap!

Crossbow bolts struck directly above my head, and to my right; people screamed in panic, scrambling in every direction, but my attention was drawn by Kianti, whose fear shot green-yellow before he ducked behind my cart.

Koi and his Falcon-trained warriors plunged through the crowd, which tried to scatter. The assassins vanished, and though I could still spot them by the roil of their auras, they had separated, and then they were lost among the spreading auras of fear and anger among the refugees.

Koi caught up presently, panting. He held up his empty hands.

"They scattered," I said. "I saw."

"They did," he murmured as he leaped up beside me. "I'm sorry we could not catch them. You unhurt? Good. I think it unnerved them, that you identified them before they could strike."

"I don't know if that will help or hurt," I murmured back, and then, after a thorough look around, I whispered, "I think Kianti thought they were going for him. Just for a moment."

Koi returned no words, but shook his head, and then, seeing his compatriots returning equally empty-handed, jumped down again, and went off with them to lay more plans.

Through the rest of the day's travel my nerves thrummed, and I reflexively scanned auras in spite of the noxious surge of vertigo. By nightfall I was too tired and dizzy to join my family, and withdrew to the tent I shared with Cray and my two maids. Minnow massaged my head, which helped, but my meridians did not release tension until Koi said from outside the tent flap, "Tell Ren that On is helping a new rumor spread, how Pangolin Ren sees evil intent like a phoenix from Suanek herself."

Whether or not that was a cause, there was no renewed attack during the remaining days.

And one morning, with spring in the air, we mounted a ridge to overlook the imperial city spread along the lower slope of Mt. Lir.

FORTY-ONE

Without trust or truth sacred ritual was an empty gourd,
As under palace towers smoke and dust were born.

BAO, WHO HAD SERVED as Watcher for the secret Falcon safe-house, appeared quietly the morning we sighted the imperial city.

His face had lined, his hair thinning around his topknot since the last time I'd seen him. He was almost as thin as Kianti, his lanky body expressive of profound though unspoken regard in his bow to Father.

Father's eyes moistened when he took both Bao's hands in order to thank him for his loyalty. "As you can see," Father said, "we are no worse for our journey in the donkey's hay cart up to Governor Gu. He has sent us back in princely luxury."

"If this your servant may offer an observation: that journey was not what your highness ought to have experienced," Bao said—though a Falcon, he was more of a traditionalist in some ways even than Father.

"It did us no harm," Father replied. "First Son and I wagered we could recite the entirety of Lao Sha's *Militias and Rebellions* to while away the time. We discovered that it has much to say to present circumstances, though written a few generations ago. We also reviewed the *Five Elements and The Dialects of Enlightenment,* which is always good to reflect upon, whatever our circumstances."

"Might this uncouth one suggest that those circumstances did not include physical ease?" Bao retorted with another bow.

"Ayoh, all these things are relative," Father answered. "Coming from prison as we did, we welcomed donkey carts as the most exquisite of conveyances."

More humor from Father! He seemed determined not to consider threats, dangers, or discomforts. Perhaps this was his way of acknowledging that he could do nothing to prevent them. I was glad to have it so. He seemed so frail—much more frail than Yanti, in spite of the blindness. Yanti even went out a few times to attempt seeds and forms with Banti, when it was not raining; though Banti was largely silent during those evening discussions, he had faithfully attended them, and I cherished the care in his hands as he hovered near First Brother, ready to catch him if he stumbled.

Everyone was on alert even more than before, knowing we would reach the imperial city well before nightfall.

Soon after breakfast, as Grandfather Gu's servants were breaking down the tents and folding them into the carts, Cray appeared, a bird fluttering on her arm. "Envoy coming," she said.

"From which of them?" I asked.

"*Him.*"

Cray hated referring to Xianti as the emperor, though he had made himself Heaven's Chosen by law and by ritual. I gave up trying to convince her that the customs and protocols, if they were to sustain a sense of order, must be maintained whether the person under the formidable cap with its swinging jade-bead curtain was good or bad. She would have none of it. Xianti was Xianti to Cray—if not a worse epithet, but at least she confined her opinions solely to me, Koi, Sun, and On.

I glanced at the note, which was from one of Bao's contacts among the secret organization run by the graywing Cedar. "Sending white flag to demand Kianti."

She said, "Why would Xianti demand Kianti now? He knows he's alive. Does he really think we'd kill him just before entering the city?"

"He wants time to interrogate Kianti, of course," I said. "Find out what we have said and done before Kianti's eyes. What secrets might have been divulged, including our numbers and organization."

"That's right," Koi said, appearing as the last of the tents was folded away. The sky had cleared, though the ground was muddy from the previous night's rain. All the snow had long vanished on south-facing slopes; I gave a thought to the northern climes we had been living in, where at this time of year blizzards still whitened the landscape.

Sun and her cranes drifted high on the air, and I suddenly wished I could go aloft. I knew the impulse for what it was: a wish for escape, leaving the tangled knots of threat and anxiety behind.

"We'll ride after them," Koi added. "We'll be implementing our own defense as you enter the city. And we'll be ready, whatever happens."

With that he strode away, weapons jingling. I longed to go after him, but I made myself turn about to seek Kianti.

There he was, listening to something Banti and On were saying. Or rather On was talking, Banti laughing, and Kianti slouched, silent, profile hidden by his black hair hanging down in unkempt strings. He had never learnt how to tend it; until recently he hadn't the strength to lift his arms over his head for any length of time.

I ran to them. "Finish dressing," I said to Kianti. "Your brother has sent a party to fetch you back to the palace."

"Proof of life *now?*" Banti asked, brows rising. "Ay! Xianti is expecting treachery at the last moment because that's what he is no doubt planning. Come here, Kianti. We'll not send you back looking like a wild hermit from a cave."

Kianti said nothing to any of us, but sat obediently as Banti, with the expertise of weeks of ship life, wound up his hair into a topknot, skewered it. Then Kianti groped in the luggage wagon for his new things.

Our cavalcade had been in motion for no more than an hour when a company of imperial guards galloped up, one bearing the imperial golden dragon banner, and another a white flag.

Koi was walking beside my cart. "Know any of them?" I whispered.

"There's one there who belongs to Grand Prince Miluo. Rest are either Xianti's or unknown."

One was enough: proof that our grand-uncle Miluo was aware of this order. There was less likely to be treachery by a desperate man who still would not communicate with us, except in ways meant to reiterate his power.

The two parties halted, banners rippling in the wind. Midway along the company there was a highly decorated carriage, drawn by four horses. It was empty inside: sent for

Kianti.

In a loud voice, the banner-bearer read out an edict demanding the release of His Highness the Grand Prince Lan Kianti" Not imperial heir, I noticed—though now Kianti was closest relative to Xianti. Did he notice as well?

I said nothing as Kianti rode past me, his things attached to the saddle. I had learned to pity Kianti, and did not wish the coming interview to be any more difficult than it might be.

"I'll ride," he said, his chin lifting a little.

The banner bearer waited until Kianti was safely among them, being saluted to on all sides, then raised his voice again. "His imperial majesty and the Grand Prince Miluo unite in welcoming their imperial relations, and request said relations to meet with them in the ancestral hall." No titles.

That was a surprising place appointed for this prospective meeting—I saw question and wonder in all faces.

"These *imperial* Lan relations accept the edict, and return greetings to his imperial majesty and his imperial highness the grand prince," Grand-Uncle Yiulo pronounced, his tone sharp on the first *imperial*.

The bannermen bowed, the company reversed themselves in perfect order, and they rode off with Kianti in their midst, the empty carriage rattling along at the back.

Koi and his group waited a time. He sent me a silent glance, then they rode after, and vanished among the budding trees.

We rode on, the city vanishing from view as we peered up at sheer limestone crag, the stone from which the outer walls of the palace was built, and a good part of the city. Presently the last of the boulder-strewn ridges and wind-scoured wildernesses gave way to rounded hills, bare in preparation for planting, and here and there small villages. A few people dared to venture out to stare, but many more remained shuttered out of sight, testament to the hard times of the previous years.

Before we entered the city, Grand Prince Yiulo gave the command for the combined defensive force to ride ahead and secure the road. It was right and proper. It must be done. But I strongly suspected that danger, when it came, would be from above.

I spared myself scanning in the Essence realm until we entered the city gates. Though we were still followed by a massive crowd of refugees, there was no crowd to greet us. It was apparent that someone had issued orders for the imperial city's subjects to stay home, out of sight. Imperial guards roamed in armed parties; they ignore the grand prince's men wearing the crimson firedragons, and Grandfather Gu's in brown. In their turn, our defenders ignored the imperial guards.

I saw none of Koi's people.

It was time to begin assessing auras. I shut my eyes to the physical world, trusting our safety to those appointed to guard it in the material world, and reached into that strange, timeless realm. I sensed a few questing entities, one or two cold voids similar to the one that had gazed out of Brother Turtle's eyes months ago. But these seemed air-borne, or rather, they had yet to hollow out a human shape. Sensing me — or perhaps more rightly sensing the sword's indefinable entities — they vanished, faster than a hawk on the wind.

We progressed along the broad main street, zigging and zagging as always, for it is long-received wisdom that demons only travel in straight lines. Was that true? I wondered as I peeped through my eyelashes at upward curving roofs, some in tiers, fine tiles gleaming from the early rain. Granny Zim said nothing; either she did not know, or she was listening in that other realm.

There. I sucked in a breath against the inward jolt that roiled my stomach. What had I caught? I reached farther, bracing my hands on the padded bench to either side, Sagacious Blade pressed against my leg. A distinct image: myself, as seen from above, seated alone on the bench behind the driver, the curtain wide open. Vertigo threatened.

"Captain," I murmured without moving — without opening my eyes.

One of Grandfather Gu's commanders rode alongside me. "Your highness?" His voice was low, instantly alert, and his aura intensified to that same lightning-brilliant blue of intent.

"That roof. Over the silk-seller..."

We were not yet in range. The captain bent to address the young warrior walking at his stirrup, who bent low, and ran along the caravan of carts on the side away from the readying shooter.

Plop, plop, plop: the distinctive clop of horse hooves on the clean-swept street. That blue-white intensified, and my hand tightened on Sagacious Blade's hilt — then the scrapes and thumps of an unseen scuffle echoed through the empty street. The blue-light had shaded to the red of the anticipation of a killing shot, then abruptly snuffed like a candle.

Suanek, I prayed, if you hear me, let him come back as a cricket, as a crane, as a shoemaker…

My cart jolted, and On whirled up to sit beside me — on the side of the would-be attacker. "What was that?" he muttered urgently. "I thought I heard orders being passed."

I told him in three short sentences, and he cursed under his breath, then said, "I think Shi Gan the hero needs a new experience: serving as target. Let them try to aim at me. You should have let me ride with you."

"The people have to see me," I said.

"But there are no refugees," On said. "And everyone else is hiding inside their houses."

"If they peep out, I want them to see me. Whatever happens," I said, my voice trembling; I rubbed my eyes, willing the bubbles of nausea away as I longed to sit still for half a breath. But we must keep on, and I breathed it out.

On waited until I said slowly, "I don't believe there will be any more assassins on rooftops."

On's brow puckered, and then his forehead cleared. "Ayoh! You don't think Xianti believed our rumor about the phoenix knowing evil intentions, eh? But Kianti surely by now would have told him that, phoenix or not, *you* know a lie when you hear one, or evil intent before they act."

I turned to On. "Do you think he'd believe Kianti?"

On's lips parted. Then he sighed. "Ayoh, ayoh, ayoh! I forgot. A man who lives lies is going to suspect the truth. But that's his favorite method of attack, is it not? The danger is not over." He sat forward, trying to make his slim body appear larger.

I forced a laugh, sensing the worry he tried to hide. "Don't puff out your chest like that. You look like you're about to spit into the wind."

"I? No, I look handsome and imposing. At least I do in my own mind's eye." He sat more normally, but still leaned forward to block me, then launched into a quotation from a clever scene he'd recently written. In this manner he heroically kept up a stream of chatter until we approached the palace gates.

The imperial guards saluted their fellow military, pretending that I and my family were invisible — but they stepped forward, weapons across their chests.

Alarm raced down the column as we approached the massive gates.

Cray appeared, to murmur, "The Ministers of the court were ordered to stay home, but they came anyway, early this morning. Now they are kneeling outside the Hall of Glorious Harmony in protest."

My meridians iced: this could only increase the tension. Xianti would not like his orders being flouted by the entire court. But would he tolerate it?

He's waiting to see what I bring to bear, I thought.

One of the guards stated in a wooden voice that only the "Lan relations" and Prince Kwai Sheion were permitted entry.

"Just think! My name! I did not expect that honor," he commented.

"Think of it as a target on your chest," Cray said sourly, and vanished behind us.

The imperial guards apparently did not count servants, and Cray had resumed the gray of palace service, thus becoming effectively invisible, along with Minnow, Perch, and my parents' servants.

After the last cart was through, we lost sight of the rest of the cavalcade. As we rolled inside the palace proper, On looked around with interest. "I have to say, the palace is quite fine. Those inlaid carvings of the Twelve Animals alone are worthy of an entire play, and this is the outer wall, is it not? But we're also quite surrounded by imperials."

"We have to trust to our people."

"I'd feel better if I could see Koi," he admitted as he snapped his fan open.

"Ah, but he's never more dangerous than when he's hidden," I said, trusting it to be true.

FORTY-TWO

The Sage Empress believed:
The dragon robe was mere cloth
Without the warp of law, the weft of ritual
And the weave, the heart-bonds of love.

ON GASPED. "'NEVER MORE dangerous than when he's hidden.' That's it! You've just given me a *very* good idea for Shi Gan...."

A brief shadow overhead, and there was Sun. Or one of the cranes. They were flying much lower, I noted.

But nothing untoward occurred as we wound our way past the state buildings—kept well away from the Hall of Glorious Harmony by a wall of imperial guards standing shield to shield, shoulder to shoulder—and the imperial garden, toward the Hall of Ancestors. That led us past portions of the imperial palace familiar from childhood. How very strange it was to be back; every circular archway, those great redbark trees, the falling plum blossoms, the budding persimmons, all brought back such intense memories.

The palace had always been quiet. Orderly. But now it was silent as a crouching tiger hidden in the grass, except for the clop of our horses and the creak of the carts, and the splat of intermittent raindrops. As we approached the Hall of Ancestors, I noted brown-clad Gu warriors interspersed with those bearing firedragons on their armor. They were matched with imperial guards, each watching the others warily.

We rolled to a halt, and imperial guards intercepted us smoothly, ignoring the spitting rain.

As I descended from the cart I kept my right hand near Sagacious Blade's hilt, though I sensed no intent around me. I couldn't scan long because I was walking. Even so, I staggered once, then gulped in air in a desperate attempt to quash vertigo-nausea.

At the door, two imperial guards crossed halberds. "No weapons," one said.

It was a tradition, maybe even a law: no one was permitted to go armed in the presence of the emperor unless specifically granted permission. I surrendered Sagacious Blade, knowing that I could call her back; with a distant spark of humor, I noticed how the one man held the sword with very careful fingers, as if expecting the blade to hiss forth and slice away madly on its own. They knew I carried a charmed sword.

The two guards permitted us to pass.

The family still living had gathered, wearing their most formal silks. It was not a large gathering. How many of those absent had lost their lives because of their proximity to the dragon throne in that great hall behind us right now?

I paused, breathing in the fragrance of mourning incense. The sight threw me back to my first introduction to the harem, when the dowager empress presided. The beauty had overwhelmed me as a small child: those graceful, golden headdresses winking in the candlelight above coils of elaborately dressed black hair, the layers of jewel-colored silks, covered with elegant embroidery; the screens depicting lofty peaks, mist-shrouded valleys, quiet rivers, and over and within these, soaring cranes and phoenixes and eagles, dancing dolphins. Framing it all, the carved pillars and beams and furnishings, enameled and gilt.

It had taken a few visits before I saw those gatherings as static. The missing element the most vital: a free flow of wit and wisdom, carried on a current of feeling. Then, as now, suppressed into silence.

Great-Uncle Miluo leaned heavily on a cane, his head turned so that his one good eye could take in the room. He had survived his father's rule, his brother's, and his son Koza's; as I glanced his way, I reflected that the law that required a whole and unmarked emperor, thus preventing him from taking the dragon throne, had probably kept him alive in his younger days. His own excellence, and the loyalty of the Eastern Fleet, had preserved his life during his brother's rule. As well as during Koza's, who had never quite dared the unfilial act of patricide, which would have caused a furor in court.

Ringing the chamber stood imperial guards—with firedragon guards and Gu defenders in brown among them. Behind this living wall stood Grand-Uncle Miluo and his wife, the princess from the east, and behind her, the Cinnabar Princess Vaha—who had saved my brother. Her gaze fixed beyond me, on First Brother I guessed, being aided by Banti. My family stood on the opposite side of the hall, behind another wall of guards.

The only unmarried princess, Taisa, was present, a few steps away from Mother; Arati's younger sisters were as yet too young. All the other princesses had either chosen to absent themselves, or more likely, had been ordered to remain with the families into which they had married.

Behind the family, against the pillars and screens, stood graywings and servants, heads bowed, eyes lowered, hands crossed before them. Living furnishings, there to serve, as were benches, cushions, and so on.

Two cushions had been set before the altar, where a pair of men knelt, alone in the wide-open space. I recognized Kianti's thin form from the back, though between the time he'd left us and now he had bathed and dressed in layers of fine robes, silver—the color of the imperial heir—predominant. His sleeves reached the floor in folds. My nerves chilled as the stronger figure next to him, swathed in rich golden and ochre silk, resolved into Xianti, wearing the dragon robe of an emperor, with a train at least the length of two tall men.

They bowed their foreheads to the floor before the altar, then rose, Xianti taking Kianti by the elbow, as if from long habit.

Then, standing there before the altar, Xianti gave Grand Prince Yiulo the slight nod of the younger generation of higher rank to an elder of lower rank. He glanced curiously at On, then shifted away with obvious indifference: Kwai Sheion, the only one left of his family, landless and poor, could not possibly be any threat to Xianti now.

He gave an even slighter nod to my father, utterly ignoring Yiuti, my First Brother (who wouldn't see it anyway) and Banti. Banti bowed correctly, followed by Yanti, who sensed Second Brother's movement. Yiuti jerked the barest bow after a flicked glare from his grandfather, his face red.

But Xianti paid him utterly no heed.

His attention was solely on me.

I bowed to them both, drew breath to speak—gallant wanderer habit— then remembered that it was long tradition, if not law, that one must not address the emperor first.

Xianti turned to Grand-Uncle Miluo. "Your imperial highness, as you see, the family is all present, and no harm has come to any." His tone implied injured innocence, but he side-eyed me, not our grand uncle, as he spoke. I strongly suspected that he was daring me to bring up that failed attempt from the rooftop.

But what would that avail? I had not seen what had happened, and I was willing to wager whoever had made that try was a hireling difficult to associate directly with Xianti. I would have to begin with unsupported accusations, after which he could mire me in having to defend what I could not prove.

No, this arrow must pass by my ear, though I felt the wind of it. I bowed to Great-Uncle Miluo, and to the various princesses in rank order, then said, "These blood relatives have come in good faith to negotiate peaceful compromise."

I braced for Xianti to come at me with laws I'd broken, and there, ready, were my words, prepared with On, about having broken none outside of bearing a charmed sword.

But Xianti chose not to begin with what was really a two-piece move on the Circle board. His opening attack came from a different direction, and it was a hard strike for its seeming amity. "Cousin Renti, I desire first to render my gratitude for curing my brother." He used the imperial pronoun for I, a word solely permitted to the reigning emperor—and it was clear in the way he pronounced it that the word had not yet lost any of its relish.

I bowed. "This cousin was grateful that her rudimentary skills were able to effect that cure."

Xianti then said, "I am willing to forgive you all if my cousin Renti becomes Kianti's physician."

Forgive *what?*

The words were there, but I breathed out the anger that this condescension—and implied threat in that "all"—kindled. Instead, I reached on the Essence level, so practiced by now I did not need to be holding Sagacious Blade. As I'd suspected, his affinities were so very like mine, though the embers of anger burned unchecked. The metal was sharp as needles. But next to him, Kianti's affinities shone with potential now that he was not struggling for breath — unbeknownst to either of them.

I bowed again. "This untrained cousin thanks his imperial majesty, but the fact remains that this cousin cannot lay claim to the calling of physician."

"You could go to the imperial medical academy," Xianti said, his glittering gaze — reflecting the hundreds of candles — searching my face. "I would grant an edict permitting you complete access to their studies."

I clasped my hands in protocol-mandated gratitude. But: "I would welcome that opportunity, once the far greater needs I see are met. Needs I promised to see resolved."

"Needs?" he repeated, his tone dubious. "Yet I have received no petitions from you, following lawful protocol."

"This cousin begs to be enlightened on the subject of lawful protocol: has it become possible for a woman to submit a petition, particularly as they are barred from the ministerial positions required before such a petition may be submitted?"

When was the last time someone had answered him back even so mildly? Had we changed places, I could have countered my question in several ways, beginning with using my rank to find a suitable person to submit a petition for me. (Which of course would not be answered!)

He seemed to be forestalling that possible argument, or some argument, or he just lost his temper, as was his habit, because he had never learned to bridle it. "You really are as presumptuous as rumor has it!" he said, raising his voice so that it echoed back from the vaulted ceiling and the back walls. "I *remember* you, creeping around the edges of family gatherings like a beggar at the gates. What made you so arrogant?"

"You did," I said as firmly, and my voice only quivered once, and I dared to drop the subordinate language. This was not a discussion, it was a duel. Though my heart thundered in my ears, I went on equally firmly. "You are a good part of why I am what you see today: your actions caused my actions. Our natures are much alike, you and I. We use some of the same tools. But we have chosen different paths."

He flushed. "Tools? You regard Guiza, and that short-sighted idiot Kandati down in Lan, and even my brother here, as tools?"

"People are people," I said. "Fire is a tool. You've used it to burn homes and habitats. I use it to cook and to —"

"Cook!" He uttered a sharp laugh. "*Cook!*"

"Cooking," I said, "is vital. We can't eat without cooking, and we can't live without eating. Cooking is an act of communal love, as Kanda exhorts us. It binds us together. Encourages truth and trust—"

"Are you," he interrupted, "actually lecturing me?"

"I am trying to share with you what it took me five years to learn. For example, how fire can be a tool to build as well as to enlighten."

"No, you are trying to gain moral ascendence by implying I know nothing of love or enlightenment," Xianti retorted, still holding Kianti by the arm as if keeping him upright. "Thus proving my point about your astounding, *ignorant* arrogance."

I imagined On urging me to avoid the trap of defending myself; I could feel intent building, and tried again, desperately, because I was losing him. "As Kanda said centuries ago, when the enlightened ruler points toward Phoenix Moon, the bad ruler merely controls the finger. To which I'll add what I have been learning, that the purest love desires to see the beloved prosper. Enlightened rulers seek the prosperity of their subjects. There is no prosperity in a burned village."

"There, you are wrong." Xianti's teeth showed in a brief, feral grin of triumph. "There is a reminder, a *lawful* reminder, of proper order. If people are obedient, they are left alone."

Are they? Then why did you keep burning, and burning, and burning?

Again the words were there, but I fought the angry spark again. Accusation would surely cause him to act. I needed to convince him.

"Hate," I said—and that snapped his attention back. "Hate is easy. It destroys. Love is difficult because it requires constant vigilance. It requires trust, and understanding, and compromise."

"Yes, lecture me about love, Lan Renti," he retorted caustically, and in that one moment, I sensed the excoriation of rejection; I kept myself from looking Princess Vaha's way. He *did* love, however that love was defined, a love that was not returned.

"Here is what this cousin has learned about love," I said, striving to ease my tone. Explain, not lecture. Find one word that would catch his ear and shift the dialogue to exchange instead of duel. "Cleverness without love is as a carved box: pretty to look at, but empty. Strength without love too easily becomes destruction. Love fosters patience. It fosters trust. It fosters hope, and willingness to reflect that love outward. It manifests in kindness."

There was no demon or other entity looking out from his eyes. He was entirely human, desperately angry, and below it a chasm of hurt far too old to be caused by rejection from the girl he wanted. Too old and corroded by the heat of rage.

Think military examples! What had Liad II said in his testament to his dead wife? "Kindness is even more powerful than love in that it demands no return, though it is written that kindness benefits both the giver and the receiver. Like anger, it is infectious, but while anger causes hates and destruction, kindness causes compassion and generosity. Both transform: anger destroys lives, kindness transforms lives."

My attention had been solely fixed on Xianti as I strove to read the minute alterations in his angry face, and to sense intent, especially toward my vulnerable family. I trusted to our defenders to guard against pre-ordered treachery just waiting for a sign, and I expected no trouble from the few Lan relations standing at either side of the Hall of Ancestors.

But I had neglected to look at Kianti.

Xianti had stopped listening; to him my words were no more than the bark of a dog. He said in the tone of intent that I'd dreaded to hear, "*You* should know better that anyone that 'love' and 'kindness' can be used as a weapon. And one thing *I've* learned is to recognize a battleground." He let go of Kianti, and gave him a push in my direction. "Now, Kianti."

Kianti stumbled toward me, within arm's reach as my gaze shifted from Xianti to his twin's face. My nerves chilled when I saw the sweat beaded on Kianti's forehead, the dark flush of red mottling the greenish cast to his skin.

Kianti brought his hands out of his sleeves, one holding a dagger; as yet no one but me, and Xianti, could see it, as Xianti's back was turned to the entire room, the dragon robe an effective screen.

Kianti drew a breath, his gaze searching mine.

"Do it, Kianti. Do it," Xianti whispered — furious, but his eyes pleaded. Then he pulled a vial from his voluminous sleeve. "It's *right here* —"

Kianti's breathing had harshened.

His fingers flexed, and the knife clattered to the mosaic tiles.

"Traitor," Xianti cried in anguish as Kianti swayed, then his knees gave way and he began to crumple.

With a sob of rage and betrayal, Xianti shoved his twin

brother at me. Kianti collapsed against me, and as the two of us staggered and fell, Xianti swung about and kicked over the nearest branch of candles. It crashed to the side of the wooden altar, sending a whirl of sparks upward. Licks of flames spread over the well-oiled surface. Clang! With two hands, Xianti threw over another branch, and another, loosing a deliberately planned conflagration as Kianti's weight bore me to the ground.

Sparks showered around us, a thousand warning stings as I struggled to pull myself from under Kianti. My frantic mind reached—Sagacious Blade smacked into my side and my vision enhanced as I hurled my awareness into him.

I understood at once what had happened: Xianti had required his brother to ingest poison, to be nullified when he stabbed me. There it was, a virulent green already threading his bloodstream, and spreading by tiny, hungry tendrils to choke the life out of his blood.

Grandfather Healer's rough old voice spoke those long-ago lessons about the five essences, the four elements of healing, and how to counter poisons. Vaguely aware of the fire all around me, I drew on its Essence, and used my own thread of fire to surround the green. *Burn only the wrong element, leave the water,* Grandfather Healer whispered in memory. *You must not tamper with the blood itself.*

A tiny portion first—it held—and flash! My Essence targeted only that unwanted element. It took the length of a breath, then I blinked myself to awareness, and found myself crouched dizzily next to Kianti, who lay, eyes open as he gazed upward.

I thought him dead until I felt the slow pulse under my fingers. Then his head turned, and the reflection of fire leaped in his eyes. I glanced up—to discover that we were surrounded by flames.

Xianti had set fire to the ancestral altar and the ranks and ranks of tablets; in order to be rid of me, he was willing to sacrifice the brother who was unwilling to stab me.

But fire was my affinity. "Come," I said, and helped him haul himself to his feet. It took more concentration of Essence to draw the heat from the fire, confining it to the blade that glowed in my hand.

Leading Kianti out of the diminishing flames, I saw Xianti's back. He was shouting at the frozen ranks of family, servants, guards, but I had not heard a word of it. As all gazes shifted from him to us, he whirled around.

He saw us as we emerged out of the dying fire.

Xianti staggered in disbelief. Then came his usual solution: "Kill…" he began to shout.

It was then that someone along the margin of the room cried thinly. Passionately. "Justice!"

And before the guards, waiting for the command to finish, could take more than a step the graywing Cedar sprang two steps toward Xianti, scooped up the poison dagger from the tile, and sank it into Xianti's heart.

FORTY-THREE

From dragon throne this lament to Heaven:
Oh, how gravely bow the men of high rank
With forehead to the floor
While never showing an honest face?

I DON'T THINK XIANTI even felt the poison. The blade had been precisely placed. He choked on a rush of blood, and was dead within a gasping breath or two of falling to the floor.

The imperial guards rushed inside the Hall, pulling weapons. Not all advanced on Cedar, who stood where he was, clearly awaiting their blades. Some advanced with the deliberation of previously-given orders on me, and Father, and Yanli.

Then Koi appeared and took a broad stance before me, one hand bearing a sword, the other high, brandishing a military tally. "Hold!"

His company ran in to spread efficiently along the walls at either side, swords at the ready as they faced the imperial guards. The Gu defenders and firebird guards now outnumbered the imperials.

Kianti swayed again, perhaps in shock. I caught his arm to steady him as I murmured, "Did he make you heir?"

"No." Kianti stared at his lifeless brother. "No," he added on an exhaled breath. "Said he would. Give me the antidote. Make me heir. But I had to prove my loyalty. Drink the poison. And kill you."

His gaze shifted to the smashed vial under Xianti's fingers, lying in a puddle of colorless liquid that I strongly suspect was water.

"He was never going to make me heir. Was he?" Kianti breathed.

It was very clear now that Xianti had not trusted Kianti ever since he'd turned up cured, and so he'd made Kianti the assassin—to draw the world's hatred if he succeeded, or suffer my Essence skills if I prevailed. But it seemed too cruel to say so out loud.

Koi held everyone in place as Kianti grappled with the realization that his brother had framed him.

I turned away from his anguished face, and caught surreptitious movement in the dissipating smoke: a pack of servants surrounding Cedar and smuggling him into the shadows beyond the pillars.

As yet everyone's attention remained on Xianti, and on Kianti and me. Most looked appalled. Shocked. Some of the imperial guards looked down on their dead emperor in impotent fury and astonishment, but most—Koi insisted much later—tried to hide a profound sense of relief.

Grand-Uncle Miluo's cane cracked on the tiles.

All turned to him as he took five limping steps, and then—with an audible grunt—he knelt before me, saying, "If walking out of a fire like a phoenix reborn is not a Sign from Heaven, I do not know what else to call it. Command, and this your subject will obey."

They all fell to their knees.

On called from behind the line of guards, "Hail Empress Renti!"

Bows. Ritual. *Order.* Falling in with tradition lessened risk. In ones and twos, then more, they cried, "Hail empress! Hail empress! Hail empress!"

I bent to help Grand-Uncle Miluo to his feet. "Please rise," I said to him. "And I beg you, let that be the last such gesture you ever make toward me."

To everyone else, "Please rise."

Grand-Uncle Miluo's quick, crooked smile reminded me suddenly of Banti's as he muttered in a rusty voice, meant only for me to hear, "In truth I do not know how many more bows I have left in these old bones."

My eyes strayed to Grand-Uncle Yiulo, hovering at the door as if uncertain whether to come in or go out. He was talking earnestly to Yiuti. Koi issued orders to the guards to stamp out the remains of the fire.

On skirted Xianti and came to me. "Yiuti's on his way to corral the ministers," he said in an urgent undervoice. "Want me to get the Upstart Prince in ahead of him?"

I wrenched my mind from the immediate. I must see the whole board. "Would you hold them until I can get there?" I asked.

"Ay! It'll be fun." He leaned forward and kissed me, quick and sweet and impertinent, then he was gone in a few steps. And I knew that however fast Yiuti might run, or even gallop, if he tried to commandeer one of the horses out in the courtyard, On would get there first over the rooftops.

"*Commander* Koi," I said.

Koi dropped to one knee, right fist to his heart. The imperial guards also dropped to their knees, some side-eyeing the others. Faction divisions? But Koi held the tally belonging to the commander of the imperial guard, and I wondered if his cousin in the guard had had something to do with that.

I said to him, "Please establish order *and safety* through the palace."

Koi bowed crisply, and I caught a flash of an anticipatory smile—he surely had a plan in place. Five plans. Such as... "What about Cedar?" I whispered.

His voice was a mere breath. "To the world, we follow the law: search, apprehend, execute. He must never return here, but vanish entirely."

He must have seen my relief in my face, for he turned away and began handing out orders for the search and for securing the palace.

The ministers had to wait another moment. First Kianti, who stood there empty of hand, his expression distraught. His was the greatest loss here. He needed something to do ... something that would preserve outward respect for his brother, who could no longer harm anyone. "Will you do us the honor of over-seeing the proper funeral arrangements?"

Kianti's hand shook as he wiped his sleeve over his face, but then he turned my way, and that vacant expression gave way to comprehension. "I will." He straightened, and with a last glance at Xianti, beckoned to a waiting servant.

I turned to Grand-Uncle Miluo, saying in a low voice. "I believe we should proceed to the Hall of Glorious Harmony."

This was the moment that Kianti ought to dispute, if he was

going to claim the heirship. But as I had guessed, he had never in life expected it.

Within moments the dispatched servant, up on the roof, began the ritual cry to Xianti's soul to return, as he waved a robe of Xianti's. Kianti's eyes closed, and tears slipped from beneath his lashes as this cry repeated, and I backed away to leave him in peace.

"Get used to the imperial 'I'," my great-uncle said as we crossed the room. "Practice it. My brother had to, not all that many years ago, though it might seem like forever to you young ones. He was exactly your age." His reminiscent voice was a reminder that those past awe-inspiring figures had been human, too—or as Mother would say, naked under their clothes.

It was also a reminder that he had survived far more violent changes of regime than this one. So far. We must now see to it that the potential for chaos ended quickly.

We passed through the bowing family and outside, into the chilly air.

Away from the hall, he continued, with a searching gaze, "He was never going to give any credence to anything you said, child. He only permitted you to speak so that that poor boy could muster the courage to act as the assassin—Xianti did not want to risk killing Heaven's Chosen himself."

My failure surged up in me again. "I wanted to convince him. I needed to convince him." And there, laid bare, my deepest fear, in stumbling words: *If I could not persuade Xianti, how could I possibly expect to rule?*

"You were never going to persuade him," the grand prince said in a low voice. "Did I not know better than anyone? No matter how hard any of us tried to make a suggestion, even smothered in flowers of flattery, he would perceive only the thorn-prick of criticism, and regard it as enmity."

I caught and suppressed a sob, though it formed a hard knot in my chest. "Why did you not interfere, since my words were so useless?"

"Because I did not know what to do outside of what I had already done, such as seeing to it that the command tally got to the right hands. Because there were some who listened to you. Because those words needed saying. You are forgetting how poisonous the palace air has become, even after the death of that woman my brother married. She had him by the ear, a far more potent poison than any she used. And she had the raising of those four. Yes, we saw you walk out of a fire, but we had a great-grandfather who could do that, too, now forgotten by anyone younger than seventy. The true miracle is that Kianti dropped that blade."

The reminder of the empress of my childhood days caused me to shudder.

We Lans needed a fresh start. A new dynasty, I thought, surveying the ruined lower row of memorial tablets. The dowager-empress's was mere cinders, the former empress's scorched.

The Lans had not been good emperors, but there were good people in the family. Father, for one. Cousin Oraiti and his father. Grand Prince Miluo. Kandati—Guiza—Princess Taiza over there, helping Father out the door as Mother and Banti guided Yanti. Arati and her silly but good-hearted sister. Lan was half of my blood.

On the other side of the courtyard, Yiuti was in urgent conversation with the grooms at the horses' bridles, with a trio of Grandfather Gu's guards facing some firedragons. They seemed to be in heated discourse, all the more for lowered voices.

Grand-Uncle Miluo gave them a glance, his lips pressed in a line, and he began to hurry himself, though he was unable to go much faster than a stiff-legged hobble.

Therefore I will leave myself pacing at his side, and shift to the Hall of Glorious Harmony, which On did reach first. On his way, he collected Sun and her companions, and in a few words he outlined what he wanted.

The unsettled weather had dampened the ministers, their assistants, and attending scribes as they all knelt before the steps into the Hall of Glorious Harmony. Their heads were bowed; many, I am very certain, fretted secretly about the rain ruining the stiffening in their hats of office, which at least was something within their control. Unlike whatever was going on at the Hall of Ancestors.

None of them noticed On until he appeared to spring up from the ground as he called from behind them, in the great court below the Hall entrance, "Open the doors for Empress Renti, may she live forever!"

The ministers, their assistants, and attending scribes looked up and around, some daring to break the silence to whisper, "Is she here?" "Is it true?" "The Phoenix…"

At that moment, a brief break in the clouds afforded a

glimpse of spring sunshine. And that was what the cranes were waiting for.

Glowing white in that brilliant beam slanting down, Sun banked low over their heads, followed by a perfect formation of young, enthusiastic cranes, plus her father, who I strongly suspect had more than a little in common with On.

They glided toward the closed doors, then uttered warning squawks before flying up. They came around again, behavior so unlike cranes in nature that the guards at the doors absolutely startled. They hastened to haul the huge carved doors open.

The cranes flew one by one straight into the hall as the ministers exclaimed about signs and miracles, and hurried after in order to witness whatever was to come, rank momentarily forgotten.

Greatly to their surprise and consternation, once they attained the hall itself, and their eyes had adjusted to the gloom lit only by a few candle branches, they discovered that the cranes had vanished. They could not know that Sun had led them beyond the throne, transformed to her human self, and scampered to open doors. The others flew through a warren of corridors to the outside, where she took to the air again in feathered form.

On strode through the middle of the ministers, silk panels swinging. He stopped on the lowest step below the dais, and turned. "I am Prince Kwai Sheion, part of the new empress's alliance for peace! Emperor Lan Xianti is no more. Long live Empress Lan Renti!"

His was the highest rank present. The imperial guards, without any orders covering this situation, stood still, weapons to hand. If there was violence, they'd know how to act. But the ministers in their robes and hats, with their jade tallies in their hands, were not fighters. Instead, they did what they knew best: got themselves sorted into strict rank order, and waited for the miracle to manifest.

While they did that, Grand-Uncle Miluo and I crossed through the imperial park. He began by saying, "This situation—you—is unprecedented, but it seems the Heavens want a change. The gods are right in that," he added. "I won't pretend to say I know how to rule. Which is not the same as commanding an action. But one thing I do know is men's hearts. These ministers are going to try you. At least half are greedy and corrupt, with eyes above their heads; the rest are stiff-necked nobles too powerful for Xianti to dislodge, and they will frown at the ascent of a young woman. The most obsequious will probably be the ones who are going to assume they can run you, the way boy emperors were run so many times in the past."

"I know," I said. "As for men's hearts—and women's—I've had an excellent education in these past six years, though little of it has been in the traditional sense." I clasped my hands gallant wanderer-style and bowed to him. "This niece of little talent and determined ambition thanks her elder for his teachings."

"Thank me by showing yourself willing to continue to learn, even after you put on that yellow silk," he retorted. "I realize that nineteen years is the sum of all your experience, but one day you will understand how very young you are. Of course you believed you could convince Xianti to reverse a path he had chosen, if you were just passionate enough. If you used words enough. But once you gain that seat, the law prohibits anyone talking back to you, and that, I assure you, is probably a worse danger than all the easterners, westerners, and demons put together. We can fight those. We can't attack the one we put on the throne without giving up our own lives—or risking chaos."

I bowed again. "I need my advisors. I know I need them. They are my greatest asset."

"Very well, girl. Very well. I am with you. Here we are."

We reached the back entrance to the Hall of Glorious Harmony, where the emperor customarily entered. There we surprised the graywings in charge, servants, and guards, who stared from one of us to the other, then—recognizing the senior grand prince—went to the floor.

"Rise," I said, and all eyes turned to me.

Grand Prince Miluo leaned on his walking stick as he addressed a waiting graywing. "Quartz, as eldest of the Lan family, I instruct you to surrender the imperial seal to her imperial highness Princess Lan Renti, whom Heaven has called to the dragon throne."

The white-browed graywing looked from him to me, and bowed. And in that moment, I believe, my rule truly began.

Yiuti burst in then. "Wait!" he yelled.

Grand Prince Miluo turned that single eye toward Yiuti. He lifted his hand toward the imperial guard. "There are standing orders about you, left from when you stole that tally years ago. You might have forgotten, but they haven't. Don't make them act on them."

Hands clasped at hilts. Seeing this — and not backed by his grandfather's people, whom Yiulo unfortunately had chosen to surround himself — Yiuti blanched and sidled away.

The moment had come. I straightened my shoulders, shrugged Sagacious Blade into place, and walked out alone, as Great-Uncle Miluo slipped along the side to the front of the ministers, and his old place as senior Lan elder.

I entered the hall dominated by that dragon throne — which I bypassed, for I would not seat myself until properly robed and crowned. This was how we must restore order, by restitching the chaotic present with the threads of protocol known to each. And I could hear in the murmur that they saw it.

I raised my voice. "Emperor Lan Xianti is dead. I, Lan Renti, declare that a new dynasty will begin with me: from henceforth, I will be known as Yslan Renti, Empress of the Thousand Islands."

FORTY-FOUR

Now spring is come
And sweet peach blossoms scatter wide.
Immortal Source pours forth
Its grace to world provide!

I DO NOT BELIEVE I need to describe that very long day.

It is from that first gathering before court, as I stood there in harness, wearing the lavender dragonfly robe that I had made myself, that I become the focus of the official records.

There are many, many eyewitness accounts of what I did and said, and even how I appeared. (They are not very flattering about my embroidery.) Some of these accounts were later embellished, and others were outright hearsay proving so popular that they were repeated as occurrence, such as the one claiming there were five dragons sighted in the sky over Mt. Lir the day of my birth. Another: how the flames in the Hall of Ancestors when Xianti started the fires glowed to life as fiery, golden scorpions, banished at a mere wave from me.

It seems petty to trumpet line by line my triumph over those who offered me lies in their flatteries. Such as Narek Ru, Narek Bin's father. Who, as his reward for insinuating his reluctant son among Grand Prince Yiulo's followers, had been appointed as Chief Censor.

Father had never referred once to this man during our journey to the capital. It was Bao who'd told me that Chief

Censor Narek, in addition to pressing his son to spy up north, had enthusiastically carried on the tradition for corruption by soliciting hefty bribes from anyone accused. Even from those Xianti had wanted condemned. They just weren't successful, he would sadly report to the hapless victim in prison.

By the time I had repeated three times, "You may now speak the truth," the word whispered through court that I could detect lies. This appeared to have more effect on those oil-tongued courtiers than the visitation from the White Crane and her heavenly attendants!

Two more ministers attempted to try me. Granny Zim was so present that I fancied a small, slightly bent shape standing next to me, evanescent as mist. Her indignation at these suasions and evasions made it clear that she was not unfamiliar with imperial courts.

At the end, I dismissed court until the fifty days of first mourning ended, which would see my coronation and a return to proper ritual. While the rooftop cry every ten days to recall a soul I think few actually wanted back took place, I'd have fifty days to reorganize the palace.

And begin on my plans for peace in the empire.

Once the ministers and their staff had filed out, the Grand Prince, obviously in pain from standing so long while I'd gone through department after department, praised me for my perspicacity and retired, surrounded by his servants.

By then the gong had reverberated, signaling the change to last dragon hour.

But the day had not ended for me.

The conversations I put my mind to recollecting and recording are with those whose voices are rarely heard in the official records. They might live useful, even exemplary lives, but once they leave their works are forgotten.

I found Cray waiting directly outside the emperor's door, with a few of Koi's defenders. "Koi told Bream, Minnow, Bao, and the others to restore your home palace. It should be ready when you get there. Have you eaten at all?"

"Yes—no—I don't know," I said. "Did you report to Dinek?"

"Just now. Hat Dove says that she would be glad to assist with seeing to those petitions we gathered on the road."

"Even though it might require an imperial position for proper authority?" I asked, in a very weak and tired attempt at humor.

Cray didn't even crack a smile. "I think her nature is more like an imperial investigator than not. But she was born a trader, so she became a trader. Give her a good position, and I think she'll stay."

"Oh, I plan to. In the censorate, if Father will have her. What else?"

"Banti promised Narek Bin they'd be on a ship soon as they could get away."

"How about the alliance princes?"

"Done," she said with a proud chin lift. "I'd had two messages readied, one for success and one for … not success." In other words, if I was dead.

"Send another to the Prince of Ran, saying that he is now above Commander Zoa, whose fleet is now to patrol the waters farthest to the northwest. I'm sure Zoa will enjoy tangling with the occasional westerner. I hope he likes ice floes. Sun seems to have disappeared. Did she say anything to you?"

"She said to thank you for the chance to make her bow before the imperial court, and they were off."

"Thank you." I caught a searching look at that, and said, "Is there something else?"

In her abrupt way, Cray pulled a shrinking figure from the shadows. This small woman in servant gray promptly went to the ground as Cray said, "Here's Eider."

"Rise, Eider," I said to my former maid. "I'm glad to see you."

She remained where she was. "This worthless one is too vile to ever deserve forgiveness."

"Eider, I'm too tired to get down on the ground to talk to you. But I will. Even though it's wet. And I hate being cold and wet. Please rise."

She peered up at me. "You always did dislike the cold, your imperial highness," she quavered.

"Eider, I know why you reported what you overheard, that day. I blamed you for the disastrous aftermath without knowing that you'd been given a direct order. And that something evil was going to happen anyway. I was very angry at first, but that didn't last. It was forgiven and then forgotten years ago."

She thanked me over and over, and when at last I could get in a word, I said—aware that that this small moment, too, was the beginning of vast change—"What happened to you is a good reminder of the necessity to alter the palace rules so that spying is not necessary. The threats are not necessary. Perhaps you can help me with that. Can you?"

"I will do anything, your imperial highness…"

It took a while, but her being entrusted with a vital task seemed to achieve what my words of forgiveness did not, and she departed for the imperial Household department, there I hoped to assure everyone that change was indeed coming. Beneficial change.

I turned toward our old home, aware that eventually the move would have to be made to Golden Dragon Pavilion. That end of the imperial palace held no good memories for me. I would change that, too.

The next encounter happened not ten steps after Eider scurried off. From between a pair of pillars, a solid form appeared, resolving in the lamplight into Imperial Princess Taisa, with her own silent guards standing well back.

"Renti," she said. "Or must this apprehensive one begin with the imperial bow?"

"Please don't. All that must come to pass, but not until Xianti has made his journey from the palace to the imperial tombs."

"That cannot happen too soon," Taisa stated matter-of-factly, glancing at Cray, but making no move to dismiss her. "This relation remembers you as a sensible girl, and hopes to lay two petitions before the new empress."

"Please," I said, and started to walk, for I was longing to sit down. As well as to eat and to drink.

She said, "First: please do not marry off this unwilling one." She lowered her voice, and slipped into informal mode. "I will help in any way I can with diplomatic matters. But I don't wish to be married. I never did."

"That seems easy enough, especially as I already intended changes in the matter: I expect it's going too strongly against Kanda, as well as tradition, to pass an edict permitting the young to choose for themselves, but I do mean to make it far more difficult for elders to sell daughters like a bag of rice. Their consent is the first step."

"May this appreciative relation admit that she is very glad to hear this?"

"Your second petition?"

"That the new and enlightened empress permit women to sit for the Imperial Examination, and thence to serve in the ministries."

"Again, done. That was in mind, too."

"I might have known," she stated, looking directly into my face. "Call upon me if you desire my opinion or reflections." She bowed, and rustled away into the night.

At last we were able to set out unimpeded. Two of Koi's guards fell in on either side of Cray and me. I looked her way. "Do you want to take over communications here, or go back to Zi Tian and Benevolence, and the Falcon life?"

"If you will agree to both," Cray said at once—making it instantly clear she had been thinking about these matters—"that is, if Zi Tian can be an outside communications chief for you, and I can take over the palace birds, then I will stay. Except for occasional visits to Benevolence, but I'll have trained replace-ments first."

"Done," I said.

It was Cray and I who had left our palace together that spring when I was twelve. Who could have predicted my return? And under what circumstances! It seemed fitting to me that it was the two of us who trod the familiar paths together.

We entered from the side.

Because our palace had been shut up, nothing had changed. The servants had been hard at work sweeping, dusting, and clearing out spiderwebs and the like. The cats were still there, though half-feral, but now the bowls of fish bits were lined up in the far yard, and I wondered if they would return with their progeny.

Ayoh! There were changes after all. Koi, of course, was absent, off somewhere prowling for trouble left behind by Xianti—and consolidating his command. In his place was Bream, Banti's new servant. And when I entered the dining room after a quick wash and a change, I discovered one more addition to the family party: Princess Vaha, her cinnabar-colored hair a rich gold-touched red in the candlelight. That red among all the dark heads was startling, but especially in candlelight, not unpleasing to the eye. The aching eye.

She sat close to Yanti with an ease that spoke of long familiarity. On my entrance she rose to her feet, making a quaint bow from the waist.

I gave her the gallant wanderers' bow, and said, "When is the wedding?"

Yanti's sudden smile was my reward, though he did not interrupt when Father said seriously, "We cannot hold a wedding until mourning is over. My suggestion is to delay for the sake of prudence. New Year's Two Moons might be best, so that any of Vaha's family who wishes to be here will have time to travel."

"I volunteer to go fetch them," Banti said promptly.

Father ignored this indecorous interruption, saying to me, "Unless you are declaring the full three years of mourning, Daughter?"

"Xianti's sisters can mourn the full three years if they wish," I said. "Or poor Kianti. As for me, the sooner the world moves on, the better. The requisite fifty days will do." I turned to Vaha. "Thank you. For everything."

She bowed again. "To save lives, I did what I could. I understand that the desire for peace is what brought you back?"

"It is. Was. And that reminds me. Did you and your mother know that Princess Namath Dhak lives as a hermit on a northern island?"

Vaha looked up, startled. "She is alive?" And on my assent, she turned to Yanti. "My mother will be so happy to hear that. She has talked much of her older sister. Though not known to her, as my mother was born much later, she learned much of her..."

The dinner was soon brought in, conversation an easy give and take that had not been the norm when I was small. This was Vaha's gift. She was so soft-spoken, so charming with that strong but not unpleasing accent and her occasional lapses in language that Yanti seemed to find delightful, that somehow my reticent, traditional parents accepted topics of conversation which I'd never thought to hear canvased in our house of order, duty, and study.

Once my parents retired, she was yet more frank. She even spoke of Xianti, generous in her pity, though he had pestered her for years, even threatened her. "I sometimes considered giving in," she said at one point, when the candles had burned low. "If I'd thought it might do any good for this people here, I might have. But my mother, she knows such men. She says, *Once he has you, he will lose interest. But he would never let you go.* I was the only one to say no to him, see you."

I remembered the anguish in his face, and wondered if that assumption might be too simple, but then I could never hope to understand Xianti. And now he was past understanding.

"Walla! Those two sisters, Siarti and Liarti, they will bring much trouble," Vaha warned, with a serious, sympathetic glance.

"Perhaps," I said, "but at least now I will be in a position to give them trouble back if they do. And they will know it. My guess is, they will both want to keep far from court, rather than be forced to bow to me. Ayoh! But first, I mean to pass a law forbidden any poisons to anyone in the imperial palace. Once found, they must take their own poison. I think that might inspire those two to keep their distance."

Vaha clapped her hands. At my request, she promised to play her armonia to us on the following day, and then we all parted for the night.

It wasn't until I reached my room that I became aware of a throbbing headache. I was alone. I'd sent the maids off to bed hours before. But no sooner had I sat on the bed when a tap came at the window.

I got up, pushing the window out, to discover On upside down, smiling at me from where he hung over the edge of the roof. He dropped lightly down and sat half in and half out the window, a slim figure whose foxy tails rippled in the Essence realm.

"You have a headache," he said, and the fox was gone. This was On, changeable as the weather but—like the air of his affinity—endlessly generous. "I can tell."

"I just discovered it. I think my heart is catching up with my head." My own emotions tumbled. "If you're here to report something, please. No more bad news. Tomorrow, duty. Tonight, ayoh! I am so tired. And more than a little dispirited. I really thought I could sway him, but I guess I was just as arrogant as he said."

"You're going to need that kind of arrogance, in my own arrogant opinion," he retorted, smiling. "No, sit back down. Listen. Koi asked me to guard you; an individual called Tiger Li is loose, and word is, he's as vindictive as Xianti ever was. Koi is searching for him now. I'd rather sit here and use all the tricks the Xuan cousins taught me to rid you of that headache, and then if you want I'll sleep outside your door."

I sighed from the insides of the soles of my feet, closing my eyes. He laid his clever hands on my shoulders, and slowly began to smooth the knots into silk as he murmured poem after poem, expressions of peace, of contentment, and of love.

From my shoulders to my temples, and then back down again to my back: I could name every one of those acupoints, but I did not have to. Instead I had to do nothing whatsoever except feel the little zings of release, until I began to float on a tide of euphoric bliss that slowly altered to urgency. And at last those patient fingers asked a question: outside the door … or not?

I answered by blowing out the light.

FORTY-FIVE

AS YOU CAN SEE by the diminished scroll, I am coming to the end of my account. If you can envision us as once young and ardent, human and high of heart in our desires and our errors, then I have in measure succeeded.

A week or so ago Fourth Great-Granddaughter said tearily to me as I rubbed salve into her small, cramped hand, "Why did you have to make so *many* sage quotations, Great-Grand-mama?"

As I assured Fourth Great-Granddaughter that I used to get sore hands, too, and that the quotations we copied were just as long, I kept my amusement hidden, for sore writing hands are serious when you are small. And though her bluntness cost me a wince, there was more pride in the reflection that she trusted me enough for honesty. In my young days, we never would have dared—and although our respectful silence was orderly, it was at the cost of a true meeting of minds. It took me several years before I won that with my own mother, catapulted from her quiet childhood to censor's wife, to rankless prisoner, thence to grand princess dowager.

Though I often think back over my reign, I don't see the utility in detailing it. There are all manner of records. The graywings, those diligent, faithful, and closed-mouthed individuals who follow the Morningstar God, have been scrupulous in recording each day what my pulse reveals to the physician who comes to check it, how many hairs remain in the comb after Minnow was done with arranging it, and how often I have my toenails clipped. Everything about me became public property — once, when Eldest Son was small, exploring the imperial archive, he counted with great satisfaction thirty-six different accounts of my coronation alone.

Yet in only one of the accounts of that event, those kept by the imperial guards, is it mentioned that Great-Grandfather Koi saw to it that I survived the day. For it was he who spotted Tiger Li among the crowds gathered along the main street, weapon in hand, and took him out so quietly and efficiently that there was no uproar to mar the festivities.

Likewise unreported except in guard records was the death of his wife Liarti; the servants pointed to the household after her corpse was found, and the household blamed the servants. It might even have been Nua Li himself, before he set out to kill me on behalf of Xianti: the case remains unsolved to this day, for no one seems to care if the perpetrator is found.

I myself most cherish many events and memories outside of my reign's official records. I'm thinking of Second Daughter's admirable collection of every one of the "On Lu" plays — plus the ones Great-Grandfather Sheion wrote under other names when he experimented. And as much of the poetry as she could find, though I know it is not possible she could catch them all. He was so very fond of composing them on a leaf, a fan, a paper umbrella, and in the sand before the tide rushed in. He insisted that the poem still existed, written on the air once leaf withered, paper tore, and sand washed smooth. Maybe he was right.

I think I will list a few treasured memories that will otherwise escape into oblivion. Such as the conversation I had with the old gardener, the day after my coronation, when all traces of Xianti were gone, and I took a walk through the entire imperial palace that was now mine. I found him in the imperial garden, working among the lovely dove trees, right then finishing their bloom. He would have bowed himself away, but I bade him continue, as I like to watch and learn.

He gave me a glance of conditional approval out of that sun-seamed face, and though his words at first were the conventional ones extolling my imperial presence among the humble plants, and attributing the beauty of the scene entirely to my grace, as I asked questions about how he chose what to plant and when to prune, he began to teach me how to view the ever-changing alteration of the scenery. "Everything is alive. They talk among themselves through all the seasons," he said, gnarled, soil-grimed fingers wide as he indicated all the trees, shrubs, and plants. "But they measure hours, days, and years differently. Our lives come and go unnoticed in the time it takes for that golden larch and these gingko to say what they want to say."

To him, the notion of ownership of land was a mere illusion. In his secret heart he saw us as caretakers, from the rock sweeper to the wearer of the yellow silk.

Another matter of importance to me that scarcely rates a mention in the records was the trip Vaha made with her quiet, loving mother to Tortor Island, to bring Namath Dhak back — once Grand Prince Miluo's enemy, during that war that neither caused nor wanted. She, who thought to die alone there on Three Ghosts Hill, instead got the chance to spoil Yanti's and Vaha's boys, and to make the old prince laugh with her tart observations until the end of his days.

Also unrecorded was my brother Banti's hurt when he realized that at least three of those handsome cranes who had so generously aided us at the end there were young males — all of whom Sun favored — and that to attempt to confine Sun in a palace as a wife would be as tragic as a swift locked in a cage. But Banti was not made for sorrow. He had flirts aplenty, and he decided that the best way to forget his disappointment was to buy a boat and sail off with Narek Bin to explore the empire's islands.

The family annals only record Banti's later marriage with dear Vaha's cousin overseas, before Banti took over as Imperial Trade Commissioner, sailing the Great Sea back and forth on that blue-painted yacht of his that all of you as children ran about on whenever he came back to us.

Another record unwritten was my father's deep satisfaction, that last year of his life, to be restored as Chief Censor. And to see his beloved department regain its reputation for probity and fearlessness in seeking the truth, before my elder brother Yanti took it over.

How impressed Yanti's young assistants were by his phenomenal memory! How they competed to be the ones chosen to read testaments to him, when Vaha had a family to draw her away from the censorate! And how vigorous his arguments with me before the court when one or the other of us thought the other donkey-stubborn!

I am only sorry that so few of you remember him; no matter how skilled Essence Physician Lan Kianti became, he could not repair health so severely broken, but we at least had the satisfaction of seeing how very fully he lived the life left to him. It was a relief to us all that he died at peace, with his beloved Vaha at one side, and his two boys at his other. What more, he said to me, could anyone ask at any age, whether forty or twice as old? He also had the satisfaction of recommending Chief Censor Taisa as his replacement, who as you know still presides as I write this, though her hair is as white as mine.

Also unwritten in the official records is my conjecture that Princess Lan Siarti's sudden death half a year after my coronation was not in fact due to spleen, though she was infamous for her temper, but due to poison. Probably given her by her husband, for she was too suspicious of everyone else, and I was told that she had never ceased hoping that he would relent toward her.

In fact, I was so convinced that Huyun Shandek had solved this problem in this manner that this is the true reason behind my journey to Lan to visit Cousin Kandati when Huyun Shandek came to make his bow before court, and thus he was obliged to make that bow before my beloved consorts, Great-Grandfathers Sheion and Koi.

The records only include my edict declaring that his excellent governance would be most contributive to the empire's good if administered from Cloud Terrace until the end of his exemplary life. Now you know the real reason he never dared again to leave his shores. I understand that while he lived he never ceased to refer to me except with fondness. The sad thing is, I could have been fond of him, too, but I could never truly love where I could not trust.

Less discerning — and scarcely mentioned again in the family annals — was wily old Grand Prince Yiulo, whom Great-Uncle Miluo had known well from their respective childhoods. It was Great-Uncle Miluo who persuaded Grand Prince Yiulo to withdraw not long after my coronation.

Though nothing could prevent Grand Prince Yiulo from attempting to meddle in the Eastern Fleet matters, as you are well aware, Grand Admiral Jai of the Phoenix Circle was expert at deflecting both him and his even more impulsive grandson, Prince Yiuti, when he duly inherited Whale Haven. Before he turned his attentions to his truly astonishing harem of consorts. Which as you've no doubt figured out is the true reason behind the penurious state of your many, many Lan cousins on that side.

As for other matters remaining outside of official records:

You now know the history of Sagacious Blade. You probably have read speculation about why I wore a sword while sitting on the throne the first ten years or so of my reign. It was not, as many surmised, to bolster my appearance before court, or to make myself look "manly". My reputation for seeing through lies I believe augmented my reputation as much as I could desire, and as for looking manly, my being tall, and after bearing five children, stout, rendered my appearance imposing enough for man or woman.

I did not really need Sagacious Blade beyond those first ten years. Which was just as well, because after the day of Xianti's death, Granny Zim was less often present. I had to call to her more often if I needed her, and in the more recent years, she has not always come.

Therefore, after I was widowed, I decided that it was time to keep my promise.

You know of course that Great-Grandfather On suffered those syncopes that caused him to long for one more journey out to sea, with his consort De Luin — who, incidentally, the first time I met him, flared with fox aura as strong as On's. But a different sort of fox. Wherever their ancestors came from, I don't think they were in the same fox clan.

What you who are not Great-Grandfather Sheion's descendants don't know is what Consort De Luin reported to me in a private interview when he returned alone. It was simple enough: in spite of all anyone could do, On had begged to be put in a little boat, while Phoenix Moon was fullest, so that he could follow its path straight to that luminous sphere resting just above the sea. He was quite content, laughing and singing until he was out of sight.

De Luin swore that he vanished, rather than sank. It was while we were recovering from the shock of him being gone that Koi, my mountain, my mighty tree, proved that he was frail human flesh: he admitted one morning that he was tired. I thought it odd, as he never complained, but when he sat down to "Catch his breath" while doing seeds and forms, and it slipped forever away, I understood too late. There was no final good-bye with either of them, which sometimes I've mourned, and other times I thought exactly right, for there was no suffering or sorrow right to the last.

But these ends made all our shared things still extant painful to me. There were the embroidered slippers Fourth Daughter had made for On, kept here when he stayed with me. And likewise here was Koi's night robe, soft from years of wear, for he saw no need for a new one. There was no escaping these reminders that would never again feel their warmth, but I could no sooner order them taken away than I could tear out my heart. That, and the unanswered question about what really had happened to On, caused me to fetch Sagacious Blade from her carved stand, and put the question.

She never answered.

I told you all at the time that my journey was to mourn in peace, which was true enough. But I also wanted to find the demon that Granny Zim had always said was awaiting her — and return the sword.

I had not traveled, except to each spring's Journey to the Clouds, since my trip to Lan to visit Kandati and his family. All of you had vital affairs to see to, and families who relied on you. The only one who expressed a desire to make this trip was Bird-Master Chief Cray's elder daughter, Nightingale. She brought her little son Piper.

Cray arranged for *Pangolin* to carry us. It was a shock to come aboard and find a young Hat standing in Dinek's place, but I knew that Dinek had retired when Fan got too stiff for winter weather on board, and the two had chosen this promising young man as *Pangolin*'s new captain.

This Captain Hat welcomed Nightingale in a familiar way, then looked at me with curiosity.

"This is ... Pangolin Ren," Nightingale said, indicating me.

The young captain seemed to about to exclaim something unfortunate, such as, *You're still alive?* He clasped his hands in the gallant wanderer bow that I discovered I had sorely missed. "Welcome!"

I had my old cabin, arranged ahead by Cray, and I relished all the old, easy habits, sitting shoulder to shoulder with crew and passenger alike, instead of up on a dais.

"Where to?" the captain asked, once we had cleared the bay for the open sea.

Instead of answering, I unsheathed Sagacious Blade, and

held her up. Granny Zin had promised long ago that the sword would lead the way. I wondered if that was still true — but then the hilt hummed with Essence, and the point swung around to the west.

"West it is," said Captain Hat, and called it out to the crew.

The days that followed were mostly pleasant, summer being over, and that year's dragon storm season a short one. We sailed west for a time, then north, until we reached one of those islands that is so picturesque in screen paintings, but in reality more uncomfortable than not, seldom affording a flat surface on which to even pitch a tent.

It was only Nightingale, Piper, and I who climbed a narrow goat path up and up — with more and more frequent stops — until I finally sat down on a flattish boulder covered with lichen. I laid the sword down, laboring to catch my breath, and then closed my eyes.

The island burgeoned with Essence. In it, shapes and shadows darted: life forms seen in the physical world and in the unseen. "Oh," I said aloud.

The two looked my way, mother and son very alike in their bewilderment. My eyes strayed to Piper, who to all appearances was a sturdy young Falcon in the making. But here, in this place, I sensed a bud of nascent Essence, within a clean, straightforward metal affinity. No tyrant here, no posturing petty king. He was just very determined. At age ten, the summit of desire was to go back to Benevolence on Hundred-Day Trees Island, having reached his next form, so that some of those older ones of twelve and thirteen would stop laughing at him for lagging behind.

"Piper," I said, "why don't you run about a little and explore? I saw some ripe dragon-fruit over that way. The biggest and brightest red I've ever seen."

Piper turned to his mother, who raised a hand in permission. He took off like a crossbow bolt, running straight uphill so effortlessly I could not suppress a sigh of longing for the days when I could do that, and thought nothing of it.

I said to Nightingale, "If you'd like to explore, do go ahead. I'm not certain what comes next, but it will probably be … odd, if anything manifests in this realm."

"This realm," she repeated, looking dubious, then she straightened up. "If you need help, you've only to shout." And she walked after her son.

I said, "Come forth, if you're going to. I can probably find you in the other realm, but I do easily get nauseated if I move about while trying to navigate between the two worlds."

Between one blink and another, a small girlish form appeared, her hair so black that it seemed more of a void than a color.

"Who are you?" I asked. "You seem familiar, but yet not. I'd know if we'd met."

"You can call me YinYin. It was the name I chose for my master, and for Bu, my friend. You know a part of me." She nodded toward the sword. "The part that binds my master into the world."

"I think she is ready to be unbound," I said. "I think. Though I am completely unsure about ... demon matters."

It was a guess, but YinYin did not deny it.

Then there, suddenly, was Granny Zim's old voice, more cracked than mine. "I must go home," she said. "I see Lu Teg. He waited for me after all!" Her voice lightened with joy. "How can that be, YinYin?"

"He is outside of time. There, then and now are one," YinYin said.

Granny Zim turned—for once again, she was nearly visible, a trick of light: a small, wizened figure. "Let me go. But don't destroy my Sagacious Blade," she said quickly. "It was so *very* good for my Bu darlings. Very, very good. Here is one now!"

Light appeared to gather in her eyes, but the little figure faded, and the light was merely the wink of sun-reflection on the shiny yellow leaves of a nearby fringe tree.

YinYin turned to me. "You have kept your covenant. Will you take the sword with you?"

"Is it just a sword, now? A pretty one, to be sure. But the..." I laid a hand to it, and smiled. "Ay, the Essence is still there. Though the voices are gone."

"My master learned from me as I learned from her. All that was good in her remains with the sword," YinYin said. "It will choose those she would have chosen."

"It is well," I said. "That is all I could have asked."

YinYin was gone in another blink, and I began making my slow way back down the trail, thinking very hard.

I had done nothing with the ban on charmed swords. For as On had said, if I lifted the ban, you could guess who would seek them first: the military. These were swords, after all. Military tools. I had also told Koi not to prosecute anyone carrying one, as long as they were not using its charms to hew bloody swathes through island after island. After all, Xianti had never had one, but that had not stopped his depredations.

And yet, did my government need another source of power?

No.

By the time we had climbed aboard the *Pangolin*, I had just about made a decision. My Yslan Dynasty was already as secure as any human construct could ever be. Education was my favorite tool. Not charmed swords. Though I had benefitted from one, my circumstances had warranted it.

These peaceful days did not.

I said nothing on the journey back, except to ask for paper and ink and brush. It was actually aboard the *Pangolin* that I began this record. Intermittently I watched the goings-on outside my cabin, observing and thinking.

When we reached the imperial island, I said to Piper, "I am old. I have no more use for a sword. Would you like this one?"

He did not scoff at taking a blade from an old woman, nor did he ask how many people it had killed. He drew the blade, bracing his young body, and admired the sweep of the scales in the sunlight, then smiled my way. The sword had accepted him.

And when they sailed away to get on with their lives, I stood on the wharf, with the beginning of this rambling memoir secure in my carryall as the inevitable imperial cavalcade waited to accompany me back into the imperial palace.

I waved goodbye to the ship I knew I would never see again.

In one of On's poems he wrote for me, soon after we acknowledged that I could no longer have the freedom of the gallant wandering world, he stated that though we cannot carry our homes with us, we can preserve the essence of home in our hearts. He and his consorts Lily and De Luin were off the next day, for he had to see a new play at Guiza's capital in Ye, where my reticent uncle had founded his music school fast gaining prestige, and some famous players had established a new entertainment house.

Those words sounded wise, but I don't think they are true for everyone. Some do carry their homes with them. Banti was such a one. He could never abide being in one place too long, and though the gallant wanderer life had never appealed to him, he happily divided his days between the east and our empire. Koi would have been another, for he never did accumulate much beyond what he could carry, but he was a settler by nature.

I continued writing this record, which in the early days assuaged some of my grief by keeping before my eye those no longer in life. I wanted to write it while memory remained sharp—and this in turn led me by degrees to the present decision to abdicate that dragon throne.

I make this decision while in full possession of my faculties, which includes the awareness that my strength is dwindling. Though he can no longer see, eyesight is not necessary to those with strong Essence skills, and Physician Kianti assures me my pulse is stable for my age, and I might have as much as another ten years in me. But I would not have a feeble sack of bones doddering on the throne while all of you, in the flower of your strongest years, must stand by and watch me wither.

Therefore, when the new year commences, it will be with my stepping down.

What will I take away as my proudest achievements? You would assume it would be the outlawing of slavery. And I *am* proud of that, but I am also aware of the river of history, whose flow is so very hard to stem, and of how humans must constantly work toward enlightenment and grace. Subjugation seems to be in our natures as well as hierarchy and order. Fight against that, and not each other! I know that it is inevitable that my dynasty will fade, as all have; and with it, perhaps, many of our works, to be invented all over again. I hope that you, my precious ones, will teach your posterity well, putting off that day as long as possible.

I am proud that I've lived long enough to not only pass the edict that daughters can inherit—which has been half true all along, what with the matrilocal exceptions—but that they can marry consorts.

As you have seen, I, in my foolish youth, declared that I would have at least nine consorts, but I only ended up with two. However, as the years gathered into decades, I believe we served as proof of family strength and amity in preference to the old ways of sneakery, lies, and false standards, creating distrust and struggles about inheritance. I know my new laws do not resolve all family problems, but what does, outside of honesty, compromise, and compassion?

I have been proud of the decades of peace after those years of Island Wars—a name I insisted the scribes use in preference to the Time of Warring Princes, as the latter seemed to retain some glamour to the young and heedless. I am aware that the new generations who have no memory of the agonies of destruction can get restless and wish to test themselves. I have officially not noticed, but I've been aware of certain noble youths leading raids far up north against the westerner raiders, for example. And of the increasing violence of some of the martial arts contests.

You probably know that I attempted by edict to curtail these for the good of all, but you might not know that shortly before he died, my beloved Koi convinced me that I was only driving into hiding those determined to risk their own lives striving against each other. That's why I rescinded that law, and leave it to the sects to govern themselves, so long as they do not importune the citizenry.

I am proud of having steadily dispersed a great measure of imperial power back to the islands through the governing councils that I appointed as guardian qilin. I still think of dispersing power to local polities as taking the firewood from under the cauldron of trouble. But I know that over time councils can go from traditional to hidebound, thence corrupt, and there goes the firewood right back to the cauldron!

Ay, my greatest pride is in *you*, my children, and their children. After long days in court I revel in family gatherings. How proud I was to see brothers and sisters painting lanterns, flying kites, and teaching the small ones the intricacies of Circle (or pitch pot, which I was never very good at). I delighted with the intensity of the sun seeing no distinctions made between Great-Grandfather Koi's and Great-Grandfather On's children—or between my five and Great-Grandfather On's children by Great-Aunts Lily and Manu. Or between the entire pack of you and your cousins with Easterner blood. You have taught your own children well in that regard, which has made festival gatherings such a joy.

But proudest of all was the moment when the five of you elders chose Second Granddaughter as imperial heir. With awareness, and gratitude, for that one true success, I can retire to the dowager pavilion overlooking the garden, where I think I might just take up embroidery again.

About the Author

Sherwood Smith studied in Europe before earning a Masters degree in history. She worked as a governess, a bartender, an electrical supply verifier, and wore various hats in the film industry before turning to teaching for twenty years. To date she's published over fifty books, one of which was an Anne Lindbergh Honor Book; she's twice been a finalist for the Mythopoeic Fantasy Award and once a Nebula finalist. Her YA fantasy novel *Crown Duel* has been in print for over twenty years.

Visit her website at https://www.sherwoodsmith.net and sign up for her newsletter to learn about new books!

ABOUT BOOK VIEW CAFE

Book View Café is an author-owned cooperative of professional writers, publishing in a variety of genres including fantasy, science fiction, romance, mystery, and more.

Its authors include New York Times and USA Today best-sellers as well as winners and nominees of many prestigious awards such as the Agatha Award, Hugo Award, Lambda Literary Award, Locus Award, Nebula Award, RITA Award, Philip K. Dick Award, World Fantasy Award, and many others.

Since its debut in 2008, Book View Café has gained a reputation for producing high quality books in both print and electronic form. BVC's e-books are DRM-free and distributed around the world.

Book View Café's monthly newsletter includes new releases, specials, author news, and event announcements. To sign up, visit https://www.bookviewcafe.com/bookstore/newsletter/